"I'll think about your proposal."

"You do that," Judah said, "and don't forget to tell the good doc your business merger's off." He crossed to the door, putting his hand on the doorknob to open the door for her—at least that's what she thought he was going to do—before pressing his lips against her cheek, his stubble grazing her ever so slightly. "Just so you know, Darla, I don't plan on mixing business with my marriage."

His meaning was unmistakable. His hand moved to her waist in a possessive motion, lingering at her hip just for a second, capturing her. She remembered everything—how good he'd made her feel, how magical a night was in his arms—and wished his proposal was made from love and not possessiveness.

Judah pulled the door open. "Next time I see you will be at the altar."

The Bull Rider's Unexpected Family

NEW YORK TIMES BESTSELLING AUTHOR

TINA LEONARD
&
AMANDA RENEE

Previously published as *The Bull Rider's Twins*
and *The Bull Rider's Baby Bombshell*

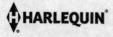

ISBN-13: 978-1-335-61744-6

The Bull Rider's Unexpected Family

Copyright © 2021 by Harlequin Books S.A.

The Bull Rider's Twins
First published in 2011. This edition published in 2021.
Copyright © 2011 by Tina Leonard

The Bull Rider's Baby Bombshell
First published in 2018. This edition published in 2021.
Copyright © 2018 by Amanda Renee

Recycling programs
for this product may
not exist in your area.

This edition published by arrangement with Harlequin Books S.A.

For questions and comments about the quality of this book,
please contact us at CustomerService@Harlequin.com.

Harlequin Enterprises ULC
22 Adelaide St. West, 40th Floor
Toronto, Ontario M5H 4E3, Canada
www.Harlequin.com

Printed in U.S.A.

Tina Leonard is a *New York Times* bestselling and award-winning author of more than fifty projects, including several popular miniseries for Harlequin. Known for bad-boy heroes and smart, adventurous heroines, her books have made the *USA TODAY*, Waldenbooks, Ingram and Nielsen BookScan bestseller lists. Born on a military base, Tina lived in many states before eventually marrying the boy who did her crayon printing for her in the first grade. You can visit her at tinaleonard.com, and follow her on Facebook and Twitter.

Books by Tina Leonard

Harlequin American Romance

Bridesmaids Creek

The Rebel Cowboy's Quadruplets
The SEAL's Holiday Babies
The Twins' Rodeo Rider

Callahan Cowboys

A Callahan Wedding
The Renegade Cowboy Returns
The Cowboy Soldier's Sons
Christmas in Texas
A Callahan Outlaw's Twins
His Callahan Bride's Baby
Branded by a Callahan
Callahan Cowboy Triplets

Visit the Author Profile page at Harlequin.com for more titles.

The Bull Rider's Twins

TINA LEONARD

Many thanks to my editor Kathleen Scheibling,
for believing in this series, always having faith in
me and editing my work with a sure hand.

There are many people at Harlequin who make my
books ready for publication, most of whom I will
never have the chance to thank in person,
and they have my heartfelt gratitude.

Also many thanks to my children, who by now are
both off to college, leaving me with an empty nest.
It's not hard to envision me writing a series about
babies—I had an extremely blessed experience
with my two kids, and I thank you for your
faith and encouragement.

And many, many thanks to the very generous
readers who are the reason for my success. I
could not write without your caring
words and loyal support.

Chapter 1

"Judah is my seeker," Molly Callahan said of her toddler son, to which her husband, Jeremiah, replied, "Then the apple didn't fall far from the tree, my love."

Judah Callahan couldn't believe the woman of his dreams was waiting in his bed. Unless he missed his guess, Darla Cameron was as naked as the day she was born.

"I've been waiting for you," she said, sitting up and holding the sheet to her chest. His throat went dry as a bone in a New Mexico desert. Blond hair cascaded over pale shoulders, and big blue eyes gazed at him with apprehension. She was nervous, Judah realized, closing the door and locking it behind him.

He wanted to say he'd been waiting for her for years.

"I'd think you'd been in the champagne, but I noticed you didn't go near it except to toast Creed and Aberdeen."

She shook her head. "It was a lovely wedding. Really beautiful. All the valentine decorations were so romantic."

He couldn't take his eyes off her. Whatever she thought was romantic about Creed's wedding was nowhere near as attractive as Darla showing up nude in his bed. A little worry crossed her face, and he realized she was afraid he might turn down what she was obviously offering.

Not a chance.

He seated himself on the foot of the bed, the sight of her creamy skin setting him on fire. "If not an excess of champagne, why tonight?"

She blushed. "I wish I could tell you."

That didn't sound like the Darla he knew. Darla was forthright. An excellent businesswoman—her new calling since she'd hung up her nurse's badge and gone into business as wedding shop owner with Jackie Samuels. "Try."

She shook her head. "Be with me."

He wasn't going to put her, or himself, through any more agony. He kissed Darla, amazed at the sweet taste of her. "Peaches," he said, his mind fogging up. "I always wondered what you smelled like, and now I know. You even taste like peaches."

She moved his hand to the sheet, and he was beset by the urge to tear it away, feel what lay hidden beneath.

"There's a hook here," he said, knowing full damn well Darla Cameron wasn't the type of woman who slept around. "Someone put you up to this, or you want something."

"I do want something," she said, her voice soft in the darkness. "Tonight I want you."

So there it was. Tonight was only a simple hookup. Outside, music played, and fireworks streaked across the sky, popping and hissing. If he opened the window to his second-story bedroom, they would see clouds streaking the moon on a cold Valentine's night. This would all be so romantic, if he wasn't suffering from the sixth sense that something wasn't right.

"How did you know I'd be sleeping in here and not the bunkhouse?"

"I know all the guests who are staying in the bunkhouse," she told him, moving his hand slightly so the sheet barely covered her breasts. He could feel heavenly softness just a brush away. Being this close to her at long last was killing him. Parts of him felt like the fireworks, ready to explode.

"And Fiona mentioned that you and some of your brothers were sleeping in the house so the guests could have privacy."

"So here you are."

"Here I am," she said, so sweetly breathless that he didn't have the heart to keep looking the gift horse in the mouth. Luckily, he had condoms in the nightstand, a groom's gift from Creed, who had a penchant for stupid gags. No silver letter opener for his groomsmen; no, just boxes of condoms with peace signs and neon inscriptions on the side. Creed's last laugh, since the brother with the most progeny won Rancho Diablo. Creed was the most competitive of the Callahans.

"All right," Judah said. "I've never thrown a woman out of my bed, and I certainly won't start now."

He didn't get why she was here, but he wasn't going to worry about it. Since the lady had hunted him down, he intended to make tonight very much worth her while.

Two hours later, something made Judah start awake. After the hottest sex he'd ever experienced, he'd fallen asleep, holding Darla in his arms, grateful for the good fortune heaven had thrown his way.

Darla jumped from the bed. "I heard someone in the hall!"

"It's all right," he said, trying to tug her back for another helping of delicious blonde.

"It's not all right!"

She eluded his grasp, so he snapped on the lamp. She was tugging on her party dress like a woman fleeing a crime scene. "Hey," he said, "we're consenting adults. No one's going to bust in here and—"

"Shh!" She glanced at the door nervously. "I think the guests have all left. Your brothers will come upstairs any minute."

"And my aunt Fiona and Burke," Judah said, and Darla let out a squeak of fear.

"Get me out of here! Without anyone seeing me. Please!"

He'd prefer it if she stayed until dawn crested the New Mexico sky, but it was clear she was determined to pull a Cinderella and disappear. He got out of bed and pulled on his jeans.

"Can you zip me? Please?" She turned her back to

him and Judah drank in all the smooth skin exposed to his hungry gaze.

"Are you sure you won't—"

"Judah, please!"

He zipped her, taking his sweet time as he pressed a kiss against her shoulder. "Even if any of my family were to see you, Darla, it's not like they'd brand you with a scarlet *A*."

"I shouldn't have done this. I don't know what came over me." She yanked on her heels, bringing her nearly four inches closer to his height. He reached for her, determined to show her how well suited they were, but she unlocked the door and dashed out before he could convince her to stay.

Shoving his shirt in his jeans, he hurried after her. He caught sight of a full blue skirt disappearing around the corner as she made it to the landing.

And then she was gone.

"Damn," Judah said. "I'm think I'm going to have to marry that girl."

Which was really funny, because of all his brothers, Judah had always known he would never marry. Not for his aunt, who dearly wanted to see all the Callahan boys married. Not for Rancho Diablo, which would go to the brother with the largest family. And not for love, because he really didn't believe in love. At least not with one woman.

But perhaps he'd espoused that view because he'd always secretly had a crush on the unattainable Darla Cameron. She'd never so much as glanced his way. She'd been a serious student in high school, gone on to be a serious student in college, gotten a grad degree and then become a serious nurse. No, she'd never really given any of the guys in town a look, so he'd figured his chances were slim. He couldn't even strike up a conversation with her.

All that changed tonight, he thought with a self-satisfied smile. And now that he'd had her, he was pretty certain he wouldn't be able to give her up.

Four months passed quickly when you weren't having fun, and Judah wasn't having any fun at all. Darla had barely spoken to him since that Valentine's Day evening. He'd tried to chat with her, done everything but go by the bridal salon and corner her, which his pride would not allow him to do. For a woman who'd seduced him, she'd certainly taken off fast. And lately, he'd heard she'd been lying low. Maybe wasn't feeling great. Aunt Fiona was no help to him, but had dared to nonchalantly ask after his Valentine's night surprise.

Obviously, Darla hadn't been as enthused about their lovemaking as he'd been.

The realization stung like gritty wind. This was worse than when he'd only worshipped Darla from afar. Now he knew what he was missing out on, and it made him hunger for her more. She was constantly on his mind. People said she wasn't taking phone calls, except from her mother, Mavis, who'd put out the word that Darla wasn't accepting visitors at her small bungalow.

He would bide his time. He *had* to have her. There was no other option. She was a treasure he alone was going to possess.

If he could just figure out how.

"The first annual Rancho Diablo Charity Matchmaking Ball was such a success, not to mention Creed and Aberdeen's wedding," Aunt Fiona announced to

Judah as he slunk into the kitchen, "that I'm in the mood to plan another party."

He grimaced, not interested in discussing Fiona's die-hard love of partying. It was all an excuse for her to marry off her nephews. The trouble with having a committed matchmaker in the family was that it was embarrassing when said matchmaker couldn't fix his problem even if he wanted her to. He was sunk. "Do we really need another social function?"

"I think we do," Fiona said. "We raised a lot of money for the Diablo public library, and we made a lot of new friends. And we irritated the heck out of Bode Jenkins, which, as you know, is my life's goal. Not to mention you could stand a little perking up."

Judah grunted. "What do you have in mind?"

"Well," she said, moving around the sunny kitchen, "we need to find our next victim. The easiest way to do that is to keep ladies visiting the ranch." She sent him a questioning glance. "Unless you know something I don't know."

"Like what?" He settled in to eating the eggs and bacon she put in front of him. There were strawberry jam-smothered biscuits on the side, and a steaming cup of brew. Life was too good to mess up with another extravaganza. The feed bag was definitely better when Fiona's concentration was on the Callahans and not on impressing females far and wide. "I'm usually the last to know anything about anything."

"That's no surprise. What I meant was that unless you know that romance is blooming somewhere on the ranch—"

He shook his head, silencing that train of thought. "Dry wells around here, Aunt."

"Then let's choose a victim and get on with it. Time is running out."

He looked up reluctantly from his breakfast. "You got Pete and Creed married off. That's a third of us who've given up the flag of freedom. Maybe no more weddings are needed. Or children," he added, knowing that was Fiona's real goal. "Pete has three, and Creed has Joy Patrice, but he brought three more with him if you count Diane's. Either way, that's a grand total of seven new kids on the ranch." He smiled, but it was pained. "Plenty, huh?"

She scowled. "Seven is hardly enough to make the case that our ranch shouldn't be sold for public land use. Bode'll never let us get off that easily. We need more."

Judah looked with sorrow at his eggs, his appetite leaving him. "Well, you could try Sam, but I think he likes the ladies a little too much to settle down with just one."

"And he's just a baby," Fiona said. "Twenty-six is too young when I've got hardened bachelors sitting around this place shirking their futures."

Judah rubbed at his chin. "Well, there's Jonas, but that would take too much work."

Fiona huffed. "You'd think a thirty-three-year-old surgeon would be a bit more anxious to find a wife, but *no-o-o.* I don't think he has the first clue about women, honestly. He's such a—"

"Nerd," Judah said, trying to be helpful, which earned him another scowl from Fiona.

"He's not a nerd. He's just a deep thinker."

That was an understatement. "You could pick on Rafe. He's next in line behind Jonas, and as Creed's twin it would make sense. He'll probably start missing that twin camaraderie now that Creed's got his hands full."

Fiona looked hurt. "Is that what you think I'm doing? Picking on you boys?"

"Oh, no. No, Aunt Fiona." Judah looked at the hurt tears in his delicate aunt's eyes. "We know you just want us all to be happy."

She nodded. "I do. And how do you think I feel about having to make you all settle down before your time—if you have a sense of time at all, and I don't think any of you boys do—when I've lost Rancho Diablo?"

"We haven't lost it yet," Judah soothed. "Sam's gotten a continuance. We may get out of Bode's trap eventually. Somehow."

"But it's better to load our deck for success." Fiona waved at him. "Eat your breakfast. It's getting cold."

Burke, Fiona's lifelong butler (and her secret husband, which she seemed keen for no one to know about, though all the Callahan brothers had figured it out) brought the mail in, handing it to her.

"Oh, look!" she exclaimed, as Judah pushed the now cool eggs around his plate. She waved an envelope in the air. "Cream-colored stock. Always a good sign!"

"Why?" he asked, his gaze on the calligraphed envelope.

"It's a wedding invitation, if I know my wedding invitations, and I think I do!" Fiona tore into the envelope. She stopped, staring at the contents. "Well," she murmured, "I didn't see this coming. No, I really didn't."

Burke looked over her shoulder, peering at the invite. "Uh-oh," he said, and Fiona nodded.

"Who's getting strung?" he asked, feeling cheerful that it wasn't him. Some other poor sack was getting the marital ball and chain, but it wasn't him. *Pity the fool who falls into the clutches of a beautiful woman,* he thought, as his aunt handed him the invitation silently.

"'Ms. Mavis Cameron Night requests the honor of your presence at the wedding of her daughter, Darla Cameron, to Dr. Sidney Tunstall, on June 30,'" he read out loud, his breath going short and his heart practically stopping. His gaze shot to Fiona's. "Didn't you know about this? She's one of your best friends."

"Mavis didn't say a word to me," his aunt exclaimed. "I can't understand why. And the wedding is in a few days, which I also can't understand. What's the rush?"

She studied the invitation for another moment, then lifted her gaze to his again. Oh, but she needn't have worn such a worried expression. He had a good idea why a woman might marry so quickly—Darla was pregnant.

The thought burned his gut.

"Oh, dear," Aunt Fiona said, her eyes huge.

Judah shoved back his chair.

"Shall I say all the family will be in attendance?" she asked, and he yelled over his shoulder, "I wouldn't miss it," as he dashed out into the hot dry wind. Darla hadn't wanted any emotional connection between them. And he, spare Romeo that he was, had fallen into her arms and dreamed of a future.

He was a fool. But not a fool on his way to the altar, and there was something to be said for that.

Still, Judah wondered if he heard an empty echo in his bravado. And his broken heart drove him onto the range, riding hell-bent to nowhere.

* * *

An hour later, Judah was positive he saw the mystical Diablos down in a canyon, well past the working oil derricks and the fenced cattle land. Legend said that the wild horses ran free on Rancho Diablo, and no one could get close to them because they were spirits. They were also a portent of something magical to come. The Callahans didn't see the herd of horses often, but when they did, they respected the moment.

They were not spirit horses, as far as Judah was concerned. He could see them drinking from a small stream that threaded through the dust-painted canyon, though his eyes blurred in the bright sunlight. Nearby, a large cactus offered a little shade, but Judah ignored it, easing back in the saddle to watch the horses. Their untamed beauty called to his own wild side.

They turned as one and floated deeper into the canyon. Judah followed, watching for snakes, hawks and other critters. He and his brothers had explored this canyon many times, knew all its secrets.

His horse went to the thin stream, too. Judah slid from the saddle and took a long drink from the pale water. When he looked up, he saw a rock shelf he didn't remember.

Closer inspection showed the opening to a cave so hidden from the main canyon path that he would never have seen it if he hadn't bent down to drink. Cautiously, he went inside, his gun drawn in case of wild creatures he might startle.

But the cave was empty now—clearly some kind of once-used mine. Judah went past a rough shaft and a basic pulley and cart.

He'd found the legendary silver mine.

But it wasn't much of one, and appeared to have been long deserted. This couldn't be why Bode was so determined to get Rancho Diablo land—unless he thought there was more silver to be discovered. Still, what difference could silver mean to the wealthy man? And even if the Callahans were forced to sell Rancho Diablo, they would make certain they retained the mineral rights.

A loomed rug lay on the cave floor, hidden from casual visitors. There was also evidence of footprints, visible in the fading light that filtered into the cave. Still deeper, what seemed to be a message in some cryptic language was written on the wall, and it looked fresh. He touched the letters, smearing them a little. Underneath, silver coins and a few silver bars were stacked on a flat rock, like an offering.

Judah realized he'd stumbled on a smuggling operation, or perhaps a thruway for travelers who shouldn't be using Rancho Diablo land.

He left the cave, grabbed his horse's reins and swung into the saddle to ride in the opposite direction the Diablos had taken, as he wondered who might be using Callahan land and why.

For the moment, he would say nothing, he decided—until he understood more about why he'd been led to this place.

The next day, Judah realized drastic steps would have to be taken. The whole town of Diablo, it seemed, was atwitter over Darla's impending marriage. No detail was too small to be hashed over—the bridal gown she'd bought from the store she co-owned with Jackie Samuels Callahan, Pete's wife; the diamante-covered shoes she'd purchased. She'd scheduled an appointment for her hair, which had been dutifully reported. It would be worn long, crowned with an illusion veil that had orange blossoms cascading at the hem, which would just touch her shoulders.

Judah was sick to death of details. He wouldn't know an orange blossom if it grew out of his boot.

Strangely, the bride had not been seen since her invitations were mailed. Nor had the groom, though he was expected in town any day now. Judah knew him. Sidney Tunstall was a popular rodeo doctor and a one-time bronc buster, a man with a spine like a spring, who seemed to be kissed by good fortune. He was also wealthy. And he'd been after Darla for some time, if scuttlebutt was to be believed. Tall and lean and focused, the doctor seemed like a guy who loved what he did and did it well.

Which pretty much stank, but that was how it went. A man could lose to a better rival if he had slow-moving feet, and Judah reckoned his feet had been slower than most.

He flung himself inside the bunkhouse, anxious to sit alone in front of the fireplace to gather his thoughts.

It wasn't to be. Jonas was like a hulking rock in the den, taking up space with Sam and Rafe. And they'd been talking about him, Judah realized, by the way they shut their yaps the instant he entered.

"What's up?" he asked, eyeing them. "Don't stop talking about me just because I'm here."

"All right," Sam said. "Are you going to the wedding?"

The wedding. As if it was the only wedding in Diablo.

Actually, he hadn't heard of any other Diablo weddings lately, and if there'd been some, Fiona would definitely have been keeping the scoreboard updated for everyone, particularly him and his brothers. He sighed. "I might. Then again, I mightn't."

Jonas shrugged. "Let us know if you need anything."

"Yeah," Rafe said, "short of a shot of pride."

Judah blinked. "What's that supposed to mean?"

Sam gazed at him. "Look, bro. It's not like we haven't known forever that you've been carrying an inextinguishable torch for Darla Cameron. What we can't figure out is why you're letting her waltz off with another man."

"Maybe that's not how I see it," Judah said, "and maybe it's none of your business, anyway."

Jonas leaned back. "We could be wrong. Maybe you haven't always been in love with her."

"Darla and I are friends. That's it."

Sam sniffed. "As long as you're cool with it, we are, too. We support you, whatever you decide. I mean, if you get an itch to crawl through her bedroom window, we'll hold the ladder for you."

"No ladders will be necessary." Judah tried not to think about the few moments he'd held Darla in his arms. "She's chosen her man, and—"

"Ah-ha!" Rafe exclaimed. "You admit she didn't choose you!"

"She didn't choose any of you, either. It's not a special situation," Judah said, feeling cranky.

"So you admit you were in a position to be chosen," Sam said, sounding like the lawyer he was. "You were a candidate, if a slightly lazy one. But there's still time to present your case. Females change their minds like the wind. And ladies love it when a last-minute challenger shows up to yodel his heartstrings under ye olde bedroom window. I say go for it. Yodel away. You can borrow my guitar."

"Darla's doing just fine," Judah said. "Everything is in the works. She's got her shoes, her flowers and no doubt something blue."

"The really blue thing at that wedding is going to be you," Jonas said, "if you don't get up off your duff and speak before the forever-hold-your-peace."

There was no use. He was going to be harried to death by the people who should have supported his wish to be a silent sufferer. And this was light treatment, Judah realized, compared to what he'd probably be treated to in town, and especially at the wedding. Pitying looks, questioning gazes—

"What about the baby?" Sam asked. "What if it's yours?"

Judah frowned, aware of a sudden urge to stuff a fist in Sam's mouth. "What baby?"

Rafe studied him. "You know Darla is pregnant."

"Is that known?" Judah asked, his heart beating hard. "Or is it gossip based on her apparently whirlwind marriage?"

"She was seen buying a pregnancy test a while ago," Jonas said with a shrug. "This is a small town, and though she sent a friend in to purchase it, the bag made a clear exchange, which was duly noted by several people."

"Who were spying like old-time geezers," Judah said, not happy to hear confirmation of his own suspicions. "It doesn't mean she's pregnant. It could have been a negative test. She could have been giving it to Jackie, for all you know. And," he said, finishing with a flourish, "there's every possibility she's getting married because she wants to, and is in love, and the lure of owning her own bridal shop finally got to her. If you owned a machine shop, wouldn't it kill you if you could never use the tools?"

"Boy, are you caging your inner lion," Rafe said. "Hey, we've got your back, bro. We know how to shine the old badge of pride. No one will ever get from us how you got left in the dust." He shook his head, more sympathetic than Judah could stand.

"That's it," he said. "I've just seen a flash of my future, and I'm taking a rain check on it. The only way to get away from you bunch of know-it-alls is to disappear on you." Judah waved an expansive arm. "With no forwarding address. Don't even try to find me. Consider me gone with the wind, in order to save the dregs of my life." He crammed his hat on his head and turned to depart, with one last thought making him swing back around to his brothers, who watched him with open curiosity.

"And you can tell everybody in Diablo that my heart was not broken, thank you very much. You can tell them that bull riding was always my only love, and is to this day." He made a grandiose exit, proud of himself for the charade he'd perpetrated.

No one would ever know he was lying like a rug.

His brothers looked at each other after Judah left.

"Are we going to tell him that the boxes of condoms we all received at Creed's bachelor party were gag gifts? Creed's parting wish that we'd all get hung by our own family jewels?" Sam asked. "It's possible Judah didn't get the joke."

"I think we leave it alone," Jonas said. "Judah

doesn't seem to want to consider that the child Darla might be carrying is his."

Rafe nodded. "*If* she is four months pregnant, as we hear she is, and the birth coincides with Creed and Aberdeen's wedding night, then it may be obvious."

"Why wouldn't Darla tell Judah?" Sam's forehead wrinkled. "That's the only thing that's not making sense. Wouldn't she just say, hey, that night of passion resulted in some passion fruit?"

"They've been running away from each other for so long, admitting that she's pregnant by Judah is the last thing Darla would do. He never acts as if he likes her, much less loves her. Ladies do not dig the strong, silent type when they need some reassurance, and Judah's been playing the role of Macho Man with gusto," Jonas said. "What woman wants a man if she thinks he doesn't love her?"

"Anyway, we're in way over our heads here," Rafe said. "We could have this all wrong. Maybe they never did the deed that night. Maybe Creed never saw them go off together. Darla could be pregnant by the bronc buster doctor, not that anyone ever mentioned them dating. It's not like we can ask her, because she's not even telling anyone she's in a family way. Rumors may be flying, but no one's going to mention them to the blushing bride."

They thought about the problem some more, then Jonas shrugged. "We'll know by November, I guess."

"Or not," Sam said. "She may choose to never reveal the real father."

"And Judah loses out on being a dad," Rafe mused. "Which would really be a loss, because he'd probably make a decent one. I mean, if Creed and Pete can do it, why not Judah?"

But there was nothing they could do about it. Darla was getting married, and Judah was gone, and neither one of them seemed to care that true love was being held captive by stubborn hearts.

"I hope I'm not that dumb when a beautiful woman loves me," Sam said with a sigh, and both his brothers immediately said, "You will be."

"But not as dumb as Judah," Sam muttered to himself, listening to Judah's truck roar away.

"I say it's time we engage Aunt Fiona," Jonas suggested, and his brothers nodded. "This situation could be dire."

"Maybe, maybe not," Sam said, "but Judah certainly isn't going to do anything to save himself."

Chapter 2

Rafe, Sam and Jonas went to the kitchen to find Fiona. As a rule, she or Burke could be found there, or nearby, at least. It was nearly the dinner hour, a very odd time for Judah to decide to depart, which just showed that even an empty stomach hadn't deterred his boneheadedness.

The kitchen was empty. The scents of wondrous culinary delights (Fiona could cook like no other, and Burke was no slouch in their shared gastronomic hobby) were absent. Rafe felt his stomach rumble and figured this might be an unannounced catch-as-catch-can night. They had those at Rancho Diablo, though rarely. Usually on the nights their fearless aunt had bingo or her book reading club or a church group, she cut them loose. But at least a pie would be left on the kitchen counter, with a note on the Today's Meal chalkboard that read something to the effect of "Tough Luck! You're Stuck!"

Tonight, all that was on the counter was a single bar of something silver. Rafe, Jonas and Sam crowded around it, perplexed.

"That's not cherry pie," Sam said.

"It's mined silver," Jonas said. "Mined and pressed into a bar. See the .925 on it?"

Rafe blinked. "Why would Fiona leave us a bar of silver?"

"All those years people have whispered about there being a silver mine on our land suddenly comes to mind," Sam said, his voice hushed.

Rafe's gaze went back to the bar. "We've been over every inch of Rancho Diablo. There's no way."

"I don't know," Jonas said. "Why else would Aunt Fiona have a silver bar?"

"Because she's putting it in her stock portfolio," Sam said. "She bought some through a television advertisement, or a jeweler, to diversify her nest egg. It's not sound to leave all one's investments in the stock market or the national currency. She's just taken physical possession of some of her holdings, I would guess."

"But what if it's not part of her nest egg?" Rafe asked. "What if there really is a silver mine on Rancho Diablo? That would explain why Bode Jenkins is so hot to get this place."

They heard Burke whistling upstairs, and the chirping sound of Fiona's voice.

"Quick," Jonas said. "Outside."

They hustled out like furtive thieves. Rafe closed the door carefully behind him. His brothers had already skedaddled down the white graveled drive toward the barns.

Rafe hurried after them. "Why don't we ask her what it is? What if there is silver on the ranch? What if Bode is sniffing around for it?"

"Then she probably wouldn't have left proof of its existence lying out on the kitchen counter," Sam said. "By now, Bode's had this place satellite mapped, I'm sure. He's had the geographic and mineral composition of the land gone over. If there was silver around here, he would know before we would."

"All I'm suggesting," Rafe said, "is that maybe it's time we quit being so worried about offending Fiona. That we just ask her."

His brothers stopped, gave him a long eyeballing. Rafe shrugged. "I mean, what the hell?" he asked. "If we have a silver mine, hurrah for us. It doesn't change anything."

"If there's a silver mine, and Fiona's been putting away dividends all these years, I don't want to know." Jonas shrugged. "Look, I love Fiona. I don't give a damn if there's solid gold under this ranch from corner to corner, and she plans to ferret all of it off like a conquistador. I really don't care. So I'm not asking."

Jonas had a point. Rafe didn't want to hurt Fiona's feelings, either. She'd given up a pretty decent life in Ireland to come take care of them, which couldn't have been easy. They had not been a snap to raise. "All right," Rafe said, "by now she's probably hidden the damn thing. So can we go back now, act like we didn't see it and go over the Judah problem with her? I'm pretty certain we need a guiding hand here."

They went back to the house, and this time, Jonas banged on the kitchen door.

Fiona flung it open. "For heaven's sake. Can't you open a door by yourselves? Three big strong men can't figure out how to use the key?" She glanced at the doorknob. "The door isn't locked. Why are you knocking, like this isn't your house?"

They stared at their tiny aunt. Her eyes were kind, her voice teasing, but she seemed truly mystified. Rafe swallowed. "Aunt Fiona, we wonder if you have a moment so we might pick your brain?"

"So you're standing on the porch? You won't pick it out there. When you're ready, come inside."

They went in, glancing at each other like errant school boys. "You bring up the joke condoms," Rafe said quietly to Jonas. "You're the oldest. I'm not comfortable talking about sex with my aunt."

Jonas straightened his shoulders. "It's not a conversation I want to have, but no doubt she's heard worse."

"That's true," Sam said. "You go for it, Jonas. We support you."

Fiona waved them into the kitchen, where they leaned against the counters. The silver bar was gone, which Rafe had expected. His brothers gave him the same "You see?" look, to which he simply shrugged. He was more worried about condoms than silver bars at the moment.

"Rafe wants to tell you something," Jonas said. "Right, Rafe?"

He gulped, straightened. "I guess so." He flashed Jonas an irate glare with his eyes. "Judah has departed."

Fiona nodded. "He said he longed to test his mettle on the back of an angry bull. I told him to have at it. Judah's been restless lately."

Rafe swallowed again. "Aunt Fiona," he said carefully, not sure how to begin, and then Sam said, "Oh, come on. It's not that hard."

Rafe gave his brother a heated look, wishing he could swing his boot against Sam's backside.

"Spit it out," Fiona said. "You're acting like you have something horrible to tell me. I've got butterflies jumping in my stomach just looking at you, like the time you came to tell me you'd burned down the schoolhouse. You hadn't, but you thought you had—"

Rafe cleared his throat. "Creed gave us all boxes of prank condoms at his bachelor party as a send-off."

Fiona looked at him. "Prank condoms?"

He nodded. "Different colors, different, uh, styles. In the box, there were 'trick' condoms. You were supposed to guess which of the twelve was the trick."

Fiona wrinkled her nose. "What ape thought of that?"

"Creed," Sam and Jonas said.

"I mean, the product." Fiona sighed. "Only an imbecile would buy... Oh, never mind. None of you were dumb enough not to get the joke, so ha-ha."

"We hear rumors," Jonas said, trying to help his brother out, for which Rafe was relieved, "that Darla might be expecting a baby."

Fiona frowned. "What does that have to do with us?"

"Well, is she?" Sam asked.

"It seems there may be a reason for the marital haste." Fiona opened the refrigerator and took out a strawberry icebox pie. She cut them each a generous slice, and the brothers eagerly gathered around with grateful thanks. "I have a Books'n'Bingo Society meeting tonight, and I intend to ask my dear friend about this rumor."

"Creed thinks," Sam said, around a mouthful of pie, "that Darla and Judah may have had a…"

She glanced at him. "Romantic interlude?"

All three brothers nodded.

"Did you ask Judah?" she inquired.

They shook their heads.

She gazed at all of them. "Do we suspect joke condoms might come into play?"

"We fear they might have," Sam said. "They could have. I threw my Trojan horse away," he said hastily. "But then, I'm a lawyer. I read fine print. When a box says 'Gag gift only, not for use in preventing pregnancy,' I hurl it like a ticking bomb into the nearest trash can."

"Too bad," Fiona shot back. "I like babies, and four of you are dragging your feet."

"Worse than dragging our feet. Judah's gone away with a broken heart," Rafe said.

"And the joke may be on him?" Fiona eyed each of them. "You believe Darla's marrying this other man as a cover for a relationship she may have had with Judah?"

"What we're theorizing," Jonas said, "is that he may have thought the condoms *were* the gag gift, not that they were useless." Jonas sighed. "I, too, threw Creed's gift in the trash. I didn't want hot-pink condom sex with anyone I know."

They all looked at him with raised brows.

"I threw mine away, too," Rafe admitted. "I'm afraid of children. At least I think I am. Or maybe I'm afraid of getting married," he said cheerfully. "When

I watched Creed go down like a tranquilized bull, I said, 'Rafe, you are not your twin.'"

"It's possible Judah tossed them as well," Fiona said. "And for all we know, Darla isn't pregnant, although I wouldn't bank on it at this point." She wrapped up the strawberry pie and returned it to the fridge. "Rafe, run upstairs and look in Judah's nightstand, since that's where he stayed that night because of the wedding guest housing situation."

"Not me," Rafe said, "I never snoop."

Fiona elevated a brow. "We can't let him go all over several states riding on the circuit and maybe scattering his seed, so to speak. If he took the condoms with him, and if he honestly needs glasses so much that he can't read a box—"

"Who reads the label on a box of condoms besides Sam?" Rafe said. "You just whip the foil packet out and—"

"Go," Fiona said. "Your brother's future may be at stake."

"I'm not doing it," Rafe said, and he meant it.

Fiona plucked three straws from a broom. "Draw," she told the brothers. "Short straw plays detective."

A moment later, Rafe held the short straw. "It's not fair," he grumbled. "I'm the existential one in the family. I believe in reading, and thinking deep thoughts, not nosing into places I don't belong." But he went up the stairs. In his heart Rafe knew that Judah and Darla belonged together. But they couldn't just fall into each other's arms and make it easy on everybody. "Leaving me with the difficult tasks," he muttered, reluctantly opening his brother's nightstand.

And there was the black box of joke condoms with the hot-pink smiley faces, peace signs and lip prints.

"Hurry up!" Fiona bellowed from the stairs. "You're not panning for gold! The suspense is killing us."

Rafe grunted. He opened the box.

There were nine left.

"Uh-oh," he muttered, and went downstairs with his report.

"Three?" Fiona said, when Rafe revealed his findings. "Three have been…are missing?" She looked distressed. "I hope Judah hasn't had more than one situation where such an item might be called for."

They all looked at her, their faces questioning.

"One woman," Fiona clarified, and they all said, "Oh, yeah, yeah, right."

The brothers glanced at each other, worried.

Rafe shifted. "What do we do now?"

They all gazed expectantly at Fiona. This was the counsel they had come to hear.

She shrugged and put on her wrap. "Nothing you can do. No one can save a man if he decides to give up his ground to the enemy. Faint heart never won fair lady and all that. Good night, nephews," she said. "Wish me luck at bingo tonight!"

And she tootled out the door.

The brothers looked after her.

"That was not helpful," Sam said.

"I agree," Rafe said. "I thought she'd give us the typical, in-depth Fiona strategy."

"She's right," Jonas said. "And we should be taking notes to remember this unfortunate episode in our brother's life."

"We probably won't," Rafe said morosely, and sat down to finish his pie. "I heard once that men are slow learners." And he wasn't going to tell anyone that it was Judge Julie Jenkins, next-door ranch owner and Bode's daughter, who had thrown that pearl of wisdom at his head.

Darla looked at Jackie Callahan, co-owner of the Magic Wedding Dress Shop. "Pull harder," she said. "I'm not letting out my dress. I just bought it."

Jackie tugged at the fabric. "The satin just doesn't want to give. And I don't think it's good for the baby...."

Darla looked at herself in the triple mirror. "I've been eating a lot of strawberries. I crave them."

"That shouldn't cause so much weight gain," Jackie said. "Not that you look like you've gained *so* very much."

"On ice cream," Darla said, aware that her friend was trying to be tactful. "Strawberries on top of vanilla ice cream."

"Oh." Jackie looked at her. "Maybe switch to frozen yogurt?"

"There's only a week before the wedding. I think the waistline isn't going backward on the measuring tape." She looked at herself, turning around slowly, and then frowned. "Something's not right."

"I think the dress is beautiful on you."

"Thank you," Darla murmured. "I'm not sure what's not quite right, but there's definitely something."

"Nerves?" Jackie said. "Brides get them. They want everything to be perfect. We've certainly seen our share of Nervous Nells in here."

"I'm not nervous," Darla said. *What I am is not in love. And that's what's wrong. I'm not in love with the man I'm marrying. And he's not in love with me.*

"Do you want to try a different gown?" Jackie asked, and Darla shook her head.

"No. This one will do." She went to change. The gown was not what was wrong. She could wear a paper bag, or a gown fit for a royal princess, and it wouldn't matter.

"Well," Jackie said as Darla came back out, "I think I know what the problem is."

She looked at her, hoping her dear friend, business partner and maid of honor didn't.

"You're not wearing the magic wedding dress," Jackie said. "You always said it was your dream gown." She smiled at Darla. "It worked for me."

Darla's gaze slid to the magic wedding dress. It was true. Ever since Sabrina McKinley had brought the gown to her, saying that it brought true luck to the wearer, she had known it was the only gown for her. It was the most beautiful, magical dress she'd ever seen. Sparkly and iridescent, it made her catch her breath.

But she couldn't wear it, not to marry someone she didn't love with all her heart. She was fond of her fiancé. Dr. Sidney Tunstall was a perfect match on paper. Even he'd said that. He needed a wife for his career, and she…well, she needed not to think about the fact that somehow she'd gotten pregnant by Judah Callahan even though she knew he'd conscientiously used a condom every time they'd made love that incredible night.

He would never believe this was his baby.

"I don't think I believe in magic," Darla said.

Jackie looked at her. "Magic is what we sell."

"I know," Darla said, "but these days, I'm concentrating on the practical." *Practical, not romantic. No magic, just the bare business proposal. And one day, I'll tell Judah the truth—after I've backed it up with a DNA test.*

She'd had hopes that he was in love with her—but she knew better. Hijacking a guy just because he'd spent one evening giving her the pleasure of her life was no way to win his heart. And especially not when he'd been so very careful with protection. Judah was definitely a hunk who didn't want to get caught. He'd always been the favorite of the ladies, and he never stayed with just one.

Practical. That was how it had to be.

Judah was into living lucky. That was his new approach. He was going to swing by his tail in the jungle of life until he beat the jungle back. He was feeling mean and tough, and resolved to win. Focused.

He put his entry in for a bull riding event in Los Rios, New Mexico, and smiled at the cute brunette who took his money.

"Haven't seen you in a while, Judah," she said. "Where have you been hiding?"

"On the ranch." He didn't want to think about Rancho Diablo right now. "But now I'm back, and I plan on winning. How many entries are there?"

"Quite a few today. You're just in time. We were about to close registration."

"Then I'm lucky," he said.

"You could get luckier," she said with a smile.

He took that in, maybe half tempted, then shrugged. "You're too good for me, darlin'," he said. He winked at her and headed off to find some drinking buddies, telling himself that he hadn't accepted the brunette's generous offer because he was in a dark mood—really dark. Refusing her hadn't anything to do with Darla Cameron.

But thinking about Darla reminded him that she was marrying another man, and he definitely didn't want to think darker thoughts than necessary, so he pushed her out of his mind. Broken hearts were a dime a dozen, so his wasn't special. He headed to the bar, glad to see some cowboys he knew.

He was welcomed up to the bar with loud greetings.

"You're in?" someone asked, and Judah nodded.

"I'm taking nine months on the circuit to see what I can do. If I can break even and stay healthy, maybe I'll stay until I'm old and gray." He took the beer that the bartender handed him, raising it to the crowd. "And one for all my friends."

His buddies cheered. Judah grinned. This was what he needed. A buddy chorus of men who understood life as he did.

The little brunette slid into the bar, sending a smile his way. Female companionship wouldn't kill him, either. He couldn't slobber in his beer over Darla forever.

He'd left his condoms at home.

And that was probably lucky, too. Judah sighed and looked at his already empty bottle. He didn't need to sleep with a female. He needed Darla, but Darla—damn her lovely just-right-for-him body—didn't need him at all. Just when he'd finally kissed the princess of

his dreams—after forgoing the temptation for years—
the princess had turned into a faithless frog.

Which just showed you that fairy tales had it all
wrong. It wasn't the woman who always kissed the
frog—sometimes it was the guy who got gigged.

Chapter 3

Darla wondered if she was making the right decision.
Her whole world reeled as she left the doctor's office.

Twins. She was having twins. It was the last thing
she'd expected to hear at her prenatal checkup. And
now she knew why she was getting so big so fast, why
her wedding gown was already tight. And her babies'
father was the wildest of the Callahans.

Her phone rang, startling her. The display read Rancho Diablo. She didn't necessarily want to talk to Fiona
at the moment, but a friendly voice was probably just
what she needed. "Hello?"

"Darla, it's Sam Callahan. Get your jeans on, doll.
We'll be by in five minutes to pick you up."

"Why?"

"We're getting up a convoy to go watch Judah ride.
He needs all the hometown support he can get. He's

in the finals, and we're borrowing Fiona's party van to take the cheering squad over to Los Rios. So get your boots on and put the cat out for the night."

She didn't have a cat, nor any reason to follow this Pied Piper. Nothing good could come of it. "Sam—"

"And we're picking up Jackie, Sabrina and Julie just for fun. You don't want to be the only girl left in town, do you?"

Put that way, no. But she was getting married in four days, and she was having twins. She was exhausted.

Then again, the last thing she wanted to do was sit around and think about how her life had spun out of control. And if everybody was going to the big event, what harm was there in going, too? "I'll bring my pom-poms."

"That's my girl," Sam said. "We'll take good care of you."

She hung up, feeling like a moth attracted to a bright, hot light. "All right, babies. We're going to go see Daddy ride a big piece of steak around an arena. Your first event. I'm so proud."

Her children might end up as bull riders them-selves, and they would never know that strong, hand-some Judah Callahan was their father. She shivered, thinking about that one wonderful night in his arms.

It would never happen again.

Fiona, Rafe and Jonas waited as Sam hung up the phone.

"No woman wants to be left out of a party." Sam grinned. "Just like you said, Aunt Fiona."

She nodded. "Now remember, when two immov-able objects are forced to move into the same space—"

"It's highly combustible," Rafe said. "Your play on physics is unique, Aunt."

She nodded again. "And remember step two...."

"I feel like a spy," Jonas said. "You'd better not ever play any of these tricks on me, redoubtable aunt."

"Oh, I wouldn't *think* of it," Fiona said, her eyes round.

Her nephews grunted in unison, not falling for that, and headed off to pick up the other ladies.

"Did you hear my oldest nephew, Burke, my love?"

"I did." He placed a gentle kiss against her temple. "I do believe he offered you a challenge."

Fiona smiled. "That's exactly what I heard, too. And I wouldn't dream of not accepting a challenge."

Judah wasn't nervous about his rides. He'd almost been carried by angel's wings on every one so far, so high did his bulls buck and thrash, so easily did he hit eight on every ride. Never in his life had he ridden so well. Somehow the bulls he'd drawn were rank, and somehow, he was unbeatable. If riding bulls could always be so easy...and yet, in all his years, he'd never ridden like this. He was living in the moment, blessed by the rodeo-loving gods.

And then it happened. He was sitting outside, thinking about his next ride, pondering the bull he'd drawn—Lightfoot Bill was known for tricks, and better cowboys than him had come flying off—when the hometown crowd came whooping and hollering over to him. It wasn't a huge scene they made, just enough to let him know they'd brought practically every one of their friends, including Darla Cameron.

She was definitely pregnant. Even he, who had little

experience with the changes of a woman's body, could see that the lady he loved was with child. Her tummy protruded despite the pretty blue dress she wore, and if his eyes didn't deceive him her breasts were taking on the shape of sweet cantaloupes.

Yum.

She was beautiful, Madonna-like. Judah's heart thundered as he met Darla's gaze.

His concentration went haywire. "Hello, Darla," he said, and she said, "Hi, Judah. Good luck."

And then she went inside the arena, and the other ladies kissed his cheek and wished him a long ride, and his brothers clapped him on the back with hearty thuds, telling him he was *the man!*

But he didn't feel like *the man.* What man wanted to see his ladylove pregnant by another guy? The thought cramped his gut.

He was a wimp. A romantic fool.

He dragged himself inside. A couple of his brothers rallied around, giving him a pep talk he didn't hear. "Why'd you bring her?" he asked dully.

"Who?" Rafe asked.

"Darla." He couldn't speak her name without feeling pain.

"We couldn't leave her behind," Sam said. "Now buck up, bro, and think about your ride. I heard Lightfoot took his last rider for a spin into the boards."

"Yeah." That rider had busted his leg and would be out for a few months. Judah put his mouth guard in, a preride ritual that always focused his mind on the next few moments.

His mind wouldn't cooperate. "She's beautiful," he said, and Sam said, "What?"

Judah couldn't form words clearly around the mouth guard and his rattled brain. It didn't matter. Darla wasn't his, wasn't ever going to be his, and that baby she was carrying was going to have a rodeo doctor for a daddy. Not him.

And then he realized why Darla was here. She hadn't come to see him. Her fiancé—husband-to-be in just a few days—was working there tonight.

"Well, I'm not going to need his services," he said, and Sam said, "What, ass? I can't hear you with that mouth guard in. Why'd you put it in if you were going to go all Oprah on me?"

Lightfoot Bill was in the chute. Judah got on the rails.

It was time to score big. All he needed was to keep riding like he'd been riding—and then it wouldn't matter that his heart was blown out.

Nothing was about to matter, except hanging on.

Darla didn't know when she'd ever been so nervous. Jackie held her hand, and Sabrina McKinley clutched her fingers on the other side. "Having any visions?" Darla asked Sabrina.

"Only that you're having twins," Sabrina whispered back.

Darla looked at her in shock. "You really are psychic, aren't you?"

"I was teasing. Nice to know I can occasionally guess right." Sabrina smiled at her. "He'll be fine. At least I hope so."

Darla hoped the row of Callahan men behind them—and most especially Fiona—hadn't heard her big news. "Don't tell anyone. I'm still trying to get over the shock."

Sabrina laughed, and Jonas said, "What's so funny? My brother's about to ride down there." So the women shared an eye roll and went back to watching the arena.

The gate swung open and the bull came out jacked and on a mission. Darla was pretty certain her breath completely stopped. She didn't realize she was squeezing Jackie's and Sabrina's hands until the buzzer went off.

The brothers jumped to their feet, cheering for Judah. So did everyone else from Diablo. Darla sat back down, closing her eyes for a moment, awash in conflicting emotions. Judah scared her to death. He loved living dangerously. He always had. Her heart had always been drawn to that. She herself was practical, calculating risks and making sure she stayed in a safe zone.

She wasn't safe anymore. She was wildly in love with Judah Callahan, and in four days she was marrying someone who was not the father of her children. Her babies' father was down there being congratulated, so far away from her they might as well be in different hemispheres.

Judah's score shot him into second place, and Darla tried to breathe.

"Man, that was something!" Jonas said. "That bull laid out all the tricks it knew to get Judah off."

"He's got to be happy with that score," Rafe said. "Now, if he can just keep it going."

Darla closed her eyes, wishing she'd never agreed to come. The nurse in her wished Judah had a safer calling; the practical side of her knew he was doing what he loved best.

Which was why she hadn't said a word to him about being a father.

"You'll have to tell him sooner or later," Sabrina said.

Darla stared at her. "Tell him what?" she asked, hoping her secret was still safe.

"That he's going to be a dad," her friend said.

"Hey, Sabrina," Fiona said from behind them. "I'm thinking about hiring you away from Bode. What would you say to that?"

They all turned to look at the older woman.

"Is that wise?" Sam asked. "Not that I don't approve, but won't that get Bode on you all over again?"

Fiona shrugged. "I'm in the mood to annoy Bode."

Burke said, "We could really use the extra help. There's been so many babies, and Fiona wants to spend all her time holding them."

Darla felt her heart drop again. Her children would never be part of the love in the Callahan household. It was their rightful place. There were a lot of people at Rancho Diablo who would love the twins, if they knew about them. And she had no right keeping Judah in the dark.

Suddenly, Darla knew Sabrina was right. She had to find a way to tell Judah—before she said "I do."

It wasn't going to be easy, and he probably wouldn't believe her. But her children deserved an honest start in life—no secret-baby surprises. Her gaze found Judah in the arena—though she should have been looking at her rodeo physician fiancé—and it seemed Judah glanced her way before he disappeared.

I'll tell him tonight.

* * *

It wasn't Judah's policy to make love to a woman the night before a big ride. He had two more rides tomorrow. He was sitting on a big score tonight—second place was sitting pretty. It left him room to chase, but he wasn't the target. Second was great.

Therefore, lovemaking was the last thing on his mind.

Well, not the last thing. Every time he glanced up at Darla in the stands, looking like a hot dream, he had to fight his mind to focus.

He wasn't planning on making love.

But when she came to him and asked him if he had five minutes to talk to her—alone—a devil jumped to life inside him. "My room's across the street."

She stared at him, her cheeks pink. Oh, he knew her fiancé was here. He'd spoken to the good doc at least five times tonight. He didn't hold a grudge against the man.

If he held a grudge against anyone, Judah thought, it was this woman. She'd snared his heart, then trashed it. He didn't feel bad about reminding her that she'd once been behind a locked door with him.

"I can't go to your room." Darla's face was pale.

"Then talk here." He crossed his arms. "I'm listening."

"I can't talk to you here," she said, glancing around. "Isn't there someplace we can talk privately?"

Judah shrugged and turned back to taking off his gear. "My room."

She took a deep breath. "All right."

He was surprised that she relented. "Here's my key. I'll be there in five." He handed it to her, and she snatched it, looking around furtively, which almost made him smile. Darla did not do sneaky well. She was more sweet than sneaky. She must have something big on her mind if she was willing to rendezvous with him. Idly, he wondered about it, decided he'd never understand the mysteries of the female mind, and promptly dismissed it. She was probably going to do the guilt trip thing, like how the night they'd spent together hadn't meant anything, and now that she was getting married, if he would keep the little detail about their evening under his hat, she'd be eternally grateful, blah-blah-blah.

He'd act as if it hadn't meant a thing to him, either, and let her go on to her newly married life with a clear conscience.

But first he let her stew in her juices for a little bit. Then he followed after her, tapping on his door. She let him in.

"Well? What's so urgent?" He put *I'm a busy man* in his voice, so she'd get her soliloquy over with, thereby sparing both of them the agony.

Darla's eyes were huge as she stared at him; he could tell she was nervous. Judah kept his gaze away from her belly. Looking at her, knowing she was pregnant, was killing him. No man should be in love with a woman and know she was carrying another man's child.

"I'm pregnant."

"I can see that. Congratulations."

"Thank you." She swallowed. "Congratulations to you as well."

"Yeah. It was a lucky ride. I need a couple more tomorrow." He didn't look toward his bed, because if he did, he'd be tempted to drag Darla there. And he was a gentleman. Barely.

"I mean, congratulations to you, because you're having a baby, too."

He laughed. "Not me. I'm—" He stopped, looked at her carefully. Her face was drained of color. "You're not saying—"

She nodded. "I'm afraid so."

He stared at her, gazing deep into her eyes. Darla was not a dishonest woman. She wouldn't tell him this unless she believed it to be true. "I don't get it. How?"

"I don't know! Maybe there was a tear." She glared at him. "You'd know better than me."

He blinked. The condoms had been given to him by Creed at his bachelor party. The side of the box had read *For The Guy Who's Large and In Charge.* Judah remembered vaguely thinking all that might be true, and that it was pretty damn competitive of Creed to try to keep the other brothers from getting themselves in the family way, just so he could stay in the lead for the ranch.

Judah sank into a cracked vinyl chair near a tiny round table. "Why are you telling me this now?"

She breathed in deeply, obviously trying to calm herself. "I wasn't going to tell you at all. But then I realized that was wrong. I don't want to have secret babies."

"Babies?" His heart ground to a halt in his chest. *"Babies?"*

She nodded. "We're having twins."

Judah's world opened up, chasmlike. His pulse jumped, more fiercely than when he'd been on the back of Lightfoot. "You say we're—"

"Yes."

He passed a hand across his forehead, realized he was sweating under his hat. "I don't mean to be coarse, but how do you know that you're pregnant by me and not by your fiancé?" He wasn't about to say the man's name.

"Because I've never slept with him."

"Why not? Not to be indelicate—"

"It doesn't matter," Darla said. "We don't have that kind of relationship."

Maybe the man was an idiot. Maybe his thing didn't work. Judah couldn't believe that a guy who was fortunate enough to get a ring on Darla's finger wouldn't be making love to her like a madman every night. "Every man has *that* kind of relationship, darlin'."

She wore embarrassment like a heavy winter cloak. "When Sid asked me to marry him, we agreed on a business relationship. That's it, and no more."

Sid. Judah leaned back, trying to take in everything he was hearing. "That's why you were so eager to get in my bed that night. You wanted a good time before you tied yourself to this *business* relationship."

She hadn't been interested in business with Judah.

A blush crossed her cheeks. "I—yes. And I'm not sorry about it. Even now."

"Nice to know you don't regret it." He couldn't help the sour tone in his voice. "So what does Tunstall think about you being pregnant?"

Darla stared him down. "It was unexpected, obviously, but he's not opposed to being a father."

Judah jumped to his feet, crossing to her. "Let me tell you something, Darla Cameron. If you're telling the truth—and something tells me you are—no one will be a father to my children but me. Let's just get that straight up front." He studied her, deciding it was time this relationship got on the right track. "Something's going to have to change about your wedding plans, sweetheart."

Darla shook her head at him. Judah was angry. She'd expected anger, but not his statement about her wedding. "What exactly does that mean?"

He went back to his chair, dropping into it with an enigmatic smile shadowing his lips. "It means you've got the tiger by the tail, and now you're going to have to tame it. I shouldn't have to spell anything out for you. You knew when you told me this that your wedding to the good doc was never going to happen."

"I know no such thing!"

"You're not marrying another man while you're carrying my children. So put all that out of your sweet head."

Darla felt her own stubbornness rise. "I'm not having children out of wedlock when I've got a perfectly good groom planning to be my husband, Judah. It's no inconvenience to you if I'm married. You're not planning on being around."

She could see by Judah's expression that he was fighting to be civil. But he didn't have the right to tell her how to run her life.

"It'll be inconvenient for you when two grooms are standing at the altar with you on your wedding day," Judah said.

"You're not suggesting that you want to marry me?"

He nodded. "If you're pregnant by me, the only man you're marrying is me. That's the way *I* do business, babe."

Annoyance rose inside her. "Not that I expect romance in a proposal, but I don't want to be told what I'm going to do, either."

"And I don't want to be told that I'm going to be a father, and that someone else is planning to raise my children." He gave her a determined stare. "I'm being very reasonable, under the circumstances."

This was awful. No woman wanted the man she loved this way. Darla wished she could walk out the door and forget these past ten minutes had ever happened. But she couldn't. Her pride couldn't be the most important thing to her right now—she had her children's welfare to consider. "I'll think about your proposal," she said coolly, going to the door.

"You do that, and don't forget to tell the good doc your business merger's off." Judah followed, putting his hand on the doorknob to open the door for her—at least that's what she thought he was going to do—before pressing his lips against her cheek, his stubble grazing her skin ever so slightly. "Just so you know, Darla, I don't plan on mixing business with my marriage."

His meaning was unmistakable. His hand moved to her waist in a possessive motion, lingering at her hip just for a second, capturing her. She remembered everything—how good he'd made her feel, how magical the night in his arms had been—and wished his proposal was made from love and not possessiveness.

Judah pulled the door open. "Next time I see you will be at the altar. Till death do us part, darlin'."

Darla stared at him for a long, wary second before stalking off.

If Judah Callahan thought she was going to marry a hardheaded, mule-stubborn man like him, then he was in for a shock.

Chapter 4

Judah had never been one to let someone else fight his battles. So it wasn't even a stretch for him to hunt up Dr. Sidney Tunstall. The good doctor was taking a breather in a bar down the street, which was good because Judah needed a drink himself.

First things first. "Tunstall," he said, seating himself next to the ex-bronc buster. "We have business to discuss."

Sidney put down his beer and gave him a long look. "Do we?"

Judah nodded. "I think it's only fair to let you know that you'll be hearing from Darla that your wedding is off."

The doctor raised a brow. "And how would you know?"

"Because," Judah said, "we just finished having a chat, Darla and I. And we came to the same conclusion. She can't marry you."

Sidney finished his beer, waved for another. "I'll wait to hear that from her, if you don't mind, Callahan."

"See, though, I *do* mind." He put down the money to pay for the beer. Sidney grunted, not about to utter any gratitude, and Judah couldn't blame him. "Darla says she's expecting my children. So that means she'll be taking the Callahan name. *My* name."

Sidney turned. "I happen to know that Darla thinks you're an ass she wishes she'd never met. And she's never mentioned you being the father of her children, so as far as I'm concerned, you're not even in the picture." He raised his bottle in a sardonic wave. "Thanks for the brew, but buzz off and let me drink it in peace."

Judah elected to ignore the insult. "What do you mean, you don't know about her being pregnant by me?"

The doctor shrugged. "We never talked about it. I don't need to know everything in her past. And until I know better, you *are* her past."

Judah slumped on his bar stool for a moment. He couldn't be mad at Tunstall—the man clearly wasn't in possession of all the facts. Just like a woman to leave out important details. Judah stood, tossed some tip money on the bar. "Look, Tunstall, you're an innocent party here, so I'm going to cut you some slack. But don't get in my way. I'll be standing at the altar with Darla, I'll be raising my own sons, and that's just the way it is."

"Maybe," Sidney said, "and maybe not."

The man had no idea how thin Judah's temper was at the moment. It was all he could do not to pound good sense into him. But Darla was the person he needed to be setting straight, so he took a deep breath and saun-tered off to collect his wits before his rides tomorrow.

It wasn't going to be easy. His concentration had never been so scattered.

He couldn't decide if it was suddenly finding him-self altar-bound or becoming a father that had him the most bent.

"How *dare* you?" Darla demanded when Judah made it to his motel room an hour later, where she was waiting outside the door. He cast an appreciative eye over the snapping fire in her blue eyes, and her long blond hair. She looked like an angel, but she was going to bless him out like a she-devil.

Which meant that Tunstall had given her the bad news. And that suited Judah just fine.

"I dare," he said, unlocking his door and stepping inside his room with her on his heels, "because that's what I do. *I dare.*"

Her lips compressed for a moment. "You have no right to interfere."

He tossed his hat into the chair. "Just one man chat-ting with another. Don't get your panties in a twist over it, sugar." Grinning, he pulled a beer from the six-pack his brothers had thoughtfully left in his room, satisfied that matters should be straight as an arrow between him and his buttercup.

"I'm not going to marry you, Judah." Darla's chin rose, and her tiny nose nearly pointed at his chin. He so badly wanted to run his finger down her face and tell her everything was going to be just fine, if she'd only settle down and let him take care of her.

"We'll talk about it tomorrow after I ride. There's a

lot of things we'll have to plan, like naming my sons. You'll need to enroll in a prenatal yoga class, too. I hear it's very beneficial for the mother and the babies."

Darla's cheeks went pink. "I'm leaving now," she told him, "and I *am* marrying Sidney. Quit trying to take over my life."

"Whew," Judah said, pulling her close against his chest. "You'll know when I'm trying to take over your life, babe. I'll say, 'Get in my bed,' and you'll go happily because you'll know I'm going to make you feel like a princess."

Irate as Darla was, she leaned into him, and for a moment, completely relaxed.

But she suddenly pulled herself away and marched to the door. "Not a chance, Judah. Goodbye."

The next day Darla carried the magic wedding dress to the back of the store where she couldn't see it. Lately, it had begun to call to her with a siren song of such temptation that she could barely resist it.

"Just try on the gown," Jackie urged. But Darla didn't want to fashion hopes and dreams through simple fabric.

"I don't need fairy tales and magic in my life. I'm making a solid, practical decision to marry a man who's as even-keeled as I am. Judah is a winter wind blowing through a canyon. I could never rely on him."

"But he's the father of your children," Jackie said. "You don't want to do something in the heat of passion, Darla."

"I already did that," she replied, "which is why I'm choosing to be quite selective with my children's futures now. Sidney will be a good father. He comes from a very small family, and has always wanted a large one. We're good friends. I'll be an organized, supportive doctor's wife." Darla stowed the magic wedding gown in the very back of the stock closet, behind back-stock dresses. It did lure her. Sometimes in the night, she could hear a faint rustle of musical chimes, like an antique jewelry box opening to play a lilting melody. The dress was beautiful.

And she wanted it so badly. But she wouldn't admit that to Jackie. Darla wanted to believe in romance and dreams and fairy tales, just like any other bride. Yet she couldn't afford any mistakes. Her whole makeup was geared toward thoughtful, careful decision making. There really wasn't any room for loving a bonehead like Judah.

Unfortunately for her, that bonehead made her body shiver and ache every time she thought of him. It was like that wild winter wind blew over her skin, reminding her of how much she loved him.

But that was the problem. She did love Judah—and she was just another responsibility for him, much like the ranch, and his family, and bull riding. Nothing special or different. Something he had to rule over, boss, command. Before their night together, he'd never spoken to her, nothing more than a passing hello and chitchat about the weather. And he hadn't so much as sought her out at the store since that night, either.

A woman knew when she was the object of a man's passions, and she wasn't that to Judah. He was too wild for her, too unsettled for a woman who liked calm rational choices in her life. Judah was her one moment of reckless abandon—and it didn't take a psychic gift to know they were not meant to be.

"Speaking of psychic," Darla said, and Jackie glanced up.

"Were we?" she asked.

"No, but is Sabrina really going to work for Fiona?"

"I think so. Why?"

"Because I was thinking about asking her if she wanted to work in the shop while I'm out after the babies are born. You can't do it all by yourself," Darla said, staying in practical mode.

"I'll be fine," Jackie assured her.

"You have three little ones. We need backup."

The door swung open, sending the bells over the shop door tinkling. Judah strolled in, the man of her dreams obviously on a mission, judging by the hot gleam in his eyes. Darla's heart jumped into overdrive.

"We need to talk," he stated, and Jackie said, "I'll be heading out for a coffee break. Nice ride last night, Judah."

He tipped his hat to her, and when the door swung shut behind her, he put the closed sign in the window.

"You can't close my shop," Darla said.

"We have to talk."

"Not while I'm working."

"The brides of Diablo will just have to wait while you take a fruit and juice break." He handed her a small bag. "Organic. Every bite."

She began to seethe. "I eat healthy, Judah. You don't need to concern yourself with my diet."

He nodded. "A husband takes care of his wife."

"Not to point out the obvious—"

He handed her a box. "Darla, you have to quit being so stubborn."

"What's this?" She eyed the small dark box as if it were a bomb.

"What a man gives a woman he wants to marry." He grinned, clearly pleased with himself.

She handed it back. "I'll keep the organic breakfast. You can keep your Pandora's box."

He put it on the counter. "If you don't want me to romance you, I'll stop."

"Thank you." She folded her arms.

He shrugged. "If that's the way you want it."

She didn't say anything to confirm his statement because it really wasn't the way she wanted it. But under the circumstances, "no" was the only option. Judah was a conqueror. He wanted to bulldoze her ivory tower and take her prisoner—but letting him do so would be a mistake.

"Why aren't you at the arena?"

"I can't ride when I'm all torn up like this."

That stopped her. She checked his eyes for signs of amusement, found none. Surely he was jesting, though. Judah wasn't a man whose emotions ruled his life. He was all action, sometimes even brave, fearless action. She again checked his expression for teasing, but he looked just as deadly serious as he had a moment ago. It was like gazing into the eyes of an Old West gunslinger in a classic movie: resolute, determined, honest.

She caught her breath. "We don't know each other at all."

He looked at her. "We know each other well enough to be parents."

"It's not enough, Judah. Marriage between two people who don't love each other is a mistake."

"So marrying Sidney would be just as big a mistake," he pointed out.

She took a step back. "I meant that marrying you when you never loved me would be a mistake. And you can't say that you do, Judah."

He remained silent, and she felt he'd conceded her point.

"If you're worried about having access to the children, you'll always have that."

"That can be taken care of legally," Judah growled. "I don't waste any energy worrying about that."

She blinked. "Legally?"

"Sure." He shrugged. "I could have Sam draw up custodial papers tonight if I was worried about you keeping me from my children. That's the least of my concerns."

"It's very nice to know that you've considered all your options, even as you bring me a token of your questionable affection."

His lips thinned. "That's not what I meant."

She turned away. "It doesn't matter, Judah. I don't want to marry you."

"Guess I'll have to take the good doc out and ask him what his secret is."

She whirled around to face him. "There isn't a secret. We have a lot in common. I like the security of knowing that I'm marrying someone a lot like me."

"Sounds boring." Judah leaned against the counter, giving her a lazy smile. "You're too sexy to be boring."

"Sexy?" She looked at him, startled.

"I think so." He shrugged. "Does Sidney?"

"I don't... I don't know," Darla said, confused. "I don't believe so. I mean, why would he?"

Judah grinned at her, and suddenly Darla felt like a mouse in the paws of a playful lion.

"I don't know why he wouldn't," Judah said. "Maybe you should ask ol' Sid." He pushed himself away from the counter, approaching her too quickly for her to step away, even if she'd wanted to, which she didn't. Not really. She was kind of curious to see what new trick he had up his sleeve.

And she wanted him to kiss her. Just once more, to see if it was as good as she remembered.

He stopped in front of her, towering like a strong redwood tree. "I'm sure almost anyone would say that the good doctor is the better man. I know you'll rest comfortably with your very prudent decision."

"Quit being a rat," Darla snapped, and Judah kissed her—on the forehead.

The jerk. She wanted his lips on hers, and she had a feeling he knew it.

"I know when I'm beat." Judah strode to the door, tipped his hat, then placed it over his heart. "Congratulations. And I'll let ol' Sidney know that I have stood aside, his bride having made her choice."

Darla stared as he flipped the closed sign to Open, and loped down the main street of Diablo. Judah Callahan was the most maddening man she'd ever met. Why she'd ever slept with him, she didn't know.

Passion. She'd wanted one night of passion, which she knew Judah would give her, before she did the practical thing and married Dr. Sidney Tunstall. She'd wanted a lusty bedding before her marriage of convenience shut her up in a gilded prison of diligent routine for the rest of her life.

"I have no regrets," she murmured, and then her

gaze fell on the small jeweler's box Judah had left on the wrap stand, next to the healthy snack he'd brought her.

She glanced once at the door to make certain he wasn't outside spying in on her, ready to tease her if she gave in to temptation. But Judah was long gone. There was a crowd on the sidewalk, so she knew that several women had run to chat with him, Judah being a female magnet like all the Callahan men.

Darla's hand rested on the jeweler's box.

Chapter 5

It was one of those days, Judah thought, as he picked himself off the ground. Some days you were the hero, and some days you were the dust between the hero's toes.

Today he might have been the dust under a very ordinary man's feet. Crazy Eight had thrown him within three seconds. It hadn't even been a decent ride. Crazy Eight hadn't been anything spectacular. But just as he'd left the chute, Judah had seen Sidney Tunstall out of the corner of his eye, and somehow his concentration had gone to hell.

He'd gotten thrown so easily a child could have ridden better. Judah slowly wandered over to the rail, slapping his hat against his leg. And somehow, he didn't seem to care. He wondered if Darla had opened the box with his offering in it. A man had to be prepared to fight like a soldier, and Dr. Tunstall was nice enough, but Judah understood women. And what he understood best about women was that a big sparkly diamond sometimes won the fair maiden.

Dr. Tunstall hadn't ponied up yet, so Judah had no compulsion about trying to get the jump on the competition. He'd called Harry Winston's and given a description of exactly what he wanted, then flown to pick it up. And it was a sparkler, like a star plucked from the sky.

No woman could resist it.

"And you know," he said to Sidney when the doc came over to check him out, "I went for the biggest star I could find."

Sidney looked at him. "How do you feel, Judah?"

"Like a winner," he said. "How do you feel, Doc?"

Sidney grunted. "Let's get you where I can take a look at you." He slipped an arm under Judah's, and helped him to a seat.

Then he passed one finger in front of Judah's face. "How many?"

"How many what?" Judah asked.

"Fingers?"

Judah sighed. "I see five fingers, which are going to be a knuckle sandwich, Doc, if you don't get your bony hand out of my face."

Sam came over to stare into his eyes. "Hey, bro. Hearing little birdies or anything? Faraway music? Fairy whisperings?"

Judah drew in another deep breath. "I don't have a concussion. I wasn't paying attention and I got thrown. That's all."

Rafe bent to stare into his face. "That was a doozy of a toss you took. Hit your head or anything?"

It was impossible to convince anybody that his problem wasn't in his head. His problem was in his heart. "If everyone will get out of here, I'm going to get ready for my next ride."

"Assuming I approve you to ride," Sidney said, and Judah glared at him.

"If you don't pass me to ride, I'll kick your ass."

Sidney nodded. "Unprovoked aggression. Loss of concentration. Could be a concussion."

Judah narrowed his eyes. "Don't pull that doctor mumbo jumbo on me. If you keep me from riding, it'll only be because you're trying to keep me from winning. You don't want me to win because you know ladies love cowboys who do. And I am in a serious position to be loved."

Dr. Tunstall shook his head. "I should let you ride. It would serve you right if I let you land on your already cracked head. Maybe it would knock some of the hot air out of you and serve to flatten that outsize ego of yours. But as it is," Dr. Tunstall said, "you're going to have to scratch."

"I will not scratch," Judah declared, and Sidney said, "Then I'll scratch you myself. Either way, your bull riding is over for the next month."

"Month!" Judah hopped to his feet, heading after the departing doctor. "You can't keep me out for a month. I need to ride to make up the points for the finals. You know that as well as anyone."

"I do." Sidney glanced at him before he went back out to the arena to observe the next riders. "Go home and rest, Judah. Don't do any handsprings or jump off any houses, and you should be fine in a few weeks."

"I don't remember hitting my head," Judah muttered, glaring after him. "He's trying to keep me out of the arena."

"Well, that's a shame," Sam said. "Now you'll just have too much time on your hands to hang around Diablo and convince Darla that you'd make a better husband than a cowboy."

Light dawned. "Yeah," he said, "that's what I'll do. I'll cede this hallowed ground and grab territory closer to where yonder princess lays her fair head."

"Oh, jeez," Sam said. "Let's get you to the E.R., bro. I think you've stripped a gear."

Darla had begun to open the box Judah left, but then, not wanting to know what she was passing up, she'd snapped it closed without getting past the first crack in the hinge.

There was no point in torturing herself, since she wasn't marrying him. Ever. He wasn't above tempting her, but she would not succumb. Especially not since she had a wedding in a couple days.

The very thought made her break out in nervous hiccups, something she hadn't done in years. Jackie had gone home, the store was closed for the night and Darla was alone with her thoughts, and a hundred wedding gowns mocking her. She hiccuped twice in rapid succession. The magic wedding gown secreted in the storeroom called to her, dragging her thoughts to it. Temptation—wondering how she would look in the gown of her dreams—tugged at her.

She hiccuped again, painfully and loudly, in the silent store.

She had to know. It would wipe the last questions from her mind, and she could go on with her marriage to Sidney, knowing that a gown was just a gown, after all. It was the groom who made the day special for a bride, a man a woman knew she could trust to be at her side and...

And what? Take care of her? She didn't need that.

But Sidney would expect to take care of her. Judah wouldn't, she mused. He would expect to make love to her most days of the week, and be the guiding light in her life.

Sidney would not expect such hero worship.

Why she was even thinking about both men, comparing them, was a mystery. One of them was about to become her husband. The other wasn't going to be anything more to her than he'd ever been, just a casual acquaintance—with whom she now shared future parenting.

"Argh!" Darla hiccupped wildly. Dashing into the stockroom, she tore the magic wedding dress off its hangar and slipped it on, entranced by the luscious whisper it made sliding over her skin. The dress seemed to enfold her in its beauty, pouring dreams into her heart. The hiccups ceased; her nerves unfurled.

Taking a deep breath, she stepped to the mirrors.

The gown was simply stunning, glinting and sparkling with sequins and crystals, and a luminescence all its own emanating from the fabric. Darla's breath caught as she looked at herself, turning slowly to see all views in the mirrors. It was everything Sabrina had claimed. The same spell that had captured Jackie was now shimmering around her, gentle motes of magic that made her feel like a real bride.

Slowly, Darla gave in and opened the jeweler's box, gasping at the lovely diamond ring. Never had she seen a ring so utterly perfect. Unable to resist, she slipped it on her finger. It fitted perfectly, as if made to order.

Her gaze bounced to the mirrors and caught. She stared, astonished to see herself transformed into a fairy-tale bride.

And behind her, smiling a sexy *you're-all-mine* smile, was her handsome prince.

Darla whirled around. He wasn't here. Her prince was a figment of her imagination—fantasy, wishful thinking, whatever. She hurried to take off the ring, shut it back in its box. She'd had no business trying it on.

And then she felt it, like a butterfly wing brushing against her neck: his lips, pressing against her fevered skin. Darla glanced into the mirror with longing as she watched Judah's ebony head dip to the cradle of her shoulder.

Before she could totally lose herself in the fantasy, she tore the magic wedding dress off and rapidly dressed, fingers shaking as she put on her own clothes. It was unsettling how much time Judah spent in her thoughts. He practically *lived* there, teasing her subconscious.

"It can't go on like this, buddy," she muttered, slipping on her shoes. "Once I'm married to Sidney, you are banished to the bin of ex-boyfriends."

Ex-lover, to be exact, but she'd fudge a little, one day in the future, when her children asked her about their real father. She'd say Judah Callahan had been a boyfriend, someone she'd cared about, but that they just hadn't loved each other....

Except she did love Judah. Darla swallowed against

a tight throat and quickly turned off the store lights, locked the door, ran to her vehicle. Of course she loved him. She'd had a crush on him forever. Once they'd made love, she was lost to him.

And, she thought fiercely, *I'm glad I'm having his babies. It's a piece of him I never dreamed I'd have.*

"Keeping in mind that you've always been a bit irascible," Fiona said, "Judah, this is irritable, even for you."

He sighed, taking the piece of triple chocolate fudge cake she'd brought him. He was going to get fat if Fiona didn't stop ministering to him. Once he'd scratched from riding—very much against his will—and come home, his aunt had appointed herself his watchful angel. He was in bed reading at eight o'clock at night only because he didn't want to hang out with his brothers, who were playing, of all stupid things, badminton under the lights with their wives.

Judah munched dutifully on the delicious cake. "Aunt, you're going to make me fat. I'm not supposed to ride, I can't even play hopscotch with the kids for exercise. Every time I open my eyes, you're stuffing my face with some delicacy." He waved his fork. "You don't have to feed me. I'm capable of making a run to the kitchen myself."

"I'm sure you are." Fiona seated herself on the foot of his bed with a little bounce. "Are you certain you're comfy? Pillow soft enough for your aching head?"

Sighing, he put the cake on his nightstand and sat up, already wishing he had a handful of aspirin. Or an aunt-chaser, like a double whiskey. "What's this all about?"

"Judah," she said, her gaze pinned on his, "I know you found the cave. And I need for you to keep its existence under your hat."

He blinked. "How'd you know I found it?"

"I found your big boot prints there. And Burke had seen you riding that way. Promise me that you won't breathe a word about it. To anyone. Not even…not even Darla."

Judah studied the determined gleam in his aunt's eyes. She was really worked up about this, hence the angelic caregiving she'd been heaping on him. He should have remembered she liked to bake when she was worried about something. "I haven't mentioned it to anybody. I've been preoccupied, and I also needed time to think about why it might be there. But I'd like to know why you're keeping it a secret. Is it because of Bode?"

"Partially," Fiona said, "and partly because we use it often."

"So is that the silver mine everybody's asked about over the years?" Judah reflected on that for a moment. "At one time or another, I guess just about the whole town has gossiped about it. Do we own a silver mine?"

"Not exactly," Fiona said carefully. "You might consider that cave a gift from a friend."

"What friend?"

She glanced at her hands. "I need to know that I have your absolute confidence."

He took another bite of cake, transfixed by his aunt's caginess. It was almost like when she'd told them childhood bedtime stories. She was spinning a great one right now—he could practically hear her thoughts churning. "I wouldn't breathe a word of this to my closest brother."

She sniffed. "Since you have five of those, I guess that's plural."

"Absolutely." He waved his fork again imperiously. "Speak on, aunt of many tales."

She gave him a sharp look. "This is not a fairy tale. More than you can realize hangs on the complete secrecy of that cave."

"I know, I know. But you shouldn't be crawling around in that place," Judah said. "It makes me nervous to think about you being there. What if you stumbled onto a snake? What if a coyote was in there? We never knew you had a secret hangout."

"Nothing will happen to me. Burke usually goes with me."

"Oh, so Burke is in on this as well," Judah said, growing more fascinated by the moment. "Do the two of you make midnight runs out there to dig up silver?"

She sighed. "I'm going to pop that concussed head of yours if you don't pay attention."

"Go. I'm all ears." He set down the plate and swigged the milk she'd set on his nightstand. The copy of *Death Comes to the Archbishop* he'd been reading fell to the floor, but he didn't notice.

"I have a friend who comes once a year to visit," Fiona began, and Judah said, "The Chief."

She nodded. "The silver is his. The cave is his home, of sorts."

"Is there a tribe around here?"

She nodded again. "But he sometimes stays in the cave. Alone. We won't ever tell anyone that."

"Is he a fugitive? Illegal?" Judah arranged a stern

look on his face. "Aunt, we shouldn't be harboring someone who has some kind of record—"

She shook her head. "The cave is his. Your parents bought Rancho Diablo land from him—from the tribe, actually. The cave and the mine stay in his hands, all of those mineral rights being signed over to him."

"Why?"

"It was a fair exchange," Fiona said simply. "Your father negotiated for the land with the stipulation that the mine remained in the tribe's possession. It will be this way for always." She took a deep breath. "And one more reason why I absolutely must keep this ranch from falling into Bode's clutches."

"Oh." Judah had the whole picture now. "So Bode really wants the mine?"

"He wants everything. The mine, which he's only heard rumors about, but which he suspects must be real. The two working oil derricks, the land, the Diablos. He wants it all."

"No one can own the Diablos. They're free."

"For now," Fiona said. "As long as they are on Callahan land, the spirits are free."

A cool breeze passed over his skin. "And if we lose the ranch?"

"Everything is lost. The mine, and the secret that the mine hides."

"Surely there's not all that much silver. It was a small cave, as caves go."

Fiona looked at him sharply, her mouth opening as if to say something. Then she closed it, before rising to put his book on the nightstand and collecting his dishes. "Try to rest. I believe the doctor said a concussion requires absolute stillness for forty-eight hours, in your case."

"Funny thing is, I don't remember hitting my head," he complained. "I swear it's a conspiracy to keep me from riding."

"You'll live to ride another day if you rest now," Fiona said with a smile. "Good night, Nephew."

"Good night, Aunt. Thanks for telling me about the cave. I'll take the secret with me to my grave."

She looked at him, her eyes deep and troubled. "You have no idea how much is riding on your ability to do just that." Then she left his room.

Judah felt restless now that he'd heard so much family lore. Inaction was never his strong suit.

What he needed was someone to annoy, to take his mind off all the family stuff. Nothing like a little late-night foray to make a man feel less starved for adventure.

Instead of staying here and allowing Fiona to put ten pounds on him, he decided to go make a different kind of midnight raid. After hearing about Bode bothering his aunt and the family treasure, he was in a dangerous mood.

Judah hesitated only once, and that was in the hall outside Jonas's old room, where Sabrina now resided. Normally, the brothers slept in one of the large bunkhouses, having moved out once they hit the teen years, though occasionally they slunk back to their old rooms in the main house if they had an injury, which, thankfully, wasn't often. But it was easier to be where Fiona wouldn't have to run out to check on them twenty times a day, which she did when they were injured, no matter how many times they told her it wasn't necessary. His brothers hadn't even asked him where he wanted to sleep off his trifling—in his opinion—concussion; they'd dumped him unceremoniously at the house.

But Jonas shouldn't be in residence, nor any of the other brothers. Judah froze outside Sabrina's room, surprised by the answering murmur of a man's voice. If he didn't know better, he'd think...

He didn't know better. He knew nothing at all, Judah told himself, tiptoeing past her room. He had bigger fish to fry tonight than who was paying a nocturnal call on Fiona's personal secretary.

He sneaked past Fiona and Burke's room without any trouble, and flitted past the family library where they held their meetings, just in case any of the brothers were hanging out in there. One never knew where a Callahan might be loitering, and Judah didn't want to answer any questions.

Then he was out the door and into his truck. Not a soul would know he was laying his pride on the line.

"Where are we going?" Sam asked through the window of the truck, and Judah swallowed a good-size howl.

"*We* are going nowhere," he said. "*I'm* taking a short, *private* drive."

"Ah. To see Darla." Sam leaned his arms on the door. "You know what your problem is?"

"Tell me," Judah said. "I'm just dying to know."

"Your problem is that she's getting married in two days, and it's not to you. Getting that concussion is the best thing that ever happened to you."

"Why?" Judah asked, irritated.

"Because you need to be defending your castle, not riding bulls."

"There's nothing to defend. I don't have a castle."

"If my lady was pregnant, there wouldn't be any discussion of her marrying another man. That sucker wouldn't dream of encroaching on my territory, because he'd know I'd knock his block off. In fact, my lady wouldn't be thinking about marrying another dude, because she'd be so wild to get into my bed." Sam gazed at him. "Like I said, you have a problem."

"Thanks for letting me know," Judah said, "because I hadn't figured that out on my own."

"You need to buck up. Now is the time for all good men to come to the aid of the party," Sam said.

"If there was a party to be had. Will you get out of my truck so I can go?" he demanded.

"You don't know of any women I could go carousing with tonight, do you?" his brother asked. "I'm in the mood for *looove*."

"Do I look like a dating service? Did you lose your little black book?" Judah was getting steamed. "Why would any sane woman want to carouse with you?"

Sam sighed. "This case is getting on my nerves. I could use a distraction."

Judah straightened. "Are there new developments?"

"Well, Bode's pretty endless with his tricks and appeals. He's got a pretty seamy team of lawyers. And as you know, law isn't my strong suit."

Judah blinked. "You're the best lawyer around. No one bites the pants off the enemy like you. You're legendary for being a butt—ah, bulldog-like in the courtroom."

"But this is personal," Sam said, and Judah realized his brother needed to talk.

"Come on," Judah said. "Let's go carousing."

"Thought you'd never admit that you need a break from hearth and home." He got in the truck, grinning.

"Fiona's driving me nuts," Judah admitted. "She feeds me like a lost lamb."

"Ah, the benefits of home life." Sam looked at him. "So where are we going? Howling at Bode's bedroom window? I wouldn't mind giving the old goat a good fright."

"How about Darla's?" Judah turned down the drive.

"That doesn't sound like much fun unless the doc is there. We could run him off. *That* would be fun."

Judah's thoughts instantly ground to a halt. He'd never considered Darla might be having company. In his mind's eye, she was tucked up in her pristine bed waiting for his embrace—not the good doctor's.

"I'm not sure this is going to be as much fun as I thought it would be," he growled.

"Kind of tame stuff," Sam said, "when we should be painting 'Bode Sucks' on the water tower."

"That's kid's stuff." Judah frowned, thinking about Darla in bed with a rangy, loose-limbed retired bronc buster-turned-doctor. He had a horrible vision of Dr. Tunstall using his stethoscope to listen to Darla's heart going thumpety-thump for him—or even worse, listening to Judah's babies cooing inside Darla's nicely watermelon-shaped tummy. "I need something dangerous."

"Thinking about Darla sleeping with the good doc after the 'I do's' are said?" Sam asked, his tone commiserating.

Judah turned onto the main road. He was loaded for bear, his mood as territorial as he could ever remember it being. He was tired of Bode looming over them; he was tired of Tunstall, nice as he might be. But nice and in-the-way were two different things. "'Hang on to your ass, Fred,' to quote a favorite movie of mine. We're going to look in the face of danger with no regret."

Sam rubbed his hands together with enthusiasm. "Danger, here we come!"

Chapter 6

"This is your idea of dangerous?"

Sam glared at Judah as he held Jackie and Pete's girls, Molly and Elizabeth, on his lap. Judah waved a small stuffed pony he'd bought at the toddlers; he'd bought one for every Callahan child, passing them out like Santa Claus.

Judah grinned at Sam. "This is definitely my idea of dangerous. What did you have in mind, bro?"

Sam allowed little Fiona to crawl up in his lap. The triplets were dressed in their jammies, and old enough to realize they were being given a special treat of staying up past their bedtime. Jackie and Pete looked on fondly and with some amusement as Judah tried on daddy skills.

"I don't know," Sam said, "maybe lobbing a peck-happy chicken through Bode's bedroom window? Perhaps heading into town and seeing if we could rustle up some female attention? That's my idea of living on the edge. Of course you *are* darling," he said to mini-Fiona. "You're my niece, so what else would you be?"

"This is plenty dangerous for me," Judah said. "I'm not good with kids. I'm not cut out for fatherhood."

Pete laughed. "No one is. It just creeps up on you and you deal with it."

Jackie gave her husband a light smack on the arm. "You *are* cut out for being a dad," she told Judah. "You're a Callahan. All the brothers have a latent dad gene. I'm positive."

Judah grunted. "I can't convince Darla of that."

"But did you try?" Jackie asked, smiling. "Did you give her a reason to believe you were interested?"

"I suggested prenatal yoga. And vitamins. And good nutrition." Judah kissed his niece on the top of her head. "What more can I do?" He glanced to Jackie, puzzled, very aware that Pete was trying not to snicker.

"You offer to go *with* her to prenatal yoga," Jackie said gently. "And offer to cook those nutritious meals for her. Things like that. And offer to rub her belly."

"She won't let me rub anything of hers," Judah said morosely. "I'm pretty sure she thinks her pregnancy is a result of my, um, mishandling of the situation."

"It was," Sam said, unable to keep from tossing in his two cents.

"I used protection," Judah said defensively, frowning when everyone started laughing. "What?"

"You never read the box, did you?" Sam asked.

"The box of what?" Judah knew he was the butt of some secret joke, but he wasn't certain why. He'd come here for a little sympathy, and a bit of no-pressure, hands-on baby guidance. Not guffaws.

"Condoms," Sam said. "Creed gave us all joke condoms."

Judah blinked. "There's nothing funny about condoms."

Sam grinned at him. "You don't read directions."

"I'm a man of action," Judah shot back.

"And you fired away and asked questions later." Sam nodded. "That's the reason you're going to be a father."

"No," Judah said, "my box said something like 'For the Man Who Has Almost Everything.' *That* was the joke."

His family laughed harder. Judah shrugged. "It doesn't matter. Even if I begged to attend prenatal yoga, or promised to attend a cooking school for pregnant parents, Darla would still be determined to marry Doc Skin-and-Bones," he said. "You'd think she'd want a fellow with a little more muscle and meat to him. Those bronc busters always look like a string bean reverberating on the back of a horse to me. I'd rather my sons have a man to look up to who has muscles," he said with a sigh. "Strength."

"Meathead," Pete said, his tone kind. "You've got to quit letting Sidney bother you. Tell Darla—without being an ape—how you really feel about her."

"I don't know how not to be an ape." Judah stood, clapped his hat to his head, kissed the little girls goodbye. "Thank you for letting me be an uncle who doesn't call before he drops in at bedtime. I promise not to make a habit of it."

"Come anytime you like," Jackie said, giving him

a hug. "We love you, Judah. We want you to be happy. You're a good man."

"Sometimes," Sam said. "When he's not a stupid man. Now can we go do something dangerous? Something that'll really rock the epicenter of wild-n-crazy? Like maybe drive to the Sonic, at least?"

Pete thumped Judah on the back. "It's always darkest before the dawn, dude. It'll work out."

"It's pretty damn dark out there," Judah said. "She's getting married in two days."

"You better rescue the princess *tout suite* then," Pete told him. "You can do it. You're a Callahan."

Judah nodded. "Thanks."

"Danger, here we come!" Sam said, kissing his nieces and hugging his sister-in-law goodbye.

Judah shook his head. Sam had no idea just what kind of danger lay in wait. And he couldn't tell him.

"You did not inform me that babysitting was your idea of dangerous," Sam said with a groan twenty minutes later, when they'd made their way to Creed's house. Sometimes Creed's sister-in-law Diane's three daughters stayed in the house with their little cousin, too, but tonight, it was just Creed and Aberdeen and their daughter, Joy Patrice.

"Not only is it dangerous," Judah said, holding out a stuffed pony for the baby, "it's essential. You should do one thing every day that scares you. It's important for your growth. And in my book, diapers are dangerous."

"Growth comes in the shape of luscious, eager females, too," Sam said, "but I can tell you're on a mission, so never mind." He sighed heavily and took the pony from Judah. "She's a baby. She can't hold a stuffed animal, idiot."

Judah gave Creed a stern eyeing. "Did you give us condoms that were basically party balloons?"

He grinned. "Seemed like a great groom's gift, as far as I was concerned."

"Why?" Judah demanded. "Do you mind me asking why?"

"To help you along. And clearly it did." Creed put on an innocent face. "It would be selfish of me to cheat you out of marital bliss. A little lambskin shouldn't stand between you and the most happiness you will ever know."

Judah snorted. "The mother of my children wants to marry someone else. Is that what you had in mind?"

"Now that sounds like a personal problem to me. Can't blame that on a neon party favor." Creed handed him a beer. "The box clearly said—"

"I know. I know. Only I'm not an owl. I don't see things in the dark, like very small print." Judah took the beer, more in the mood to bean his brother with it than to drink it. "I just thought that if a lady bothered to make love with a guy, then surely she had some kind of feelings for him."

Aberdeen looked at him with sympathy. "Darla does have feelings for you, Judah."

"What those feelings are could be anything," Creed said unhelpfully, and Sam laughed. Judah hugged the baby in his arms, setting down his beer to gaze into her face. "Hey," he told her, "your uncles are pigs. But me, I'll rescue you. Don't worry, little princess. You'll always know Uncle Judah had your back."

"Knowing you," Creed said, "you've tried overwhelming Darla with your machismo. You've even given her the ol' I-know-what's-best-for-you treatment." He glanced at Judah. "So that only leaves romancing her socks off."

"Darla doesn't wear socks," Judah said, and everyone groaned.

"You have to go slowly for him," Sam said. "He's not the sharpest knife in the Callahan knife block."

"So, romance," Creed said, speaking slowly for Judah's benefit, as if he didn't know what to do with a woman, "is done with a gentle conductor's baton, a wand, if you will. Not a crashing bull-in-a-flower-bed thunderclap."

"Like you did with me?" Aberdeen said sweetly, and Judah and Sam hooted at their brother. "Judah, don't let Creed tell you he had all the answers, because he didn't."

"But he still won your heart," Judah said. "Though I don't know what you see in him."

That earned him a glare from Creed, which made Judah feel better.

"He won my heart by being persistent."

Creed stared at his wife. "No, I didn't. I won your heart by being the most awesome, irresistible—"

Aberdeen waved at Creed to be quiet. "Trust me, your brother made some mistakes in the wooing process. He was not a perfect prince. Nor was he a love machine, as he might lead you to believe."

Sam and Judah snickered as Creed was put in his place.

"But," Aberdeen said, "he hung in there, no matter what hoops I made him jump through, and I admired that. It made me realize that he actually loved me, in spite of all the doubts I had about us being together. And so he won my heart." She smiled at her husband, and Creed perked up like a plant in the sunshine.

"So how do I hang in there, when Darla doesn't even want me hanging in there? I left her a ring—a ring I was guaranteed would make a lady jump into my arms. And I got nothing," Judah said sadly. "Not even a phone call."

"Well," Aberdeen said, "perhaps it would be good to present your case in person."

"Yeah, dummy. You don't just leave a ring for a woman and hope she gets the clue. It takes more effort than that," Sam said. "Now can we go do something dangerous?"

Judah kissed his niece on the head. "Why is it that all we have on the ranch are baby girls?" he asked, thinking about the sons who would be in his arms before he knew it. A few months was nothing. He could hang in there.

He *could* hang in there. Just like Aberdeen said.

"We have baby girls," Creed said, "because it takes a real man to pack pink booties. Deal with it."

"Where's the danger?" Sam asked, when Judah pulled in front of Darla and Jackie's wedding shop. "This is just a dress store. It's a *wedding dress* store, but unless there's man-hunting brides around—and there's not, since it's nearly midnight—then I don't see the danger. Enlighten me."

Judah took a deep breath, wondering if he was going to be standing at an altar in two days or not. It was going to take everything he had to do it. "The danger is that you get to find a ride home," he told his brother. "I travel alone from here."

Sam gawked at him. "You would leave me in town with no ride?"

Judah nodded. "You wanted danger."

"I get it." Sam hopped out of the truck, wearing a sour expression. "This is not my idea of danger."

"Yes, but your day is coming." Judah waved at his brother. "I'm going to go find an ex-nurse and see if she wants to take my temperature."

"Huh," Sam said, "good luck with that."

He loped off, heading toward the town's only secret night spot, in the back of Banger's Bait and Tackle. Judah drove away, thinking about everything he'd seen in his brothers' homes. It was true that they probably hadn't had the smoothest routes to the altar. They were certainly not hard-core princes.

But they had made it across the finish line.

And that's where Judah wanted to be.

Chapter 7

It was rude to pay a visit at midnight, particularly without calling first, but time was of the essence. Judah figured he could blame his lack of manners on his nonexistent concussion, which he considered overcautiousness, and maybe even passive-aggressiveness, on Sidney's part. The bronc buster had known that Judah was winning. He hadn't wanted to give his rival any reason to look like a hero, so he'd scratched Judah.

Therefore, it was completely legit to be here. And there was a lamp shining in the window, so a tap on the door would let him know whether Darla wanted company.

There were no vehicles in the drive, and Judah figured she had no nocturnal guest sleeping over. "That's a good thing," he murmured. "I would have hated to toss ol' Sid out on his bony butt."

He knocked.

"Who is it?" Darla asked, and Judah took a deep breath.

"The father of your children."

"Judah," Darla said through the door, "it's late. I have work tomorrow, and I have a doctor's appointment. I don't have time for fun and games."

Fun and games? Was that how she saw him? "I could play the pity card and tell you I had to scratch from my ride due to a slight concussion, and that only a nurse would understand, but—"

The door opened. She looked out at him, her expression wary. "Did you really?"

"Yes. And no. I actually don't think I hit my head, but Tunstall scratched me, and the E.R. said I had a hairline concussion, or stage one. Something like that—I wasn't paying attention." He shrugged. "I think it was Tunstall's evil plot to get me out of the event."

She shook her head. "Sidney's not like that."

"I was fine," Judah insisted. "I've ridden with worse injuries."

She sighed and opened the door. "Come in, but only for five minutes."

He took off his hat and sat awkwardly on the sofa. She looked so cute in her blue robe and little flip-flops. Okay, maybe those weren't sex-goddess garments, but he liked her comfy. It felt homelike here. "This is a nice place."

"No room at the inn." She crossed her arms. "Judah, what did you want to talk about?"

He forced himself to pay attention to why he'd come in the first place. "I don't think you should get married.

It's too soon. You could be making the biggest mistake of your life, which will affect my sons."

She frowned. "I don't know the sex of my children, because I haven't asked the doctor. I don't want to know until they're born. So please don't refer to them as males."

"They'll be boys," Judah said. "Pete and Creed might not be capable of manly offspring, but I am."

Darla sighed. "Judah, I'm getting married in two days. Whatever you think about what I'm doing isn't important."

"Can I get a restraining order or something?" Judah pondered this. "There has to be a law where a man can stop a woman from making a foolish mistake in his sons' lives."

Her frown deepened. He could see he'd landed in deep cow droppings with that tack. He decided to change course before he got thrown out on his ear. "What I'm trying to say, Darla, is that I don't think you've given us a chance."

Once he'd said it, it was like a cork popping out of a bottle. "We've started off on the wrong foot for a number of reasons, but there's a spark between us."

"And we should blow on that spark and see if it bursts into flame or goes out altogether?" Darla didn't look convinced. "Judah, there isn't one compelling reason you can offer for me to call off my wedding. I'm not convinced you and I have any sparks, but where you're concerned, I'm pretty flame-resistant."

Well, wasn't that just a pearl every man wanted to hear falling from his beloved's sweet lips? She didn't think there were sparks.

There was only one thing to do. He could be run off by his pumpkin's frosty ways, or he could be a fireman.

He pulled Darla into his lap and said, "I don't know why you're fighting so hard. Maybe you just like a chase. But I'm good at running. And as long as I know you haven't returned my ring, I'm going to believe that you're just fighting your practical side."

She slid from his lap onto the sofa. "You make me sound…like a tease."

He kissed her neck. "Mmm, you smell delicious. And don't put words in my mouth. You're a hot little number, Darla Cameron, and I'm not afraid of a little teasing. You tease me all you like, and I'll tease you back. Although, that night we shared might have been a one-off, come to think of it," he said, angling for a kiss, which he adroitly stole. He noticed she wasn't exactly fighting him. "What's holding us back from having a really kinky lovefest, anyway? Just me and you and a bowl of fruit, maybe?"

"Sidney."

Judah raised a brow. "Didn't you tell me that you and Tunstall aren't exactly burning holes in the bedsheets?"

She stiffened like a dress mannequin with a pole up its back. "That isn't how I phrased it, thank you, speaking of putting words in someone's mouth."

He leaned back comfortably against the sofa and indicated she should go on with her explanation. "I think a woman who is planning on a sexless marriage—a business arrangement—probably has a very good reason for locking herself in a gilded cage."

"You don't know everything," Darla said, "and it's really none of your affair. Now, if you don't mind, I have to be at work early in the morning. We have a shipment of gowns arriving."

He nodded. "And you need all the beauty sleep you can get before the wedding. I understand. It's a bride thing." He stood. "Not that I think Tunstall's much of a catch, but—"

"It doesn't matter what you think," Darla said. "Anyway, what's wrong with him?"

"Nothing," Judah said, a tad too quickly. "Nothing at all."

"You're just annoyed because he made you scratch. That's why you're here, isn't it?"

"No," Judah said, "I'm here to kiss you good night."

He kissed Darla like he might not ever kiss her again. He held her, framing her face with his hands, touching her skin, telling her with his kisses how he felt about her. He couldn't bear the thought of her marrying another man. Darla belonged with him, and he couldn't imagine why she didn't see it the same way he did. He kissed Darla with his whole heart and soul, thrilled to finally have her in his arms. So it was a horrible shock to his soul when banging erupted on the front door.

Darla jumped away from him as if she'd been zapped by a cattle prod. "Who is it?"

"Sidney."

"He can't find you here!" She started shooing Judah toward the bedroom.

"I'm not hiding," he declared. "But even if I would hide like a weasel, don't you think the bedroom is the last place he'd want to find me?"

Darla shook her head. "He won't come in here. Don't move! If you do, I swear I'll…you'll wish you only had a slight concussion!" She closed the bedroom door.

Judah shrugged. "Well, this wasn't how I planned to get in here," he said to himself, "but I'm okay with it." He pulled off his boots, his shirt, his jeans, his socks, hesitated at the black Polo briefs, then shrugged and tossed them on the pile, too. What the hell. He didn't sleep in anything at home; no reason to stand on ceremony now. No telling how long Boy Wonder would be pressing his case with his not-gonna-be-bride, so Judah slid into Darla's bed wearing nothing but a grin.

"Now *this* is living dangerously," he said in the dark, briefly wondering if Sam had made it home and was as comfortable as Judah was at this very moment. Impossible. This bed—Darla's bed—was simply the best place to be in Diablo. And then Judah fell asleep in Darla's soft, cozy, clean smelling sheets, wondering when she'd remember that Judah's truck was parked out front where even Tunstall couldn't miss it.

Sam was right. It was huge fun living dangerously.

"Do you have company?" Sidney asked, and Darla glanced nervously at the bedroom door. She wasn't certain she could trust Judah not to come popping out like a jack-in-the-box to annoy Sidney. Even now, she was pretty sure Judah had his big ear pressed flat to the door, listening to every word, carefully choosing his moment to spring.

"I actually do have company," she said, unable to lie to Sidney. He'd been too kind to her. He really was a nice man, and they made a good team. Sometimes she suspected that he felt a little more than friendly toward her, and then other times he was strictly professional.

Yet Judah wouldn't play nice and understand the unique situation she was in. *Stubborn ass.*

"Do you mind me asking who it is?" Sidney asked, and Darla sighed.

"It's Judah."

"He's in there?" Sidney jerked his head toward her bedroom.

"He'd be happy to come out, if you want. I told him to go in there while you were here. I wasn't aware you'd planned to stop by." She looked at him, gauging his reaction, but he seemed like the Sidney of always, calm and unconcerned.

Not in love with her. Which was a relief.

"No." Sidney sat on the sofa, making himself comfortable. "I'm happy for him to cower in there if you're okay with it."

Darla sat at the other end of the sofa. "So what's on your mind?"

"I just want to make certain you still want to go through with this, now that Judah knows he's the father." Sidney looked at her. "I'd completely understand if you feel that your circumstances have changed."

"There's nothing between Judah and me," Darla said. "He wants to be a father to his children, which I'm grateful for. But there's no reason…" She stopped, thinking about the beautiful diamond ring Judah had given her. She remembered the satiny feel of the magic wedding gown as she'd slipped it on. It had felt so right, so real, like she was meant to wear it and be a beloved bride.

Then she thought about Judah standing behind her in the mirror, his handsome face gazing at her with love and passion—yes, she'd seen passion in those dark blue eyes—and she shivered. He'd made love to her with an intensity that had rocked her. She knew that side of Judah Callahan.

But not much else. And she didn't want a man who simply felt that she should be his because he'd made children with her. "Nothing needs to change between us, Sidney. You still need a wife to satisfy your inheritance, and I'm more than willing to be a stand-in."

Sidney looked as if he was about to say something, then closed his mouth. His lips, she noticed, weren't full and capable of being demanding—like Judah's. Sidney's lips were thinner, almost nonexistent, as if he was used to holding back his emotions a lot. She considered his dark brown hair, dark eyes, kind face. "Sidney, why haven't you ever married, anyway?"

He shrugged. "I'm always on the road. I have a house that's nice enough, but no woman wants to go home alone at night for months on end."

"That's true, I guess." Darla thought about how nice it was that Judah was so close to his family. They were always around. Sometimes they aggravated each other, but most of the time it was obvious that they all loved each other a lot.

She really wanted a big family for her babies.

"I guess I'll be alone much of the time," she murmured.

He winced. "If you marry me, that's unfortunately part of the deal. I will take very good care of you, when I'm around. And financially you won't lack for anything. Nor will your children, whom I'm willing to adopt as my own."

She took a deep breath. She really didn't need to be "taken care of," as nice as Sidney was trying to be. She'd always taken care of herself just fine. What she really wanted was a father for her babies, a name for them to own, so that they wouldn't grow up wondering why they'd had no daddy.

But she hadn't counted on Judah being so determined to be a father. He was Mr. Footloose, Mr. Don't-Tie-Me-Down.

The huge diamond he'd bought her almost made her change her opinion of him.

Almost.

She owed it to the children to find out. "I think," Darla said softly, "maybe I'd better wait and see how this turns out, Sidney." She looked at him. "I'm so sorry. I hope you can forgive me."

He shrugged. "Nothing to forgive. I completely understand. It's why I came out tonight."

She nodded. "You're a good doctor. And a good man."

"I know," he said, standing. "You've heard that good guys always win, haven't you?"

She smiled. "It's true. You'll win."

He pressed a gentle kiss against her knuckles. "I have half a mind to go in there and tell Judah that I lied about his concussion."

She blinked. "You did?"

"I said I thought he had one. I felt it was important to get him off the road. The hospital never really found anything, either. They just told him he needed rest. He ran with the advice—quickly, I might add, right to your door." Sidney glanced toward the bedroom. "Part of me wants to go in there and tell him we've decided to elope tonight, and would he mind keeping an eye on the house while we're gone." He grinned at Darla. "What do you think he'd say?"

"I don't know," she answered.

"I do." Sidney smiled at her, tipped his hat and left. She listened as his truck gunned to life and he drove away.

Then she went to her bedroom, opening the door abruptly just in case Judah did have his ear pressed tight to it. She fully intended to smack him a good one for being so nosy.

But he was asleep in her bed—nude, judging by the pile of clothes on the floor. And obviously not worried one bit by what was transpiring in the other room.

It stung. He could have been pacing a little at least.

All he really wanted was to be a bad-ass. And it wasn't going to work with her.

But here they were, bound together. She placed a hand on her belly.

Her babies' father was sleeping blissfully, unconcerned that he did not love their mother. But he would do his duty, just like any of the Callahans would.

There was only one option that would solve their dilemma.

Chapter 8

Dear Judah,
You and I aren't in love. You want to get married because of the babies, but I have a proposal of my own for you. Let's agree to stay together until after the twins are born, and then we'll re-evaluate the situation. That's the best deal I can come up with right now, because I really don't think we're meant for each other as married partners. But we'll try it your way for the sake of the children, if only temporarily. If you agree to a divorce after the babies are born, I'll be at the altar in two days, ready to say I do.
Darla

She put the letter in an envelope, decided to leave it on the kitchen counter where Judah would easily find it. She laid his beautiful ring beside the letter. The diamond caught the light from the overhead hanging fixture, sending prisms dancing over the counter. Her breath caught just looking at it. A princess would wear such a lovely ring.

She was not a princess. She was an unwed mother with a scoundrel for a one-night-stand daddy. "Oh, boy," she murmured, and closed her eyes for a moment. Did she really want to be married only until the children were born? It sounded so prenup, so planned.

At least she was giving him the freedom to leave. And for the sake of her pride, she had to know that he had an escape hatch built in to their agreement. She felt tears pool behind her eyes, told herself she'd spent far too much time staring at dreamy white gowns. She'd gone from a no-nonsense nurse to a woman who dreamed fairy-tale dreams—and it hurt.

Strong arms closed around her, making her jump. Warm lips pressed to the back of her neck, sending sizzles zipping along her skin.

"Is that a Dear John letter you're leaving me?" Judah asked against her nape, and Darla closed her eyes.

"Not exactly." His hard body pressed against her and her knees went weak. "Please tell me you're wearing something."

He kissed the side of her neck. "I think you'd be very disappointed if I was wearing clothes, Darla. You don't have to pretend you're a straight-laced nurse who'll read me the riot act for making a pass at you. Although if I was one of your patients, I definitely would have tried—"

"Judah," Darla said, unable to think about where he was going with that while he was driving her out of her mind with kisses. "I could have a better conversation with you if you weren't nude."

"I don't want to chitchat, doll. I want to hold you and make you scream like a wildcat. Which I know you can do very well." He nipped her shoulder lightly, then ran a tongue over the spot he'd bitten. "The question is, are Dear John letters supposed to be written on pink stationary with a purple pen? It seems to send a romantic signal, dressing it up like that. Black and white would be a lot more impersonal for bad news, I would think. But I wouldn't know," he added, his voice husky. "I have to admit no lady of my acquaintance has ever tried to write me off."

"I'm sure." Darla didn't dare turn around. He was rascal enough to not have a stitch on, and she didn't want to see his firm, well-muscled body. She wasn't strong enough to deny herself a naked Judah whose body was carved by a master sculptor.

"Where's the good doc?" he asked, his breath warm against her neck, tickling the tiny hairs at her nape. "Not trusting me alone with the treasure, is he?"

"Judah, I'm not treasure. And yes, Sidney would trust me. Totally."

"I guess he was trusting you when you sneaked into my room that night?"

She swallowed. "Sidney… Sidney and I aren't getting married anymore. So quit bothering me about him. And please put something on! And leave. I want you to leave."

He took the envelope from her fingers. "Is that what this says? Go away, big bad wolf, and never come back?"

She didn't nod, because she hadn't written anything

of the sort. Now she felt foolish for what she had written. Why hadn't she realized how unwise it was to try to bargain with a devil? She tried to snatch the envelope away from him, but Judah eluded her easily.

"Ah," he said, running the envelope down her back so it rasped along her zipper, "you don't want me to read something that has my name on it? I find that strange, Darla Cameron. And one thing you usually aren't is strange."

"Judah, there is a robe in my closet. If you'll at least put on a robe, we can have an adult conversation."

"Now, my love," he said, kissing the shell of her ear, "being an adult is one thing no one's ever accused me of. Besides, I like your backside so much. I remember it fondly."

She closed her eyes, wishing she wasn't pressed against the kitchen counter. He'd teased her enough, she decided. She was going to turn around, was going to face this strong, naked man and tell him she'd changed her mind. She just wanted her letter back, and to give up her unwise attempt at taming this lion.

She was melting, knowing full well what wonderful pleasures lay in store for her if she just gave in.

She couldn't.

Whirling around, she kept her eyes forcefully averted from the masculine glory. "Judah, give me back that envelope right now." Her gaze ran the length of him in astonishment. "You're not naked! You're fully dressed!"

"Disappointed?" he asked, grinning as he stole a kiss. "Sorry about that, babe, but I've got to go. Duty calls back at the ranch. Sleep well." He waved the envelope at her before tucking it in his shirt pocket. "I'll save this for my nightly bedtime reading. I'm sure it'll prove to be interesting, even fascinating. I never expected a letter from my lady." He winked at her, so devil-may-care it was maddening.

"I want it back!"

"Ah, no. I bid you good night. I would stay, sugar, but at this hour, I'm afraid I only have one thing on my mind. And I'm sure you know what that is." He stole another kiss and departed, leaving Darla lathered up and pink-cheeked.

She spun around and saw that the ring was still there, sparkling on the counter. He knew she wanted it. He knew it tempted her. He knew *he* tempted her.

In fact, she was drowning in temptation.

There was nothing she wanted to do more than run after him and beg him to come back, spend the night with her, make love to her. He probably knew that about her, too. He'd so shamelessly teased her about his nudity, making her think about him naked, making her remember. Oh, he was baiting her, and it was working.

She didn't know how she was going to sleep tonight.

"Well, if it isn't Roughriding Romeo," Sam said when Judah dragged himself into the bunkhouse well after midnight. "Mr. Danger himself."

"Glad you made it home, bro. I figured you would." Judah hung his hat on the hook in the mudroom and looked at his brothers in front of the fireplace. Jonas, Rafe and Sam stared at him with raised brows and expectant expressions.

"So, did you find any danger?" Sam asked.

"Nope," Judah said, "nothing but lambs and cotton candy in my world."

"What's that pink thing poking out of your shirt?" Jonas asked.

"This," Judah said proudly, "is my first Dear John letter."

"Nothing to brag about there," Rafe said. "You weren't even a 'dear' as far as Darla was concerned in the first place. So if she's writing you off, you're going backward, bro."

"This Dear John letter means," Judah said, running it under his nose to smell the scent of Darla's perfume, "that she cares about me enough to try to run me off. She's fighting it, brothers, every step of the way. And that's the way I like my lady."

"Reluctant? Distant? Icy, even?" Sam said. "You always were the peculiar one of us."

"Darla's none of the above." Judah threw himself on the sofa lengthwise, cradling his head on a sofa pillow. "She's fighting herself. And she's losing."

"You can tell all that without even opening the letter? Maybe you've picked up some of Sabrina's psychic skills. But I advise you to read it before you go crowing about how hot your runaway bride is for you," Jonas said.

"She won't run from our wedding, that's for sure. She'll be too practical for that. I'm a catch." Judah shrugged and tore open the envelope to hoots from his brothers, pulling out the letter to read it. "This is better news than I'd hoped, even," he murmured. "She's given the skinny bronc buster the wave-off."

"Really?" Sam perked up. "He's cleared the field for you?"

"And she's planning on marrying me in two days. I

told you!" Judah looked up at his brothers in triumph. "I hope I still fit in my tux."

"Dummy," Rafe said. "Sidney wasn't going to wear a tux. Why should you?"

"Why not? It's a special occasion. It calls for a tux." Judah was pretty certain that in spite of her protestations to the contrary, he and Darla would be married forever. He planned to make rock-solid vows in two days, and no way was he ever letting her give him the slip like she'd given Tunstall. Oh, she might think that was what she wanted, and certainly he would agree to her darling little last-ditch attempt to keep herself from falling head over heels in love with him. But this agreement she wanted bought him time. And he could do a whole lot of convincing in four or five months. Judah squinted at the ceiling. "Which one of you dunces wants to be my best man?"

"I'm not feeling it," Jonas said. "Something tells me nothing good can come of marrying a woman who's Miss Reluctant."

"I'm telling you she wants me. Read it for yourself." He handed the letter to Jonas, who snatched it and read it before passing it to his brothers. They all looked at him with worried expressions. Judah shrugged at their hangdog faces. "Don't worry. She's crazy about me."

Rafe sighed. "If I have to, I'll be the sacrificial lamb who stands next to you at the altar while you sign on to get burned a few months hence. But it doesn't feel like happy ever after to me."

"Thanks, tough guy." Judah closed his eyes, annoyed. He waved the letter in the air again. "This is my ticket, my golden chance, my checkmate, if you will. I win."

"We see," Sam said. "We see that you're nuts. Darla's telling you up front she has every intention of marrying you so her babies will have a name. Then she's divorcing you, dude."

"So? I'd rather her marriage-of-convenience be with me than with Sidney. That puts me in her bed, and therefore, in medal contention."

"You think of everything in terms of winning or losing," Sam said. "I don't know if that's healthy."

"Yeah," Rafe said, "what if Darla gives you the boot, as per this agreement? Don't you have to be a gentleman and honor that? Or else it's not valid. She doesn't have to say yes until you agree."

Judah shrugged. "Just be ready in two days to toss birdseed, bros. That's your only job."

His brothers grimaced, then went back to what they'd been doing, which looked to be high-stakes, boring Scrabble. Judah smiled to himself. They had no idea that he had everything completely under control. And they could keep their bachelor jealousy to themselves. He was going to be in contention for Fiona's ranch-o-rama, and they weren't.

Darla was going to be Mrs. Callahan, and he was going to be the hero with strong boys who'd ride bulls just like him. A bull rider and his bundles of joy—how great was that? He knew all about what Darla wanted, and what the practical side of her wanted was a fab dad. Once she saw how great he was with the little lads, she'd never want to let him go.

Just two days.

It seemed like forever.

Chapter 9

"I'm worried about Judah," Jonas said, after Judah had conked out. "He thinks he's got this all planned down to a script, but I think the situation's more explosive than he realizes." Jonas squinted at the Scrabble board, considering his options.

Rafe nodded. "I was thinking the same thing."

"Still," Sam said, "it's his business if he wants to get burned like an onion on a grill. We can't save him from being stupid."

"The problem," Jonas said, glancing over at the peacefully snoring Judah, "is that he believes he can convince Darla that she loves him. The two of them have lived in the same town almost all their lives, and never even played doctor with each other."

Rafe and Sam blinked at him. "Doctor?" Sam said.

"Yeah." Jonas grimaced. "You know. Doctor."

Rafe considered that. "I've never played doctor with any of the girls in this town. Spin the bottle, maybe. Pin the tail on the donkey, definitely." He frowned at Jonas. "You don't strike me as the type to play doctor, Jonas."

Sam snickered. "I played doctor. I also got slapped. Ah, good times." He looked at Jonas. "Is that why you became a doctor, because you liked playing it so much?"

"No," Jonas said, "I became a doctor because I'm smart, and I like helping people. I like puzzles."

"It had nothing to do with beautiful nurses," Rafe said. "Good thing, too, or that would have been a waste of your time, considering you've never brought a beautiful nurse home. Or any nurse."

Jonas sighed. "All I was trying to say is that Judah and Darla never had the hots for each other before. So why get married?" He glared at his brothers. "There, was that plain enough for you boobs?"

"Plain enough for me," Rafe said. "I don't think we can save him, though. He's on a mission to marry."

"I think we should test that mission," Jonas said, "to make certain true love exists. After all, it's easier to call off a wedding than to get a divorce later on. Some people have marital counseling, you know, to help them decide if they're on a successful path with their chosen—"

"Bah," Sam said. "I say let him fall on his face."

Jonas looked at Rafe. "That leaves you the deciding vote."

Rafe appeared troubled. "I see your point about saving pain for him and for Darla and for the children later by not putting them through a divorce. I also see Sam's point about it being Judah's business what he does. How exactly do you plan to test this marriage-of-convenience adventure?"

"Simple," Jonas said. "We tell Judah we think he's making a mistake. We just be honest. Nothing underhanded, just plain old honesty."

Rafe shook his head. "I don't want to be punched, thank you."

"Me, neither," Sam said. "I'm the brains of this outfit, you know. I'm trying to save us from Bode. Since it's your idea, it should probably be you, Jonas. You are eldest, after all."

"And I'm the surgeon," Jonas said, "who will stitch Rafe up when he busts his lip on Judah's knuckles."

Rafe shrugged. "Anyway, I still say the deciding factor is it's his life. The truth is, those babies do need a name. And it is all Creed's fault that a Callahan got Darla into this mess, so a Callahan should bail her out."

Sam and Jonas looked at him. Then they looked at Judah, who was snoring, his chin practically pointing toward the ceiling.

"He really isn't much of a catch," Rafe said. "I guess if all Darla needs is a name for her children, I can do the marriage-of-convenience thing as well as anybody. If it would save Darla from making a disastrous mistake."

"You mean Judah," Sam said.

"I mean Darla," Rafe retorted. "He really isn't much of a catch, like I said."

They sat silently, mulling over the situation. Then Jonas leaned over, kicked at Judah's leg with his boot. Judah's eyes snapped open.

"What?" he said. "Are you losers still playing Scrabble? Don't you know how to spell a word longer than three letters?"

"Rafe has something to tell you," Jonas said.

Rafe looked miserable. "We think marrying in haste means repenting in leisure."

"Whatever." Judah moved his hat down over his eyes and shifted to a more comfortable position on the leather couch.

"We think," Rafe said, trying again bravely, "that marriage isn't your style. You're more of a drifter."

"No, I'm not," Judah said from under the hat. "I'm a pragmatic romantic."

They went dead silent for a moment. He grinned, but the felt of his Stetson covering his face kept them from knowing he was laughing at them. They thought they were being so Fiona, but they weren't. No one could plot like Fiona, and Judah had learned at her knee.

"I'm going to tell Darla I'm willing to marry her so her babies will have a name," Rafe said.

Judah rolled his eyes. "You do that."

Silence met his pronouncement. Judah snickered. His brothers were always trying to help, though not successfully, and he had to admire their ham-handed ways.

"You don't mind?" Rafe asked, sounding a little less sure of himself.

"Nope," Judah said. "Have at it."

"I vote we resume this game later," Jonas said, and Sam said, "A fine idea, since Rafe has to be somewhere."

Sam said it importantly, as if Rafe was about to run right over and pop the question to Darla. *These goofballs,* Judah thought. *I don't know what they're up to, but Darla would never want to marry anyone but me. She wants me bad.*

"Okay," Rafe said, "see you later."

The door opened, and Judah heard boots moving out the door. "Called your bluff, didn't I?" he said, sliding the hat from his face. He was alone. They'd gone, ostensibly to scare him into thinking Rafe was actually heading off to save Judah's princess from her self-declared dilemma. But Darla wanted only one cowboy. *And that's me,* he assured himself.

He glanced over at the Scrabble board, seeing a lack of imagination in the chosen spellings. "'Marriage, wife, convenience, bad idea,'" he said out loud, eyeing the tiles. "Oh, very funny. You guys are a laugh a minute." He went back to sleep, completely unconcerned. He had everything under control.

"Marry you?" Darla asked twenty minutes later, when Rafe had hotfooted it over to her house and banged on her door. He'd told her he'd just left Judah, after telling him he was going to propose. Darla didn't know what to think about the Callahans anymore, except that maybe they were just as crazy as everyone said. "Why would I want to marry you?"

"You'd like me better in the temporary sense," Rafe said, "and after all, it was my twin's gag gift that got you into this dilemma. I feel a certain irony to putting matters right."

She frowned, wondering why Judah hadn't told her about a gag gift. "Gag gift?"

Rafe nodded. "Judah didn't tell you?"

She shook her head.

"Creed gave us all prank condoms as groom gifts.

Clearly, the joke was on Judah." Rafe stood straighter. "Like I said, I'm here to put things right."

Darla's heart was sinking. "Judah didn't mind you proposing to me?"

Rafe shook his head. "No, he said to have at it."

Darla wondered what new game Judah had up his sleeve. Her pride came to the fore as she said, "I don't understand why this would solve anything."

"Well, if it's a temporary situation you're looking for, and I guess it is, due to the pink ultimatum you gave Judah, it would be better to marry me, because I am all about temporary. Short Term is my middle name. In fact, No Term is what they should have named me—"

"You don't think Judah will honor the divorce?"

"Nope," Rafe said. "We're territorial in my family. He's not going to give you up once he has those little cherubs under his control. I mean his, uh, loving guidance."

Darla considered that. "But Judah doesn't love me."

Rafe shrugged. "Hasn't he told you that he does?"

"No." Darla looked at Rafe. "I can raise these children on my own. I don't need anyone to help me with that. I want to marry for love."

"I know. But it may not happen." He looked properly saddened by this revelation, which didn't make her feel any better. "As you know, you're like a sister to me. I've always loved all women, but you have a special place in my heart. I don't want to see you get hurt." Rafe wondered if he was carrying his role a little too far. The more he talked, the more he believed his story. The truth was, Darla and Judah didn't love each other;

getting a divorce after the babies were born was going to hurt them, their children and the family.

But if Rafe married Darla, and she knew he was doing it to give her children a name, then there was no ulterior motive. But there was the small matter of him carrying a super-secret torch for Judge Julie, Bode's daughter. He sighed deeply.

"Darla, I'm here for you if you don't want to marry Judah, and probably no sane woman would want to, I suppose."

"I guess you're right," Darla said, thinking that she'd have loved to marry Judah, if things had been different. If they'd fallen in love gently and slowly, finding each other of their own will and choosing, not this slamming together of their separate galaxies. "It's nice of you to offer, Rafe, but actually, I don't want to marry you, either."

He blinked. "Either?"

She sighed. "No. I don't want to marry you, of course, because you're right. You are a brother to me. And I don't want to marry Judah. I'd always feel like the wallflower that got asked to dance because the guy felt sorry for her." She felt tears prickle her eyes, but stood her ground. "Thank you for coming by, Rafe. It's been helpful."

"It has?" Rafe wasn't certain the conversation hadn't gone wildly off the guided track. She wasn't supposed to be saying she didn't want either of them. She was supposed to insist that Judah was the only man for her, once she realized it was true. Clearly, she'd realized something of a totally different sort. "So what are you going to do?"

Darla smiled. "What I should have done all along."

* * *

"I have to give this back to you," Darla said, laying the magic wedding dress carefully over the bed in Sabrina's room at Rancho Diablo. "It's lovely." She gave Sabrina a smile she didn't realize was sad until she felt it on her face. "Thank you for offering it to us. Jackie felt like a princess when she wore it to her wedding."

Sabrina studied Darla. "Do you want to talk about it?"

"There's nothing to talk about. I think our customers just aren't looking for gowns that are quite so vintage."

"I meant do you want to talk about your wedding? Or anything else?"

Darla shook her head. "There won't be a wedding. For one thing, Sidney and I have decided to remain simply friends."

"And Judah?"

"Judah and I have a complicated situation. We're still trying to figure out how to say hello to each other without feeling awkward."

"Is there anything I can do?"

Darla shook her head again. "I don't think so. Callahans are different types to deal with, as I'm sure you know."

Sabrina smiled. "It's true."

"Do you think you and Jonas will ever—"

"No." Sabrina shook her own head. "You and Judah do not have the market cornered on awkward."

Darla smiled. "Why that makes me feel better, I don't know."

"Misery loves company."

Sabrina hung the gown in her closet, closing it away. Darla fancied she could still hear the lovely song of its allure calling to her. It was like looking at a sparkling diamond a woman dreamed of one day owning—

"Oh!" Darla jumped to her feet. "I'm sorry to cut this short. I just remembered something I have to do."

Sabrina nodded. "Judah's in the bunkhouse. And if you change your mind about the dress, it'll be here, ready to go on short notice."

"Thanks," Darla said, thinking that short notice and her wedding would never go together. She'd learned about being hasty—and next time, if there ever was a next time she planned a wedding, she was taking the long route.

"So then what did she say?" Jonas asked. Sam was glued to Rafe's every word. They sat around the Scrabble board, but they weren't playing. Judah was nowhere to be found. There were chores that had to be done—ASAP—but at the moment, Jonas and Sam were spellbound by Rafe's bungling of the Darla Problem.

"She said she didn't want to marry me or Judah," Rafe said. "She was pretty definite about it, too."

"Judah's going to kill you," Sam said. "You were supposed to help Darla see that Judah is the only man for her."

"She doesn't think like most women," Rafe said in his defense. "She's pretty independent. And I think Judah annoys her fiercely."

"What does that have to do with anything?" Jonas demanded. "We don't care if she's annoyed. We care that she takes Judah off our hands and keeps him forever."

"It was scary," Rafe said. "For a minute, I thought she was going to take me up on my offer." He shuddered. "I don't think Judah understands how thin a thread he's hanging by with Darla."

"This isn't good." Jonas considered the information about Judah's precarious nuptials. "We could talk to Fiona, tell her that the lovebirds are planning to get a divorce *inmediatamente*. That would frost her cookies. I think that falls under the heading of no fake marriages, and puts him out of contention for the ranch. She won't be happy."

Sam swallowed. "I've got to have a fake marriage if I play the game. I'm never letting a woman lead me around by the nose."

Rafe sighed. "If you don't think that women are doing that every day of your life already, you're dumb."

Sam sniffed. "Well, we can't tell Fiona. She'd just throw a party. That's her answer for everything. Party, party. It's her stress buster."

"Any news on the filing?" Jonas asked. "What's the update on our legal status?"

Sam shrugged. "We could stand for Judah to get married and populate this joint. If we had a small city of kiddies here, maybe we could make a case that we are the people. The people would be best served by us keeping the ranch and opening an elementary school for the community. Something like that, anyway."

Rafe straightened. "That's a great idea. We need an elementary school. I like kids. I like school bells. Let's build a school with a school bell!"

Jonas sighed. "Let's not put the bell before the babies, all right? First we have to get Judah to slide over home plate."

"Yeah," Rafe said, "and since he told me I could

marry the mother of his children, I'm pretty sure he's not in love. It would stand to reason."

"Yeah," Sam agreed. "You wouldn't even need a lawyer to make that case. If I was in love with a woman, I wouldn't let any of you fatheads near her. Probably not even to offer her a glass of water."

"You're selfish, though," Jonas said. "Maybe Judah is more generous."

His brothers blew a collective raspberry at him.

"Judah's not in love," Sam said, "or he would have kicked Rafe's ass when he told him he was going to pop the question to Darla."

"Yeah," Rafe said, "and my ass is un-kicked. It's depressing."

"Look at that," Jonas said, waving at his brothers to come to the bunkhouse window. "Darla just came out of the house. She's heading this way." He glanced at Rafe. "Suppose she's changed her mind about you?"

"Hide me," Rafe said. "She's got a gleam in her eye that doesn't bode well."

"Where's Judah?" Jonas asked. "We need him front and center to catch this incoming fireball."

"Probably in the tub with his rubber ducky. How would I know?" Sam asked.

"Let's sneak out the back," Jonas said. "They'll find their way to each other eventually, and I don't want to be in the path of love."

"Or not," Rafe said. "Last one out the back door has to tell Fiona we screwed up Judah's life."

The brothers did their best Three Stooges impersonation getting out the door. Judah heard the back door slam, looked out his bedroom window in time to see the trio of siblings running for the barn.

"Immature," he muttered, pulling on a shirt. "Always competing."

"Judah?" a female voice called, and he grinned. *I knew that little gal couldn't resist me.*

"Hi," he said, framing himself in the bedroom doorway. "Little Red Riding Hood must be looking for her wolf," he said, taking Darla by the hand and tugging her into his room. He locked the door. "Lucky for you, I just happen to be *very* hungry."

Chapter 10

"Very funny." Darla swallowed her unease. "I'll wait out in the den."

"Don't be scared. I'll be good to you. No biting."

Warily, she removed her hand from his. She hesitated to be anyplace that contained Judah and a bed, but he was hardly going to jump on her and eat her like a chocolate bunny. As he said, no biting.

"I brought you this," she said, trying not to look at him as she set his ring on the nightstand. She glanced around, curious in spite of herself. His bunkhouse room was sparsely furnished, but he kept it neat. The quilt on the bed was vintage, a beautiful patchwork pattern that must have taken months. Someone had cared deeply about the project. But Darla could hardly pay attention to the room's decor when Judah's shirt was open and he was zipping up his work jeans. She wished she hadn't accepted his invitation to enter his lair.

Bedroom. It was just four walls. Four walls and a bed where they could be together.

There was a time she'd dreamed of nothing more.

"I'm not marrying you, Judah," Darla said, and he grinned at her, a slow, confident grin that unsettled her and got her off her planned script.

"I got that part." He jerked his head toward the ring. "Rafe talk you out of it?"

"No." Darla frowned. "Did you want him to?"

He shrugged. "Only if you could be talked out of marrying me. I knew you wouldn't say yes to him. He's too wild and woolly for a straight-laced little mama like you."

She raised her brows. "You're not exactly tame yourself."

"But the difference is," Judah said, sitting on the bed to pull on his boots, "I'm willing to be tamed."

"I'm pretty sure every single woman in this town has set her cap for you at one time or another," Darla said, "and you've never been available for more than a one-night stand. Two nights at the most, according to gossip."

Judah grinned. "I wouldn't pay attention to gossip, darlin'. This town loves to talk, but talk's cheap."

"It may be cheap," Darla said, "but it's usually pretty much on the money."

He laughed. "Let's just say I'm trying to mend my ways, then."

"Anyway," Darla said, "let's go back to being the way we were before we ever…you know. Next time I talk to you—"

"I'll be a father?" He winked. "I think you're going about this all wrong, sweetheart."

"What do you mean?"

He leaned back, lounging on the bed. "This Dear John business. It's premature."

She edged toward the door, not trusting the look in his eyes, which had turned distinctly predatory. "How so?"

"Usually a Dear John letter is reserved for people who are breaking up, which implies that there was a relationship of some sort. We have no relationship. I would suggest, therefore, that you don't know what you're missing out on."

She blinked, trying to follow his thought process. "What exactly *am* I missing out on?"

He moved off the bed and took her in his arms. "Let me show you what you're trying to write off, babe."

She could feel warmth, and strength, and full-on sex appeal radiating from him. It made her weak in the knees, faint in the heart. The problem was, she'd always been in love with this man. She couldn't remember a time she'd ever wanted someone else. He ran his hands along her forearms up to her shoulders and she froze, mesmerized by his touch. She had no wish to escape him; she'd wanted to be in his arms for too many years. "This isn't a good idea."

"We don't know that it's a bad idea, either."

He kissed her on the lips, and she melted into his embrace. It hadn't been a dream; she hadn't imagined the overwhelming passion that swept her when he held her. At some point, she wondered why she was bothering to fight him when she wanted to be with him so much.

It was something about pride, she reminded herself, and not wanting to trap him. But it felt as if he was trying to entice *her* into a trap. "Judah," she said, breaking away from his kiss, "parenthood isn't a good reason to marry."

"It's not the worst reason. Ships have been launched because of babies, fiefdoms have risen and fallen. I say you let me kiss you for a while before we try to solve the world's big questions. Let's just figure out if you even like kissing me before you Dear John me." He slipped his hands along her waist, holding her against him. "You'd hate to kick yourself later for giving away a very good thing."

He was so darn confident that he held all the keys to her heart. Darla supposed he was like this with every woman. "Maybe the only way to prove that you're not as irresistible as you think you are is to prove you wrong."

"I'll take that dare," Judah said. "What time do you have to open the shop?"

She looked at him, her blood racing. "What difference does that make? You just kissed me, and I can live without it," she fibbed outrageously. "There's nothing between us that neither of us can't live without."

"I never said that," Judah said, "and you need to stop thinking so hard, my jittery little bride. I haven't even begun to kiss you."

Two hours later, Darla opened her eyes. "Oh, no!" she exclaimed, trying to leap from the bed, where Judah had seduced her until she was nothing but a boneless mush of crazy-for-him. He lay entangled with her so that she couldn't free herself from him, possessive even in sleep. He'd made her gasp with pleasure, cry out with delight, and then the man slept practically on top of her, assuring himself that she wouldn't get away without him knowing. She tried to move his big arms and legs off her, and he opened sleepy eyes, grinning at her.

"Move, Judah," she said, pushing at him. "I'm late to open the store!"

"Bad girl," he said, running a lazy hand over her hip. "Have the customers been waiting long?" he asked, kissing her shoulder.

"An hour." She felt his sneaky hand caress her backside, slip a finger inside her. She pushed at him with a little less enthusiasm, and he licked at one of her nipples, teasing it into instant hardness.

"Ready to tear up that Dear John letter yet?" he murmured.

"No," she said with determination. "Just because we had sex does not mean we're right for each other, Judah."

"Hmm," he murmured. "Clearly I have more convincing to do. The customers will have to wait while I plead my case."

He pressed her into the sheets, kissing her, torturing her with sexy passion, giving her no room for thinking of anything but him. Darla felt herself giving in once again. He knew exactly what he was doing to her.

The problem was, she didn't know if she worked the same magic on him.

"What if there's no such thing as forever?" Darla asked Jackie that afternoon. "What if forever is just smoke and mirrors?"

Jackie glanced at her as she put away hand-beaded garters. "If you're talking about being audited, I'd say forever would be a real pain and I would hate it. I'd break the mirror and blow the smoke away."

Darla wrinkled her nose. "Forever as in marriage."

"Sometimes you have to throw caution to the wind. We sell the prepackaging to the dream here." Jackie waved a hand around the room. "We never thought we'd be so successful when we were planning this little adventure. We said, 'let's give it a shot and see how dumb we are to give up a good job, and try to sell dreams in a bad economy.'"

Darla nodded. "We did jump off a cliff without knowing what was beneath us."

Jackie nodded. "Marriage is the same thing."

Darla stared at her. "Does Pete know you feel like this? That you just took a leap of faith?"

"He took a leap of faith, too. I think it's harder for guys." Jackie giggled. "They don't know if we're going to decorate with lace doilies and leopard-skin rugs. They don't know if we're going to cook for them, or if we can. When Pete married me, he knew little about my cooking and less about how I might decorate. And then there's the biggest question of all."

Darla's eyes went wide. "Do men have all these deep thoughts? Or do they just dive in and hope it goes well?" Judah was probably a "diver." He didn't seem interested in her cooking or decorating. "What's the super-question?"

"Whether we're going to give them a lot of sex after marriage, or if we're just trying to drag them to the altar with lassos of lust."

Darla blinked. "They worry about that?"

Jackie shrugged. "It's a fact that there's a lot more nookie going on in the beginning than later. But that could be for any number of reasons, not necessarily lack of enthusiasm on the female's part."

"Have you been reading these bride magazines?" Darla sank onto a cabbage rose-printed sofa. "I don't think Judah worries too much about lovemaking."

"Because he's in romance mode right now. But on a subconscious level, he's figured out whether he wants to make love to you all the time, and if you'd like it. They like enthusiasm, too."

"Gee," Darla said, "all I was worried about was whether there was such a thing as forever."

"You're thinking romantically. Guys think logically. With their need barometer." Jackie giggled. "The comforts of hearth, home, kitchen, bed."

Darla liked being in bed with Judah—too much, if anything. "But there has to be more."

"Not for men. They don't get caught up in the fairy tale. It's pretty cut-and-dried."

"It doesn't sound very romantic."

"A moment ago you were wondering if forever was practical. It's not an illusion if both people have the same goals." Jackie laid some white gloves in the case. "Have you ever listened to the brides who come in here? They never talk about how wonderful their guys are. They talk about the dress, the flowers, the cake. Nothing that lasts."

"That's true," Darla said.

"They're in love with the icing," Jackie said, "when they should be focused on the cake."

"I don't remember you being so focused," Darla said. "When did this happen?"

"After I let Pete sweep me off my feet." She smiled.

"You should let Judah sweep you. Trust me, it's a whole lot of fun to be romanced by your man."

Jackie and Pete had gotten married after Jackie had a surprise pregnancy. Pete appeared to be gaga over his bride—still.

"Even with three newborns, the romance is—"

"Hotter than a pistol." Jackie closed the cabinet. "I wouldn't worry about forever so much, Darla. I'd be enjoying my nights, if I was you. And coming in late every once in a while is a good thing, too. I can cover opening the store."

Darla blushed, wondering if Jackie knew that she hadn't been late because she'd overslept. Darla never overslept. "I can't think about anything else when he makes love to me," she admitted. "I'm holding out to see if we have anything in common that's not physical, but I'm not sure I'm going to be any good at telling him no. I gave Sabrina the magic wedding dress back, and then I found myself in bed with Judah. And it was wonderful."

"You *are* running in place, aren't you?"

Darla blinked. "You're right. I need a new plan."

Chapter 11

Darla called Judah that night and told him she was rescinding her offer of a marriage of convenience.

"Good," Judah said. "I'll be right over."

He hung up. Darla stared at the phone for a moment before racing to brush her hair. She should have anticipated him jumping the gun! She'd meant to tell him that she'd decided that they should wait to get married until after the children were born, when they'd had time to get to know each other better—and naturally, he'd drawn the conclusion he preferred.

Which was pretty much how it always was with Judah.

When she opened the door to him, she redoubled her vow to stick to the plan: no-nonsense laying out of the rules. It wouldn't be easy with him looking like a dark renegade cowboy ready to ravish her at any moment. She hadn't changed out of the comfy, dark gray sweat bottoms and pink polka-dotted halter maternity top, and still he looked at her as if she were edible.

"Tonight we lay everything on the table," Darla said.

"I'm all about tables," Judah said, "and I'm glad you're loosening up a bit. Let me show you what tables are best for, love."

And then to her shock, and beyond her wildest imaginings, Judah made love to her on the beautiful antique dining table where she usually laid out holiday dinners. "I'm afraid I'm too heavy for you," she whispered as he carefully placed her over him. He said, "No, baby. You're just right." And it was completely all right.

She felt like a million dollars as she collapsed with delicious shivers in Judah's arms.

"No more of that," Darla said, after the storm of lovemaking had abated. "We have to talk." She picked up her panties from the floor, collected her sweatpants from a chair and her halter top from the fruit bowl. Her sweats had been far too easy for Judah to take off—*she'd* been too easy. Far too much so.

He grinned. "I know talking is important, but I've always preferred action. I speak better with my hands."

She backed away from his dark appeal. "It doesn't surprise me that you would say that."

"Anyway," he said, "I can't really talk on an empty stomach. Can what you have to say wait until we eat?"

"Eat? At eight o'clock at night?"

He grinned. "Yeah. If this is a girlie chat, you really want me to have a full stomach."

"Girlie chat?" Outraged, she said, "First, just because you're near a table, Judah, doesn't mean all your needs have to be satisfied. Second—"

He kissed her to interrupt her, and pulled her close as he leaned back against the table. "Now, listen, missus, when you *are* my missus, I'll expect you in nothing but an apron, until my children are old enough to know that their mom is a dedicated nudie. Once the kiddos are off to college, you can return to cooking for me in the buff." Kissing her neck, he massaged her bottom, holding her tightly against him. "Questions?"

When she tried to open her mouth to give him the scolding of his life, he kissed her until she was breathless. He sighed, enjoying her quivering with rage. "Your limo driver will be here in about ten minutes. My guess is you'll want to change."

Darla's ire was drowned out by curiosity. "Limo driver?"

Judah released her, waving a negligent hand. "Or coachman. Whatever you romantic gals prefer to call them. I think they were called coachmen in the fairy tale, but they were mice first, and I thought ladies didn't like rodents and things. However, we will be attended by a first-rate rodent tonight."

Darla stared at Judah, wondering what kind of loose cannon had fathered her children. "What in the world are you talking about?"

The doorbell rang, and Judah bowed. "Better get your gown on, Cinderella. It's time for the ball."

"Ball?"

"Our date." Judah grinned. "Every woman wants to be swept off her little glass slippers, doesn't she? Though again, you'll have to forgive the rodent who's driving us." He flung open her front door. "She's not quite ready, bro," he said to Rafe, who walked in wearing some kind of chauffeur's uniform, or maybe a pilot's. Darla wondered what was going on. Rafe had proposed to her in sort of a bee-in-Judah's-eye way not twenty-four hours ago—why was he here now?

"Women are slow to get ready," Judah told Rafe. "And this one wanted to talk first," he said in a loud whisper to his brother.

Darla's gaze jumped to Judah, assessing whether he was trying hard to be a jackass, or if it just came naturally.

She decided it was the most natural thing in the world to him.

Rafe tipped his hat. "Can you hurry it up a bit, Darla? You look lovely the way you are, but I booked a flight plan, and there's a certain window of opportunity I should probably follow."

"Shh," Judah said, "don't give her too many details. She argues when she has detail overload." He went over and kissed Darla. "Hurry, darling, the rodent gets nervous around midnight. He has a phobia about leaving on time."

She opened her mouth to argue, but Judah had claimed she liked to argue, so she really had no choice except to go into her room to examine her options.

There weren't many, she decided, as she tossed off the sweats and took a quick rinse. She wanted to talk, and Judah had left the door open for that. All he wanted to do was eat, he claimed, and though she had some organic veggies in the fridge, she sensed that wasn't what he had in mind. She slipped into a casual dress and tied her blonde hair up in a ponytail. Maybe this was his boneheaded way of being romantic. Judah probably didn't understand that a man didn't barge into a woman's house, ravish her on the dining room table and then announce he wanted to eat.

Yet it sounded romantic, as if Judah had put some thought into whatever his plan was. She slipped on some high heels—it would help her look him almost in the eye when she told him *no* the next time he tried to undress her. Had Rafe said something about a flight plan?

She went back into the den.

"Five minutes flat," Rafe said to Judah. "Dude, you can't do better than a girl who can beautify in five minutes."

Judah's gaze went from Darla's face to her dress, then slowly made its way up again. He grinned at her, and Darla knew instinctively he was thinking *dessert*.

She blushed. Or maybe *she'd* thought it.

"Come on," Rafe said, laughing. "There's so much electricity in this room there's going to be a fire."

Judah opened the door for her, and they left. She went to the Callahan family van, which was apparently serving as the limo tonight.

As soon as Rafe opened the door for her and Judah, she heard giggles and squeals.

"We're going to Chicago!" Sabrina exclaimed, and Darla saw that Jonas was in the back with her. "This is my sister, Seton," Sabrina said. "Seton, this is Darla Cameron, who is engaged to Judah." Sabrina smiled as Rafe took his place behind the wheel, next to her, completely missing the uncomfortable look on Darla's face. Judah slipped in next to Darla and whispered, "Are you okay with this?"

"Almost," she said. "Let me get over the shock."

He squeezed her shoulders gently. "I thought you might enjoy something fun."

No one else could hear Judah over the light jazz music softly playing and the excited chatter in the van, but Darla noted the kindness in his tone and realized he'd been acting like a rascal in her house just to bait her, knowing he had a romantic evening all planned, which delighted her. Dessert in Chicago would be so much fun.

And it was so much better than talking.

In fact, just about everything Judah wanted to do was better than talking. She sent a sidelong glance his way, enjoying him laughing as the girls teased him, and Rafe and Jonas ribbed him about being a worse date than he was a bull rider. And before long Darla felt herself falling for her man of action.

She'd fallen, she realized, completely under his spell.

It was too late to do anything but enjoy the ride.

"You shouldn't have let her get away from you like that," Bode Jenkins said, over a gin and tonic that same evening. Sidney Tunstall shrugged his shoulders, not certain what difference it made to one of the wealthiest ranchers in these parts whether he got married or not.

It made a huge difference to Bode. He intended to make certain the nuptials of Darla and Judah never happened. If there was one way to thwart Fiona—and he knew all about her little plan to grow her own zip code—it was to derail this wedding. "Your inheritance is all tied up in you getting married, and as the executor of your grandfather's estate, I have to make certain everything is proper." He gave Sidney a pensive look. "Who are you going to marry, since you've let Darla get away?"

Sidney shrugged. "I don't know."

"You have only another month before it all goes to charity." Bode shook his head. "It sure would be a shame to lose out on a couple million bucks."

Sidney shrugged again, not happy about the situation, but not fighting it, either. "That's just pocket change to some people, I guess. I lived without it before, and I can keep living without it."

Bode slammed a palm down on the mahogany table, one of the few nice furnishings he'd bothered to splurge on for his home. Julie had insisted on it. Lately, she'd been decorating a lot, despite his propensity to groan over the money spent. "You younger generation don't know what money is. I wouldn't let a penny get away from me, much less two million." Bode considered the man across from him. "You don't throw away a fortune, son."

"Under the parameters it was left to me, I can." Sidney straightened. "There's nothing wrong with waiting until I find the woman I love, Mr. Jenkins. And in a world where people now live to be a hundred, being a thirty-five-year-old bachelor isn't an emergency."

"Well, your grandfather thought you were dragging your feet. That's all I know." Bode shrugged, wondering how he could get the good doc to get off the dime and grab Darla away from that wild-eyed Callahan. Fiona's nephew had just stormed in there and thrown Sidney off the train, and apparently put stars of romance in Darla Cameron's eyes. He'd heard all about that from her mother, Mavis, who was the silliest, most cotton-headed woman he'd ever met. It was all love-this, and love-that, and Bode'd had it to the back teeth with all the Callahans and their ability to get everything they wanted. "If you liked Darla, why'd you surrender your ground, son?"

"Because I liked her," Sidney said, "I didn't love her. And she didn't love me."

"I see," Bode said thoughtfully. "You were going to take the money and run."

"No," Sidney said, showing a flash of temper, "I was going to take the money that was left to me, and be a husband to Darla and a father to her children. That's what the plan was."

"And you were never going to divorce?"

Sidney looked at him. "I suppose no one could ever say never, but I don't know why anybody would want to give up Darla. She's a nice lady."

Bode blinked, lit a cigar. "I do not understand your lack of competitiveness."

"I don't understand your thirst for it, so we're square." Sidney looked at Bode. "Is there anything else you need, Mr. Jenkins? I should probably be out looking for another wife, don't you think?" He said it sarcastically, and Bode caught that, but what he also caught was the *angle.*

"It will be hard to get another so quickly," Bode said, "one who has so much going for her. A man can find a woman anywhere, they're like fleas on a dog. But a good woman is tougher to find."

"Not exactly, Mr. Jenkins," Sidney said, getting his gentleman's ire up, which was just what Bode was hoping for. "They're nothing like fleas on a dog."

"Now, now, what I meant was that they are numerous, but not necessarily quality."

"I don't know what you meant, but it sounded pretty demeaning to me."

Bode laughed. "I never remarried after I lost my wife, Sidney. I think I know the value of a good woman."

Sidney looked at him, not appeased.

"Now, take my daughter, Julie—"

Sidney stood. "I'll find my own wife, Mr. Jenkins, if it's all the same to you."

Bode nodded. "Well, be quick about it. I'm very eager to write this check out to you instead of a charity. To be honest, I don't think much of charities, Sidney. I'm not certain that all that lovely money ever gets to the deserving folks who need it."

Sidney, white knight that he was, looked outraged. "There are many charities that do necessary, vital work."

"Yes, and it would be better in your pocket where you could decide on the charities of your choice. I'm not much for charity, as I said."

Sidney stared at him. "Are you trying to say that you decide where the money goes, if not to me?"

Bode pretended surprise. "Who else would?"

"My grandfather left no directive?"

Bode shook his head. "Nope. He figured you'd want the money badly enough to find your way to an altar, son. So maybe you ought to rethink letting Darla go, since the two of you had this nice little thing worked out."

Sidney sighed. "Tell me again how my grandfather came to choose you to be the executor of his estate?"

"Business, Sidney. We did business together. You might say we understood each other's world view, to a certain extent. And we went to school together, so we went back a long ways. He knew he could trust me."

Sidney looked at him a long time. "You're not trying to jump this will, are you, Mr. Jenkins?"

Bode grinned at him. "Sidney, from where you sit, two million dollars is a world of money. You can do a lot of good with it. You can have a nice house, send your kids to college. But for me, now, because I never let a penny go that had my name on it—unless Julie makes me—two million is good money, but it's not going to change my standard of life."

"I'm not sure you have a standard."

"That's where you're wrong." Bode smiled. "Your grandfather was a good man. And I always honor my friends."

Sidney put his hat on. "Thanks for the drink."

Bode nodded. "By the way, I have my doubts about Darla and Judah working out."

Sidney stopped. "What do you mean?"

"A little bird told me that they're planning to divorce as soon as the children are born. Now if you ask me," Bode said, his gaze sad, "that's a crying shame."

"I don't believe you."

"Ask Darla," Bode said, and Sidney said, "I will." He closed the door.

Bode grinned and hummed a wedding march.

"It was a lovely evening, Judah," Darla said at her front door when the "limo" returned her home. "Thank you."

"My pleasure," Judah said. "My truck's here, so I can leave, but of course, I can also stay if you want company."

Darla thought about the dining table and how she'd never be able to eat there again without remembering Judah loving her into a delirious frenzy. "It's been a long day. I have to be up early."

He nodded. "I understand."

She wondered if he understood something she wasn't necessarily saying. "Judah, why did you really plan the surprise trip tonight?"

He shrugged. "We haven't ever dated, for one thing, and for another, I'm kind of hoping that tomorrow will be the day we get married."

A truck door slammed, and Sidney appeared.

"Hello, Darla," he said. "Judah."

She glanced at Judah, then at Sidney. "What are you doing here, Sidney?"

"Just feeling a bit wistful. Tomorrow's supposed to be our big day," he said. "Hope you don't mind me saying so, Callahan."

"Not at all," Judah said, "but I guess this is awkward. You two probably have things to discuss. Plans to end."

"Actually, I need to talk to both of you," Darla said.

Chapter 12

Darla seated her beaus on the sofa, gave them some tea, wondered if she should serve something stronger. They looked at her expectantly.

"Sidney," she began, "you and I were making a deal when we agreed to get married. That wasn't fair to you."

"I was okay with it," Sidney said. "I still need a wife. In a really bad way."

"There's a lot of women running around Diablo," Judah said helpfully. "Let me introduce you to some."

"I like this one," Sidney said, and Darla could tell he was baiting Judah.

"And Judah," she said, "there are some things between us that make me nervous. The condom prank, for one thing, which you never told me about. We shouldn't even be in this position." She took a deep breath. "I'm still in shock that I'm having twins."

"I'm a Callahan," Judah said. "Magic happens for us."

"Awkward," Sidney said. "And as a doctor, may I remind you that the female is responsible for some of the genetic coding?"

Judah shrugged. "But babies by the bunch are what we do at Rancho Diablo."

He said it in a *top that!* tone, and Darla sighed.

"Also," she said, "Sidney wasn't honest with you about your concussion."

Judah looked at Sidney. "Tunstall, you're a dirty dog. You made me think I'd cracked my nut. Did I even have a scratch?"

Sidney shrugged. "Perhaps there was something minor. Maybe." He sighed. "No. But I saved you from yourself. You needed to be here, with Darla, figuring out your future."

"You see," Judah said, "he's a gentleman, if not a good M.D."

Sidney shrugged again. "Whatever. I've had crankier patients."

"So," Darla said, interrupting their digging at each other, "this is my dilemma."

"No," Judah said. "You're having *my* children. There is no dilemma. We will find Sidney an appropriate bride of his own. I'll lend him my tux, but nothing else."

Sidney put his palms up in surrender. "I'm thinner than you, so the tux wouldn't fit. However, I can see that Darla has made up her mind—"

"I haven't made up my mind," Darla said quickly, feeling bad for Sidney, "because what I'm trying to tell both of you is that none of this started out right with either one of you."

"I don't care how it started out," Judah said. "I'm pretty happy with how things are proceeding. But if Sidney tries to marry the mother of my children, I'll give *him* a concussion he won't forget."

"He probably would." Sidney stood, went to the door. "He's a caveman, Darla. And I'm a gentleman. But ladies have always been attracted to bad boys. I know when I'm beat."

"That's right," Judah said, and Darla glowered at him.

"You're not beat, Sidney," she said softly, "but he is a caveman."

"I just took you to Chicago," Judah protested.

Sidney kissed Darla on the forehead. "You guys have a lot to work out. I'll shove off."

"Both of you shove off," Darla said in annoyance. "I think you two have a lot to work out."

"What?" Judah asked. "You can't expect us to be best friends. We're both too manly for that."

"It's hard competing for a woman," Sidney said. "So I'll have to agree with him."

"Both of you go," Darla said. "Now."

They looked at her, neither one happy.

"And don't come back until you've resolved your issues. I'm not having any hard feelings over a day that should be the happiest of my life."

"But—" Judah started, and Sidney said, "All right."

"Now, look here," Judah said, "this game of yours of always being Mr. Nice is tiresome. I can be nice, too."

Sidney shrugged. "If you own that emotion, own it. No one's standing in your way."

Judah frowned. "He's not going to fight fair," he

complained to Darla. "I don't trust skinny bronc busters. He's already tried to put one over on me about my nonexistent concussion."

"That was your own fault," Sidney said righteously. "Even you should know if you bumped your head or not."

"I've had other things on my mind," Judah said with a growl Darla's way.

"Good night," she said, closing the door on both of them.

"What about tomorrow?" Judah called through the door.

"Tomorrow is another day," Darla told herself, and went to bed alone, already wishing Judah was there to hold her in his arms.

"We're going to have to be careful," Sidney said. "She might find another guy to marry."

"What are you talking about?" Judah wondered if the top of his head was about to blow off. Was the doc crazy? In Judah's opinion, Darla loved no one but him—even if she hadn't realized it herself yet.

"If she has to choose between us," Sidney said reasonably, "she might opt for a third party."

They leaned against Judah's truck, chatting under the dark night sky as if discussing the stars. Judah grunted. "I'm not worried. I wouldn't let that happen."

"She's suffering with a guilt complex where you're concerned, so you might not have a say in the matter. Guilt doesn't make for an easy path to the altar."

Judah didn't care. "I'm getting her to the altar tomorrow. I have the rest of our lives to let her make up to me for all that guilt she's worried about."

"I don't know if that's the proper approach."

"You're my shrink now? My love doctor?"

"Someone's got to do it," Sidney said. "Look, I don't mind helping you, but I'm in a ditch. I need her, too. So don't push me."

"What's your deal?" Judah asked. "What's it going to take to get you convinced that Darla is not the bride you want? Because frankly, you're not going to have her."

"Remember I was first," Sidney said. "That flower arch in her backyard has my name on it, so to speak."

"What flower arch?" Judah's head turned like it was on a swivel. "I don't see an arch."

"Notice that all the little elves have been busy while you were chasing romance in Chicago."

In his haste to try to get past Darla's front door to-night, he hadn't noticed the lanterns strung along her porch, and candles wrapped with pink ribbons along the drive. "Okay, what's the plan? I'm open to sugges-tions right now. Because she returned the ring to me. And I heard she gave Sabrina some stupid magic wed-ding dress, not that I believe in magic." Judah thought about the wild horses that ran across the far reaches of Rancho Diablo. They hadn't been seen in a while. Maybe good luck had left him behind. "I do believe in magic," he said after a moment, "and right now, I need some."

"Yeah, me, too." Sidney nodded. "I was sent here tonight to break you two up."

Judah didn't let himself show his surprise. "So you're the villain in my fairy tale."

"There's nothing Bode Jenkins would rather see more than you and Darla calling things off."

"Over my cold dead body will that happen."

Sidney nodded. "I thought so. Anyway, that's why I came over tonight. Hope I haven't confused matters between you and Darla."

"What do you mean?"

Sidney shrugged. "Just in case she's in there right now having second thoughts. Third thoughts."

"She's not."

"Bode's determined to get at your family. I should probably keep my mouth shut, considering he holds some of my purse strings at the moment, but he's playing foul."

"Look," Judah said, "I don't know how to help you with your problem. I wish I did. But don't let Bode talk you into a wedding you don't want."

"Yeah," Sidney said, almost reluctantly. "I don't want it. And Darla doesn't love me, either. She's always loved you."

"Not me," Judah said, and Sidney said, "Yes, you. You're the only one who doesn't know it."

Judah blinked, considered whether Sidney knew what he was talking about or was trying to dig himself out of a pounding courtesy of Judah's big fists. "Did Darla tell you that?"

Sidney got in his truck. "You'll have to find out on your own. I've done all the repairs on my conscience I intend to. I'll be here tomorrow, waiting to move in if you don't do the job properly, though. And if you don't mind, keep this conversation under your big hat. I don't want Bode deciding to claim my inheritance. You have a trustworthy aunt who oversaw your affairs. Bode is a different proposition altogether."

Judah tipped his hat. "Be here with your tux on," he said. "I need a best man, and you'll fit the bill just fine."

Sidney looked at him. "Are we inviting gossip?"

"Just letting everyone know that the bride's a smart lady. She's got good taste in men. And you can show Bode he doesn't own you."

"He does, in a way, but that's out of my control now." Sidney backed his truck up. "Let me know if you come across an extra bride."

"By chance have you ever met Diane, Aberdeen's sister? She's not exactly looking for marriage, but you might change her mind. Anyway, good luck." He waved, and when the doctor's truck had disappeared, he marched to Darla's bedroom window. He tapped and a moment later she appeared, looking none too pleased to see him.

"Judah! What are you doing?" she asked through the glass.

"Serenading you."

She slid the window open. "Go away."

"I can't. We have to talk."

"So talk."

"Let me in, Darla."

She shook her head. "Not a chance, buster."

"What is it?" he asked, his voice innocent. "What's got my bride thinking less than happy thoughts the night before her wedding?"

"I'm not getting married tomorrow," Darla said, "even though everyone is conspiring to make it happen."

"I got blood drawn. I'm ready to rock," Judah said. "It looks like the decorating is done, and you've got a dress. We can go get a marriage license in the morning, and be ready to say 'I do' at sundown."

She shook her head. "I'm not a girl who rushes in to things."

Judah put his hands on the window ledge and hauled himself into Darla's bedroom. "Whew, I'm getting too old for this," he said. "I hope you plan on being a more agreeable wife than you are a fiancée."

"I'm not your fiancée. And you're not supposed to be in here." Darla closed the window and pointed a finger toward the den. "Go out there if you want to talk."

"It's dangerous for you out there, too," Judah said. "I like variety."

She didn't reply, but he could tell she wasn't exactly rejecting his suit. "So back to this guilt thing," he said. "I don't care if Creed's stupid condoms failed. I'm going to have the most beautiful babies in the world. And I don't care about Doc trying to give me the shove. I like him. He's entitled to want the most beautiful woman in Diablo, too. So," Judah said, crossing to take her face between his hands, "can we put all this guilt business behind us? Because you really, really want to marry me, and frankly, putting me back out in the stream to be fished by other ladies is a move you'd always regret."

Darla closed her eyes, allowing herself to relax in his grasp. "Let's sleep on it. I'm too tired to think tonight."

"I've waited a long time to hear that. Come on, love, let me put you to bed."

He pulled Darla toward the bed, pressing her down into the sheets. He lay down next to her, tugging her up against him spoon-style, and rubbed her back until she fell asleep. Once she was breathing deeply and he could tell she was out like a light, he cupped a palm under her tummy—under his boys—and fell asleep himself, feeling like a million bucks.

Chapter 13

Darla would have liked to pretend that she surrendered, but when she stood at the altar the next evening after a whirlwind of last-minute preparations, she knew she was marrying Judah because she'd always dreamed of it. Whatever they were letting themselves in for, he was going to be her husband, and she was going to be Mrs. Judah Callahan, exactly what she'd always wanted.

She wasn't strong enough to resist her dreams another day. She couldn't imagine not marrying him. In that, Judah was egotistically right: she didn't want to return him to the dating pond for other women to catch. She wanted him all to herself.

Maybe he wasn't the marrying kind, but she had to take a chance that he was.

Everyone was happy, smiling at the wedding. The

evening was lovely, the air sweetened with romance. Judah was breathtakingly handsome and sexy; she couldn't believe he was actually going to be hers.

"Are you ready?" Jackie asked, coming to her side.

Darla nodded. "Thanks for being my maid of honor."

"I'm happy to have a sister." Jackie hugged her. "Judah's out there pacing. If we don't get you down the aisle, he's going to come get you."

Darla smiled. He'd been gone this morning when she'd awakened, but he'd left a note on her pillow telling her that she was the luckiest woman in the world, and she'd always be the envy of every other woman in town.

Typical Judah.

"I'm ready," Darla said.

"Just a small warning," Jackie said, "so you won't be surprised. Bode's here."

"I didn't invite him." The news did nothing to calm her nerves.

"Bode is like the troll that no one ever invites, but he manages to hang around. I vote ignore him, and completely ruin his day. Fiona told him that if he did one thing to upset you, she'd have him tied to a cactus. And I won't tell you what Judah said about it."

Darla felt better. "Let's hurry before something bad happens. I distinctly feel an urge to speed this along."

Jackie waved to Diane, who was in charge of overseeing the music. Diane motioned for the harpist to begin, and serene music filtered through the air, joined by a traditional piano wedding march. Darla took a deep breath and headed down the aisle as Diane's little daughters scattered rose petals from white baskets along her path.

Judah was smiling at her, eating her up with his eyes as she walked to the beautiful altar. An excited tingle shot up her spine. This sexy man was about to tell the world that he was making her his wife. It was all her dreams come true.

A shot rang out, and in front of Darla's horrified eyes, Judah fell back against Sidney, who helped him to the ground. Guests cried out, scattering, and the wedding march ground to a halt. The little flower girls ran to Diane, and suddenly, Darla was grabbed by big strong Callahans and dragged away from the altar—and Judah. She protested, wanting to be at his side, but Sam held her back, keeping her out of danger.

Darla shrugged Sam off and ran to Judah's side. She could hear Sidney calling for an ambulance as he worked to stop the bleeding in Judah's arm.

"Judah," she said, kneeling down next to him, despite the hands trying to pull her back, "don't you *dare* die on me!"

He gave her a weak smile. "I've been shot before. This is just a flesh wound. Don't get my babies all upset over nothing."

"How do you know it's a flesh wound? Sidney, is it a flesh wound?" She didn't wait for an answer. Her heart was painfully tight in her chest as she watched the blood oozing from him. "What do you mean, you've been shot before? You never told me that!"

"Hunting accident," he said. "Anyway, it wasn't important. We had a lot more important things to talk about."

"That's it," Darla said. "As soon as you're patched up, you're moving in with me. I'll make sure you stay out of trouble."

He closed his eyes, and Sheriff Cartwright's men surrounded the wedding party, moving everyone away in case the shooter was still out there. "Go," Judah told her, "I don't want you getting shot. Do what the nice lawmen tell you. Isn't that right, Doc?"

"That's right," Sidney said, and Darla said, "Shut up, both of you. I'm not going anywhere until I know you're not exaggerating about your flesh wound."

Sidney waved to the Callahan men, who were standing around helplessly. "Get him inside," he said, "not near windows, until the ambulance arrives."

But that wasn't necessary. The ambulance pulled up, its sirens wailing, and two EMTs jumped out to take over from Sidney, who looked gravely concerned.

"I know we've had our differences, but I hope you know I didn't do this," Sidney said.

"I know you didn't," Judah said.

Sidney watched protectively as Judah was placed into the ambulance. "I'm going to ride with him."

"I'm going, too." Darla shoved her way into the vehicle behind Sidney.

"All this stress isn't good for the babies," Sidney warned, and Judah said, "Stay here, Darla."

She shook her head. "My children would never forgive me if I didn't stay with their father when he'd been shot."

"More guilt," Judah said, and Darla said, "That's right. Now just lie there."

"I'm going to love being married," Judah said, his face creased with a smile even though he closed his eyes wearily.

"I'm hoping this wasn't your way of getting out of marrying me," Darla said, and Judah's eyes snapped open.

"Not a chance, sweetheart. Not a chance."

Darla looked at the blood on her wedding dress and wondered if she should have worn the magic wedding gown, after all. She'd definitely seen Judah standing behind her in the mirror. He'd been smiling, handsome, tall and virile. Not shot by a sniper. Gooseflesh jumped onto her arms, and she rubbed them, not able to rub away the unease as the ambulance raced to the hospital.

"You see what I mean," Sabrina whispered to her sister, Seton. "There's a dark cloud over Rancho Diablo."

Seton nodded. "I've been keeping an eye on the Jenkins's place, but I have to be honest with you, I don't think the old man did it. He seemed shocked when Judah got hit. Not displeased, necessarily, just shocked."

Sabrina blinked. "Who else would have done it?"

"Maybe the best man set it up. Weren't they romantic rivals?"

"You'd have to get to know Sidney to understand that he wouldn't hurt anyone," Sabrina said. "The man is gentle. He's a healer." She could see that in his peaceful aura, in the kindness in his eyes. He'd never borne any ill will toward Judah, and she knew Judah liked the doc, too. "No, it wouldn't have been Sidney."

"Any other ideas?"

Sabrina shook her head. "The Callahans are well-liked in the town, as you might have been able to tell by the number of guests who showed up to the wedding. And that was for a wedding no one thought would actually happen."

"Well, it didn't." Seton glanced around Darla's property, watching the guests help clean up the yard and put away chairs. "The thing that puzzles me is that whoever shot Judah either wasn't a practiced assassin or didn't mean to kill him."

"Why? What are you thinking?"

Seton shrugged. "I think someone just wanted Judah—or the Callahans—to know he was out there. Scare them a little bit. Or, and the possibility is remote, it could have been a random misfire from a hunter. But I don't think so. It didn't sound like a large firearm."

Sabrina sighed. "Hold that thought. Bode and Fiona are having a row, and since I've been employed by both, I'd better see if I can run interference."

"I'm telling you," Bode said angrily to Sheriff Cartwright as Sabrina walked up, "I didn't have anything to do with the shooting. And she hit me! That's assault. And I want to know what you're going to do about it, Sheriff."

"Not much, Bode, and you're not, either." The sheriff rocked back on his heels. "Do you have an invitation to be here?"

Bode's mouth flattened. "One doesn't need an invitation to attend a wedding of a local favorite. It was known by all that a wedding would take place here today."

Fiona looked at him. "Bode, one day, things are going to turn out badly between you and me. I suggest you keep your dealings with my family on the professional level, and quit being such a pest."

Bode didn't reply and Fiona left, with Sabrina following her. "Fiona, let me drive you to the hospital. We'll check on Judah and Darla."

Fiona nodded. "I'd appreciate that. They don't need

me at the hospital, I'm sure, but if I stay here, I'm going to have more fighting words with that scoundrel."

"We don't want that." Sabrina steered Fiona toward the van, waved at Burke so he'd know they were leaving, in case he wanted to ride along. He did, and so did Seton, which made Sabrina feel better, having her sister around. Diane said, "I'll hold down the fort," and Fiona shouted, "Thanks!" out the window, and off they went to see how Judah was surviving his big day that hadn't turned out the way anybody had hoped.

"I'm fine," Judah said for the hundredth time, thinking that having a nurse for a fiancée had its blessings and its curses. Darla hovered over the nurses, she hovered over the doctors, she hovered over Judah. No one escaped her watchful eye. He reminded himself that this was one of the things he'd known about her, that she was efficient and businesslike.

But he was a man, and he didn't want to be fussed over. Not about a gunshot wound, anyway. The truth was, dark thoughts kept running through his mind, torturing him, and he wanted to reflect on them.

What if the bullet had hit Darla?

What if his babies had been injured?

His blood ran cold, keeping him shivering, as the worries punctuated his blood loss.

"If you're cold, I'll get a heated blanket," Darla said, and a small redheaded nurse said, "I'll get it," anxious to stay out of Darla's path. She was as protective of him as a lioness, and Judah closed his eyes, not wanting to think about how much he wanted to marry her.

He was glad now that he hadn't.

"Darla," he said, as they began to wheel him toward an operating room, "today was not our day."

Tears jumped into her eyes. He hated to see her cry. If he had his way, a tear would never form on his behalf in her eyes, ever again.

"We'll have another day," Darla said. "We'll work something out."

He gave her a small grimace of a smile before he was wheeled to the O.R. so the bullet could be removed. He didn't care about the bullet. He cared about what had been taken from them today, which was romance and innocence.

It made him angry. Worse, the shooting had given him crystal-clear perspective. Until today, he hadn't really thought through what he was doing to Darla by marrying her.

But now he remembered. And now he knew what he had to do.

Chapter 14

Sam waited until Bode walked up the drive of the Jenkins place before he launched himself at him, landing on top of the elderly man. Bode cursed, trying to throw a punch, but Rafe caught his hand.

"Mind your manners, Jenkins." Rafe held him down and Sam took a seat on the man's back.

"*My* manners?" Bode spit some dirt out of his mouth. "I'll have the law on you so fast it'll made your head spin if you don't get your ape of a brother off me. You Callahans have never been anything but trouble, you and your crazy aunt, too."

"Crazy!" Sam said. "Brother, did you just hear him insult our aunt, who raised us when no one else would have?" He leaned over from his seated position on Bode's back to look him in his eyes. "Bode, we're curious just how far back your animosity goes."

"It goes back years. Why the hell wouldn't it?" Bode demanded. "If you need a carbon dating, you could probably date it to the time your parents arrived here."

"We wonder what really happened to our parents," Rafe said as Jonas walked out of the neatly manicured bushes around Bode's property.

"There's no one here and Julie doesn't appear to be home," Jonas said to his brothers. "You're free to conduct yourselves as you see fit."

"And you call yourself a lawyer," Bode snarled in Sam's direction. "Get off of me, you hooligan. All of you are insane, like your silly aunt."

"Ah," Rafe said with a sigh, "I'm just dying to hit him."

"But we won't," Sam said, "because that would be against the law. We're just having a chat with our neighbor." He bounced on Bode's back, drawing another snarl.

"I don't know what happened to your parents," Bode said. "That I swear."

"Your word's not really good with us," Jonas said, "if you don't mind me pointing out the obvious."

"What do you think I would have done with them? And if you really want to know, why don't you ask Fiona?" Bode tried to get up, but Sam was too heavy to be budged. He patted Bode on the head, comforting him like a child, and the old rancher cursed at him.

"Someone shot Judah tonight, and no one would do that but you. You're too clever to get caught," Jonas said, "so you hired some punk to do it. Luckily for you, Judah isn't dead, or you'd be joining him in pushing up daisies."

"Why would I want to kill your brother? Why don't

you suspect the man he stole Darla from?" Bode demanded.

"That's too easy," Sam said. "First of all, Doc wouldn't hurt anybody. Second, you want us gone, scared off. When the ballistics on the bullet come back, we're going to have Sheriff Cartwright search your house for a match, and any records for a weapon that's been sold to you, licensed to you, ever fired by you at a tin can."

"I didn't do it. I really don't want any of you boys to come to harm. I swear it."

Sam bounced on Bode's back a little harder, and the rancher *oofed* into the dirt. "You say that now, while we've got you cornered. But we know you sneaked into our house and locked Pete in the basement. You threaten us constantly, and our aunt. So we know to come to you when we so much as find a piece of bread missing from the pantry."

Bode shook his head. "I'm not talking any more until I have a lawyer and the sheriff here."

"Why? We're not arresting you, Bode. We're just asking a few friendly questions. The truth is, we want to save you from yourself," Rafe said.

"How so?"

"Because you really don't want to be the jackass that you are," Jonas said. "We know deep inside you beats a heart that doesn't want to harm anyone. Isn't that right, Bode?"

"I want your land," Bode said. "And that's it. But I can figure out a hundred ways to get it besides killing people. I'm too smart for that."

Sam glanced around at his brothers, then got off

Bode and rolled him with his boot so that he faced three angry Callahans.

"Bode," Jonas said, "just so you know, we'll do whatever it takes to keep you from owning one inch of our land."

"It's too late," Bode said, the corners of his mouth lifting with glee. "Your aunt is broke. She has no money. She made bad investments, and it's only a matter of time before I put all of you out on the road with nothing but your belongings. And I look forward to that day, boys. Your aunt and Burke, too, and all those hobos you take in."

Jonas sighed. "Pride goeth before a big-ass fall, Jenkins. Just remember I told you that."

"Maybe," Bode said, "but some of us don't fall."

"We'll see," Sam said, and the brothers walked away.

"There's going to be war on the ranch," Fiona said to her friends as they sat in the back room of the Books'n'Bingo shop. "It may not be quite full-blown war, but I'm really afraid it's coming."

Mavis stared at her. "How can we help you?"

"I need help plotting more than anything else. There's got to be a way to think myself out of the box I'm in." She sipped her tea, and glanced around at the faces of her three best friends. These women had been with her through thick and thin from the day she'd arrived in New Mexico. Their friendship had strengthened and sustained her over the years at Rancho Diablo. Now she needed it more than ever. "The worst part is that the wedding had to called off. I'm so sorry about Darla's big day," she told Mavis.

"I'm confused," Corinne Abernathy said. "First I ordered a tea set for a wedding gift to give Darla and Dr. Tunstall, and then I had to change the card to make it to Darla and Judah, and now I don't know what to do!" Corinne blinked. "I think I'll take it back to the store. It's not a lucky tea set, for certain."

"I suppose you could give it to one of your nieces," Nadine Waters suggested. "Seton or Sabrina might like it."

"Don't worry," Mavis said. "Darla might be my late-in-life child, but she's always quick to resolve her dilemmas. And that tea set is lucky, I'm certain, Corinne." She patted her friend's hand.

Fiona sighed. "This is all my fault."

"There is no fault." Mavis shook her head. "It's just that Bode Jenkins can't leave well enough alone."

"I beaned him pretty good with my purse at the wedding. And it had Burke's pocket watch in it, too, which as you know is no light thing. I heard it go thump on Bode's thick skull."

"Why were you carrying Burke's watch?" Corinne asked.

"Sabrina had taken it somewhere to get it cleaned a couple months ago. She knew of a person who specializes in antique pocket watches. Burke does so love his timepiece," Fiona said with a sigh. "That watch has been running for over half a century now."

"Like you," Corinne said with a giggle.

"That's true," Mavis said. "Hope you didn't mess up the watch by using it as a nunchuku."

Fiona shook her head. "The watch has a gold case. It's like a rock, a lucky Irish rock." She looked around the sitting room of the Books'n'Bingo shop, taking in all the volumes of beloved books, the various teapots lining the walls for decoration and for use, and sighed at the coziness of it all. "I just wish everything would settle down for just a little while. Mostly, I want Darla and Judah to get married. I want you to be my in-law," she told Mavis. "Even though you're all my sisters, I was really looking forward to adding one of you to my family tree. And I do so love Darla. She's just always so nice to me. Everybody in our family likes her so much."

Mavis blinked. "To be honest, as much as I think Sidney is a great doctor, I was really pulling for Judah. I think those two have been making secret cow eyes at each other for years."

Corinne nodded. "At least you'll be getting more grandchildren, Fiona. That's more than I can say for myself. Goodness knows neither Seton nor Sabrina are interested in being altar-bound."

Fiona contemplated that over a sugar cookie. "I was just positive it was a stroke of brilliance for me to hire Sabrina to light a fire under my boys, since they have no idea you have nieces, Corinne. The fortune teller bit was priceless. And it's a bonus that Seton is a private investigator, because now I can spy on Bode to my heart's content."

"But none of it's working," Nadine said. "Bode's still being ugly, and only two of your boys jumped at the chance to own the ranch. I mean, I think Judah will still make an excellent groom, Mavis," she hurriedly said, "when he gets over being shot."

"Being shot does slow a groom down." Fiona threw out that last bit to comfort Mavis, but the truth was, she feared that a wedding postponed might be a wedding canceled for good. "I'm all for striking while the bride is hot, though."

Mavis gasped. "Darla will always be hot! There are good genes in our family!"

"I meant iron," Fiona soothed. "You know Darla is a silver-blond beauty, Mavis. Don't get in a twist. I'm just so nervous and rattled my mouth is running off like a rabbit." She did feel completely rattled, and it wasn't fair. She didn't like not being in control. "I've always pushed my boys to do what I believed was best for them, and I want Judah right back at the altar before Bode figures out a way to…to—"

She couldn't bring herself to think about the fact that Bode had tried to kill her nephew. "You know, they said the bullet was small, not meant to do anything more than incapacitate, but I don't believe that. Even a .22 can kill."

"Shoot, even a BB gun can kill a person," Nadine said morosely. "My husband used to shoot varmints with BBs, and you'd be surprised the damage they can do."

"I don't want to think about it," Fiona said, swallowing against a rush of coldness seeping into her body. What would her brother, Jeremiah, and Molly say if she let something happen to one of their sons? She had to keep the family whole and together—and at Rancho Diablo. "Judah will go home from the hospital tomorrow, and then we'll see what he's planning."

"I hope he's planning another wedding," Nadine said, and Fiona nodded.

"Me, too. I've about run out of lures to convince these boys that marriage is the holy grail." Fiona put down her teacup and pursed her lips for a moment. If

Bode had gone to the trouble of harming Judah, basically scaring him away from Darla, then her plan of getting the boys married off was working.

She just didn't know why. "Why wouldn't Bode want Judah to marry Darla?"

"Because your family is growing and his is not, and he's a jealous old coot," Corinne said with some heat. "You don't think he'll ever allow his daughter, Judge Julie, to leave his house, do you? So while you've got grandkids popping out all over, he has no hopes whatsoever of having any at all. Because he'll never allow Julie to leave his home to marry someone. And pity the poor man who ever does try to take her off Bode's hands."

Fiona snapped her fingers. "That's what we need to do."

"What?" Nadine asked, lost. "What are we doing?"

"If we find a beau to hang around Bode's, eager-beaver for Julie, Bode won't have time to be in my business!" Fiona said with delight. "I believe the shock would almost end his ability to do harm to anyone on the planet."

"Except for the poor suitor," Nadine said. "You couldn't pay a man to date poor Julie."

Fiona blinked. "There's that."

Corinne nodded. "For every plot, there's a twist."

"But maybe the best way to declare war," Fiona said, "is to take it right to his door."

"We don't know a bachelor brave enough nor stupid enough to… Why are you looking like that?" Nadine asked. "Fiona, it appears as if someone turned a light-bulb on over your head."

Fiona smiled. "I have three nephews left, and all of them are very brave, and not stupid in the least."

Her friends stared at her.

"Can you imagine how upset Bode would be if one of my nephews started coming around his place? He wouldn't be able to focus on anything but Julie, and we could plan another wedding!" Fiona clapped her hands. "I just knew we'd come up with an answer if we brainstormed enough!"

"It could work," Corinne said. "In fact, it's impressive. I do see one tiny problem, however."

They all looked at her expectantly. Corinne shrugged. "Which one of your nephews would you sacrifice to the dragon, Fiona?" Just as she posed the question, the store bell tinkled and Darla walked in, locking the door behind her.

"Darla!" Mavis exclaimed. "What are you doing here?"

Darla accepted a cup of tea from Fiona and took a tufted chair in the circle. "This is the only place where I can come and have a good… I don't know. I don't want to cry, but I definitely want to talk to women who've been through everything."

The four women looked at her carefully, and Darla felt comforted by their interested perusal. If anyone could give her solid advice, it was these four.

She hoped they had some advice.

"Are you feeling all right?" Corinne asked.

"The babies are okay?" Nadine inquired.

"Did you just come from the hospital?" Fiona demanded.

"Yes, yes and yes," Darla said. "Judah is raising

Cain with the doctors to release him, so he's in peak form."

"As I expected." Fiona nodded with satisfaction. "All the Callahans are tough nuts."

Darla nodded in turn. "Tougher than you think. Judah broke off our engagement."

"What?" The women exclaimed as one and began offering sympathy in huge doses, which Darla needed.

"That scoundrel," Fiona said. "Honey, he didn't mean a word of it. You just give him a day or two to cool off, and he'll be throwing himself at your feet again, if I know my nephew."

Darla's heart was heavy as she shook her head. "I don't think so this time. He said there are too many things that endanger me and the children for him to marry me. He said there are too many family ghosts, and until they're laid to rest, he can't put me in jeopardy."

"With two little babies on the way he doesn't want to marry you?" Mavis asked, proud mother coming to the fore. "Fiona, I don't think your nephew is being honorable."

Fiona puffed up like a small bird. "If there's one thing Judah is, it's honorable, Mavis Cameron Night." She leaned toward Darla. "It sounds like shock to me, Darla. We have no family ghosts, not really, not of the variety that would harm anyone, anyway."

Everyone stared at Fiona. Darla said, "I'm not afraid of ghosts. He is."

"Silliest thing I ever heard," Nadine said. "Ghosts at a wedding, indeed. Fiona, you tell Judah to buck up."

Darla's heart hung heavy in her chest. After all of Judah's romancing her through her own case of cold feet, she had never expected to hear him say that the wedding was off.

He felt that she was safer without him.

It broke her heart.

Fiona looked uncomfortable. "I think there's been a miscommunication."

Darla shook her head. "After the surgery, he distinctly said, 'I can't marry you, Darla—'"

"Pain pills," Nadine sniffed. "Sounds like they fed him a handful, and I wouldn't listen to a word he said, Darla. You were a nurse. You know how drugs can make people time travel right out of their normal dispositions. I've never seen a man crazier for a woman than Judah is for you."

"He said it's not safe," Darla said, not drawing any comfort from their words. "He said that in order to keep me safe, he has to keep away from me."

"I don't understand," Fiona said, blinking. "It's like he got shot with the opposite of Cupid's arrow."

"Yeah, it was called Bode's bullet," Mavis said.

"Oh, dear," Fiona said. "Darla, I'm so very sorry. Surely this will all pass after my renegade nephew gets out of the hospital. He was never very good with injuries, you know that. Look at the last one he had. He thought he had a concussion when he didn't. I'm not saying Judah's a wienie, but he's not a patient patient, and—"

"It's all right," Darla said, even though it wasn't. Her heart was shattered.

"Well, it just shows you should have married Dr. Tunstall," Mavis said hotly. "Dr. Tunstall wouldn't have put you through all this nonsense. He's a steady man with a good income, and no one would shoot at *him*."

Fiona stiffened. "That's my nephew you're calling unsteady, Mavis."

"That same nephew who can't be bothered to read a big-ass label that says Party Condoms on the side," Mavis returned, her cheeks pink.

"Prank Condoms," Darla said. "And it was just as much my fault as is. I seduced him."

The women went quiet, staring at her.

"I did," Darla said. "I've been wanting to for years, and I'd do it again in a heartbeat. In fact, I'd seduce him tonight if he didn't have an injury. But it really doesn't matter. Judah has vowed to stay five miles away from me until all the ghosts in your family have been laid to rest. That's what he said, and I could tell he meant every word."

"What are these ghosts, Fiona?" Corinne asked. "I don't remember anything phantasmagoric hanging about your place."

Fiona cleared her throat. "I think Judah means the whole Bode problem."

Darla shook her head. "He muttered something about aunts who keep secrets."

"Well," Fiona said uncomfortably, at her friends' curious perusal. "Pain pills are powerful."

Mavis gathered her teacup and purse. "You'd best talk to your nephew, Fiona. We have another suitor in the wings, and we're not going to wait around for Judah. To be frank, it sounds like the man got a case of winter-cold feet. Darla shouldn't be dumped and humiliated—"

"Mom," Darla said, "I'm not humiliated."

"You will be when your children are born and people wonder why you and Judah were getting married and then didn't." Mavis glared at Fiona. "This is what happens when you meddle, Fiona. Clearly, you hurried a man along who wasn't ready to accept his responsibilities. Getting shot is no excuse. Darla's a nurse, for heaven's sake. If anybody could nurse a man back to health, it's her."

"Oh, dear," Nadine said. "We need more tea. And cupcakes."

"Ladies," Corinne said, "I vote we adjourn our chat before fur really begins to fly, and words are spoken that can never be taken back."

"Goodness," Fiona said, "this is all a tempest in a teapot."

"A cracked pot, if you ask me. Come on, Darla," Mavis said, and swept from the store.

Darla blinked, then hugged Fiona goodbye. "It's not your fault," she whispered. "I always knew he didn't really love me. Not the way I was in love with him."

Darla followed her mother. "Mom, you shouldn't have said those things to poor Fiona. It's not her fault someone shot Judah."

"She raised a back-sliding nephew," Mavis said, "and it's high time she get her house in order over there."

Darla sighed. There was a house that needed to be put in order, and it was her own. Her mother wouldn't want to hear that right now—she was too upset over everything that had happened, and Darla understood. Everyone was upset. People would be talking in Diablo for weeks.

But she didn't care. All Darla knew was that Judah had pursued her, finally convincing her that she was the only woman for him. Even if it had been all about the babies, he'd still pursued her.

Now she intended to pursue him. She owed it to her children, and to their father, to make certain that they all ended up as a happy family, no matter how many ghosts Judah thought he had to protect her from.

She was in love with him, and he was just going to have to deal with that. *And I've never been afraid of ghosts, or anything else that goes bump in the night. What I fear is losing the one man I know in my heart is a good man, the right man, the only man, for me.*

Chapter 15

The next evening Fiona walked into the bunkhouse and gave her four nephews, who were trying to resurrect their lagging game of Scrabble, a baleful stare. "Judge Julie's got herself quite the conundrum," she said. "She's trying to get that longhorn you brought from El Paso untangled from the fence, and she's wearing a tight dress and fishnets. I guess that's what a beautiful judge wears under her black robes." Fiona bleated a pitiful sigh—theatrical, to Judah's ears—and said, "I never knew why you boys had to have that longhorn, but if I was you, I'd go save it from the judge. Julie looks fit to slip it on the grill."

Jonas, Rafe and Sam abandoned Judah on the double, as Judah was certain Fiona had hoped they would. She looked at her nephew. "Why aren't you at the main house?"

"I'm fine here," Judah said.

"Usually when you boys have some kind of issue, you stay at the house."

"I don't have an issue," Judah said, not about to be lured by coddling.

She put her hands on her hips, staring at his arm, which he'd propped on a pillow. He preferred that to wearing the sling the doctor had given him. The sling made him feel like an invalid, and Judah wasn't giving in to any weaknesses when he most needed to be strong.

"You do have issues," Fiona said. "What in the world did you mean by telling Darla about ghosts?"

Judah shook his head, in no mood to be questioned the day after his wedding had taken a sinister turn. He leveled a wary eye on his aunt. "You should know about ghosts, Aunt."

"Well, I don't. I've never seen a ghost in my life," she snapped, and he grunted at her truculent tone.

"I don't know what all you've been keeping to yourself, Aunt Fiona. All I know is that Darla might have taken a bullet that was meant for me. And until I've got everything figured out, I'm not putting her in harm's way."

"The only harm that's going to come is when she decides not to wait for your silly butt." His aunt glared at him. "You do not take a bullet and then use that as an excuse, a pitiful one, not to marry the best woman that's ever been placed in your path. Trust me, even a woman who owns a shop full of wedding regalia doesn't put on the old satin-and-lace lightly. You should rethink your situation when you're not chock-full of hallucinogens."

"I haven't taken any pills," Judah said. "I don't like pain pills. So don't worry."

"You're not thinking straight, and I hate to see you make the mistake of a lifetime. You're going to look quite the ass when Darla marries Sidney."

"She won't," Judah said, though he didn't admit to a twinge of unease. But Darla's safety had to come first. "I'd almost rather she marry Sidney. Then I'd at least know she's safe."

"What?" Fiona exclaimed. "Don't talk like a quitter! I can't stand quitters!" She sank into a chair across from him. "One thing I won't have people saying is that I raised a bunch of lily-livered, weak-kneed men." She passed a hand over her brow, rearranging her hair a little, as if that would help reorganize her thoughts.

"There's been nothing but craziness around here for a while. I'm sorry to say it, Aunt Fiona, but your plan has definitely not been conducive to communal calm."

Tears jumped into her eyes, brightening them as she stared at him remorsefully. "I just want the best for you and your brothers."

"I know you do," Judah said softly, "but you don't give us all the facts. You wouldn't even have told us you and Burke were married except that we figured it out."

"You boys were so young when your parents…well, you know." Fiona sniffled into a tissue for a second, then stiffened. "Burke and I made the decision that we didn't want to confuse you. He always loved you boys, but he knew he couldn't take the place of your father, nor could I take the place of your mother. We felt it was best if we always were just aunt and bodyguard to you."

"Bodyguard?" Judah frowned. "Burke isn't your bodyguard."

"He was quite the fighter in his youth," Fiona said. "A street fighter for the cause. Things changed for us when we came over here to take care of you boys. We had to make fast decisions. Maybe we didn't make them the best we could, but I stand by them." She wiped at her eyes and put her tissue away. "I'm not going to say we didn't make mistakes. But there's a lot we didn't want to burden you children with."

"We're not children anymore."

"True," Fiona conceded. "Which is why I don't want you babbling about ghosts. You just marry Darla and raise your babies, and that'll be more than your parents were able to do for you." She sighed heavily. "People don't always get the chance to do what they really want to do."

Judah felt as if a knife had been stabbed into his gut. Never had it occurred to him that his father had been unable to raise him and his brothers. It was almost like an unbroken chain of missed parenting, he realized. The shock of being shot at, and being determined to keep his little family safe, had made him think that the best thing to do would be to let Darla have a life far away from Rancho Diablo and its spiraling misfortunes.

But should one bullet keep him and Darla apart?

He thought about the cave, and the secrets he knew were there, and the silver bar that had been in the kitchen, and the ancient Native American who visited their home every year. He thought about Sam coming after their parents were gone, as Jonas had pointed out years ago, and he wondered if it wasn't family ghosts he should fear, but far-reaching skeletons that had never rested comfortably. "I don't know," he murmured. "This isn't the way I envisioned a marriage beginning."

"That should be up to Darla, I would think. But you do what you think is best. Heaven only knows I'm all out of ideas."

Fiona left the bunkhouse, hurt and unsure, and Judah felt bad for the words he'd spoken to her. But then he got thinking about Darla for the hundredth time that day, and wondered if all his brave words about breaking up with her to protect her were really based in the fact that he'd never known a father growing up—and maybe he didn't know what being a father actually meant.

Not thirty minutes later, Judah's jaw dropped when Darla wafted into the bunkhouse, wearing a blue dress and looking like something out of his most fervent dreams.

"This is the simplest decision you've ever made," Darla said. "Get up and get in my truck, Lazarus. Where's your overnight bag?"

"I'm not going anywhere," he said, just to test her, and she looked at him with a patient, determined gaze.

"Yes, you are," she said sweetly. "Because if you don't, I'm staying here, and I'm pretty certain a lady isn't welcome among bachelor men in a bunkhouse."

Darla would be. His brothers would welcome her with open arms. They liked Darla a lot, and they would feel that if she wanted to coop up here with the father of her children and the man she'd nearly married less than twenty-four hours ago, that was certainly her priority. Shoot, they'd probably roll out a red carpet and the family crystal.

But he could think of a bunch of places he'd rather Darla be than holed up with his brothers. As a crew, they were a fairly unimpressive group. They played Scrabble, and sometimes bridge. Some of them read books by foreign authors, and sometimes they watched movies in French, not to learn the language of love so much as enjoy it. They were basically nerds, and if there was one thing Judah didn't consider himself, it was a pencil-carrying nerd. "Where are we going, and for how long?" he asked, grumbling to show her he didn't appreciate being taken charge of, though secretly he thought it was sexy.

"Just get in my truck and you'll find out."

He shoved himself off the sofa. "Did Fiona put you up to taking me off her hands? She's worried about me."

"Everyone's worried about you because you've gone weird. But Fiona doesn't know I'm rescuing you from yourself."

He blinked, hesitating as he tossed some random clothes into a duffel. "I don't need rescuing. I don't need nursing, either," he said stubbornly.

"Good, because Jackie can't take care of you and three babies and her husband, and she's the only nurse in the family I know of who'd be willing to take care of you. Can you carry that duffel or should I?"

He glared. "Only one of my arms was shot, thanks." Actually, he'd hang the bag around his neck like a Saint Bernard if he'd been shot in both arms. A man could stand to look only so weak in front of his woman.

"Good. Then come on. There's no time to waste."

"Why?" Judah strode after Darla, getting in front of her to open the driver's door for her. "What's the rush?"

"Would you believe me if I said I can't wait another minute to get my hands on you, Judah Callahan?"

He smirked. "Now that's more like it," he said, and closed the door. Tossing his duffel into the truck bed, he hurried around to get in the truck. "What took you so long?"

"So long to what?" Darla backed down the drive, waving at Sam and Jonas as they loped back to the bunkhouse, looking a little worse for wear. "What have they been doing?"

"I think they rescued Judge Julie from our long-horn." Judah squinted at his brothers, noting torn and dirty pants on both of them. "I'm kind of glad I didn't make that rescue. I wonder if they left Rafe for dead."

Darla turned on the main road. "Why would they?"

"Depends on how dead he was, and if an angel was smiling on him." Judah focused his attention on Darla, not worried about his harebrained brothers. "Anyway, what took you so long to realize you couldn't keep your hands off my rock-hard body? I should make you wait for playing hard to get." He tweaked her hair. "It would serve you right."

Darla laughed. "My, you talk big, cowboy."

Judah leaned his head back and grinned, happy to let Darla drive him to her house. "But I can back up every word, sweetheart."

"This may not be the kind of visit you think it's going to be. As you pointed out, I need protection, and so protection you're going to be," Darla told him. Judah waved at Judge Julie as they went by, and at his brother Rafe, who was lying on the ground, probably looking up the judge's tight dress—if Judah knew his brother, and he was pretty sure he did—and thought life was sweet when you had a hot blonde like Darla who was gaga for your lovemaking. Of course, if she wanted to pretend it wasn't all about the loving, and that she needed a bodyguard to keep her warm, he'd be her muscled protector—just for tonight. He'd rather keep an eye on her than listen to his brothers argue over words on the Scrabble board.

And he wouldn't be lying if he bragged that he could make love with one arm tied behind his back.

Two hours later, Darla parked Judah in a room at the StarShine Hotel in Santa Fe. He'd protested, but he ceased his halfhearted carping when he saw that she'd reserved the honeymoon suite. She detected a fairly enthusiastic gleam in Judah's dark blue eyes, and a certain curiosity at what the little woman might be up to now.

The cowboy was in for a surprise.

"Why are we here?" he asked, in a tone that suggested he already knew, and Darla smiled at him blithely.

"It was the only room big enough for the both of us," she told him, her voice ever so sweet.

He raised a brow. "I mean, why are we in Santa Fe?"

"Oh." She waved a hand. "I knew you were worried about me being at Rancho Diablo in case someone tried to kill you, and I knew you'd be worried about being at my house in case someone tried to kill you, so I thought it'd be best to bring you someplace no one would be able to try to kill you. You know. In case someone tries to kill you." She smiled at him. "And we never planned a honeymoon, so this seems as good a place as any. I always wanted to stay here," she said, slipping off her shoes and coat. She noticed she had Judah's attention, so she pointed to the bed. "Why don't you make yourself comfortable while I take a bath? Be sure to prop that arm up."

"You didn't bring your nurse's uniform by any chance, did you?" he asked, his tone hopeful. Trust her guy to be the one with a nurse fantasy. Darla headed for the bathroom, planning to lock herself in and draw a nice, full tub.

"I'm sorry. I'm off duty. But you don't need anyone to take care of you," she called. "You just relax and let me know if anyone comes to the door."

"Are we expecting someone?" Judah asked.

"No. But just in case someone does come and tries to, you know, shoot you or something. I don't want to be in the tub when it happens."

She thought she heard him mutter, and smiled to herself.

Thirty minutes later, when she came out of the bathroom, Judah was sound asleep, which had been her plan all along. She grabbed her robe and her things and slipped into the room across the hall, locking the door behind her.

Judah awakened twelve hours later, if his watch was right. He thumped on it to make certain it was still working. Apparently it was, because it corresponded to the clock radio next to the bed, which Darla had tossed a towel over for reasons he couldn't decipher.

Had he made love to her? Was that why he'd slept so long? Nope, he hadn't had so much as a kiss or anything pleasant like that. He passed a hand over his stubble, testing his arm. It was sore as hell, but not so sore that he couldn't pleasure Darla to the depths of her being.

So what had gone wrong with his little lady's seduction?

He felt the bed beside him, patting around for a soft, round body. There was time enough before checkout to give Darla a rousing dose of what she'd clearly wanted last night. After all, he was a stud, not a dud.

There was no sexy, warm female next to him, and the bed felt suspiciously undisturbed on her side. He flipped on the bedside lamp, realizing that not only had he not made love to Darla, she hadn't even slept in the room.

He tapped his watch again. No, twelve hours really had elapsed, and she hadn't spent them with him.

Which made him wonder if he'd said something to upset her. "Bath," he said, "and I fell asleep. Possibly I should have offered to bathe with her, but she seemed determined to be alone."

So that wasn't the problem.

"I'm pretty sure I shouldn't have been sleeping alone," he muttered, and went to find Darla. There was a door that looked as if it connected to another room in the suite, so he banged on that, and a moment later she opened it, wearing a stunner of a white nightie. His breath left him.

"Yes?" Darla said, and he frowned.

"Why are you in there?"

"Where else would I be?"

He took in her pretty pink toenails, and sweet lace in a V down her front, almost to her belly. In fact, if she shifted just right, perhaps he could see a little bit more of Darla. The peekaboo effect really had his attention, so he decided to play it soft and smooth. "Shouldn't you be with me? In that nice comfy bed?"

She shook her head. "No, that's a honeymoon suite. I'm not on my honeymoon."

"Oh," he said, "*that's* what this is about. You're annoyed." He had a sneaking suspicion he was caught in a plot, which shouldn't be happening in a honeymoon suite.

Other things should be happening, like lovemaking.

"Any chance I can convince you to let me order you breakfast in bed?"

She smiled. "I'd like that. Ask them to bring it to the B suite."

He glanced over his shoulder. "Am I in the A side?"

"Yes," she said, her tone like cotton candy. "A is for ass."

He blinked. "Oh. This isn't a weekend for seduction. This is about showing me what I'm missing out on."

"I always knew you were smart, cowboy." Darla smiled at him, and his gut tightened. "We could be on a honeymoon, but we're not, because of a tiny bit of lead. We could be making love, but we're not, because you broke up with me, because of a fractional piece of lead. And so," she said, "I'm sleeping without a husband, which I hate, because I really had my sights set on a certain cowboy. And so my children will be born without their father's last name, all because of a teeny weeny, miniscule—"

"That's it," Judah said. "If you went to the trouble of getting a honeymoon suite, you probably also went to the trouble of making certain there was a justice of the peace around who would marry us after you drove me insane with that bridal nightie."

Darla smiled. "Maybe."

"Did you bring a dress and all the rigmarole a bride needs? I'd hate for you to marry me without feeling like a real bride." Ten years from now, would she look back on their marriage as a quickie, low-budget affair? He tried to buck himself up to hero status in her eyes. "If you're determined to do this, we could fly to Hawaii."

She handed him a menu. "Order breakfast. You'll need it to fortify yourself for giving up your bachelor-hood. Fiona packed your tux. You'll find it hanging in the cabinet. I can't wait for Hawaii, Judah, because you might get shot. Although I can get you a bulletproof vest for under your tux, if you're worried."

She closed the door.

"I'd like to think she's worried about me being shot," Judah muttered, "but I think she's trying to tell me something."

He went to order breakfast and then locate the tux the little woman had thoughtfully commandeered on his behalf. Who was he to tell a lady wearing a white lacy nightie that he wouldn't run through a hail of bullets for just one night in her bed?

Chapter 16

Fiona peeped in after Darla closed the connecting door between suite A and suite B. Jackie followed, as did Aberdeen, and Darla's mother, Mavis, with Corinne and Nadine waiting behind them. All her friends were here, and for Darla, sandbagging Judah like this couldn't have been more perfect.

"Is he gone?" Fiona asked.

"With his marching orders," Darla said. "Come in."

"We'll get you into this beautiful gown post haste," Jackie said, "though I'm not afraid Judah's going to change his mind."

Darla wasn't afraid of that, either. Not anymore. If she'd learned anything, it was that her man was stubborn and opinionated, and if Fiona said he really wanted to be caught, because he was too worried about the danger to Darla to go willingly, then maybe she was on to something.

"Judah did say once that he'd never be caught dead at an altar," Darla said as Jackie eased her into the magic wedding dress, and Fiona said, "Well, he nearly was dead at the altar, so he was almost right, for once. We're just not going to tempt Fate a second time."

"If it wasn't for the children," Darla said, "getting married wouldn't matter to me so much." But the instant she said the words, she knew it wasn't true. The magic wedding gown sparkled on her, drew in light, making her catch her breath. "I love him," she murmured. "I always have."

"I know," Jackie said. "That's why this time we're not taking any chances. It's all about the gown."

It was true. The moment she'd waited for was here, and right. Deep inside herself, she knew Judah wasn't afraid of marrying her, he was afraid of hurting her. "Thank you all so much for helping me," Darla said. "I treasure your friendship more than you can ever know." She hugged her mother, and then, hearing Judah pound on the door adjoining their rooms, said, "You hide in here until we've left."

The ladies concealed themselves in the large bathroom and the huge walk-in closet, and Darla opened the door. Judah, just as handsome as he'd been last night in his tux, stared at her. "New gown?"

"The one from last time had a few bloodstains on it," Darla said. "I thought I'd wear something else for good luck."

"The luck is all mine. Wow." His eyes glittered as he took her in. "We could see how fast I can get you out of that gown now, and then go to the J.P."

"No, thank you," Darla said quickly, more than aware of the listening ears concealed in her room. "I'm not sure what time the office closes."

Judah nodded. "That's probably a wise plan, but you know, you could change my mind. I'm easy."

"I know." Darla was blushing all over, and if she ever got the nerve to tell Judah where the wedding guests had been hiding, he would probably blush, too.

Or maybe he'd just be proud of himself.

"Then I guess we're going to run this route," Judah said, "if you're sure you want to marry me."

"I'm not one hundred percent certain," Darla said coyly, "particularly as you once told me that marriage was for whipped men, and you wouldn't be caught dead doing it."

"Got you into bed that night, didn't I, though?" Judah kissed her hand as Darla blushed again. "I knew you were the kind of girl who just couldn't resist a challenge."

"Come on," she said, knowing that later on she was going to get a lot of teasing from her lady friends—and heaven only knew what her mother thought about everything she was hearing. Fiona was probably shocked, too.

Judah smiled at her. "You're the most beautiful bride I've ever seen."

"Really?" Darla asked. "Have you seen many?"

"My fair share," her sexy rascal of a man said, "but somehow, you're the only woman who's ever made me feel like getting married is magical."

"Let's go before the magic wears off, then," Darla said, and Judah just smiled as he took her hand. He walked past the closet and banged on it, and then the bathroom door and banged on that, too, and said, "Ladies, don't be late to the wedding!" and Darla wondered if he'd just played hard to get to see if she wanted him enough to drag him to the altar.

He was the most infuriating man she'd ever known—and she was head over heels in love with him.

Judah wasn't certain why he knew this moment was the best of his life, but the second that Darla Cameron said "I do" he felt like a new man. A better man. He couldn't have explained the emotions that swept over him as he watched her face while she spoke the words. All he knew was that something he'd waited for all his life had just agreed to be a part of him forever, and it was a very precious thing. He couldn't imagine not having Darla beside him at this moment and every other, and when he slipped the ring on her finger and she gazed up at him with wide, beautiful eyes, he just knew the moment was magic.

And he wanted it to last forever.

Weeks after the wedding, gifts were still arriving at Darla's house, which now contained one cowboy husband and a bunch of well-wishers. Of course, everyone in Diablo wanted to know why she and Judah had married out of town. Darla simply told everyone that they'd decided to take a leaf from Aberdeen and Creed's wedding manual. Folks were satisfied with that, except that they were dying to see a wedding at Rancho Diablo.

Her house had become a shrine to weddings and babies. Darla had never seen so many presents. "These children will lack for nothing," she told Judah, and he grinned as he unwrapped a pair of tiny pink snakeskin cowboy boots.

Then the smile slipped from his face. "Wait. Why are these pink, Darla?"

She glanced over at the boots. "I don't know, but they're darling."

"I know that." He studied them, mystified. "But they should be blue. Blue is for boys. My sons will not be wearing pink boots, even if they're in a cradle where I can cover them with a blanket."

Darla laughed. "Babies don't wear cowboy boots in a cradle. They're for later on. Toddler age."

"We'll have to take these back."

Darla put down the crystal bowl she'd just unwrapped and went to look at the card. "The boots are from your brothers. Every single one of them signed the card. And there are two pairs of boots." She giggled. "I never realized the Callahans are so into gag gifts."

"I'm tired of gag gifts," Judah grumbled.

Darla looked at him. "What do you mean?" she said, wondering if he was referring to the gag gift that had brought them together in the first place.

Judah dropped the boots back into the box. "Uh-uh," he said, "you're not going to catch me that easily. I love gag gifts. I love my brothers' insane sense of humor." He kissed her cheek, her neck, finding his way to the buttons of her dress, which he casually popped open. "Don't worry that I meant the original, granddaddy of them all gag gift, because I didn't."

"You'd better not." She pulled away from his interested perusal of her cleavage. "Keep unboxing. We have a lot of thank-you letters to write."

"This house isn't going to be big enough for all of us and all this stuff," Judah pointed out.

Darla smiled. "Jackie and Aberdeen warned me this conversation would come up."

"Why?" He shook his head. "By the way, I'm not writing the thank-you letter for these pink boots. You can do that one."

Darla ignored his anxiety over the baby-girl boots. "Because somehow Jackie and Aberdeen said they found themselves eventually moving out to Rancho Diablo. I intend to hold firm, however."

"But it's such a great place to live." Judah held up a fluffy white baby blanket embroidered with a pink giraffe. "Why are we receiving pink things, Darla? Am I the last one in town to know something?"

She giggled. "It would be both of us. Unless my doctor has dropped a hint…"

They stared at each other.

"He wouldn't have," Darla said.

Judah shook his head. "No. Doc Graybill wouldn't."

"Unless Fiona wormed it out of him," Darla said.

Judah started to deny the possibility, then closed his mouth.

Darla sighed. "Let me know if anybody gives us something blue. But you see, there are reasons not to live at Rancho Diablo while we're still getting to know each other, Judah."

He gave her a look of innocence. "Did I ever hint that I wanted to move to the ranch?"

"You just claimed my house is too small."

"It is," Judah said, "but I like being as close to you as possible, Mrs. Callahan. In fact, I'd like to be a lot closer. Let's downsize and get a smaller house and a much smaller bed." He grabbed her around the waist, lifting her so that she had to put down the gift she'd been unwrapping, after which he carried her to the bedroom.

Darla laughed, enjoying her husband's antics, thinking that there was nothing more wonderful than making love with Judah on a summer afternoon in August. But then pain sliced across her belly, and she doubled up. Worried, Darla waited for the pain to go away.

"What happened? Are you all right?" Judah asked, leaning over her as she took deep breaths through her nose, trying to stay calm.

Another cramp racked her. "Probably just a little baby kick or two. Maybe we're having dancers. I don't think it's something I ate."

"We had oatmeal," he said. "Plain organic oatmeal with a tiny bit of brown sugar, nothing exciting, so that means, Darla, my love, that you get a trip in my chariot to see the doctor. We'll let him tell us if you've got garden variety gas cramps. Or just a lot of baby fun going on in there."

"I think you're right," Darla said, letting Judah lead her past the presents to the door, feeling her whole world shake around her.

"I'm no coward," Judah told his brothers, who'd gathered around him to wait at the hospital, where Darla had been instantly sent by her concerned doctor, "but I'm shaking like a leaf right now. And if somebody doesn't come out of that room soon and tell me something about my wife, I'm going Rambo."

"Easy," Jonas said. "Darla needs you in a Zen state, not all whacked out. Everything's going to be fine."

"You're a cardiac guy, what the hell do you know about that end of the female body, anyway?" Judah snapped, appreciating his brother trying to ease his fears, but unable to do anything but bite down on any hand that reached out to comfort him. Like a feral wolf. That's how he felt: feral, primitive, caged. This is when he ran. Always separating himself from fear, anxiety, doubt.

This time he couldn't. He had to sit here and wait. Darla wasn't far enough along to be having the babies. He knew that, though Jonas hadn't proffered any professional opinion. Judah had seen his brother hanging around the nurses' station, ferreting information out of them. Medical terminology was way over Judah's head at the moment. He wanted a simple "your wife is fine, your babies are fine."

He wanted to be with Darla, but Darla had said she wanted him to stay in the waiting room. Had insisted.

The anxiety was killing him. He wondered why she hadn't wanted him with her. Shouldn't a wife want her husband? If he didn't hear something soon, he was going to make everybody mad by barging into his wife's room, and damn the consequences. Of all people, Darla knew best that he wasn't a patient worrier. He wasn't patient about anything.

At least he had his brothers with him to wait this agony out. "So, you guys are butts for giving Darla and me pink cowboy boots."

"You're having two babies," Sam pointed out. "We thought it was a priceless idea. Rafe came up with that one. I was rooting for pink baby dolls, but then Rafe suggested pink ropers and we immediately ordered them."

Judah grunted. "Why not blue?"

His brothers smirked at him.

"Why would you be the one to have the boys in this family?" Creed asked.

"A precedent has been set, if you haven't noticed," Pete said, "and we figure gambler's odds on pink being the order of the day."

"We'll see about that." He'd be happy to have babies of either sex—babies born healthy and yelling the ears off the nurses, though not tonight. They weren't quite ready to come out of the maternal oven. "What could be taking so long? Darla was just having a bit of a stomach ache."

The brothers turned their gazes to Jonas, who shrugged.

He was saved from answering by the doctor coming out. "Mr. Callahan?" he said, and all the brothers said, "Yes?"

"Sorry," Rafe said, "we're strung tighter than guitars. This is Dad." He pointed to Judah, who stood, with nervous pangs attacking him.

"I'm Darla's husband," he said. "These are my brothers."

"Why don't you step back here so we can talk, Mr. Callahan?" the doctor suggested. "I'm Dr. Feske."

"Can I see my wife?" Judah asked.

"You can, but let's talk first." They settled in a small room, and from the unsmiling expression on Dr. Feske's face, Judah knew the news wasn't good.

"Is Darla all right?"

"Your wife is fine. Your daughters were born pre-maturely—"

Judah tried to bat back the small specks of blackness dancing in front of his eyes. "Prematurely? They've hardly had time to grow."

"The success rate with preemies is quite good, though they'll be in the hospital for some time."

"Is something wrong?" Judah pressed his palms to-gether, trying to keep his hands from shaking.

"We're running tests to make certain everything is as it should be, in the range for the amount of time they spent—"

"Doctor," Judah interrupted, "is Darla all right?"

He nodded. "Mr. Callahan, the prognosis is good for your entire family. Yes, the babies are young, but they seem well-developed and within the norm for what—"

"I'm sorry," Judah said. "But I can only take in about half of what you're saying, and I really need to see my wife." He wasn't certain he'd ever felt this desperate in his life. Fear gnawed at him, driving him crazy.

"I understand, Mr. Callahan. Would you like to see your wife, or visit the neonatal—"

"Darla," Judah said. "I need to see my wife."

The doctor led him to Darla's room. She was pale, and had a sheet pulled up to her neck.

"Hey, beautiful," Judah said. "How do you feel?"

"Like I've been through a washer." She looked at him as he tucked a strand of her hair behind her ear. "Have you seen the babies? What do you think?"

"I came to see you first." Judah kissed her forehead, then her lips.

"Well, apparently your daughters were anxious to

see you," Darla told him. "They get their impatience from the Callahan side of the tree."

He tried to smile for her sake. "Everything's going to be fine."

"I know," Darla said. "They're Callahans. They're tough."

Judah nodded, his throat tight. He hoped so. God, how he hoped so.

Chapter 17

When Judah saw his daughters ten minutes later, he honestly thought his heart stopped. He felt for his chest, wondering if he'd imagined a skipped beat. His daughters weren't tough at all. They were tiny, half the size of footballs maybe, with more tubes than a baby should endure taped to teeny appendages.

He wanted to cry. Pete's daughters had gone longer in the womb than these, and at their birth, Judah had been totally unnerved by those tiny little babies. He was overcome now by the urge to hold his daughters, but he knew he couldn't.

He had to stay strong for Darla.

"You're as beautiful as your mother," he told his twin girls through the glass. "You don't know this now, but she's a nurse. She can help you grow big and strong."

Then his shoulders began to shake, and he started

to cry, wondering what he could have done differently to help his tiny babies grow. The doctor didn't have to lie to him. Judah could tell that these babies might not make it, and if they did, they might not be strong, barrel-racing, boot-scooting cowgirls. "You've got me on your team," he told them, "and I'm a big, tough guy. Daddy won't let anything happen to you. Nothing at all."

But he thought they needed guardian angels, too.

"Don't worry," a voice said next to him.

Judah turned, startled to see Fiona's Native American friend standing at his side.

"Do not worry," he said, his black eyes sure and calm as he met Judah's gaze. "These are blessings, and they are meant to be here. They are meant to make you strong."

Judah blinked. "You mean, I must make them strong."

"No." He went back to perusing the tiny bassinets.

After a moment, he surprised Judah by taking out an iPhone and snapping a picture. "I will say prayers," he told Judah, and then ambled down the hall.

Judah stared after the man, who disappeared around the corner before he had a chance to say anything else, stunned as he was by the sudden visit. Then he glanced back at his daughters, his gaze searching, but strangely enough, he felt calmer now.

"I'm going to go take care of your mother," Judah told his daughters. "But I'll be back. Every day you'll see my face at this window. For now you just rest, and when you're ready, I'll be here to hold you. Daddy will always be around to hold you, until finally it's your turn to take care of me."

Judah loped off to find his wife. It was just beginning to hit him that he was a father now, for real. Those tiny bundles were his, and he felt as if he'd just been handed the world's biggest trophy and the shiniest buckle ever made.

"He's changed," Fiona told Burke a week later. "I don't know what's come over Judah, but he's seems in permanent 'ohm' mode. Have you noticed the calmer, more relaxed Judah? When he's not at the hospital, that is."

"Guess he likes being a father." Burke put away the last of the dishes and smiled at her. "He just didn't know how much he would, maybe."

"He's different." Fiona considered her nephew with some pleasure. "Nothing rattles him anymore. He never even mentions being shot. I've got the ballistics report from the sheriff, but Judah never talks about what happened that night, so I'm sure not going to bring it up."

Burke shrugged. "The shooting wasn't important to Judah, as long as Darla was fine. I think he believes it was an accident, and if it wasn't, Sheriff Cartwright'll let him know. All Judah cares about is that he married Darla with no static from next door, and he has his daughters. That's all that matters to him." Burke looked over Fiona's shoulder at the paper she held. "So what does it say?"

"That the gun was a .38. It's not registered to Bode or anybody else in this town. Likely it was black market." Fiona frowned, her thoughts moving from the pleasant aspect of her two new great-nieces to the rumblings on the ranch. "Which scares me, because it means we don't know what we're dealing with. It's a new element. I was hoping it was Bode," she said, "because we could have easily handled him."

Burke frowned. "Does the sheriff have any theories?"

"They found no footprints, and no new vehicles coming through town that they noticed that night or since. No one's been in town asking questions, and nobody has contacted the sheriff's office with any tips. And everyone knows about the shooting, because most of Diablo was there. So if somebody strange was hanging around, Sheriff Cartwright would get a call in a hurry."

"Why would someone we don't know want to take a potshot at Judah?" Burke asked.

Fiona and he looked at each other for a long time.

Then they turned back to cleaning the kitchen, both to their own tasks, without saying another word.

Since Darla had required a C-section, her mother and all her friends wanted to come over and take care of her. Judah found he didn't have as much time alone with his wife as he wished, thanks to the steady stream of callers. He'd asked Darla if she'd like for him to start screening her visitors a bit, trim her social time, so she could rest—and so he could spend some time with her.

Darla had said she enjoyed the company and knew he needed to be working, so he might as well go do what he had to do and let everybody else look in on her if they wanted to. He'd tried to act as if he had a whole lot he could be doing, but the truth was, his brothers were covering for him, and shooed him away from the chores if he ever came to help.

It was getting depressing. There was nothing for

him to do at the hospital except stare through the glass at his daughters, and because he was there so much, it seemed to him that they never grew. He didn't detect any changes at all, which gave him the nearest thing to a panic attack he could ever recall having.

In fact, staring at his babies and not being able to do anything to help them was worse than a bad ride. He'd rather be thrown any day of the week than be helpless, as he was now.

And Darla didn't want him hanging around. That much was clear. She said she had "lady" moments he couldn't help with, which he'd decided was code for *I'm trying to figure out pumping breast milk, so I need Jackie and Aberdeen more than you right now.*

Although he would have been more than happy to help with that. He was pretty sure Darla's breasts were a lot bigger right now, and he wouldn't have minded re-acquainting himself with them, which he supposed was a chauvinistic thought, except that he missed his wife and wanted to feel he had some connection with her.

He felt like a roommate. He wasn't even sleeping with her, having banished himself to a guest room so she could rest, and so he wouldn't accidentally turn over in the night, forget and reach for her, and crush her stitches or something. He didn't know if she had stitches. He wasn't certain how a C-section was performed, exactly. He did feel that his wife was in a fragile state right now, and the best thing he could do was not roll over on her in his sleep.

But she hadn't invited him into her room, either.

Forced away from chores on the ranch and outnumbered by females in his house, Judah slunk off to the bunkhouse to try to center himself. He flung himself onto the leather sofa and closed his eyes in complete appreciation of the quietude.

Which lasted all of five minutes before the door blew open on a strong gust of wind. Judah didn't open his eyes until he realized the door hadn't closed.

He sighed upon seeing his visitor. "It would be you, Tunstall. An ill wind blows no good."

"Your brothers said I'd find you here," Sidney said. "Mind if I talk to you?"

Judah sat up and motioned to the sofa. "Sit."

He waited for Sidney to unload. Hopefully, this was about anything other than Darla. Right now, Judah wasn't in the mood to discuss his wife, or his life, or much of anything. He didn't even want company.

"Congratulations on the twins," Sidney said.

"No doubt you wish Darla was married to you. Probably, you figure that as a doctor, you could care for them better than I can," Judah said sourly.

"Problems?" Sidney asked.

"Do I look like I'm having problems?"

"You always look like you're having problems, Judah." Sidney smiled. "Your daughters are going to be fine."

Judah crooked a brow. "Do you think so? Or are you just blowing smoke up my ass for your own nefarious purposes?"

"Now, Callahan," Sidney said. "Darla told me you were having a few little worries about your girls. I just came to reassure you."

Judah grimaced. "Because you're a pediatrician or a wizard, and know so much."

Sidney shook his head. "Look. I know all this animosity isn't because of Darla. I know you're worried.

Darla loves you. She just wants you to lighten up so she can quit worrying about *you*."

"Did she send you to tell me this or are you applying for a job as a marriage counselor?" Judah couldn't have said why he was so ornery. Pretty much anything Tunstall said was going to rile him. His brothers could give testimony to the fact that just about everything annoyed Judah lately. "Okay," he finally said. "I'll admit I'm a little worked up. But that doesn't mean I want you here ladling out advice and words of comfort I don't need."

Sidney nodded. "All right."

"So you can go." Judah waved a hand toward the door.

"I haven't finished."

Judah raised a brow. "Then would you get on with it? I don't have all day to listen to your clichés."

Sidney laughed. "You really have it bad, don't you?"

"Have what bad?" He frowned.

"Never mind," the doctor said. "Listen, what I wanted to ask you is…" He lowered his voice, even though there was no one else in the bunkhouse. "Well, I've been talking to Diane lately. And I was wondering—"

Judah held up a hand. "No. You can't marry her to fulfill the terms of that inheritance that's hanging over your head. Diane isn't Darla. Darla was being… well, she was trying to be helpful because she's like that, and you caught her at a difficult time in her life, and… I don't want to talk about it."

"I wasn't talking about Darla. You were," Sidney said. "All I want to know is if you think Diane is ready to date. I didn't say I wanted to marry her. Jeez."

Judah lowered his eyelids, considering him through

slitted eyes. "You're kind of a snake in the grass, aren't you?"

"I resent that!"

Sidney really did sound riled. Judah grunted, realizing he'd drawn blood, when he hadn't drawn any with all the other barbs he'd flung at the doc. "All right. Why Diane?"

"I like her," Sidney said with a sudden flush of his angled cheekbones. "I like her little girls."

"Those are Creed and Aberdeen's little girls, too," Judah said. "And Diane is… I don't know about Diane. Why the hell are you asking me?"

Sidney shrugged. "I'd like to do this right." He stood. "Anyway, sorry to take up your time. Good luck with the twins and—"

"Hang on a minute," Judah said, motioning for him to sit back down. "Don't go off all offended."

"I'm not offended," Sidney said. "You're always a little rude, but I understand why."

"I am not rude," Judah stated. "I pride myself on being a gentleman."

"Whatever," Sidney said. "As long as Darla sees that side of you, I don't care how you are."

Judah took a long, hard look at his one-time rival. "Diane had a difficult road to hoe. If you ask her out, you take good care of her. Which I know you will," he said generously. "You're an okay guy, and I'd probably feel all right about you if you hadn't tried to marry my girl."

"Darla wasn't your girl," Sidney said, "and as I recall, at that time you had your head so far up your ass you couldn't see daylight. Darla didn't want to be unmarried and pregnant. This is a very small town, and everyone knows her and her mother, and that's why she was willing to help me out. But it had nothing to do with love or sex or anything but a bargain between friends. You were not her friend, you were a butthead, and she wasn't going to sit around and wait for you."

Judah listened to Sidney's soliloquy, then shook his head. "I've been in love with that woman for years."

Sidney's eyebrows shot up. "Are you serious?"

Judah nodded. "Yep."

"Does... Darla know this?"

"I don't think so," Judah said, trying to remember if he'd ever gotten around to telling her that she'd held his heart for so long he'd sometimes thought he might not ever get it back. "Things have been moving pretty fast."

"Yeah, well." Sidney walked to the door. "If I had a prescription to offer you, it would be to sit down and talk to your wife instead of hiding out over here. You don't want to be in the bunkhouse, you want to be with Darla."

Judah nodded. It was true, and the fact that he didn't want to stomp Sidney's head in for implying he wasn't handling his love life very well was a great sign. "Hey, good luck with Diane."

Sidney smiled. "Thanks." He disappeared out the door.

Judah got to his feet, took a deep breath and turned off the lamps.

It was time to go home. It was past time for some honesty between him and the lovely Mrs. Judah Callahan.

If he could shoo all the well-meaning friends and family out of the henhouse.

Chapter 18

When Judah entered the house, Darla was surrounded by about sixteen ladies giving her a baby shower. He walked in tall, dark and handsome—and Darla could tell at once that something was wrong with her man.

He looked darker than usual.

"Hi, Judah," Darla said.

"Have some punch, Judah," Fiona added, handing him a crystal cup filled with pink liquid.

"And a cucumber sandwich." Mavis passed him a plate with tiny, triangle-shaped, crustless sandwiches. Judah looked perturbed, as if he didn't know what to do with such insubstantial food.

"And a petit four," Corinne Abernathy said. "The frosting is so sweet it'll give you a cavity on contact. But it's so good!" She put two on a tiny dish she stacked on the other plate he was holding.

Nadine Waters handed him a pink napkin. "We decided to decorate the nursery. Which meant a shopping spree! And of course, a small party."

Darla smiled at Judah. He looked overwhelmed, ready to flee. And she didn't want him to go anywhere. She wanted him to stay and relax for a change. He never relaxed around her; he never relaxed *here*. She was pretty certain he had complete fish-out-of-water syndrome in her house.

"Let me show you what the ladies did for our nursery, Judah." She got up, and Judah practically dropped all his plates, plus the crystal cup, rushing to press her back down on the sofa.

"Don't get up. You're supposed to be resting," he said. "In fact, I'm not sure all this excitement is good for you."

"I'm fine," Darla said with some exasperation. "I'm not made of china."

"I can find the nursery myself," he said, tipping his hat at the ladies as he escaped down the hall. He'd left his food untouched on the table, and Darla suspected he was happy to be away from all the females.

"Excuse me," she said to her friends. "I have to go tend to my husband. I hate to cut this short—it's been lovely—but I need to settle him down or he'll never feel like this is home."

Fiona grinned. "We completely understand. We'll clean up in here, and you go calm a cowboy."

"Thank you." She looked around at her friends. "I can never thank you enough for everything you've done. And the nursery is a dream come true."

Corinne touched her hand. "We'll be quiet as mice, so don't mind us at all."

Darla went down the hall. Judah wasn't in the nursery; the door hadn't been opened. She found him in the guest room, sitting on the bed he'd commandeered for his own. "Hey, husband," she said.

"Hi." He glanced up morosely. "You should be resting. Not having company all the time."

She sat down next to him. "Judah, I can take care of myself."

"I'd like to take care of you."

She gingerly put her face against his. "You need to work. The ladies are happy to keep me from losing my mind while my babies can't be here."

"I can be here." Judah allowed her to stroke his cheek, then caught her fingertips and pressed them to his lips, kissing them. "I want to be here."

"And I want your life to go on as it was, unchanged, until our daughters come home. I want you to stop worrying. There's nothing you can do here, Judah. I'm learning about my body, and healing, and figuring out why some parts of me work differently than they used to. Some of it's a little strange. I'm a bit embarrassed by it all."

"Why?" He lay down, pulling her alongside him and cradling her head on his shoulder. "I want to get to know my wife."

"All right. No more company. You can do everything for me from now on. You can help me pump breast milk—"

"You're not scaring me."

Darla smiled. "And you can watch me while I nap, which is a lot of excitement—"

"I can do that."

"And you can help write our thank-you letters for all the wedding and baby shower gifts."

He leaned down to kiss her. "We don't have to go all crazy."

Laughing, she pushed him away so she could recline on his shoulder again. "You don't want to be stuck here all the time. You'd be bored out of your skull. You're a man of action, not a couch cowboy."

"True," he said, "but if I can talk you into being naked, and just the two of us watching soaps together, I could learn to like being king of the couch."

"Ugh." She closed her eyes. "I'm not going to be the queen of the couch. I can't wait to get back in my jeans so I can ride my horse."

"Let's move out to the ranch," Judah said. "There's a bunkhouse that we're not using for anything right now. We could call it home. Then I wouldn't be away from my job. You'd be there and I'd be there, and we'd have more room, and the babies would have all the family and friends around they could stand."

"I thought the ranch might be sold."

"Maybe," Judah said, "but I've got faith in Sam. He's got a lot of aces in his boot. But even if it was, we'd still be together."

"Just homeless," Darla said, loving the fact that she and Judah were lying together, dreaming about the future, comfortable with one another. This was how she wanted it to be. She wanted them to slowly grow together and bond.

"Do you doubt me, wife?" Judah cuddled her, kissing her neck—but not touching her.

"I won't break if you hold me, Judah."

"You can't lure me that easily. The doctor said rest,

and rest you shall do." He nipped her neck lightly, then moved back to her lips. "Quit avoiding the subject."

Darla gave a small moan, wishing she were healed and that she could make love to her husband. "What subject was that?" she asked, distracted with lust from all Judah's kisses. *I could fly, he makes me feel so light, so gauzy.*

So in love.

"Do you doubt my ability to provide for you?"

"No," she said. "When were we talking about that? I never asked you to provide for me."

He sighed. "Typical new-age female."

She kissed his forehead, troubled but not sure why. "Typical old-fashioned male."

"Darn right," he said, and then Darla drifted off to sleep, vaguely aware that she'd missed something important, but not sure what.

When Darla awakened, Judah had slipped away. The sun was shining brightly outside, and birds were singing, and—

"Heck," she said, and hopped from the bed. She remembered what they'd been talking about. He wanted to move to the ranch. She'd been giddy with lust.

"Yes, Virginia, females lust. At least I do, for Judah," she muttered, and jumped in the shower. She bathed carefully around the stitches, glad that Judah wouldn't ever see her like this—she wasn't about to let him—and then put on a comfy, oversize pair of shorts and a T-shirt that she would normally only wear for cleaning.

She went into the nursery, doubtful that Judah had even glanced in here to see the ladies' handiwork. He wasn't coping well with the fact that his daughters had come early. None of it was real yet—or he was scared. Men like Judah avoided what bothered them.

But it was a beautiful nursery now, all pink iced confections gracing smooth white furniture. She couldn't wait to bring her daughters home. Their new room was like a music box, and—

Judah hadn't looked at this room because it wasn't real. In fact, this wasn't his home. He wasn't comfortable here, and he never would be.

She was going to have to fix the situation, if they were ever going to truly be two halves of a whole.

Fiona wrinkled her nose and hung up the phone. "Judah Callahan, what have you done to that wife of yours?"

He blinked, caught in the act of lifting a piece of pound cake from the covered glass pedestal as he headed out to the barn. "Let me think about it." Squinting, he took a bite of fragrant cake, sighing with happiness. "Haven't done anything to my wife. Doctor's orders."

"That's not what I meant," Fiona said. "Corinne just called and said Darla is listing her house with her."

"Listing her house?"

"As in preparing to sell it." His aunt put her hands on her hips. "When we left that house last night, you two were supposed to be cozy as bugs in a rug."

"We were." Judah raised his cake to her. "This is delicious."

"Then why is she selling her house?"

"Beats me." He shrugged. "I've never understood the mysteries of the female mind. And that includes yours, Aunt." He kissed her cheek. "Though I do love you."

She brushed him back. "If she moves farther away from me, I'll be annoyed with you. You go over there right now and be a gentleman. Tell her you don't want her to move."

"I can't," Judah said. "She has a mind of her own."

"Did you tell her you wanted her to move?" Fiona shot him a suspicious glance.

"Yes, but…" He stopped, put down the cake. "But she wouldn't do that for me." Would she? "I asked Darla to move to the ranch, and she'd said she didn't want to in case we lost the place, and then I asked her if she doubted my ability to provide. And that was that," he said. "Honest. Moving barely came up."

Fiona glared. "You can't guilt your wife into moving when she doesn't even have her babies home from the hospital, Judah. She hasn't recovered from giving birth!"

He felt like a heel. "I admit it probably wasn't the right time to bring up the topic."

"And now she's listed her house." Fiona shook her head. "You need to tell Darla that she doesn't have to sell it."

"Why?" Judah asked. "Isn't it a good thing that she's willing to make me happy?"

Fiona closed her eyes for a second. When she opened them again, she just shrugged. "Nephew, you'll have to figure this one out on your own."

Which didn't sound good, if Fiona wasn't in the mood to dish out wise counsel. It sounded as if she was adopting a new, mind-my-own-business strategy, and Judah knew that could only mean one thing.

He had stepped in it big time.

"Hey," Jonas said as he walked by.

"Hey." Judah fell in beside his brother. "If you might possibly be in the doghouse with your lady, but you're not sure, and yet you don't want to be in the doghouse if you're not actually there—"

"Jeez," Jonas said, "I haven't had my coffee yet. Could you speak in some other format besides riddle?"

"I'm not sure if Darla is making a big decision because of me," Judah said, following his brother into the barn. "I don't want her doing something she'll regret. So I'm wondering how to approach this. Is it a flowers situation? Or a turquoise bracelet situation?"

"Boy, you're dumb," Jonas said. "The fact that you're even asking shows that you have no idea of the workings of the female mind. What did you do to Darla?"

"I didn't do anything to her!" Judah was up-to-here with everyone assuming that he'd done something to his wife. "All I said was that we should move out to the ranch. Next thing I know, she's put a call in to list her house. I hear all this from Fiona. Darla didn't tell me."

Jonas slumped on a hay bale. "The problem is that you're slow."

Judah hesitated. "Slow?"

"Slow to figure things out." He waved a hand majestically. "Obviously Darla thinks you're an ape and is moving as far away from you as possible."

Judah's heart nearly stopped. "I did not do anything to upset my wife!"

"Did you ask her?"

He shook his head. "No."

"If you did, she'd probably tell you that she liked her little house, but since you used faulty condoms and got her pregnant, now she's going to have to sell her house and live out of a cardboard box with you."

"Cardboard box?" Judah blinked. "Rancho Diablo is no cardboard box."

"Yeah, well, that's if it doesn't become Rancho Bode." Jonas shrugged. "I guess she's taking a leap of faith that you'll provide."

That's what he'd asked her: if she doubted his ability to provide for her. Judah felt a little guilty about that.

"So, I'm guessing turquoise bracelet, huh?" Judah asked, and Jonas sighed.

"I'd go ahead and make it sapphires," his brother said. "And make good friends with the jeweler. I have a feeling your marriage is going to require a frequent-shopper discount."

Judah snorted. "Why am I asking you? You've never even had a girlfriend," he said, and stomped off.

Jonas was wrong.

But just in case, maybe it wouldn't hurt to make a quick stop on the way to Darla's.

When Judah got to Darla's house, the place was empty. No note, no nothing. A shiver ran across his scalp. He didn't even have her cell phone number.

Jackie did. He could ask her, but then everyone would know that he and Darla hadn't gotten to the point of even exchanging information, and he'd look pretty much a dope, which was how he felt at the moment.

He didn't know if she was at the bridal shop or the hospital. "She's not supposed to be out of the house," he muttered. "Doctor's orders."

Fear jumped into him, and he hurried to his truck. What if she'd had a problem? What if something had gone wrong and he hadn't been here to help her? After he'd sent her friends and family away, and made a big deal of how he could take care of her, he hadn't even bothered to ask for her cell number.

He tore down the driveway and nearly collided with Jackie's truck as she was pulling in. Darla was in the front seat. He was relieved, but still plenty unhappy.

He hopped out of the truck and strode to Darla's window. "Where have you been?"

"What?" she said, while Jackie stared at him, almost gawking. "What do you mean, where have I been?"

Judah tried to cool his jets so his blood pressure wouldn't pop out of his head like a fountain. "You scared me. I didn't know where you were."

Darla blinked big blue eyes at him. "I had my two-week doctor's appointment, Judah. Goodness."

"Oh." Sheepishly, he stepped away from the window, and the mirth in Jackie's eyes. "Sorry about that. Hi, Jackie. Thanks for driving Darla."

"Hi, Judah," Jackie said. "Mind moving your truck so I can get by?"

"I'm going." Okay, he was going to be the laughingstock of the town. He'd just made a superior ass of himself. He backed up, parked, then followed the ladies to the house. They didn't pay a whole lot of attention to him as they went inside. Darla slowly seated herself on the sofa, and Jackie got her a glass of ice water.

"I'm going now," Jackie said to Judah. "Think you can handle it from here?"

"Yes," he said, his tone gruff, his gaze drinking in his tired wife. "Thanks, Jackie."

"No problem. She has another appointment in a couple of weeks, so put that on your calendar so you don't give yourself a coronary." His sister-in-law smiled at him and waved goodbye to Darla as she popped out the door.

"Sorry," Judah said. "I've lost my mind."

Darla sighed. "I didn't think to tell you because it wasn't important."

"Yeah." He took a seat beside his wife. "I won't always be like this. I don't think so, anyway."

"You won't," Darla said, "or I'll put you back in the pond, toad."

"Speaking of ponds," Judah said, "Fiona told me you might be looking for a new one."

She closed her eyes, leaning her head back. "It's as good a time as any, I suppose."

"I thought we talked about the fact that you're not supposed to be doing anything, not even so much as moving one of those tiny, pink-painted piggies of yours," he said with a frown.

"Judah, I only made a phone call. I didn't lift weights or pull a truck." Darla sighed. "Are you always going to be difficult and overbearing? Because I'm not sure I saw this side of you when I let you sweep me off my feet."

"Who swept who?" He brought her hand to his lips and kissed it, then took the plunge. "Are you thinking about moving out to the ranch?" He ran a lock of her silver-blond hair between his fingers, mesmerized by the silkiness of it, as he waited for her to give him the answer he wanted so badly.

"I've always wanted to live in a renovated bunkhouse," Darla said.

"Have you really?" Judah asked, and she said, "No. But I'm willing to give it a shot."

He grinned, the happiest man on earth. "Thank you," he said. "If you're sure."

She rolled her head to look at him. "I'm not completely sure."

"Oh." He didn't know what to make of that. He just knew he'd feel better if she was at the ranch, where more eyes could be on her, and on his daughters.

"But I've always been practical." She gazed at him. "Something tells me my downside risk is minimal."

"Can I have your cell number now that I've talked you into moving into a run-down bunkhouse with me?" he said, and Darla smiled.

"Exchanging cell numbers seems like a very serious step."

He kissed her nose. "Commitment is fun. You'll see."

The next morning, Judah was feeling slightly better about things. He and Darla had spent a pleasant evening together, even sleeping in the same room. It was a milestone for him. He was becoming less afraid of hurting her, and the future seemed pretty rosy. One small step at a time, baby steps, he told himself, whistling as he went to the barn. *And soon my babies will be coming home, too.*

"Hey, did you hear the big news?" Sam asked from the barn office. Jonas and Rafe were sitting in there with him. They all wore half-moon grins.

Judah paused. "I never hear any news. What's the news flash?"

They all laughed, practically waiting to pounce on him *en masse.*

"That you got your wife's cell phone number!" Sam

said, guffawing like a pirate. "You're really slick now, bro."

Rafe nodded. "Jackie told us all about it. She said you were in a panic when she brought Darla home from her appointment yesterday. That you were breathing like a woman in labor."

"I was not." Judah slung his hat onto the desk. "I just… I mean, what the hell was I supposed to think?"

"We're just ribbing you. The news is that Sidney and Diane eloped," Jonas said.

"What?" Judah's jaw went slack.

"Yep," Sam said. "Just think, if Sidney had married Darla, he'd probably have had her cell number by now. But that's okay. We're not embarrassed by you or anything. Every family's got its runt in the love department."

"No one has to tell me that the small details have been known to get by me." Judah looked at his brothers. "Is this good news about Sidney and Diane?"

They all shrugged.

"It's not bad news," Sam said. "It's just news."

"I guess." Judah sank onto a chair. "But it's so fast."

"Maybe for you," Rafe said. "But not every man is frightened of women."

"I am not—oh, hell. Why do I bother?" He was a little afraid of Darla, he supposed. He definitely had her on a high pedestal, keeping her out of reach. "I don't feel like I'm standing in knee-deep mud. It feels like I'm running pretty fast."

"But you're not getting anywhere." Sam nodded. "We understand. We're trying to help you."

"I don't need any help." Judah got up. "We get plenty of help. More than we need."

"But Sidney bagged his female and is off on a beach in Hawaii, while you're making your wife move into a little-used bunkhouse," Rafe said. "We think your romance quotient is low. We've been theorizing about where you went wrong."

"I haven't," Judah said, heading off to the stalls, wondering if he had gone wrong, when he wanted everything to be so right.

Chapter 19

"So the ballistics showed that the bullet was from a .38," Fiona told Judah as she swept out the bunkhouse. "Sheriff Cartwright doesn't think it was a random hunter's bullet."

"I could have figured that." Judah watched his little aunt getting the bunkhouse ready for his brood to take over. "What can I do to help?"

"Stay out of my way," Fiona said cheerfully. "I think I'm going to have to take down these red-and-white gingham curtains. They're too bunkhousey for a new family. I know Darla will want to decorate your home, but she doesn't have any time right now, and this can all be changed later. So I think we'll do plain white lace curtains Darla can replace."

Judah helped his aunt move some furniture. "You work too hard. Let me have that broom."

"You just take care of your arm. Don't think I haven't noticed that you bark at Darla but haven't exactly been taking care of yourself."

He shrugged. "It was a scratch."

Fiona sighed. "Judah, remember when you found the cave?"

"Yeah." He pushed the furniture back and waited for Fiona's broom to land in a new spot so he could try to help her. "If you tell me what needs cleaning, I can do this, Aunt Fiona."

"You're not paying attention." She wrapped a rag on the end of the broom and gestured to the overhead fans for him to dust. "You didn't mention the cave to anyone, did you?"

"No. Not even my daughters, whom I spend every waking moment with when I'm not with my wife." He grinned. "They're making good progress. And the doc says in a month or so they'll be over five pounds and can come home."

His aunt smiled. "Maybe home will be here, if Darla doesn't change her mind."

"Why would she?" He frowned but didn't look at Fiona as he dutifully moved the broom around the wagon wheel chandeliers and fans.

"I don't know." She watched him with an eagle eye to make certain no dust was missed. "Anyway, if we can keep to one subject, Burke and I have been talking it over, and we think there's possibly a connection between you getting shot and the cave."

Just talking about it was making his arm hurt. Or maybe reaching for dust and cobwebs was doing that. Judah ignored the pain and kept dusting, wanting everything perfect for Darla. He was so happy she was willing to live here that he could hardly stand it. And then, in time, he'd build her the house of her dreams.

Their family would begin here, at Rancho Diablo.

"Did you hear me?" Fiona asked, and Judah snapped his thoughts away from Darla.

"Yes, dear aunt. You said the cave is the reason I got shot. But that makes no sense, because Bode doesn't know about the cave, and he wouldn't shoot me at my own wedding, anyway." He handed the broom back to his aunt. "Clean enough even for a nurse."

Fiona looked at him. "Bode didn't do it."

She had his full attention now. "How do you know?"

"A feeling I have."

Judah snorted. "You don't act on feelings. You've always been too practical for anything but data and hard evidence. Even when we were kids, you didn't believe anything you heard about us until you saw proof that we'd painted a neighbor's goat for the Fourth of July, or that we'd been smoking in the fields outside of town."

Fiona's lips went flat. "If I'd believed every rumor I'd heard about you kids, you would have been doing chores for the rest of your lives."

Judah shrugged. "So it makes no sense that you'd be dealing in hunches now."

"Except that it's not really a hunch. There are things I can't tell you—"

"Why?" Judah demanded. "We're all full-grown men, Aunt Fiona, not little boys. You don't have to bear the burden of protecting us any longer."

"I know." She nodded. "I'll tell you eventually, as soon as I know the time is right. And I know that time is coming very soon. I knew it the night you got shot."

"I just don't understand what it has to do with the

cave. I know someone would love to help himself to the silver. But why pick me?" He looked at her for a moment. "Because I found it and whoever it was didn't want me to?"

She didn't say anything. Judah's blood began to run cold. "You're not trying to tell me that Darla and the girls might be in danger, are you?"

"I don't know," Fiona said. "I didn't expect anyone to try to harm you. Frankly, I'm scared to death."

He sank onto the old sofa in front of a fireplace that hadn't been used in years. "What does Burke say?"

"That you should be careful," Fiona said simply. "We don't know what we're up against now."

"But it has nothing to do with Bode trying to run us off."

She shook her head. "We think Bode is the type of man who tries to buy everything he wants, or cheat people of it, but he wouldn't kill anybody. I know I cracked him with my bag that night, but once I cooled down, I realized how unlike him it would be to use foul means. He's too much about the thrill of destruction. He likes being able to take people down legally, and sometimes a little bit under the law. I'm not saying he'd bring us a loaf of bread if we were starving. He'd enjoy watching a family be run off. But he wouldn't physically harm any of us. He wouldn't want Julie to see him in a bad light."

"So you're telling me I'm bringing my wife and kids here, and we have a murderer running around?" Anger assailed Judah as he thought of what he would do if anybody ever tried to harm Darla and the babies.

For the first time, he knew he was capable of harming another human. And it scared him. But he knew he would protect his family at all costs. It made him keenly aware of how Fiona must have felt all these years about the family for which she'd been responsible.

"We were at Darla's for your wedding that night," she said softly, reminding him. "We weren't here."

His throat went dry; blood pounded in his ears. "You're right. I've always thought of Rancho Diablo as the unsafe place because of Bode." But Fiona was correct. Whoever shot him—if it had been on purpose—had followed him to his own wedding, a time when he would have had his guard down completely. It felt like a warning.

"Darla's alone at the house," Judah said, and ran for his truck.

Darla let out a screech when the back door crashed open. As Judah burst into the living room, she wanted to bash him with the baby name book she was holding. "What in the world, Judah?"

He slowed down, his eyes crazy, his dark hair blown and wild around his head. He was, unfortunately, handsome as all get-out, but she wanted to slap him silly. Maybe she would as soon as her heart slowed down.

"What are you doing?" he demanded.

"What does it look like I'm doing? I'm trying to pick baby names. For heaven's sake, Judah, you frightened me!" She glared at him. "I thought we talked about this. You were going to calm down." She worked herself up into some righteous anger. "You just can't keep acting like a madman. You've been crazy ever since you found out I was pregnant, and it's only gotten worse." She bit her lip, then said, "Or maybe I never really knew you."

"Of course we didn't know each other," Judah replied. "I could never get you to even talk to me."

"Well, I'm talking now, and I swear, if you don't calm down…" She looked at him. "Why did you come in here like you were running from the devil, anyway? What is your problem?"

He put his good arm around her, holding her. She could feel his heart beating hard in his chest, ricocheting in panic. "What is wrong with you, Judah?"

"I don't know," he said. "Actually, I do know, but some things are better left unsaid."

She pushed him away and went to stare at him from the sofa. "I don't know that I can live with a crazy man. You literally frightened me out of my wits. I didn't know who was coming in the house." She frowned at him. "Why did you use the back door, anyway?"

"I overshot the driveway," he said, a little embarrassed. "So I came in the rear. I was in a hurry." He gathered her to him once more, ignoring his wounded arm. "I worry about you, I guess. And did you know that Sidney and Diane eloped?"

She pushed him away a final time and said sternly, "The driveway is not a speedway. You nearly hit Jackie's truck the other day." Darla gave him a long look, thinking it was a shame that her handsome husband had such race car driver tendencies. "Look. Is there anything I can do to make you feel less insane?"

"I don't think so," Judah said. "I think it's the new me."

She sighed, trying to be patient, which wasn't easy. "You can't be jealous if Sidney and Diane have eloped, so what's bugging you now?"

He shrugged. "I wouldn't say I'm done being jealous of ol' Sid. Sometimes I wonder what women see in that bony bronc buster. But as far as what's bugging me, it's not Tunstall. I haven't figured everything out yet, to be honest. It's a work in progress."

"So maybe you're always going to be a fat-headed ass?" Darla was in no mood to let him off the hook. "You're going to have to get a grip."

He would, but not today. He'd been a dad for only four days—and as far as he was concerned, he had over a month to change. He could do it. "Keep the faith, wife."

On the first of August, Judah could honestly say that "Coming Home Day" was the best day of his life. "Miss Jennifer Belle Callahan," he said proudly, laying daughter number one gently in her bassinet, "and Miss Molly Mavis Callahan." He placed his second daughter near her sister in a matching bassinet.

Instantly, both babies began to cry. "They don't like their names," Judah said, feeling helpless.

"They want to be together." Darla sat up in bed and motioned for him to hand her his daughters. Gingerly, as if he was handling small, fragile pieces of china, he passed the girls one by one to their mother. Darla made sure their blankets were wrapped properly, then put the girls side by side next to her on the bed. Instantly, they stopped fussing, and Judah's nerves stopped jumping.

"I don't like it when I don't know what they want."

"You'll learn. We'll learn. Right now, I'm sure the girls just want to feel like they did in the womb."

He nodded. "Looks good to me. Any room for Dad?"

"Come on." Darla motioned to the other side of the twins.

"I don't know," Judah said, hanging back. "I read that it was bad for Dad to sleep in the bed with babies."

"It might be, but you're not going to sleep," Darla said. "I haven't seen you sleep for weeks. Do you ever?"

He thought about it. "Now that you mention it, I don't think so."

Darla smiled. "Just don't roll over on them, and everybody will be happy."

He stared down, wanting very much to get in but not sure it was safe. The bed seemed so big, for one thing. And it was full of females. While this was normally a good thing, these females were all in a very delicate state. "I think I'll wait until everyone is a little more, uh, ready for company," he said, backing away. "I'll sit over here in the rocker and watch you ladies enjoy having the bed to yourselves. It won't last forever, so take advantage of it while you can."

Darla shook her head at him. "You're afraid of your daughters."

"Sometimes I'm afraid of you. I'm not ashamed to admit that." Judah waved his hand and then reached for a pink baby blanket to roll up behind his head. "The guy who can't admit the truth isn't much of a man."

"That's nice. Did you make that up?" Darla asked. "I've never known the philosophizing side of you."

He yawned. "I think so. Then again, I might have plagiarized it from somebody smarter than me."

And then he fell asleep.

Darla looked at her knocked-out husband and smiled tenderly down at her babies. "He's going to be better now, I think, girls. Bringing you home was the best thing that could happen to him." It was true. The moment he'd held his daughters and brought them home, she'd sensed a change in him. He wasn't frantic or rattled up anymore.

Judah seemed content.

Darla kissed each of her daughters on the head, falling in love with all the new people in her life, and the magic she could feel binding them together as a family.

When Judah opened his eyes, he found Darla and the babies gone. Pushing himself out of the rocker, he went to find his family. They were quietly nursing on the sofa in the den, and he was amazed that he'd apparently slept through baby calls for breakfast. "Sorry. I guess I was tired. What can I do to help?"

"Hold a baby," Darla said with a smile, and he thought he'd never seen her look more beautiful. He found himself literally gawking at his wife.

"I want to marry you," he said, and Darla laughed.

"We are married."

"I know. But I'm afraid you'll get away from me. Maybe I'll marry you once a month just to make sure you're holding tight to our commitment." He sank onto the sofa and trailed a finger over his daughter's face as she nuzzled her mom. "Remember when you used to talk about our marriage as something you wanted to do until the girls were born?"

Darla nodded. "Is that what's making you all nervous and weird?"

"No, this is my natural state now," he said, and she nodded.

"Probably." She handed him the daughter who'd gone to sleep on her breast.

"So," he said, taking the baby tenderly, "if you don't mind, I'd like to make this a solid, no-holds-barred commitment. I have a feeling you're going to like being married to me."

Darla laughed. "Well, confidence isn't your short suit."

"So, I'll go rustle up some breakfast. What are you in the mood for, little mama?" The least he could do was grab some grub, since she was doing all the work—and as lovely as that work was, she didn't seem to need him all that much.

"Fruit," Darla said. "I'd kiss you for fresh fruit."

"Really? Does a truckload rate more than a kiss?"

Darla smiled at him, and Judah tried to ignore the fact that she hadn't said a whole lot about staying married to him longer than the time it took to give his daughters his name.

Which was now.

"Oh, that reminds me," he said, "speaking of gifts and whatnot—"

"We weren't," she said. "We were just talking about breakfast."

"Well, I know, but a guy has to work in opportunity when it presents itself." He handed her the jeweler's box he'd picked up in town. "It's not a banana or an apple, but it's something."

She indicated the baby on her breast she was supporting with one arm. "Would you mind opening it for me? My hands are full at the moment."

Okay, so maybe his timing wasn't all that great. Judah told himself it didn't matter—timing wasn't everything.

Or maybe it was. He snapped open the lid, and Darla gasped.

"Judah!"

He laughed when she freed a hand to grab the box so she could look at the sapphire bracelet more closely.

"It's gorgeous," she said. "But what's it for?"

He chuckled and took the box back. "To thank you for my babies? To work my way out of the doghouse I land myself in occasionally? I don't know. Maybe it's because I love you."

She looked at him, cornflower-blue eyes assessing him. "Do you?"

"I might," he said, putting the sapphire-and-diamond bracelet on her wrist. "Maybe. When you're ready."

She looked at the bracelet, then smiled. "Thank you. It's the most beautiful thing I've ever owned."

"I don't know about that." Judah stroked his daughter's tiny head. "Our babies look like their mom. So they are the most beautiful things I own."

Darla's eyes sparkled, and then she broke eye contact. "Thank you," she murmured.

"You're welcome. So," he said cheerfully, feeling better about his place in the world already. "Bananas? Apples? Peaches?"

"All," she said, looking back at him, "and when does the moving truck arrive?"

Chapter 20

"About that moving truck," Judah said. "I think it's too soon, don't you?"

Darla touched the lovely bracelet he had given her, and wondered why he was so worried about every little thing. She was fine; their daughters were fine. He'd asked her about making a real commitment, and that commitment was best made in a home they started out in together. Maybe Rancho Diablo was just so much a part of him that he couldn't relax until he was there.

"If you're worried about me, Judah, don't be. I've waited a long time for us to be a family. You don't have to stress out all the time."

"I do," Judah said. "It's a new husband, new dad thing."

"All right," Darla said. "But the sooner you're not feeling like a fish out of water, the sooner you'll de-stress."

"I don't know. I'm accepting stress as my due in life

at the moment. But," he said, clearly trying to take all the blame for his unease, "I would feel better at the ranch, although not for the reason you assume. I'm not unhappy here with you, Darla. If things were different, this house would be fine for a month or two. At least until our daughters start needing some elbow room."

Darla gazed down at their diminutive babies. "I think that'll be a while, don't you?"

"Nah. They're going to be tall like their mother and father."

"That's probably true, but I don't think it'll happen overnight."

"The way they're chowing, I wouldn't underestimate them," Judah said enviously, eyeing his breast-feeding daughter.

Darla smiled. "So what's the reason?"

"What reason?" He appeared momentarily disoriented from staring at her breasts, and Darla shook her head.

"The real reason you want to move to the ranch, if it isn't for a bigger house to raise your family in."

"Oh," Judah said, bringing his gaze back to her eyes. "I don't know."

She frowned. "Yes, you do. You're a pretty practical guy. You know why you do things. So quit hiding it."

"Uh, I have to get breakfast for my love right now," he said, edging toward the door. "Don't you worry about a thing while I'm gone, and when I get back, I'll watch babies so you can shower."

He escaped out the door, and a second later she heard his truck roar off down the driveway, no slower than he'd driven in. He was always in a hurry. Darla looked down at the bracelet on her arm, mesmerized by the twinkling diamonds and deep blue sapphires, and wondered why Judah wouldn't just tell her what he was thinking.

"Maybe he's one of those men who keep everything inside," she murmured to her daughters. "The strong, silent type. Which will be hard to deal with since I'm not a mind reader."

She knew he'd wanted her out at the ranch yesterday—but he'd just said it wasn't because of building their life together in a bigger house. Darla closed her eyes after a moment, deciding to relax and not think about her mysterious man. Judah was Judah—and he moved to a drummer that only he seemed to be able to hear.

"Well, look at you, making the doughnut run," Bode Jenkins said as Judah loaded the groceries he'd grabbed onto the checkout counter. Bode glanced over his purchases. "Hungry wife?"

Judah grunted. "Bode, mind your own business."

"Hey, that's no way to talk to a neighbor."

Judah ignored the comment, paid his bill with cash and departed. Bode followed, trying to keep up with Judah's long strides.

"I mean to give you a wedding gift," the older man stated, and Judah said, "Don't bother."

"Callahan," Bode said, his voice changing to a more insistent tone, "you really ought to be nicer to me."

"Why?" Judah asked. "Nice really isn't my deal, but most especially not to you. And I don't have time to chat this morning, Bode. If you have a complaint with me, lodge it with someone who cares." He got in his truck, tossing the groceries on the seat next to him.

Bode stood at the window. "Listen, I think I know who shot you."

Judah hesitated in the act of turning on the engine, surprised that Bode had brought up the shooting, and wondering if he should even bother to listen to anything the old man had to say. "If you think you know, why don't you tell the sheriff?"

"Wouldn't you rather I tell you?"

Judah scrubbed at his morning growth of beard, wishing he had a magic club he could beat Bode over the head with and make him disappear. "Jenkins, if you knew anything at all you'd be shouting it from the rooftops, not trying to keep me from my family when you can see I'm on a mission." He started the truck. "To be honest, I don't care who shot me. You can't scare us off our land, Jenkins. Callahans don't scare."

"It involves your aunt, and some other things I think you'd be interested in."

"All right," Judah said, "spit it out so I can get home to my hungry wife and kids."

"Ask your aunt," Bode advised, and Judah said, "What?"

"Ask your aunt who likely shot you."

"Jump, Jenkins," Judah said, "'cause this truck door'll swing open in two seconds and knock you flat to the ground."

Bode jumped away from the vehicle and Judah drove off, swearing under his breath. He cursed colorfully, using words he rarely said, and told himself it was against the law to back up over an old man, even if Bode deserved it. Judah pressed the pedal down, peeling out of the parking lot, eager to get home. Never had he been more anxious to see his wife and children.

* * *

Darla heard Judah's truck roar up the drive, and was mentally ready when the front door blew open with a great sucking sound. "Shh," she said, "the babies are asleep, Attila."

"Attila?" Judah handed her the bag of fruit. "Who's he?"

"He was a man who was always on a conquering mission. You've just about conquered my driveway and my door frames. I'm going to need to have everything Judah-proofed."

"Sorry," he said, and she sighed.

"You were going to start acting like a human being?"

He shrugged. "Maybe it takes a while."

"Hmm." Darla went to the kitchen and got out plates. "Thank you for the fruit. It's beautiful."

"Babies are beautiful." Judah threw himself onto the sofa, looking rattled even for him, Darla thought. "Fruit is just appetizing. Or not."

She shook her head and cut the fruit into two bowls. "Are you all right?"

"Yeah." He got up, went to her fridge. "Any beer in here?"

Darla's eyes widened. "At eight o'clock in the morning?"

"Maybe just a fruit chaser." He found a Dos and opened it gratefully.

"That's older than you want, like from a picnic last summer. How about some coffee instead?"

"I'm jacked enough already." He opened the beer and took a swig, made a face and sucked down another swig before pouring the rest down the drain. "That was just what the doctor ordered."

Darla shook her head and handed him a bowl of fruit. "Are you all right?"

"Never been better," Judah said, but Darla had the strangest feeling he wasn't being honest.

And it wasn't the first time she'd felt this way.

She heard a tiny cry from one of the babies, and set her bowl down.

"I got it," Judah said. "Eat."

She hung back in the kitchen as he'd told her to. It would be all right. Judah would call her if he needed help. No sound came from the other room. She chewed her fruit halfheartedly, listening, and when she still heard nothing, she peeked around the corner.

Judah had both babies on his chest as he lounged on the sofa. He peered down one baby's back, hooked a finger in her diaper and peeked. "Nothing there, Dad," he said, talking for the baby, then hooked a finger in the second diaper. "Nothing here, either, Dad," he said, still being a baby ventriloquist.

Darla smiled and brought him his bowl. "What do you know about changing diapers?"

"Just that it needs to happen often or everybody's unhappy." Judah smoothed a hand over tiny heads. "And I did a lot of babysitting in high school. Fiona was a big believer in us working whatever odd job came our way. Babysitting, wrangling, bush hogging. Didn't matter. She said it was good for us to respect a buck."

Darla didn't know where to put herself. She wanted to sit next to Judah, but something held her back. "If you're good with the girls, would you mind if I grab a shower?"

"Go. The babies and I are going to watch an educational flick." He turned on her television, flipped channels with the remote and chose the movie download. "For our first foray into intelligentsia," he told his daughters, "we're going to examine the societal differences between *Little Women* and *Gone with the Wind.* I'll expect spirited discussion during intermissions."

Darla laughed. "Oh, you'll get spirited discussions, but they'll all be concerning dinner."

"Switch out the lights, please. We must have the proper surroundings to begin the study of our topic of females in society."

"Okay," Darla said. "By the way, your aunt will be here in thirty minutes."

"Why?"

"You'll see," Darla said with a smile, and left the room.

"When you become literary bra burners," Judah told his daughters, "please remind yourselves that men don't like surprises." He said it loudly enough for Darla to hear in the next room, and she rewarded him by saying, "Men like spice, girls. Never forget the spice."

And then Darla put tape on the final packed box in her room, sealing it and marking it "Darla and Judah's bedroom."

We'll see how well my husband handles surprises.

Thirty minutes later, Judah had just gotten comfortable watching *Little Women* when the door banged open.

"We're here!" Jonas called out. "Darla, we're here!"

"Hi," Fiona said, poking her head into the living room. "What are you doing here, Judah?"

His brothers and Burke piled in behind Fiona.

"Have you guys ever heard of being quiet so as not to wake sleeping babies?" Judah said with a growl.

"Not those two. They sleep like puppies." Fiona came to kiss each great-niece on her downy head.

"Anyway, what do you mean, what am I doing here?" Judah didn't appreciate the inference that he might not be where his wife and daughters were.

"Well," Sam said, "we thought you'd be off doing something stupid, like trying to solve the universe's problems. We're trying to give you a surprise party."

"Party?" Judah raised a brow. "What kind of surprise party? I don't like surprises."

"And yet it's been one after another for the past several months. Good morning, girls," Rafe said, touching a palm to each of his niece's tufts. "Miss me?"

"No, they don't," Judah said. "We are trying to have a literary discussion."

"Oh, your favorite movie." Jonas laughed, and when Darla came into the living room he told her, "Judah always wanted to be Laurie."

"Didn't happen, though," Sam said. "Judah was never polite enough to be Laurie."

"True. He's been a little on the crabby side lately." Darla smiled, and Fiona said, "Are we ready?"

"Everything is boxed up." Darla took them back to her room, and Judah tried to spy down the hall to see what they were doing. He couldn't move the two tiny bundles on his chest, however, because they were so warm and satisfied right where they were.

"What's happening?" he demanded as Burke went by with a wheeled dolly.

"We're moving your wife and girls to the ranch," Jonas said. "Surprise!"

Chapter 21

Once they had Darla and Molly and Belle moved into the bunkhouse, Judah really did feel peace come over him. There were so many people coming and going all day long at Rancho Diablo that he knew his ladies were safe.

Which meant it was time to talk to Fiona. He caught her heading to the basement, her favorite haunt besides the kitchen. "Whoa, frail aunt, let me carry those for you."

She sniffed and gave him the box of party lights she'd hung in June. "I'm not frail. You're frail."

"In what way?"

"You're making your wife do all the heavy lifting."

He stared at Fiona as they made their way down the stairs. "What lifting?"

"She's making all the sacrifices."

It was true. "Not much I can do about that right now."

"You could take her on a honeymoon. Let me keep the babies."

He hesitated. "Uh, she's breast-feeding."

"True, but trips aren't planned in a week, Nephew. Good ones, at least. There are logistics involved. And I'll probably have to fight Mavis tooth and nail for baby time, so I want to get my request in first."

She sniffed again, and Judah said, "Catching a cold, Aunt?"

"No. I'm merely allergic to bone idleness."

"I suppose you have the name of a travel agency you prefer?" he asked with a sigh.

"I do. But I refuse to pick a destination. You'll have to ask Darla what she wants. I can't do everything for you."

He smiled. "Thanks for thinking of it. I'd forgotten."

"You've had a lot on your mind." She showed him where to shove the box, and pointed to another she wanted.

"I thought you were going to have a monster garage sale and get rid of all this."

"I might, if we ever have to move. But right now, Sam's doing a bang-up job. I'm only fifty percent worried these days. And Jonas has become quite the financial investor, something I was never aware of before. Guess he has to have something to do now that he's not cracking open people's chest cavities."

Judah winced. "Aunt, speaking of cracking things open…"

"Oh, let's don't," she said. "I hate to think of it. Only eggs should be cracked open."

His gaze slid to the dirt patch that was unlike the rest of the basement floor. They'd asked Fiona about it when they were younger, and gotten some water-seeping-in, covered-over-mold story. The boys had told each other ghost stories about the dead body in the basement, but these days, Judah wondered if he could dismiss any tale about his fey aunt.

"What about safes? Safes get cracked open."

"No," she said dismissively, "not unless one is a thief, and we have none of—" Her gaze met his, and then slid to the floor where he'd been looking. "Now, Nephew," Fiona said. "Don't go odd on me just because you're lacking sleep due to your darling daughters. In fact, you should go—"

"Bode says I should ask you about who might have shot me," Judah said quietly, and Fiona stared at him.

"Bode's a fool. Why would he say such a thing?"

"You tell me."

She put her hands on her hips and glared at him. "Whose side are you on, Judah?"

"Callahan side, ma'am," he answered, "but why are there sides?"

She pursed her lips. "I always think of everything that's happened as Jenkins versus Callahan. That's all I meant."

"Do you have a theory as to who shot me?" Judah was determined to know just how much Fiona was hiding.

"I have theories," she said, "and they're about as good as any that are floating around. I've had people ask me if you accidentally let your own gun go off."

"Why would I be carrying at a wedding?"

"See how much sense it makes to listen to gossip?"

She moved to inspect her rows of pickled vegetables, breaking eye contact. "I've heard that it was Bode. That it was a hunter. That it was Sidney." She shrugged. "We're probably never going to know, Judah."

And yet he sensed she was holding back on him.

"And who else might it have been?"

She looked at him for a long time. "Put those boxes on the dining room table, please," she said, and marched up the stairs, leaving him in the basement, knowing that something wasn't adding up.

"Tonight's family council is necessary," Fiona said, "because lately I've noticed a lack of faith among my nephews in the job I've been doing. Not that I blame you, because I alone got us in the mess we're in."

The six brothers and Burke watched Aunt Fiona as she struggled for words six hours after Judah had tried to talk to her about Bode down in the basement. Of course, he'd known that Bode was intent on stirring up trouble. Yet it was his aunt's lack of heat in the denial that had sparked his curiosity. Now she was calling a family council, and his curiosity was even greater. They had these meetings at least once a month to discuss family and ranch business, but this one had been called out of schedule.

Now they sat in the wood-paneled library. Burke passed out square cut-crystal glasses of fine whiskey, and Judah drank his gratefully.

"First, Burke and I want to tell you that we're married," Fiona said, "just so you know that I'm walking the walk and talking the talk when I try to set you boys up for lifetimes of happiness with someone you love. I know you already know, have known for a while, but I'm making it official."

The men applauded, congratulated Burke and Fiona, acted surprised, as if they hadn't figured it out years ago.

"Now I'm here to answer any questions you might have," Fiona said, "and I know that, based on a discussion I had with Judah this morning, that you have some. Anything we can clear up, Burke and I are here for you. Always."

The brothers glanced at one another. This was new, Judah thought. This new transparent Fiona was an unexpected metamorphosis.

And yet she'd specifically told him never to talk about the cave's existence. He wondered how far this transparency would go.

"All right, I'll bite," Judah said. "Where are our parents buried?"

The room went deathly silent. Fiona's gaze leveled on him, seemingly dazed, and then, without any warning, she fainted.

"She scared the living daylights out of me," Judah said as he lay in bed that night with Darla and their two angels. "I really thought I'd killed her."

Darla giggled. "It's not funny, I know, but it kind of is. You know Fiona is tough as cowhide. I don't think you can hurt her, Judah. Don't worry."

He winced. "I do worry. She's not so much cowhide as she once was. I feel terrible about the whole thing." His brothers had piled on, telling him that Fiona's offer had been more rhetorical and polite than anything, and was he trying to give her a stroke?

"Don't worry. Fiona knows you love her." Darla gave a contented sigh. "I love living in this bunkhouse," she said, and Judah's attention was totally caught.

"Are you being serious?"

She nodded. "Much more than I thought I would. It's really ideal for a growing family. There's so much storage space. And Mom and her friends came over today and set up the nursery just the way they had it at my house." She smiled at Judah. "It's perfect."

"I'm glad." His tone was gruffer than he meant it to be, but so much emotion was flooding over him that it practically choked him. "Thanks for being okay with this, Darla. I feel better with us being here."

"Yeah, Sam told me." Darla closed her eyes, enjoying the peace. "He said that ever since you got shot, you've been a bit of a wienie."

Judah sighed. "He's probably right."

"And he said that this is your place. Your piece of the universe." She rolled her head to look at him. "I didn't really have a piece of the universe. I loved my house, but it was just a house."

You're my home, he thought, *my whole life. My real universe.*

"Want to honeymoon?" he asked, and Darla grinned at him.

"Maybe the Bahamas," Darla told Jackie the next day when she came to see the new digs and bring a housewarming gift. "Judah says I can probably find a white skirt and he'll wear a white shirt with palm trees on it, and we'll have vows said under some kind of coconut tree or something." Darla smiled. "He's gone all romantic since we moved into the bunkhouse."

"Rancho Diablo suits these men." Jackie pulled out wedding dress vendor photos for two years out. "I figure we might as well start looking these over."

"And I need to decide what to do with the magic wedding dress," Darla said. "I suppose we should sell it. Sabrina says the magic has to keep moving."

"Do you really believe all that stuff she talks about sometimes?"

"I don't know," Darla said, "but I do know that I'm happier than I've ever been, and if a dress can bring a little luck, I'm all for sharing it. I'm a romantic at heart."

"So am I." Jackie looked at the photos and drawings. "You're still okay with the wedding dress shop, partner?"

"Why wouldn't I be?" Darla was surprised by the question.

"I thought Judah didn't want you to work."

"Well, not while the babies are so tiny." Darla stiffened. "I didn't mind changing houses, but I would never give up my shop for a man. Not Judah or any other guy."

"Just checking."

Darla frowned, not sure where all this was going. "You've got triplets, so why wouldn't I keep working, too?"

Jackie shrugged. "Pete doesn't mind me working."

Darla wondered if Judah cared if she worked. If he did, he was going to get a fat lip. "This dress shop was my brainchild, and I wouldn't give it up for him. I don't think he'd ask, either."

Jackie nodded. "I was pretty certain you'd feel that way."

Tickles of unease ran over Darla. "You're not telling me everything. What happened?"

Jackie sighed. "Judah came to me and offered to buy out my half of the shop."

"What?" Darla couldn't believe what she was hearing. "Why?"

"Well, Pete says Judah was planning on giving it to you as a wedding gift."

Darla thought about that. "But I don't want to own the whole store. I like the way we have things set up." She frowned. "How dare he?"

"I think Judah has your best interests at heart, Darla," Jackie said calmly. Her efforts to soothe her weren't working, however, because Darla was practically quivering with anger.

"Why?" she asked her friend. "Why do you think that?"

Jackie's face wore a how-do-I-get-myself-out-of-this expression. "Pete says if you own the whole store, you can sell it and have more time for the babies."

Darla began to quiver again. "I haven't even thought that far ahead. Why would Judah think he has to be involved in my business?"

"Because he's a man, and because he's a Callahan, and because he honestly thinks he's doing the right thing."

"By thinking for me?" Darla soothed Molly and Belle, who were beginning to get restless from the angry tone of their mother's voice.

"He says he doesn't want you too tired out." Jackie nodded. "And you know, Darla, when we bought the shop, we were single women, and now we're married with children, and your babies are very delicate—"

"Don't give me that. You don't want to sell your half," Darla said. "I know you too well."

"No, but if it's best for you—"

"It's not," Darla said, her tone dark with finality. "Just forget my husband ever brought this up."

"Oh, dear," Jackie said. "I don't want to cause trouble."

"You didn't. Judah did."

And the moment her man got home, he was going to get his chauvinistic tendencies trimmed way back. There was a difference between diamond-and-sapphire bracelets and buying out one's sister-in-law—a difference her handsome husband was about to learn.

"Storm brewing to the east," Rafe told Judah as they put away the last of the horses. "We'll pull the barn doors shut when we go."

"Okay." Judah glanced over his shoulder at the bruised sky. Winds were swirling the clouds, sending them scudding across the dark heavens. "When's Diane coming back?"

"She and Sidney return tonight. They'll take the girls to their new house in Durant, where Sidney lives." Rafe put his saddle away, and Judah did likewise. "I'm going to miss the heck out of the little girls."

"Whoa," Judah said, an arrow of sadness shooting through him. "I guess I should have expected that." The girls had been going back and forth from Jackie to Fiona to Aberdeen while their mother was gone, with Aberdeen keeping them at night. Still, Judah was going to miss the sound of their young voices.

"It's sad, but nothing stays the same. Eventually, all little birds fly away," Rafe said.

"We didn't."

"Our jobs are here," Rafe reminded him. "But you tried to fly. You just got your wings clipped."

"I think of it more as if I got my wings retooled. They're better now." Judah was proud of how he was handling his new settled life. He couldn't wait for the big All's Clear from the doctor—he was going to make love to his wife until he gave out. "Life's great. You should try marriage."

"Not me," Rafe said. "I don't do relationships."

"Neither did I," Judah said, pretty cheerful about the new him.

"So, about the other night," Rafe said. "What made you ask about our parents?"

He shrugged. "I'd like to know. Wouldn't you?"

"I don't know. I'm a year older than you. I understand that there are some things we'll never know. At twenty-nine, you decide it's too late to know some things."

"When you're looking down the barrel at thirty, you mean?" Judah shook his head. "Not me. I'll always want to know what happened. How did they die? Where were they?"

"They died," Rafe said, "of some funky illness."

"I thought it was a car accident." Judah frowned. "You know, it's not that hard to request a death certificate. Sam probably has done so a thousand times for clients."

Rafe turned to look at him. "Do you think Fiona would have told us, if we really wanted to know?"

"You mean we don't want to?"

Rafe shrugged. "Do you?"

"I—yeah."

"Then order the certificate." Rafe walked out of the barn into the storm, leaving Judah to wonder why he was the only one in the family who asked questions.

Finding out more about the cave was going to be first on his to-do list, Judah thought. After exiting the barn, he turned to slide the doors shut behind him, and suddenly felt a splitting pain in his skull, followed by blackness.

Inside the kitchen, Fiona had the entire family scattered about, perching wherever they could find space. "This is our last meal as an extended family," she said over the din, "because tomorrow night our three little ladies go to their new home in Durant. So I cooked their *faborites*—" she stressed the word, imitating the little girls' pronunciation "—SpaghettiO's. Real sauce and real pasta shaped like Os." She kissed them on their heads. "And now, Judah will lead us in the blessing. Since he's the most newly married, he may have the honor. Judah."

No one said anything. Fiona glanced around the room. "Darla, where's your husband?"

Darla shook her head. "I haven't seen him all day. And if someone does, will you tell him I want to talk to him?"

Everyone hooted at that. Fiona shook her head. "Someone please call his cell phone and tell him it's rude to be late to the little girls' going-away party, especially when their aunty has made them a pink-and-white cake with kitties on it."

"I will." Jonas rang his brother's phone, then said, "No answer. He'll be along soon enough."

Rafe said, "I left him in the barn, so maybe he went to do something else."

Rain pelted the windows. Fiona glanced outside, shaking her head. "All right. I guess we'll eat without him." But she wasn't happy about it.

They were all eating, deep into the spaghetti, when the kitchen door opened. Judah stumbled in, blood running down the side of his face.

Darla screamed and ran to her husband. She waved everyone away as he sank to the floor. "What did you do, Judah?" she asked, grabbing a wet paper towel from Jonas, who hovered near his brother, looking over the wound.

"You've got a mighty big goose egg back here, son," Jonas said. "You're going to need a few stitches. Maybe even a staple. Rafe, check the barn, since you were out there last. Sam, go with him. Look for…look for things," he said, with a quick glance at Fiona.

Judah groaned and slumped toward his wife, and Darla knew at once that everything he'd been worried about had been real. There was trouble, and he didn't want her to know, but was carrying the burden himself.

Her heart grew cold with fear.

"Don't move," Darla said two hours later, after Jonas brought Judah home from the hospital with a bandage tightly wrapped around his head. "You stay right in that bed. And no TV until I can ascertain that you aren't going to have latent swelling or something. You just sit there and don't move." She was being unreasonable, but she couldn't help being afraid.

"Yes, Nurse," he said. "But will you at least put on

a crisp white nurse's uniform with a real short skirt if I have to put up with your bossing me?"

"You're trying to joke about what happened, but it's not funny. First you get shot—"

"Just some kids playing with their daddy's gun, for which they owe me three months' hard labor on the ranch. And I intend to work them harder than my brothers and I ever worked, not to mention mucking. We've got sixteen horses, you know."

She ignored his effort to make light of the situation. "But then you took a knock on the head, and teasing about it just isn't funny right now." She burst into tears.

"And I'm not laughing, either, my love." He patted the bed. "Come over here and let me look down your blouse, and I'll feel ever so much better. The medicine I need is a little naked wife."

Tears streamed faster, so she grabbed a tissue. She hated crying, but couldn't quit. "You scared me!"

"Darling, I scared myself." Judah perked up. "Was it a two-by-four? It felt like a house. Tell me it was at least a really big board."

She nodded. "Sam found it out by the barn. What were you doing, getting in the way of a thick, long piece of lumber?"

"I don't know. Silly of me, wasn't it?"

"Yes! Because you said that if we moved out here, we'd be safer, but clearly you're not!" Darla shrank onto the bed and curled up next to her husband so she could indulge in a little crying on his shoulder. "And you tried to buy Jackie out of her half of the wedding shop, so I really wanted to be angry with you, but now I can't because your head's all bandaged up, so I'm really upset!"

He laughed and tugged her closer. "Now there's the bright side."

She sniffled. "It was horrible when you came into the kitchen all Lon Chaneyish. Never do that again." Darla hiccupped, which she hated to do. But once it got started it always took a while to stop, so she sat next to Judah and hiccupped, aware she sounded pitiful.

"Your daughters aren't as needy as you are," he teased, and Darla stated, "I know. They're angels."

"About the wedding dress shop," Judah began, but she said, "I don't want to fight right now."

"We're not going to fight. I was just trying to buy it for you to help Jackie out. Pete says she's overwhelmed with the triplets right now."

"Oh." Darla thought about that for a few seconds. "Pete told Jackie you were a chauvinist pig who didn't want his wife to work. Not in those words, of course. Those are my words."

"I'll put my brother in the corner with his dunce cap on later. You were really going to tell me off, weren't you?" Judah asked, planting kisses against her hair, and Darla smiled through her tears.

"Yes."

"But since I'm not a chauvinist pig, I get to see you naked for a reward?"

Darla kissed him on the forehead. "The jury's still out on the pig part. Although you're starting to look more like a prince all the time." She got up to go check on the babies, who were nestled in their tiny bassinets.

"Hey," Judah called after her, "what does a guy have to do to prove to his wife that he loves her even when she's not properly dedicated to his nursing care?"

Darla popped her head back in the room. "What did you say?"

"I said…" Judah tried to remember what he'd said that had made Darla return so quickly "…uh, what do I have to do besides take a beating with a two-by-four to get some attention from my wife?"

"Go on," Darla said.

Pain was throbbing at the base of his skull. His long hair had been shaved off in back for the stitches, and his pride was pretty bent about that. Still, Judah tried hard to think. "Oh," he said with a grin, "you're trying to get me tell you that I love you."

"No, I'm not." Darla shook her head. "I'm not trying to get you to *do* anything."

"I love you, Darla," he said. "I loved you long before you ever sneaked into my room and made wild love to me."

"You did?"

She sounded genuinely surprised. Judah nodded, feeling better already. "Why else would I have failed the condom test? I say it was all subconscious."

She advanced on him, her gaze lit with mock anger and a lot of laughter. "When were you going to tell me?"

"When I was certain I'd caught you." He held a pillow in front of himself for protection from his wife. "I love you madly, Darla Callahan, but it was darn hard waiting on you to finally leave your slipper in my path."

She got on top of him, straddling him, and he tossed the pillow away. "Mr. Callahan, are there any other surprises you'd care to share with me?"

He shook his head. "I just want you to know that you're not the only one capable of keeping one's cards to their chest." He gazed at the front of her blouse reverently. "Or breasts, even." He caught one finger in the top and tugged. The blouse fell open, and he sighed with pleasure. "Nurse, I have a terrible ache."

Darla smiled. "I can help you," she said, leaning over to kiss his lips, "but you'll have to undress so I can fix that ache."

He kissed her all over, so passionately that Darla knew she was the luckiest woman on earth. Which was really no surprise at all, because she was married to the man she'd always loved, with all her heart.

Epilogue

"Sheriff says you've had some bad luck," Darla told Judah once they'd taken out the stitches a few weeks later. "He says you shouldn't get in the way of flying boards like that. The storm really kicked up some things."

Shingles had been ripped off the roofs of some houses. Fences had blown down. One of their cows had mysteriously moved onto Bode's property. He'd returned it promptly.

"Don't want you calling me a cattle thief," he'd said, and Fiona had humphed at him.

Judah was glad it was just a board that had hit him, and not one of his brothers, his aunt or his wife. "There are worse things to be in the way of, I guess. Are you packed, wife? Itty bitty bikini and everything?"

Darla laughed. "There will be no bikini. Just a one-piece."

"One-pieces are great. Lots of leg." He rubbed his hands together.

"Did you bring your swimsuit?" Darla asked. "I want to see hunk for the whole week."

He puffed out his chest. "I'm your hunk, darling."

Darla laughed. "Shall we go say goodbye to the girls?"

Judah's face fell. "I'm not sure if I can. I'll miss them too much."

It was true. They were up with him at the crack of dawn when he ate breakfast. He'd make bottles for them, since he'd talked Darla into changing to bottles a bit before their trip. The girls had grown by leaps and bounds. They might have started out slow, but the pediatrician said they were catching up quickly on the growth chart. He said it was amazing. Judah thought it was his wife who was amazing.

Even he was flourishing, living with her.

"When we get this lawsuit settled," he told Darla, "I have a surprise for you."

"Tell me now, just in case," she said, and he grinned at her. "Nah. I like making you beg. It's so much fun."

She swiped at him. "I thought you didn't like surprises."

He swept her into his lap while they waited for Rafe to drive them to the airport. "Well, once I realized surprise was your game, I decided to turn the tables on you."

Darla smiled. "So tell me."

"I'm going to build you your own house."

His wife stared at him for a moment. "Here, at the ranch?"

He nodded. "I don't want to get your hopes up, in case we do lose the ranch."

She kissed him. "I love the bunkhouse, but thank you for thinking of such a wonderful gift. I love you, Judah Callahan."

"I know, Mrs. Callahan. I feel it every day."

"And you know something else?" she said, wrapping her arms around him so she could pull him close, to tell him something she'd long been wanting to tell him, for his ears only. "I had a dream about you last night."

He perked up. "You did? Did it involve naked you and whipped cream and maybe even some cherries?"

She kissed him on the lips. "Even better," she said. "I think we're pregnant."

His jaw dropped.

"Surprise," she said.

Judah laughed and pulled her into his arms, the luckiest, happiest man alive.

When they had put their suitcases in the car, and Rafe was driving them away from Rancho Diablo, Judah saw the Diablos running like the wind, faster than the wind, disappearing on the painted horizon.

And he knew he'd found all the wealth and happiness a man could ever hope for, because the only treasure that truly mattered was love.

* * * * *

Amanda Renee was raised in the northeast and now wiggles her toes in the warm coastal Carolina sands. Her career began when she was discovered through Harlequin's So You Think You Can Write contest. When not creating stories about love and laughter, she enjoys the company of her schnoodle, Duffy, as well as camping, playing guitar and piano, photography, and anything involving animals. You can visit her at amandarenee.com.

Books by Amanda Renee

Harlequin Western Romance

Saddle Ridge, Montana

The Lawman's Rebel Bride
A Snowbound Cowboy Christmas
Wrangling Cupid's Cowboy
The Bull Rider's Baby Bombshell

Harlequin American Romance

Welcome to Ramblewood

Betting on Texas
Home to the Cowboy
Blame It on the Rodeo
A Texan for Hire
Back to Texas
Mistletoe Rodeo
The Trouble with Cowgirls
A Bull Rider's Pride
Twins for Christmas

Visit the Author Profile page at
Harlequin.com for more titles.

The Bull Rider's Baby Bombshell

AMANDA RENEE

For Brad,
Thank you for the inspiration.

Chapter 1

Call Jade.
I can't do this.
Please forgive me.

Jade Scott read her sister's note for the tenth time since arriving in Saddle Ridge. Almost an entire day had passed since Liv had vanished, leaving behind her month-and-a-half-old triplets. Jade would've arrived sooner if there had been more flights out of Los Angeles to the middle-of-nowhere Montana. She'd ditched the godforsaken town eleven years ago and had sworn never to return. But her sister's children had annihilated that plan. Especially since Jade had been partially responsible for their existence.

"I didn't call the police like you asked, but now that you're here, I think we should."

"No!" Jade spun to face Maddie Winters, her sister's best friend and the woman who had taken care of the children for the past twenty hours. "As soon as we do, Liv's labeled a bad parent and those girls go in the system."

"Nobody will take them away with you here." Maddie checked to see if there were any new messages on her phone. "I'm really worried about her."

Jade scanned the small living room. A month ago, it looked like a baby—or three—lived there. Today it looked cold and sterile, devoid of any signs of the triplets. The crocheted baby blankets and baskets of pastel yarn were gone from the corner. Once covered with stacks of photo albums her sister couldn't wait to fill, the coffee table now sat bare. Embroidered pillows with their cute mommy and baby sayings no longer littered the couch. Her sister had even removed the framed pictures of the girls along with their plaster hand-and footprints from the mantel. Except for the video baby monitor, nothing baby related remained in sight. Why? She knew Liv's desire for order was strong thanks to their chaotic upbringing, but she'd never thought her sister would wipe away all visible traces of her children.

"I'm worried too. We don't need to involve the police though. She wasn't kidnapped." Liv was a chronic planner and everything about the situation felt deliberate. "She made a conscious decision to walk away. She wrote a note, she called you to babysit and then left on her own accord. If we call the police, the girls go into the system. Hell will freeze over before I let that happen."

Jade knew all about the system. She and Liv had

spent fourteen years in foster care, bounced from place to place until Liv had been old enough to become her guardian. Being two teenage girls on their own had forced them to grow up fast. Too fast.

Jade's phone rang inside her bag jarring her back to the present. It wasn't her sister's ringtone, but she reached for it to be safe. It was her office in Los Angeles. She answered, praying Liv had called there by mistake instead of her cell and they were patching the call over to her. "Yes."

"I'm sorry to bother you," Tomás, her British assistant, began. "I just wanted to let you know the Wittingfords have finally decided on their venue for their summer opener."

Jade's heart sank. Tomás's call was great news, just not the news she wanted to hear at that moment. The Wittingfords were the most extravagant clients her event planning company had seen to date. And their showstopping party guaranteed to outshine all the celebrity weddings she'd produced this year.

"I'm glad to hear it. I just wish I was there to oversee it." Jade tugged her laptop out of her bag and opened it on the dining room table. "Email me the contract and I'll review it. I want you to look it over first. Flag anything you question. I need you to be my extra set of eyes while I'm away. And please call my clients and tell them I've had a family emergency. Give them your contact info and make sure they understand I haven't abandoned them. But they need to phone you with any issues or changes and you can fill me in later."

"I'll get on it, straightaway. Any news about your sister?"

"Nothing yet." Jade lifted her gaze to see Maddie

glaring at her from the living room. "I need to go. We'll talk later."

"I can't believe you're putting work first." Maddie picked up the baby monitor from the coffee table and checked the screen.

"I'm sorry you don't approve of my multitasking." Jade turned on the computer. "I know my sister. She doesn't do crazy. Wherever she is, I'm sure she's safe. While I try to figure out what's going on with her and where she ran off to, I still have a business to maintain."

"And walking out on your newborn triplets isn't crazy?"

Not unless you knew the whole situation. "All right, tell me again. What time did you come over yesterday afternoon?"

"A little after three. Liv sounded frazzled when she called. I asked what was wrong, but she kept doing that answer a question with a question thing that drives me up a wall. I got nothing out of her." Maddie ran both hands through her hair, on the verge of tears. "I tried to talk to her, but she took off the second I walked in. I found the note taped to the nursery room door a few minutes after that."

"When did she remove the baby things from in here?"

"I don't know." Maddie shook her head wildly. "I'm trying to remember the last time I came over."

"What do you mean? You're her best friend and you didn't check on her? When I left, you assured me you would. You only live next door."

"She insisted on space so she could learn how to take care of the girls on her own. I guess it's been a little over a week since I've been here. I'll be honest, her abrupt dismissal hurt. I had been staying in the guest room after you left. I should have noticed something was wrong."

Uneasiness grew deep within Jade's chest. "I keep thinking the same thing. I missed our video chat on Sunday night because I was too busy with work." Many of Jade's ex-boyfriends had accused her of putting her career before anyone else. Had she selfishly done the same with her sister? Jade scanned her inbox, hoping to find an email from Liv. Nothing. "I'll check her office. Are you able to stay for a little while longer?"

"For however long you need."

Jade continued to walk around the old farmhouse. Her sister had set up three bassinets in the room next to her office in addition to an equal number of cribs in the former master bedroom, now the nursery. Liv had been prepared. Some may even say overprepared. She'd read every parenting book and magazine she found. Took infant care classes and had insisted Jade learn infant CPR too. From researching the best laundry detergents and baby shampoos to memorizing the symptoms of childhood illnesses and diseases, she'd planned for every contingency. It didn't make sense why she left. Outside of neither of them not knowing what good parenting was.

Their father had been a drifter and their mother had been behind bars on and off since Jade was two. They'd seen the inside of more foster homes than they could count. Some good, some bad. Whenever they had made it into a decent one, their mother had gotten out of jail, claimed to be ready to raise them again after completing her therapy and halfway house program only to fail miserably weeks later and wind up right back in jail. Her mother had always wanted what she couldn't have. That included Liv and Jade. Once in her care, she'd discovered they were too much work to support. Besides, her drugs were more important. She wanted those more than anything. More than her children.

The court system had reached a point where they said no more, and Jade and Liv had mixed emotions the day they learned they wouldn't have to live with their mother ever again. Liv had handled it better than she had. Jade had been angry. All the time. It hadn't helped that kids had picked on her constantly at school. One kid had been the ringleader. The one she had trusted, and then he betrayed her. And she had never forgotten him. Wes Slade.

Jade opened the bottom filing cabinet drawer and scanned the hanging folder tabs. The last one had *BABY* scrawled on it. The generic word surprised her. At the very least, she'd expected all three girls' names to be written on the label, if not three separate files. She removed the thick folder, laid it on the desk and began looking through it. On top was the first ultrasound picture of the triplets. Jade ran her fingers over the black-and-white image. She could still see her sister holding up the photo to the screen during their video chat. Liv had been shocked, but thrilled just the same. She was finally getting the family she had always wanted. And it had been a long time coming.

Liv had battled fertility issues for years. Married at twenty-three, she and her husband had tried everything to get pregnant. There was just enough wrong with each of them to prevent a successful pregnancy. Kevin had wanted to adopt, but it had been important to Liv to carry her children and have a physical connection to them. He'd refused the donor idea and their constant baby battles wound up destroying their marriage.

Jade sat in Liv's ultralux, oversize perfect-for-pregnancy office chair and glanced around the room. Her sister had always been neat and organized. Not a pen or paperclip out of place. She peered inside Liv's desk drawers hoping to find a clue to her whereabouts. Everything related to her job as a financial planner. Liv still had another two months of maternity leave until she had to return to work full-time. Working from home would help the transition although Liv had considered hiring a nanny during the day so she could talk to clients without interruption.

Her sister had a plan. A definitive plan on how her life would run smoothly as a single mom of three children. Walking away was completely out of character.

Jade continued to flip through the contents of the folder. The only item left was Jade's egg donation contract giving her sister the biological link to the babies she wanted. She just hadn't expected Liv to use all the embryos at once. Because of her sister's long infertility battle, the doctor had believed her best chance for a successful pregnancy was to implant them all in hopes one would survive. The surprise had been universal.

"Dammit, Liv, where are you?"

She stood to put the folder back in the drawer when she noticed another one lying on the bottom of the cabinet. Sliding the other files forward, she removed the thin, unmarked and probably empty folder. She flipped it open to double-check and saw another donor contract. Why? Jade had been the only donor. Liv had used a fertility clinic for the father.

She began to read the document:

This agreement is made this 22 day of July 2017, by and between Olivia Scott, hereafter RECIPI-ENT, and Weston Slade, hereafter DONOR.

"No, no, no!" Jade's heart pounded in her chest. "Liv couldn't have." She continued to read the contract. But she had. Wes Slade was the donor and the father of Jade's biological children. Her sister had fertilized Jade's eggs with the man she despised more than anyone.

A few hours later, Jade stood in front of the check-in clerk at the Silver Bells Ranch lodge. The woman whispered into the phone. "One of Wes's fans is here to see him."

"Excuse me. I am no fan of his."

The clerk cupped the mouthpiece and whispered, "She may be an ex-girlfriend."

"Are you kidding me?" Jade reached over the counter and snatched the phone. "This is Jade Scott. I need to speak to Wes concerning my sister, Liv. It's…um… an emergency of sorts."

Still reeling from her discovery, Jade needed absolute confirmation Wes was the triplets' father. She prayed he had backed out or that Liv had changed her mind at the last second. Anything…just not this.

"Oh hey, Jade. It's Garrett, Wes's brother. It's been what, ten years or more? I saw your sister and the triplets last week. They sure are beautiful. Reminded me of my two when they were born."

You have no idea. Jade swallowed hard. "I'm staying with the kids for a few days while Liv is—is away on business. She's unreachable today and I have a problem at the house. Since she and Wes are friends, I'm thinking he might have some ideas." At least Jade assumed they were friends. Who would ask a casual acquaintance to father their children?

"He's out with our guests on a trail ride. He should be back soon. You're welcome to wait or maybe I can help you."

"Uh, um. No. I appreciate the offer, but I need Wes. I don't mind waiting." Yeah, she did. The longer she waited, the more questions churned in her brain. "Where's the best place I can catch him?"

"The stables." Garrett paused. "Do you have the girls with you? I'm sure my daughter would love to me—"

"They're with the sitter." The last thing Jade needed was to introduce the triplets to their cousin.

The entire time Liv had been pregnant, Jade kept her part in the process tucked neatly away in the dark recesses of her brain. Surprisingly, Liv had carried to almost thirty-seven weeks. The day of her sister's scheduled cesarean, Jade had been by her side in the operating room, cheering her on. But the moment Jade had held those tiny bundles of perfection and stared into their blue eyes, reality hit. She was the biological mother of three little girls and she had wrestled with it during the rest of her stay in town. They were Liv's children. Not hers. It wasn't until she was on a plane flying back to LA three weeks later that she finally breathed easier. Once she had returned to her normal routine, any lingering thoughts of being their mother faded and she gladly slipped into the role of auntie.

Until today.

She needed to find Liv...fast.

* * *

Garrett took the reins as Wes dismounted. "Thanks for helping out."

"No problem." Wes didn't mind filling in for other employees while he was visiting the ranch, considering they had covered for him plenty during his last few months of employment on Silver Bells. It had been an unbearable period in his life and he'd wanted nothing more than to get away from Saddle Ridge. And he had. He'd moved to Texas and escaped the drama he once called home.

"Oh, I almost forgot." Garrett snapped his fingers. "You have a visitor. Do you remember Jade Scott?"

Wes damn near tripped at the mention of her name. Even though he couldn't think of one person he despised more than Jade, it was her sister he didn't want to think about.

"What is she doing here?"

"I guess she's babysitting the triplets while her sister's away on business. She has some emergency at Liv's house. I offered to help, but she insisted on talking to you."

"Keep your distance from the Scotts." Wes swallowed hard. This was exactly why he hadn't wanted to come home for his brother Dylan's wedding and his niece and nephew's christenings. "They can call someone else. I have no business with Liv or Jade."

"What's with the attitude?" Garrett asked. "I thought you and Liv were good friends. Besides, it's too late. Jade's about ten steps behind you."

Wes turned to see her weaving through the ranch guests walking back to the lodge. His stomach somersaulted at the sight of her and he wasn't sure if it was because of their past or how much she had transformed since high school. The mean girl who had once made his life miserable had gone from a rough, chip-on-her-shoulder teen to a California knockout.

Sleek, rich mahogany waves replaced the frizzy curls she used to have. But that body and those curves…good Lord Almighty! Her black polka-dot chiffon blouse revealed just enough of her ample cleavage to make any man look twice, and her tailored black pants hugged her hips in perfection. She exuded an edginess combined with old Hollywood glamour and if she had been any other woman on the planet, he would have moved in for the kill. Their past made her off-limits and his connection to her sister sealed that deal.

"Wes." Deep blue eyes held his gaze before traveling the length of him and back.

Transfixed upon her matte ruby-red lips, it took every ounce of strength he had left to respond. "Jade."

"Hey, kids. A conversation requires more than that." Garrett laughed. "Try hello, how are you." He nudged his brother in Jade's direction before walking away.

"What do you want?" Wes hadn't meant his tone to be as harsh as it sounded.

"It's about Liv. Is there someplace private we can talk?"

Wes stiffened. "I have work to do." He turned to tend to his horse, but it wasn't there. Silently, he cursed his brother.

"I thought you were on vacation from your job in Texas."

He reeled to face her. "Who told you that?"

"The rodeo school where you work." She stepped toward him and wobbled in her ranch-inappropriate four-inch heels. He reached for her arm to steady her and instantly regretted the contact. "I looked you up online. I need your help."

Wes released her and rubbed his palm, wanting to erase all traces of her from his body. "On second thought, I don't care what your reasons are. I'm asking you as politely as possible to leave."

"Wes, please." A half-foot shorter, even in those ridiculous heels, she stared up at him.

"What could you possibly need my help with?"

"Tell me I can trust you first."

"No. You can't trust me, so let's end this now. Goodbye, Jade." The intoxicating scent of her perfume wasn't enough to entice him to hear more.

"I know."

It wasn't so much the words, but the firm way she said them that stopped him in his tracks. "Do you care to expand on that?" He prayed it wasn't what he thought.

"I found the contract today at my sister's house," Jade whispered. "Before I go into details, promise me everything I tell you will stay between us."

Wes wanted to argue and deny his role in Liv's daughters' paternity, but the worry etched into Jade's face gave him pause. "Okay, you have my attention. And yes, you can trust me."

Jade assessed him sharply, making him more uncomfortable than he already was. She had no reason to take him at his word considering their past had thrived on a mutual loathing of one another after their brief high school romance. Her shoulders sagged as she closed her eyes momentarily, shielding him from the pain that reflected in them.

"Liv left the triplets with Maddie yesterday and hasn't returned."

"That doesn't sound like Liv." Wes's heart dropped into his stomach. "Have you called the police? Or checked the hospitals?"

"I called every hospital within a two-hundred-mile radius while I waited for my flight last night. I don't want to involve the police. This isn't a case of her getting in a car accident. She left a note saying she was leaving. Do you have any idea where she might've gone? Has she ever mentioned a place she enjoyed going to when she was under a lot of stress or anywhere she always wanted to visit?"

"Not offhand. I can't believe she left the girls." Wes propped a booted foot up on the fence rail and stared into the corral. "I was afraid this would be too much for her."

"Wait a minute." Jade grabbed him by the arm and forced him to look at her. "You suspected she was in trouble?"

"That's not what I'm saying." Wes checked over his shoulder to make sure they were still alone. "I was long gone before those babies were born. And for the record, this wasn't an easy decision on my part. There was never anything romantic or sexual between your sister and me. We were good friends. She was there for me during the darkest time of my life."

"So how did you get from point A to point B?" Her face soured. "She told me she used an anonymous donor."

"Liv hated the thought of a stranger fathering her children. I had initially said no, then I realized she wanted this more than anything and relented. I felt I owed her for being there for me over the years. But that's where it ended. I couldn't continue our friendship, knowing she was carrying my—" Wes shook his head. "They are not my children. I refuse to say they are."

"I'm not asking you to raise them." Thick sarcasm laced her assurance. "Just tell me what happened."

Wes hesitated before answering, not wanting to sound callous. "Liv and I went our separate ways. She called me once I was in Texas and told me she was having triplets. I'll admit, I had my concerns and asked if she could handle that many babies. She said she was a little overwhelmed by the news, but even more excited. I could hear it in her voice. She also had you and her friends. So, I continued on with my life."

"Turns out she was more overwhelmed than we both thought." Jade's phone rang. She removed it from her bag, checked the screen and then rejected the call. "No matter how long it takes to find her, I'm not abandoning those babies. You can't, either."

"I am not getting involved. I did my part and then got out of town for a reason. Many reasons. They are not my responsibility. She should have gone with an anonymous donor like she had with the eggs."

"She didn't use an anonymous egg donor."

"Then whose were they?"

"Mine. You and I are those girls' biological parents."

Chapter 2

Jade never saw a person pale so fast. "Don't you dare faint on me."

"For God's sake, I've never fainted a day in my life. A bull has knocked me unconscious a time or two in the rodeo ring, but I've never fainted." Wes's hazel eyes narrowed. "You're the biological mother of those children?"

"Believe me, when I saw your name on the donor contract I was none too thrilled. It's like the universe was playing some cruel joke on me."

"On you?" Wes snapped. "You're the last person I would have chosen." His abhorrence for her darkened his features. Features she probably would've found attractive under normal circumstances.

"At least I provided a biological link. You, on the other hand—"

"Go on. Finish what you were going to say." The muscles along his jawline pulsated.

"No, because regardless of our feelings toward each other, we created three beautiful lives. I will not insult them by insulting you."

Wes tilted his hat back, revealing an errant lock of dark blond hair. He folded his arms across his chest, causing his formfitting gray T-shirt sleeve to ride up and expose the hint of a colorful tattoo on his biceps. Biceps that were much larger than she remembered from high school.

"As much as I want to argue with you, that's a very mature attitude and one I should adopt myself." Wes stepped away from the fence, giving her his full attention. "When I agreed to do this, I did so under one condition. Total anonymity."

"I have no intention of saying anything." Jade had wanted the same condition, but she and Liv had discussed the possibility of one day telling the children. Especially if a medical reason arose. That was most likely why she wanted the father to be somebody she knew. Just in case. "The truth may come out, regardless."

"It can't." Wes's eyes widened. "I had second thoughts shortly after I did it. First of all, I never wanted kids of my own. And second, my family would never forgive me for not being involved in their lives. Even though that's what Liv wanted."

"Yeah, I'm not so sure about that." Jade wondered if her sister's feelings for Wes ran deeper than she'd admitted. "Had you already planned to move away when she asked you to be the donor?"

"No. I mean, we discussed how unhappy I was living in Saddle Ridge for reasons I won't get into right now. My bull riding schedule keeps me on the road a lot too, so she knew I wouldn't be around much."

"How did she react when you told her you were moving to Texas?"

Wes winced and rubbed the back of his neck. "I told her over the phone after I had already left. It was all of a two-minute conversation. One I purposely kept short because I couldn't handle being involved in her pregnancy or the baby's life. Then she called and told me she was having triplets."

"You had to have been as shocked as I was." The thought of Liv carrying and raising one of Jade's children had been surreal enough. And even though she'd been fully aware they'd harvested three of her eggs, Jade never saw beyond one child. She'd automatically assumed it was a one-time deal. At the very least she'd expected her sister to have told her they'd used all three the day of the procedure.

"That's an understatement. Look, I just came off a full week of competition and I'm only here for another week and a half before I head back to Texas. My family has two baby christenings this weekend and Dylan's wedding is the next. And I'm competing midweek in South Dakota. I'll help you in whatever way I can, but I'm not going anywhere near those babies. I can't do it. Despite what you think Liv's intentions may have been, she stressed I was to be a donor only. Nothing more. I can't get emotionally involved."

"I don't know what to do. Maddie said Liv had been adamant about caring for the babies on her own, so she sent her home. Aside from some brief text messages over the last two weeks, I haven't really spoken to her.

Based on the little information I have, Liv may be suffering from postpartum depression."

"Oh man." Wes shoved his hands in his pockets. "That's pretty serious."

"I don't think she'd harm herself, but Liv doesn't do well with failure." They'd grown up with failure in every way imaginable and they both worked hard to avoid it now. "I'm wondering if she recognized what was happening to her and removed herself from the girls to protect them. Possibly to get help."

"Would she have had that much clarity?"

"She called Maddie and asked her to come over and babysit. And then there was the note she left telling Maddie to call me. When I checked her room, her luggage was missing. Her closet and quite a few drawers were partially empty leading me to assume she packed for a trip of some sort. She planned every step. It's not erratic behavior. She's either on a long vacation or she checked herself in somewhere."

"What did the note say?" Jade withdrew the folded slip of paper from her bag and handed it to him. He read it, then turned it over as if expecting to find more. "This is all she wrote?"

Jade nodded. "That's it."

Wes scrubbed the day-old scruff on his chin. "This sounds permanent. I'll talk to Harlan and see what he can find out."

"Your brother? Why? What can he do?"

"He's a deputy sheriff."

"Then keep him out of it." Jade snatched the note back from him, suddenly wishing she hadn't come to see Wes. "The police and social workers always believe they're doing what's best for the children when they don't see or understand the whole picture. I'll handle this."

He stared at her as if she had two heads. "Look, I don't like the idea of involving my brother, either, but you can't do it alone. Triplets are hard enough for a conventional family, let alone a single parent. Your sister's a prime example of that. Do you have help at the house?"

"Maddie said she'd be willing to stay for however long I need her."

"Unless Maddie quit her job since I left in January, she works full-time."

"Are you offering your help?"

"As in physically be there with you?" Wes held up his hands and stepped back. "Oh no. I don't want to see them and please don't force them on me."

"I would never force a child on anyone. They deserve better than that. I only came here because I thought you might have an idea where she went. My mistake."

Jade trudged back to her car, almost twisting her ankle in the process. What the hell had possessed her to wear high heels to a ranch? Stupidity along with vanity. She'd wanted to show Wes that despite the horrible rumors he'd spread about her in school, she had made something of herself. Eleven years later and she was still letting his opinion matter.

For a small town, the drive back to Liv's house felt like an eternity. Except for a handful of neighbors, her sister lived fairly isolated on the outskirts of Saddle Ridge. Maddie greeted her at the door, tense in anticipation of good news.

"How are the girls?"

"Still asleep. I expect them up soon. Once one's awake, the rest follow. Did you hear anything?"

"No." Jade slipped off her shoes and kicked them aside. "I ran into a friend of hers, though. Wes Slade."

"He must be home for the wedding and christenings."

"You know about them?"

"They only invited the entire town."

Of course, they had. There was nothing like living in a small town. "So, they were good friends?"

"Until he moved to Texas. His leaving really upset Liv since he hadn't even bothered to say goodbye. He's a hottie and a half, but the two of them never hooked up. Probably because he was hooking up with everyone else in the county." Maddie's face turned pink. "Present company excluded."

Jade was all too familiar with Wes's libido.

"My sister never mentioned him. When did they become friends?"

"I'm not really sure since I didn't live here then, but based on different things she's said, I've always assumed it was around the time Wes's father was killed."

"I remember Liv mentioning that, but I didn't realize they knew each other that well." Jade had never discussed Wes or the rumors he had started. The rumors that led to one of his friends assaulting her. Liv had had enough going on between school and working whenever she could to save for college. Regardless, Liv had to have heard the rumors from her friends. Saddle Ridge was too small of a town not to. Was that why she kept her friendship with Wes from her? Or had Wes said something?

"I tried calling Liv again, and it went straight to voice mail. I left a message telling her you were here and that the girls were fine."

"Nothing about them missing her?" Jade asked.

"I—I don't remember exactly what I said. Should I have?"

Jade dropped her bag on the antique hall table in the foyer. "If she's suffering from some form of postpartum depression I'd like to believe hearing the children miss her would prove how much they need her. That's just speculation on my part." She wondered if her sister would interpret their being fine as confirmation she'd done the right thing. But Maddie blamed herself enough already. Jade didn't need to add to it. "Why don't you head home, take a shower and relax for the night. I appreciate you going above and beyond like you have."

"Are you sure?" Maddie gnawed on her bottom lip. "I realize you were here when the girls were born, but do you know how to take care of an infant? Let alone three?"

"I'm sure I can handle feeding them, changing a few diapers and putting them to bed." Jade's hands flew to her chest. "Oh my God! Liv was breast-feeding."

Maddie shook her head. "No, it didn't work out. She wasn't producing enough milk and was unbelievably sore. They started on formula pretty early."

Jade had headed back to LA eight days after the girls were released from the hospital. "She never told me."

"She probably wouldn't have told me if I hadn't been staying here. It really upset her."

"I bet." Jade imagined her sister thought not being able to breast-feed as the ultimate failure.

"Have you ever mixed formula before?"

"Can't say that I have." Jade sighed.

"Come on." Maddie motioned for her to follow. "There's kind of a formula to making formula and it all starts with boiling water."

By the time Maddie walked her through the steps, Jade understood why women opted to breast-feed. Even though the can came with directions, she took detailed notes, not wanting to risk a mistake.

"Just remember to toss out any mixed formula after twenty-four hours. You can make a large batch of it, but it's not like milk. You can't keep a gallon in the fridge for a week. If any of them don't finish their bottle, toss it because their saliva can contaminate the formula."

"Got it. I'm assuming this is the bottle sterilizer?" Jade pointed to a large dome-shaped appliance sitting on the counter.

"Yes. You can also run their pacifiers through there. But—" Maddie opened the cabinet next to the sink and removed three bottomless bottles and a box "—it's more convenient to use these with the liners. That way the nipples are the only thing you'll need to clean. Just toss the liners in the trash."

After a crash course in infant feeding, Maddie left for the night. Jade peeked in at the girls before heading to the guest room to change. She stood in the doorway as she'd done earlier, almost afraid to get any closer to the children who were biologically hers. She still had a tough time wrapping her brain around it. If she intended to take care of them until Liv returned, she needed to remember Liv was their real mother, not her.

She tiptoed across the room to their cribs, choking back tears. They were beautiful, and she'd help create them. The inexplicable desire to hold them overwhelmed her. She wanted to tell them how much she loved them and that she'd never abandon them. How bad had things gotten for her sister to walk away from her children?

She reached over the side of the crib and lightly ran her hand over one of their matching white-and-pink cotton bunny onesies. *Matching!* How would she tell the girls apart? They were fraternal triplets, but they looked alike to her. Especially at this age. Liv and Maddie could tell them apart, but Jade hadn't spent enough time around them yet. If it wasn't for the large *A*, *H* and *M* stenciled on the wall above their respective cribs she wouldn't have known who was Audra, Hadley or Mackenzie.

"What if I mix them up?"

Hadley stirred at the sound of her voice but didn't wake up. Jade scanned the room. She needed something to distinguish them from each other. Nail polish came to mind, but she feared they'd chew it off. She ran back downstairs to Liv's office and dug a black permanent marker out of the drawer. She'd have to write their first initial on the sole of their foot until she researched a better solution online. Maybe the pediatrician could offer a suggestion. She had to call there anyway to find out when the babies' next appointment was. First, she had to fabricate a plausible excuse as to why she was calling and not her sister. She didn't want to arouse suspicion about Liv.

One triplet began to cry as she reached the top step. She ran into the room, pulled off the marker cap with her teeth and wrote a large *H* on the bottom of Hadley's foot when the odor of a full diaper smacked her square in the jaw.

"Good heavens. For a tiny little thing, that is one big stink." Jade lifted Hadley into her arms as Audra began crying. Within seconds, the room was full of shrieks and smelly diapers. She couldn't pacify or change the girls fast enough. She wasn't even sure how to get them downstairs to feed them. Maddie would. Jade went to pull her phone from her pocket before remembering she left it in her bag. "Okay, I guess we're going down one at a time."

Mackenzie started crying louder than the other two before she reached the hallway. "What is it, sweetheart?" She cradled her against her chest, afraid to put her down. "You have a clean diaper and I will feed you in a few minutes." Mackenzie's tear streaked face turned red while her tiny arms flailed in the air. Jade adjusted the baby's position and sat in the rocking chair. "Shh, I've got you. I know you miss your mommy, but I'm here."

Mackenzie's cries continued along with her two sisters and Jade wondered if Liv had postpartum depression or if she'd needed a sanity break. She easily saw how this could try even a saint's patience after a while. Jade couldn't do this alone. She needed help.

Wes sat in Liv's driveway for ten minutes before he got the nerve to walk up the porch stairs and knock on the door. Once he did, he heard a baby cry from inside. He hadn't even considered he might wake them up. He hadn't considered much on the drive over except that he hadn't given Jade his phone number and he didn't have hers. His concern for Liv was worth the risk of seeing the girls.

Wes's heart pounded in his chest as a cold sweat formed across his brow. His biological daughters were inside that house. It was the closest he'd ever been to them and all he wanted to do was run. Why hadn't he called Liv's house and left a message on the answering machine if Jade didn't answer? Because he hadn't thought this through. The reality he'd created three children with the bully responsible for the beatings he'd received in the high school locker room struck him harder than a runaway Mack truck.

"Maddie, I need you!"

A chill ran down Wes's spine at the sound of Jade's desperate plea. He grabbed the knob and flung the door open, causing it to bang against the interior wall. "Jade!" He ran toward the baby cries, uncertain what he might find. He stuck his head in the numerous rooms that branched off the center hall of the old farmhouse. "Jade, where are you?" he asked as he reached the kitchen, only to find Jade, barefoot and disheveled holding one screaming infant in her arms while the other two wailed from bouncy chairs perched on top of the table.

His heart stopped beating at the sight of them. His daughters. His. They had his DNA, his genes, his— Wes grabbed the doorjamb.

"Thank God you're here." She took a step toward him.

He shook his head, trying not to break eye contact with her for fear he'd look into the eyes of one of his daughters. "Why are they crying?"

"Wes, meet Audra." She held the infant out to him. "Please help me."

His arms rose automatically to take her without hesitation as his body betrayed his will. He closed his eyes, not wanting to see the life he'd helped create. The weight of Audra in his arms made her all that more real. Her cries stopped as a soft mew emanated from the tiny bundle. He didn't want to look. But he couldn't not look. He needed to see his daughter.

"Oh my God." His heart sprang back to life.

"What is it?" Jade frantically asked.

"She's beautiful," he whispered.

"They all are. We made quite the heartbreakers."

He lifted his gaze to hers. The edginess had faded to a gentle softness. Even with her stained blouse and what appeared to be a black marker streak across her left cheek, she exuded beauty. "I guess we did." He lowered his eyes to the other two girls contentedly sucking on the bottles Jade held for them. And then he saw more black marker. "Did you write on their feet?"

"I had to. I couldn't tell them apart. They're not identical, but they sure look that way to me."

Wes cautiously stepped forward as if walking on ice. He'd held a baby before. He'd been around plenty of children in his twenty-nine years. Somehow, these three seemed more fragile than any of the others combined.

"The nose on that one is a little more upturned." Wes glanced at the infant's foot. "What does the *M* stand for?"

"Liv never told you their names?"

"She sent me a birth announcement, or what I assumed was one. I never opened it."

"Wow, you really haven't spoken to her in months because she chose those names in January."

"I stopped taking her calls when she told me she was having triplets." He reached for the third bottle sitting on the table and held it up. "May I?"

"Be my guest. She refused to eat for me."

Wes sat in the chair across from her and held the bottle to Audra's tiny lips. She hesitated for a second before eagerly drawing on the nipple. Her eyes reminded him of Jade's…big, blue and the color of the Montana sky on a bright summer day. He wished somebody would pinch him because feeding his daughter was the most surreal experience of his life.

"I hate that I didn't call. It bothered me then, but it bothers me more now. I can't help wondering if my abandonment contributed to her leaving."

"I won't criticize you for walking away because if Liv and I weren't sisters, I may have done the same thing."

Jade's candor surprised him. "So, you still haven't told me what the *M* stands for."

"Mackenzie and the other is Hadley."

"Audra, Mackenzie and Hadley." His cheeks hurt from smiling. "It's a pleasure to meet you. I'm—" He wasn't sure how to introduce himself.

"You're a friend of their mother. That's all we can ever be."

Ten minutes ago, Wes didn't even want to be a friend to anyone connected to the children, now it hardly seemed enough.

"How is this supposed to work? You can't even feed the three of them on your own."

"That's not fair." Jade held a bottle up to the light

to see how much formula remained in the liner. "This was my first try. Although I'm not sure what my sister was thinking when she told Maddie to call me. I'm not exactly mother material. My job's super demanding and consumes most of my time."

"What do you do?"

"I own a high-end event management company in Los Angeles. You could say I'm a party planner to the stars. I'm surprised my sister didn't tell you."

He would never have guessed she'd chosen that career path. He figured she would have chosen… Wes stared at her, not recognizing the woman she was today. He'd never given much thought to what she did after high school. Once she'd moved away, he had been thrilled to have her out of his life. Even though her cruelty still stuck with him.

"Your sister rarely mentioned you."

Jade recoiled at his comment. "Well, that's nice. At least you didn't tell her how much you hated me."

Just as much as you hated me. "I met your sister the day of my father's funeral. We were both at the Iron Horse, saddled up to the bar. She recognized me and offered her condolences. At the time, I was too lost in my grief to realize who she was. That was the night she and her husband called it quits. She was hurting and I couldn't see past my anger over my father's death."

"I'm so sorry you had to go through that, but I'm glad you two found comfort in each other."

Wes nodded. "That old saying about misery loving company is true. We were two lonely souls drowning our sorrows. The next day I didn't even remember her name, but we kept meeting there night after night and as time went on, we met less at the bar and more in a booth with coffee and a bite to eat. It was only then I realized she was your sister. I couldn't have gotten through those days without her."

"I tried talking her into moving out to LA when Kevin left. She refused to leave this place. We'd bounced around so much in foster care that once she had this house, hell would freeze over before she left it."

"She didn't really discuss where you two had lived while growing up, but I got a real sense that home meant everything to her." Liv had sidestepped most references to her childhood, and he'd assumed she'd wanted to keep that door closed forever. He understood where she'd been coming from and never pressed further. "Our friendship started out consoling each other over what we'd lost. My father and her husband. Once we got that out of our systems, our conversations shifted to the future and what we wanted out of life. She talked a lot about wanting a family of her own."

"Liv's not one to dwell in the past." Jade sat both bottles on the table and lifted Mackenzie into her arms.

"No, she's not." Wes waited for Jade to grab a burp towel, but she didn't. "You need to hold her a little more upright and against your shoulder. And you should have something to protect your shirt because she will spit up." He stood, still cradling Audra in one arm while he opened and closed drawers until he found what he was looking for. He draped a towel over Jade's shoulder, noticing the softness of her hair against his hand as he did so. "Watch me." Audra had finished her bottle. He set it on the counter and shifted her in his arms. "Hold her like this and lightly pat her back."

"How did you get so good at this?" Jade mirrored him.

"I've had practice. More than a man who never wants kids should." Wes had seen enough dysfunction in his own family to kill any desire he'd ever had of settling down. His father's death had fractured the final fragments that had held the Slades together. Getting tossed off a bull hurt a lot less than losing someone you love. Three of his four siblings had maintained a close relationship to each other, but their mom had taken off for sunny California. Much like Jade had. Nevertheless, he'd learned to keep an emotional distance ever since. "Any more thoughts where your sister might be?"

"Tomorrow I'll call every postpartum depression treatment center I can find, including over the border in Canada just to be on the safe side. She's an adult, so I'm not sure if anyone can legally tell me if she's there, but I at least have to try."

"Well, the reason I came here tonight was to give you my phone number and to get yours."

"You could've called the house and given it to me seeing as you didn't want to meet the girls."

"That dawned on me while I was knocking on the front door." Wes sniffed the top of Audra's head. She smelled like new car smell for humans. "From the looks and sounds of things, it's a good thing I did. Where's Maddie?"

"I sent her home. She'd been here for over twenty-four hours. The woman hadn't even had a shower or change of clothes."

"It looks like you could use the same."

"Thanks a lot." Jade attempted to smooth the front of her shirt.

Wes laughed as he settled Audra into the empty

bouncy seat and lifted Hadley into his arms. "I didn't mean that to sound as insulting as it did. It was a poorly worded offer to watch the girls while you take a few moments for yourself."

"Are you sure?"

"Considering I made a commitment to help bring these three into the world, I think I can commit to babysitting while you shower."

"Thank you."

"But…this is a onetime deal, Jade." He didn't want to delude her into thinking he'd changed his mind about being involved in their lives. "I'm here now, but once I walk out that door, I'm not coming back."

He couldn't—wouldn't—risk his heart. It was already on the verge of shattering into a thousand pieces.

Chapter 3

Jade awoke with the worst backache of her life. She eased her body out of the rocking chair she had tried to sleep in last night. Staying in the guest bedroom down the hall proved futile after hours of tossing and turning. It didn't help that she kept getting up and checking on the girls every few minutes. The video baby monitor was great during the day, but it was difficult to see at night when the only light in the room was an elephant lamp on the dresser against the far wall.

How had her sister done it alone in a house this size? It was the middle of summer and the place creaked whenever the wind blew. She could only imagine how loud it was during the blustery Montana winter. There was too much house, too much baby and not enough time to breathe.

Liv had surprised Jade when she'd first mentioned

in vitro. It had been one thing to want a baby with her husband, but as a single parent? Their mom had failed at single parenting ten times over. And she couldn't help wondering if their mother was part of the problem. She had never bonded with them and vice versa.

Jade tried to remember the days after the girls were born. Liv had stayed in the hospital for three days and the girls had been in the neonatal intensive care unit for almost two weeks. It had been so hectic that she hadn't noticed if Liv had bonded with the girls. Could she have missed the signs? Even though she'd been sore, Liv had been determined to get up and move around when she needed to. In hindsight, Jade shouldn't have left so soon. Work had beckoned and despite her connection to the girls, she should have sucked it up and stayed an extra couple of weeks with her sister.

Jade quietly slipped out of the nursery and grabbed her phone off the charger in the guest room. It was a few minutes after five in the morning. Los Angeles was an hour behind them, but knowing Tomás, her assistant was probably awake. The man had been her shadow for the last five years. His attention to the finest of details and endless amount of energy kept her business running smoothly. He was the only person she would ever trust to handle any given situation the way she would.

The hardwood floors groaned as she made her way to the narrow staircase leading to the kitchen. She hesitated on the top step and listened for any sign that she'd woken the girls. Confident they were still asleep, she continued downstairs and beelined for the coffeemaker. Once the caffeine began coursing through her veins, she dialed her assistant.

"Good morning, gorgeous." Tomás's chipper voice

boomed through the phone. "And how is our temporary *mummy* holding up this morning?"

"Let's just say I made it through the night in one piece." For the next fifteen minutes, she sipped coffee and filled Tomás in on yesterday's events, including Wes. Tomás had been the one person she had completely confided in about her past. He knew the good, the bad and the ugly.

"Oh, darling. You've been holding out on me." He lowered his voice to a whisper so not to wake his husband. "I just pulled up your cowboy online, and that's the finest male specimen I've seen in forever. He just oozes testosterone and ruggedness."

"Tomás!" Jade nearly knocked over her mug. "Do I need to remind you what he did to me?"

"No, but I think I need to remind you he was only a teenager back then. Now..." Tomás clucked his tongue. "He's a hundred percent man."

"I don't care when it was. Cowboys never did it for me."

"Your cowboy is a champion bull rider and his earnings last year were almost four times more than what I made."

Jade straightened in her chair. "You can see how much he made?"

"I sure can." He gave her the web address and she pulled up his stats.

"I had no idea bull riders made so much money." Jade continued to scan the page. Turned out Wes was one of the top bull riders in the country and fifth in the standings this year.

"It also seems your boy is active in social media. That's quite a good morning."

"What are you talking about? How did you find that out?"

"I went to his website, westonslade.com."

Website? "I didn't realize he was that popular."

"I thought you said you looked him up online."

"I did. But I used one of those people directories, so it showed me his place of employment first. And that's where I stopped."

She typed in the address. Okay, the website was impressive. Professionally done and sexy, yet unreservedly masculine. She clicked on the first social media account and wondered if he had a team posting for him as she did. Nope. A selfie of him lying in bed with the caption Good Morning had posted a few minutes earlier and it already had close to a thousand likes. The hair on the back of her neck rose as she read one erotic reply after another. Most from women although there were a handful of men on there too.

"I swear, Tomás," she warned. "I better not see your name pop up."

Tomás cleared his throat and the sound of him rapidly hitting a key on his computer reverberated through the phone.

"I can't believe you."

"It's not like I hit Send."

She continued to read the posts and noticed Wes hadn't responded to any of the comments. "Okay, so maybe he's just a narcissist."

"If I didn't know any better, I'd say your kitten claws have come out."

A flicker of movement on the baby monitor caught her attention. Hadley's legs were beginning to kick.

Judging by last night's diaper changes, that was the sign another was coming.

"I'll have to call you back. The little ones are waking up."

"Okay, love. You take care of those beauties and I'll touch base with you sometime this afternoon."

An hour later, Jade was either on the verge of tears or a nervous breakdown. She couldn't do this full-time. And she was used to dealing with difficult. But Hollywood bridezillas were easier to handle. And potty trained.

When Maddie stopped by around six thirty, Jade almost threw herself at her feet and begged for mercy.

"Oh, Jade." Maddie's eyes trailed up and down the length of her. "What have they done to you?"

Jade thrust Mackenzie into her arms. "How can anyone in their right mind think having a baby is a good idea?"

Maddie laughed. "You must've had some night if you're swearing off kids altogether."

"I've never wanted children. Never. I'm too busy and too active to be tied down. And so was my sister up until she decided to do this. She and Kevin were always off backpacking or flying to Europe for the weekend. It was constantly go, go, go. And even after they split up, she would tell me about the spontaneous weekend trips she would take to Texas or Wyoming or— I'll be damned."

"What?"

"She was following Wes on the road, wasn't she?" Jade couldn't for the life of her figure out why her sister hadn't mentioned his name or at the very least, that she was going to rodeos.

"I wouldn't say she was following him. She met up with him if his competitions fell on the weekend."

"And there wasn't anything between them?"

"No. I can honestly say I don't believe they ever even kissed."

She didn't think Wes was capable of having a platonic relationship with a woman. She thought she knew her sister better than anyone did. She couldn't have been more wrong. It didn't make sense.

"I take it you haven't heard from Liv?"

"No." Maddie smiled down at Mackenzie in her arms. "I wanted to call, but I don't want to drive her further away."

Jade had fought the same urge throughout the night. "I didn't, either. Once the kids fell asleep, I called a bunch of treatment centers specializing in postpartum depression. They were all in-patient facilities within a day's drive from here."

"And nothing?"

"It was an exercise in futility. No matter how much I pleaded, privacy laws prevented them from releasing any information. I left the same message for Liv at each place in case she's there, 'Just let us know you're safe.' I'll call out-patient facilities today and do the same thing. Other than that, I'm at a loss. This can't go on indefinitely." Jade hated to involve the police, but the more time passed, the more concerned she became. She honestly thought Liv would have reached out by now. "One day, okay, I get it. There's a lot of stress involved with caring for triplets. But we're going on two days and postpartum depression or not, a text message would have been nice."

"What happens if she doesn't come back? Can you legally take them with you to California?"

"I'm not sure." The same scenario had played through Jade's head earlier. "If I just leave with them and she returns in a frazzled state, she could accuse me of kidnapping."

"You don't think she'd do that, do you?"

"Yesterday, I didn't. Today, I'm realizing there's a lot I didn't know about my sister. Before I can leave with them, I would have to report Liv missing and the kids would go in the system. They'll probably have to evaluate me and my home in LA before releasing them to me. I'm Liv's only relative so I hope that counts for something, but I can't be a hundred percent certain the girls won't go in foster care. I need to contact an attorney."

"I can put together some names, if you'd like." Maddie eased Mackenzie into her bouncy chair.

"Thanks, but I'll call the one Liv used to set up the donor paperwork."

"You know who she used?"

"Ah." Jade froze. Her brain short-circuited as she tried to cover her slip. Liv had wanted everyone to believe she used two anonymous donors. "She mentioned someone a few times. I'm assuming she has the name and number in her office. I'm sure I'll recognize it when I see it."

Maddie nodded, seemingly unconcerned. "Before I forget, today's garbage day. Monday, as well."

"That was on my list of questions to ask you." She'd made many lists in between phone calls, ranging from to-dos to how-tos. There was satisfaction in checking off a task as she went about her day. "Would you mind watching the girls for a few minutes while I get it together?"

"Sure, I don't have to be to work until nine o'clock so I have time. Take a shower and get yourself cleaned up, including whatever that black mark is on your cheek."

"Black mark?" Jade walked into the small half bath off the kitchen and flipped on the light. "Are you kidding me?" She had a three-inch-long black permanent marker streak starting at the corner of her mouth going toward her ear. "I can't believe he didn't tell me."

Jade had taken such a quick shower last night while Wes had watched the girls, she hadn't bothered to look in the mirror.

"He was here for quite a while." Maddie's voice lilted with implication.

Jade rolled her eyes. Maddie must have seen his truck in the driveway. "We were just comparing notes, and he watched the kids long enough for me to shower and change."

"Apparently it wasn't long enough. You have some time, go do what you have to do."

Jade ran upstairs and grabbed the bathroom garbage along with the bag from the Diaper Genie.

"I never thought to ask what you do for a living," Jade said as she returned to the kitchen and lifted the lid off the trash can alongside the counter.

"I'm a court reporter. It's nowhere near as glamorous as your job. I can only imagine what it's like meeting all those celebrities."

Jade inwardly laughed. Her job was far from glamorous. "I don't just have celebrity clients, but they are the majority of my business. And let me tell you, those happy smiles you see plastered on the pages of magazines aren't always real. Underneath they have the same fears and concerns as the rest of us. Sometimes I feel sorry for them. Every move they make, especially when it comes to their wedding, gets photographed and scrutinized. I can't even begin to tell you the lengths we have to go to sometimes just to get a client to a venue. It can be a logistical nightmare. Some days seem like they'll never end, but I wouldn't trade it in for the world."

How was she going to run a business and care for Mackenzie, Hadley and Audra? She never wanted kids and now she had three. No. She squared her shoulders and tied the garbage bag closed. She had to stay positive. Liv would come back and everything would be fine. Jade opened the back door off the mudroom and almost tripped over three car seats sitting on the top step.

"Okay, we need to find a better place for these."

"Oh my God!" Maddie jumped up. "Those are from Liv's car. When did she put them there?"

"I have no idea." Jade moved one aside and ran down the steps into the yard, hoping to find her sister.

"They are a little damp from the morning dew," Maddie said. "They've been out here for a while."

Jade wanted to collapse in the grass and cry. *Where are you, Liv?* She took a deep breath and plodded back up the stairs to the mudroom. "I don't think I opened this door yesterday. Did you?"

"I did when I put the garbage in the can. That was sometime in the early afternoon. It had to have been after that."

"Then she came back." Jade's heart rose to her throat. "But when?"

Jade closed her eyes and hoped it wasn't when she and Wes had fed the girls in the kitchen last night. Liv would have had a clear view of them from the steps. Seeing the biological parents together with their children was the last thing her sister needed. She just prayed it hadn't pushed Liv further over the edge.

Wes had thought the worst mistake of his life had been the day he miscalculated Crazy Town's spin direction and damn near died when the bull tossed and trampled him. He'd changed his mind when Liv told him the embryo transfer had been a success. It still hadn't compared to the mistake he made last night.

There had been an uncontrollable force driving him to Liv's house. He'd gone and done the one thing he'd sworn he never would. And now that he'd met his daughters, he couldn't get their tiny cherub faces out of his head. His heart couldn't handle seeing them again knowing they weren't his to keep. Not that he wanted to keep them. Just the opposite. The sooner he got out of town, the better.

He'd spent most of the night down at the stables to avoid Garrett's countless questions about Jade and her emergency. He wished Jade had just called and left a message instead of talking to his brother. Then again, if she hadn't stalked him at the ranch, he never would have spoken with her and she knew it.

His phone rang, and he was almost afraid to check the display. It was half past nine and it could be anyone, from his management team to one of his friends. But his gut told him it was Jade. The thought alone both frightened and excited him.

He braved a glance at the screen. Her name flashed

at him like a rodeo clown waving a red flag. He froze long enough for the call to go to voice mail. He couldn't talk to her. Talking would lead to seeing his daughters again. His daughters. They were no longer a concept. Even after their due date had passed, Wes had refused to think of them as tiny humans almost two thousand miles away from his new home in Ramblewood, Texas. Now he had no choice.

He had held them in his arms and they had imprinted themselves on his heart. How could he walk away and go back to life as usual? Especially when they were growing up in his hometown where every time he visited his brothers and their growing families he ran the risk of running into them. And what would happen when they got older and started driving or playing sports? He was bound to see their names in the newspaper or mentioned by a neighbor or friend. Saddle Ridge was a small town and nothing escaped anyone.

Wes stormed to the tack room. He needed to go for a ride and clear his head. The voice mail notification chimed from his back pocket. As much as he wanted to ignore it, he couldn't. His finger hovered over the play button, praying Jade had called to say she had found Liv and everything was fine.

"Wes, it's Jade. I know you have your phone in your hand because you posted a pic online less than five minutes ago. At least it was better than the tacky one of you in bed. Anyway, I'm calling to tell you Liv came back to the house sometime yesterday or during the night. I don't know when or how long she stayed, but it may have been when you were here. Please call me as soon as you get this. I'm scared of how she may have reacted if she saw us together with the girls."

* * *

Wes took the front porch steps of Liv's house two at a time. Jade opened the door and pulled him inside before he had a chance to knock. He told himself repeatedly on the drive over he was there only for Liv's well-being. Any attachment to the girls was off-limits.

"Thank you for coming. I know this is the last place you want to be."

Wes followed her into the small living room off the main hallway. He'd half expected to see Audra, Hadley and McKenzie when he turned the corner, instead the room looked exactly as it always had.

"It doesn't even look like a baby, let alone three babies, lives here."

"Exactly." Jade paced the length of the small off-white area rug. "We were so busy feeding the girls yesterday I didn't get a chance to show you this." She grabbed his hand and led him down the hall to a narrow closet. The gesture was innocent enough, but her palm against his felt more intimate than a kiss. Within seconds she released him, and damned if he didn't miss her touch already. He balled his fist, refusing to feel anything for the woman. "This is what I mean when I say Liv knew what she was doing."

She swung the closet open and flipped on the overhead light. There were numerous neatly stacked, transparent lidded bins with index cards taped to the front of them listing each one's contents. Baby toys, baby blankets, baby photo albums…all generically labeled.

"Why is everything in the closet?"

"These had all been in various rooms when I left a little over a month ago. Sometime between now and then, she ordered storage containers and packed everything away."

Wes wandered around the first floor of the house, peering into each room. "I've never been upstairs, but nothing down here looks any different from before she got pregnant. The place was always spotless. Is it possible she took the bins out when she needed them?"

Jade shook her head. "It doesn't make sense. Those photo albums used to be on the coffee table. She couldn't wait to fill them. I looked inside and there are three, possibly four pages' worth of photos. And the baby blankets…she was so proud that she'd learned how to crochet for her daughters. Those are shoved in a box too."

"What about the nursery? Did she change anything in there?"

"No." Jade started up the stairs, but Wes's feet refused to follow. "Are you coming?"

"Aren't the girls up there?"

Her shoulders sagged at the question. "So that's it? Last night was a onetime deal and you're never going to see them again."

"I thought I already made that clear." What part of not wanting to be a parent didn't she understand? He had to set boundaries before she expected more from him. "I'm not here for them. I'm here because you said Liv came back to the house and you're afraid she saw us together. I'm here because I'm worried about her. I'm not worried about the girls. I trust you with them."

"How very big of you." She closed the distance between them, her eyes blazing with anger and fear. "Hell, I'm surprised you haven't snapped a picture of them and posted it all over the internet to see how many likes and follows you can get."

Wes put a hand on her arm. "I know you're upset, and I meant what I said yesterday. I'll do whatever I can to help you find Liv. But please, don't take it out on me. This isn't my fault just like it isn't your fault."

Jade dropped her gaze. "It is our fault. We missed the signs. You taking off to Texas is no different from me flying back to LA as fast as I could. We both abandoned her."

"We were only donors." Wes bit back the bile he now associated with the word. "Those kids aren't ours. And you didn't abandon Liv. You were there when the babies were born. You helped bring them home. You're caring for them night and day. You're living in the same house with them. They're the first thing you see in the morning and they're the last thing you see at night. I don't even have to be here to recognize you're getting attached to them."

"Of course I am." Tears filled her eyes. "I never wanted to feel this way, but they're our daughters. How can you not get attached?"

"They are your nieces, but they can't ever be anything to me. That's how Liv wanted it."

Jade tried to pull from his grip, but he refused to let go. Not when she was in so much pain. Her heart beat wildly against him as he held her tight to his chest. Despite the past or the resentment he still felt toward her, he wanted nothing more than to ease the guilt she carried.

"It's okay." He smoothed her hair and rested his cheek against the top of her head. "It's going to be okay. We'll find Liv, make sure she gets the help she needs and bring her home to her children."

"I'm scared she's not going to be okay or that she'll do this again." Jade sobbed against him. "She came back, Wes. She was here, and she left. She walked away twice. How could she do that?"

Wes eased her onto the couch, summoning every ounce of strength he had not to panic. Between the abandoned triplets he'd never wanted to be involved with and Liv's fragile emotional state, he felt the overwhelming need to protect the Scott women, even if that included Jade…the woman who had made his life pure hell.

"Tell me what happened."

After Jade explained about the car seats she'd found earlier, he figured there was a fifty-fifty chance Liv had seen them together. Since she'd purposely kept their identities from the other, he understood how watching him and Jade with the girls might upset her.

"I'm not trying to belittle your concerns in any way, but why do you think seeing us together would push her over the edge?"

Jade shifted on the couch to face him and tucked her bare legs underneath her jean-short-covered bottom. Coupled with her deep V-neck white cotton T-shirt, she wore ultracasual extremely well. A little too well since his jeans felt snugger than they had a minute ago.

"I think my sister had a thing for you and maybe still does."

Wes threw his head back and laughed, knocking his hat on the back of the couch. He removed it and set it brim side up on the coffee table while running his other hand through his hair.

"Trust me, your sister was not interested in me romantically."

"How can you be so sure?"

"Because she's still in love with Kevin. That's one broken heart I don't think she'll ever get past."

"She divorced him years ago."

"He divorced her," Wes corrected, surprised she didn't know. "I was with her the night she was served. And she was served very publicly in the middle of the Iron Horse."

Jade's mouth hung open in disbelief. "Is she so afraid of failure that she has to hide her pain from me? Or am I that cold of a person she didn't think I would understand?"

Wes couldn't believe the words coming out of her mouth. "Get over yourself. It isn't about you. From the little she told me about both of your pasts, she was the one taking care of you while you did whatever you wanted."

"That was hardly the case."

"Really, because the Jade I remember was constantly getting into trouble. You were an angry kid. And mean. God, you were mean."

"I'll own up to having an attitude, but I was mean to only you and that's because you said I'd slept with you. Your lie almost got me raped by your friend."

"What?" His fists clenched. Wes couldn't imagine any of his friends forcing themselves on a girl. "Who are you talking about?"

"Oh, come on. You know damn well I'm talking about your buddy Burke. Every time I saw you two together afterward you were laughing at me."

"Burke tried to rape you?" A slow rage began to

build in his chest. Burke had been more of a rival than a friend. They'd competed against each other in all aspects of their lives. From bull riding to girls. "When?"

"Our ninth-grade fall harvest dance. How can you not remember?" Jade jumped up from the couch as if it was on fire and faced him. "You two were sitting on the gym bleachers laughing and pointing at me. I'd had enough and decided to leave. Burke followed me into the hallway, threw me against the lockers and reached under my skirt. He tore off my underwear!" Her eyes filled with tears. "He told me he wanted what I gave you. I physically had to fight him to break free. He had his zipper down and was ready to go."

Wes's stomach churned. "He said you two had hooked up. He even showed me your underwear. I was crushed you chose him over me. Jade, I had no idea what really happened."

"It wasn't consensual! Torn underwear should have been your clue?" Jade shook her head in disgust. "It happened because you told everyone we had slept together. You told everyone I was easy. He assumed I was shareable when you and I had only kissed."

"Yeah and we had dated for almost a month." The words came out of his mouth before he could stop them.

"So that meant I owed you sex?" Jade's face reddened. "We started dating, like, my second week of ninth grade. Liv and I had just come out of another group home and had moved in with a new foster family. I hadn't even told my sister about you. I was trying to learn everyone's name and get acclimated to a new town. I was fourteen years old and you kept pushing me to go further than I was ready. And then you broke up with me because I wouldn't. Do you have any idea how that made me feel?"

"I'm sorry," Wes whispered. He lifted his gaze to hers. "Everything was a competition to me back then. I was hurt that you didn't like me as much as I liked you. I didn't even know what sex was. I mean I did, but I hadn't done it yet. Burke had. So I lied and said I had too. He was the only one I told." He rose from the couch, torn between wanting to comfort her and beating the crap out of Burke. His old rival had moved to New Mexico after high school, but the next time they crossed paths on the rodeo circuit, he'd be damn sure to teach him a lesson.

"Burke taunted me every chance he could, and you were right there next to him. We had just been placed with a really nice foster family, and Liv and I finally believed we had a place to call home. As nice as it was, it was never easy. At least not for me. I felt like I had a scarlet letter emblazoned on my chest, thanks to you. And two years later, on Christmas Eve when my foster mom's brother tried to force himself on me, I believed it was my fault, because it had happened to me once before."

"Please tell me he didn't—"

"Rape me?" Jade violently shook her head. "No. Liv walked in, saw what was happening and kicked his ass. But when the police came, they didn't care what I said. He claimed I had been the aggressor and they took his word over mine."

Wes felt sick. One of his brothers had recently dealt with a serious bullying issue involving his daughter and Wes had been so angry when he heard that, he had wanted to drive straight through from Texas to Montana to confront her attackers. He'd never considered himself one of those people. But he had been. And so had Jade. As much as he wanted to confront her about her bullying, he refused to turn his apology around on her. "I never intended to put you in physical danger or make you feel like any less of a person."

"That rumor followed me around until the day I graduated. I'm sure your brother is a great deputy sheriff, but any faith I had in the system disappeared that night. Instead of arresting my attacker, they sent me to a group home. Liv was eighteen then and she immediately petitioned the courts for guardianship. Within the month, the state had released me into her care." Jade began to pace the length of the small room. "We struggled to survive after that, but we did it. Liv worked two jobs and still managed to attend college full-time on the scholarship she'd won. I worked every day after school and on weekends to help pay the bills. I owe my sister for all she did back then, and I refuse to let her down." She stopped less than a foot in front of him and folded her arms tight across her chest. "And after what you did, I think you owe me too."

He'd call them even after what she'd done in retaliation all those years ago, but the determined set of her chin left him fearing where her next sentence would lead if he disagreed. "Fine."

"We created those three lives upstairs. And despite our donor contracts or how we feel about the situation, we have an obligation to Liv to make sure they're cared for. I can't do this alone. Outside of hiring a stranger, you're my only choice. Since you're in town, I'm asking you to help me. You can stay in one of the guest rooms."

"Whoa, you want me to move in here?" Wes may have been willing to handle the grocery shopping or running whatever errands or chores she needed done, but living under the same roof with her and the girls was out of the question. "That would send up all sorts of red flags to my family."

"I just told you I can't do this alone." She stared up at him. "I highly doubt you want to run the risk of the girls not getting what they need or heaven forbid, getting hurt because I only have two arms? What if there's a fire? I thought about that last night. I don't know what Liv would have done in that situation."

Guilt trip launched and on target. "Fine, but kindly keep my time with them to an absolute minimum. I'll take care of the laundry, run wherever you need me to go and clean the house. Once this is over, you'll still be around the girls. I won't. There's no room for me in their lives so let's not make this any harder than it needs to be."

One of Jade's perfectly arched brows rose. "Of course."

Frustration coursed through his veins. She was handling him just like she probably handled her troublesome clients and he didn't appreciate it. He couldn't leave her to deal with this mess on her own, either. He had a week and a half until Dylan's wedding, and then it was back to Texas. This time he had no intentions of ever returning to Saddle Ridge.

Chapter 4

Jade should probably have her head examined for asking Wes to move in with her and the girls. While she'd never forgive him for the past, their talk last night had lessened her anger about the situation. She doubted she'd ever have full closure over the event that had spiraled her teen years out of control, but at least she'd discovered his intentions hadn't been as malicious as she'd thought.

Wes stayed true to his word. Since yesterday morning, he'd helped her around the house, made sure all Liv's bills and utilities were up-to-date and even washed, folded and put away countless loads of laundry. But when it came to the girls, he slept downstairs on the couch and excused himself from the room whenever they were near. Like now…he was in Liv's office researching other treatment centers and contacting some of their mutual friends while she prepared another round of formula. Now that she had mastered feeding the girls with the help of a rolled-up towel to support the bottles, she didn't need Wes at mealtime. But, despite their history, some company would've been nice. Caring for triplets had quickly become an isolated job. He could have at least helped during diaper changes or bath time.

The house phone rang, and Jade almost broke her neck tripping over a chair when she ran to answer it.

"Hello?"

"May I please speak with Jade Scott?"

She shivered at the direct tone of the man's voice. "This is Jade."

"Ms. Scott, this is Jacob Meyer, Olivia's attorney. We met last year. Your sister asked me to contact you."

"Have you heard from Liv?" Her pulse began to beat erratically. "Is she all right?"

"Olivia asked me to call you and let you know she's safe."

"Thank heaven she's okay." Jade slumped against the counter, but her relief was short-lived. "If my sister is all right, why are you calling me? What happened?"

"Liv has checked into a recovery center and she'll be there for a minimum of thirty days, possibly longer."

Thirty days? She couldn't possibly stay in Montana for that long. "What kind of recovery center? What's wrong with her and how can I get in touch with her?"

"Contact is forbidden during the first week of treatment. She has authorized me to tell you she checked herself in for postpartum depression."

"I knew it. I should've seen the signs sooner." Jade looked up to see Wes standing in the kitchen doorway.

She covered the phone with her hand. "It's Liv's attorney. He says she's in a treatment center."

"Where?" Wes asked, avoiding all eye contact with the three tiny faces fixated on him.

Jade shrugged and uncovered the phone. "Can you at least tell me where she is?"

"She asked me not to. I can tell you that I met with her yesterday and she has granted you temporary guardianship and power of attorney until she is able to return."

"Yesterday? That means she must be close. Unless she flew there. Then in that case—"

"Ms. Scott, please refrain from trying to contact your sister. Even if you called every PPD treatment center in the country, legally they are unable to acknowledge her residency. You'd be wasting your time and theirs."

"But she does plan on coming home." Wes crossed the room to her, every bit as eager for the answer as she was.

"Most definitely. Your guardianship is a temporary solution to an unfortunate situation. If it's any consolation, this isn't the first time I have had a client with PPD. They've all recovered, but the length of time in which that happens varies from person to person. Your sister's situation is more unique because of the donor aspect and the fact she's dealing with triplets. Considering the role you played in their births, I have to ask… are you prepared to be their guardian?"

Jade squeezed her eyes shut and exhaled slowly. "Without a doubt, but do those documents allow me to take them to California?"

"California? Part of your sister's recovery involves

exposure therapy and a slow reintegration back into their lives. You and the children need to be available for all family sessions."

"That's further proof she's someplace relatively close."

Jacob cleared his throat. "Ms. Scott, you have to remain in Saddle Ridge. I hope you can make the necessary arrangements. Your sister's counting on you."

"I refuse to allow those children to go with anyone else." She wasn't sure how she'd make it work, but she didn't have a choice.

"I'll need you to stop by my office to go over these documents. Are you available around two this afternoon?"

"I'll be there."

Jade's body went numb as she hung up the phone. Her sister was safe, but unreachable. Now she was responsible for her biological children. Children she already felt too attached to.

"What did he say?"

"Not a lot except Liv is in an undisclosed postpartum depression—PPD as he called it—treatment facility and she'll be there for at least thirty days, if not more. He has guardianship and power of attorney papers waiting for me. Apparently, he met with Liv yesterday, so I'm assuming she came in to see him, although I guess he could have gone to wherever she is. He told me I have to stay in town so Liv can have visitation with the girls."

"That means she's close and this will be over soon." Relief swept across his face and it prickled her a bit, even though she felt the same way. They were both thinking too much about protecting themselves and not about what was best for the girls.

"I should do some shopping after the attorney's office." Jade slid onto the chair closest to Audra. She lightly squeezed the infant's chubby little toes. "I wasn't prepared to stay here for a week, let alone a month. I only packed a few things and most of Liv's prepregnancy clothes are too tight on me."

"I want to help in whatever way I can, but I can't stick around for the entire month. I have to get back to my job in Texas."

"And I have a job waiting for me in California. Correction…a business that I happen to own and June is our busiest month. Never mind all the planning that goes into each event or the millions of dollars we pay our vendors. Because you are so right, bouncing around on top of a bull for eight seconds is much more important. I don't expect anything from you past this upcoming week. And honestly, it doesn't even sound like you'll be around much anyway."

"Is this how it's going to be? Your job is more important than mine?" Wes kept his voice low. "We need to work together, not fight. I realize it's difficult to put the past aside. I also realize I need to remain a stranger in the girls' lives. Liv wanted you to be their aunt. She never wanted me to be a father beyond their creation. Once this is over, I don't plan on seeing them again. I won't be returning to Saddle Ridge."

"You're never coming back?" The thought alone sent her into a slight panic. "What about your family?"

"They are more than welcome to visit me in Texas. I have a small house down there with a guest room."

"That's it? You've already decided?"

He jammed his hands in his pockets. "I can't put myself or them through it. The more they see of me, the more questions they'll ask later."

Jade knew he was right, she'd just hated the thought of him walking away from his hometown forever. Not that she should care. But Wes had deep roots in Saddle Ridge. Something her damaged past never allowed her to have. He belonged near family. And Liv belonged near her. There was nothing tying her sister to Montana and Jade genuinely believed Liv would be happier in California. "I hate to ask you this, but since Maddie's at work, I really need you to babysit them this afternoon while I run into town. I promise not to be long."

Wes's cheeks puffed out and for a second she thought he'd give her an argument. "Do what you have to do." He strode across the kitchen and grabbed a bottle of pop from the fridge as his mini fan club watched from the table. Jade already saw little bits of him in Hadley. Especially her stubbornness. "Something's been bothering me all night. Didn't Liv have a baby shower?"

Jade nodded. "It wasn't that big though. I'm assuming you know her circle of friends. You, Maddie and Delta are the closest to her. Or at least you were until you moved away. And Delta's been battling cancer for the past few months. I don't even think she was at the shower. Liv has a few friends in town and some from her old job, but now that she works from home and her company is based out of Nebraska, she doesn't have the comradery she used to have. She made a lot of major life changes since she and Kevin divorced."

"Thanks for squeezing that subtle guilt trip in there." Wes braved a glance at the triplets, but his face showed zero emotion. How could he not smile when he looked at them? "What I was trying to get at, don't women usually receive baby swings and all sorts of big items at their showers? My sister-in-law had a huge baby registry. Aside from what you showed me in the closet, I don't see any other gifts in the house."

"I bought her the car seats and a triplet stroller along with a monthly diaper subscription. Her friends gave her gifts, but there was never a swing. Aren't they too small for them?"

"Are you kidding me?" Wes sat his drink on the counter. "I bought Belle this awesome Bluetooth infant seat that swings and rocks, mimicking the mother's movements. You can control it from your phone and adjusts in multiple positions so they can sleep, play, eat...you name it. I even gave one to Dylan's fiancée, Emma, for their new daughter. Here—" Wes tugged his phone out of the front pocket of his jeans and tapped the screen. "This is the video I took the other day of my nephew Travis—Belle and Harlan's kid—in his."

"Wow. He looks so much like the girls. Especially Mackenzie." Jade looked from the phone to the triplets who remained entranced by the man continuing to ignore them. Wes growled under his breath and Jade returned her attention to the large automated infant seat. "That looks really nice. The girls would love that. Where can I order one or three?"

Wes took the phone from her. "I got it covered." He tapped the screen again. "What's the address here? I can never remember the house number."

"You don't have to do that. They look expensive." For a man who claimed he didn't want kids, Wes certainly knew his way to an infant's heart.

"I can afford it." A hint of annoyance evident in his

tone. "It's something I should have done months ago. Liv was my best friend and I never even bought her a baby gift. Regardless of my part in this, I shouldn't have shut her out the way I did."

"Seventy-five."

"Seventy-five what?"

"You asked the house number. Seventy-five Brookstone Lane."

"Oh." He entered the address into his phone. "I was expecting another guilt trip. My mistake."

"Let's just say I was silently agreeing with you and leave it at that."

"Fair enough. Unfortunately, I can't get next day air shipping since today is Friday, but they will be here on Monday."

"When do you go to South Dakota?" Not that she cared what he did. She hated to admit it, but last night she'd felt more comfortable with him there. A floor separated them and they had barely said a word to one another after he agreed to stay. Regardless, she'd worried a little less. Then again, she probably would have felt the same way if Maddie had stayed over. And since she had volunteered, maybe that was a better idea.

"Tuesday evening. I will be back sometime on Thursday. Don't forget I have two christenings tomorrow, a family celebration tomorrow night and a prewedding party on Sunday. I don't expect to be around much during the day."

"About that. I may have overreacted. You're home for such a short time and this is a special week for your family. You should be with them. Especially since you don't plan on coming back to Saddle Ridge. Maybe it is best if I hire someone."

Wes stared at her, causing her to shift uncomfortably. Sarcasm or some other retort would have been better than nothing. With Maddie around at night, she'd only need help during the day. Possibly even two people, since she needed time to work. There had to be a nanny service nearby where she could hire someone reliable and less…less Wes. She didn't want to like him, but after their talk last night and his infant seat gesture, she found herself doing just that. Although she owed him an apology of her own after what she did to him in school. "About last night—"

"I thought you didn't want a stranger around." Wes's tone bordered on accusatory.

"Only because I didn't want to explain Liv's absence. The guardianship papers make it legal and I don't have to worry what anyone else thinks. Not that I want my sister's personal problems broadcast around town." Although people might be more sympathetic to postpartum depression than Liv skipping out on her babies for a month because of a job.

"What are you going to say when someone asks where she is?"

"I don't want to lie. It makes things more complicated. I'm sure she assumed people would find out the truth. A thirty-day absence is hard to hide."

The girls finished their bottles, and she rinsed out each of the plastic liners before tossing them in the trash. She'd learned her lesson yesterday after the garbage can stunk to high heaven. The liners were more trouble than they were worth. She'd use regular bottles for their next feeding.

"I don't know how I'm supposed to feel about any of this."

Jade turned off the faucet and dried her hands before facing him. "You and me both. I think it was a mistake to involve you. I should've thought it through. Hell, I should've thought everything through." Jade prided herself on efficiently moving from one thing to another. That principle worked great in business, not so much in her personal life. "It bothers me that my sister was so emotionally distraught she had to abandon her kids in order to get help. You're telling me what you should've done for her and I'm thinking to myself how wonderful I thought I'd been by donating my eggs and enduring all the hormone injections and doctor visits. My body was bruised and my mood swings and hot flashes triggered by the hormones almost caused my entire team to quit. Never mind all the time I had to take off work."

"I had no idea it was that involved. My part was over in—well, you know." A tinge of pink creeped up his neck as he quickly reached for his drink.

"Despite my research, it had been more involved than I'd ever imagined. But she called me a hero for doing it and kept thanking me for the sacrifice." Jade lifted Hadley into her arms. "I thought I'd been this great sister by taking off even more time for the delivery, plus all the things I'd purchased for Liv and the girls. I was so busy congratulating myself, I missed the obvious. I should have been more aware of her needs and made sure she had the proper help. And I shouldn't have left so soon after the girls came home from the hospital."

"If she didn't want Maddie's help, what makes you think she would've welcomed someone else's?"

"Because Liv had talked about hiring a nanny once

she went back to work, even though she was working from home. I can appreciate why she wouldn't want a nanny during those initial bonding months, but the point is I hadn't noticed a problem because I was too busy trying to escape."

Wes exhaled a slow breath and stared at Audra. She met his gaze and held the stare. And then smiled.

"Oh my God, did you see that?" Wes laughed. "She smiled. She actually smiled."

"Or she has gas. Either way, that's the first time I've seen any of them make that face. I think she likes you."

"Yeah, well." Wes cradled the back of Audra's head and scooped her into his arms. "Don't get attached to me, kid." He sat in the chair across from Jade and slowly rocked the infant. "I sympathize with your guilt. I'm sure Maddie does, too. But from what I've read on the postpartum depression websites, a lot of women try their hardest to cover up how they're really feeling because they don't want anyone to know they're not bonding with their children."

"And many times they are crying for help and nobody's listening." She had replayed every phone and video conversation over in her head last night and one thing stuck out more than anything else... Jade had purposely kept the calls short. She had made one work excuse after another to get off the phone, ignoring her sister's needs.

"You can analyze it to death, but it won't change anything. All we can do is accept what's in front of us and take it day by day. As much as I want to walk away, I can't. Whether we like it or not, we're a temporary team."

Jade hated temporary. The first sixteen years of her

life had been filled with temporary. Temporary meant loss. And nine times out of ten, loss brought pain along for the ride. Even if she left tomorrow, there would be pain. As unconventional as they were, sitting around the kitchen table and holding the daughters they'd created felt natural on some alternate plane. If her heart wasn't ready to let go now, how would it ever be ready in a month?

Wes had never been more terrified in his entire life. He thought he could handle being alone in the house with Hadley, Audra and Mackenzie, but he'd underestimated their cuteness factor. Jade had tried to put them down for a nap before she left, but they were having none of it. So Wes relented to baby playtime on the mat in the center of the living room. Thank God they were too young to roll over and crawl away giving him some semblance of control. Gripping his finger was one thing. Gripping his heart was altogether different.

He checked the wall clock. Jade had only been gone for fifteen minutes. That was barely enough time to get to the attorney's office. He groaned. And she was clothes shopping afterward…he was doomed.

Mackenzie intently watched the musical, plush butterfly mobile he had set up over their play mat. Jade hadn't been kidding when she said Travis and Mackenzie looked alike. They were cousins, born days apart from one another, yet they would never know it. Wes choked down the unfamiliar lump in his throat. The startling realization that Travis and the triplets would be in the same grade, possibly even the same class all through school sucker punched him in the gut.

"How did I miss that before?" If they looked alike

now, he could only imagine the resemblance as they got older. People were sure to question it. Jade had already asked Liv to move to California. Somehow he needed to convince them both that was the best thing for all of them. Then maybe he could visit his family freely again. Although in the back of his mind, he already knew he would forever associate Saddle Ridge with the three girls he would never see after this week.

Wes's eyes began to tear. "How could you do this to me?" he asked the triplets. "You weren't supposed to be cute. You weren't even supposed to let me like you. How can I not like you? Have you looked in the mirror?" Audra smiled again as if she understood. "You're adorable. I see a lot of your mom in you. I guess I shouldn't call her your mom since Liv gave birth to you. She's your mom. But your aunt Jade, she's a special woman. She went through a lot to help bring you into this world. And your mom, she's going through a lot too. But when she comes home, she'll be better than ever." At least he hoped so.

He couldn't help but have the same fears Jade had. What if Liv relapsed? What if raising triplets on her own proved to be too much? Jade's lifestyle and work schedule didn't mesh well with raising children. She'd even admitted to not wanting kids of her own. And neither did he. But once he retired from bull riding next year wouldn't he have the time for a family?

Wes rocked back on his heels. What the hell was he thinking? He'd never planned on having kids and even if he had, his daughters weren't his to raise. Liv didn't want him parenting her children. She'd made that painfully clear when she proposed the idea. Up until that point, he had only casually mentioned not wanting kids. So when Liv became adamant about him not being in the girls' lives, it hurt. Not because he wanted to be a father. But because she thought so little of him. The fact she had been hurt and shocked when he moved away had surprised him. How could she have expected them to stay friends? In the back of his mind, he'd wondered if Liv would try to rekindle her relationship with Kevin once the babies were born. Even more reason for her to be happy he was gone. The Liv he knew had become a walking contradiction.

Wes ran his fingers lightly over the bottoms of Audra's feet. "Are you ticklish yet?" Her big blue eyes reflected innocence at its purest. "There's a big world out there waiting for you to conquer it." Her little legs kicked, and he noticed her foot was marker free. "Did your aunt Jade finally figure out how to tell you apart? I always knew. Yes, I did." He lifted her into his arms. "And I'll always remember you as being my first daughter to smile at me."

A tear rolled down his cheek, and he quickly wiped it away. Contrary to what his former ex-best friend thought, Wes enjoyed being around kids. He adored Harlan's eight-year-old daughter, Ivy, and a good 50 percent of his job at the rodeo school in Texas involved him training young children to compete.

Liv had insulted him when she'd assumed it wouldn't bother him to run into his own kids. If that hadn't screamed how she really saw him, he didn't know what would. In hindsight, that should have been his sign to turn Liv down. If she had used an anonymous donor, they could have stayed friends after he moved. Instead he chose to sacrifice it all to give his friend what she wanted most in this world. A known biological father to her children, even though he was technically unnamed.

None of what he did changed how much he hated the idea of marriage and settling down. That had more to do with his parents' dysfunctional marriage. A detail his brothers managed to leave out whenever they remembered the good times. A fight usually followed every one of those good times. Ironically, the only brother who understood was the one who had killed their father.

"You're going to have the best life. Even if I can't be here to see it, I'll make sure you're okay. Better than okay. Think of me as your fairy godfather. I'll always watch over you."

As the girls began to fall asleep, Wes attempted to figure out the logistical nightmare of getting three infants off the floor and down the hall into their bassinets. "How did Liv do this?"

He wished he had thought to bring the car seats in from the mudroom. It would have made baby transport much easier. That reminded him. He needed to install the car seat bases into Jade's rental car. Would they all fit side by side? Two yes, three…no way. Liv had talked about leasing a large SUV but he didn't know what she had eventually chosen.

He tugged out his phone and one-hand typed a quick text message to Jade.

Swing by rental car company after attorney. Need a larger vehicle to fit three infant seats in one row.

Since he wouldn't be around much this weekend, he wanted Jade prepared for any emergency. She and

Maddie didn't need to fumble with fastening the seats into two cars if the unexpected happened. He'd take the vehicle down to the sheriff's department and have Harlan or one of the other deputies double-check he'd installed the seats properly. Besides, it would give him a chance to explain his disappearance to his brothers. By now they had probably assumed he was shacked up with one of his old girlfriends while he was in town. If it hadn't been for Jade, he would've been. Unfortunately, for the past two nights, she'd taken center stage in his dreams.

That wouldn't have been a bad thing if he hadn't still resented her for the pain she'd caused him in school. He understood her reason now, and he felt horrible for the role he had played, but it hadn't lessened the damage she'd done. He had been beaten up many times in the locker room after she'd spread around that he had used her as a front because he was gay. The rumor had followed him on the high school rodeo circuit and home. While his brothers only ribbed him about it in the beginning, his father had taken the rumor as gospel and had berated him daily. Her lie had made it impossible for a friend of his to come out because he feared the same treatment from their classmates. Her cruelty had affected far more than just his life. The sad part was, he had started their feud.

After opting to use the bouncy chairs, he successfully made it into the downstairs nursery. Then a whiff of something rotten almost caused him to gag. "What is that?" He covered his nose. "Did something crawl in here and die?" He quickly scanned the room and inspected each crib. "I can't leave you girls in here." He slid their bouncy chairs into the hallway and the odor followed them. Hadley kicked her little legs and made a sour face. "Is that smell coming from you?" He leaned closer and gave her the stiff test, almost passing out in the process. "Oh, that's just not right. How can someone so small and beautiful smell so rotten?"

After changing Hadley's diaper, he decided he'd be proactive and change the other two, just in case. By the time he'd settled them down for a nap, he needed one himself. He also needed to fumigate the room. Located in the back corner of the house, the nursery's open windows offered a nice cross breeze. Northwest Montana got hot in the summer, but most of the time they didn't need to run air-conditioning.

Unwilling to leave them alone in the room, Wes eased into the antique rocking chair in the corner. He ran his hands over the worn wood. He had been with Liv when she stumbled upon it at the county yard sale. He never imagined sitting in it and watching his children sleep. Now he didn't want the moment to end.

Chapter 5

Other than the few minutes he'd spent with Jade when she returned from the attorney's office yesterday, he hadn't seen her or the girls. Maddie had stepped in his place as soon as she'd gotten off work last night. He hadn't even been able to say goodbye when he dropped off Jade's new rental SUV after he had the car seats inspected at the sheriff's department. He'd phoned Jade twice, but she kept reiterating she had it covered and she didn't need him. Once again, he felt cut out of the triplets' lives. And while that had been the original plan, he didn't like it so much now.

Watching Harlan and Dylan stand up as godfather for each other's children left him a little sad and lonely. Three of his brothers had kids—five among them— yet they'd never asked him to be a godfather. Dylan and Garrett had done it twice. That just showed how his brothers saw him. He guessed he couldn't blame them. His reputation had been far from stellar and he had begun to distance himself from them after their father's death. They were always cordial to each other and even joked around some, but the closeness they had once shared continued to fade. Harlan had made more of an effort recently, but now it was too late for Wes to stay in Saddle Ridge. Even if he wanted to be the girls' father, Liv didn't want that. And he couldn't risk his heart breaking every time he ran into them.

When he had stood in the church earlier, he envisioned Audra, Hadley and Mackenzie's christening. Who would be their godparents? He assumed Jade, but who else? And why was he jealous of a man he didn't even know. Did Liv even plan on having them christened? Maybe they had been already. As much as he wanted to know the answers, he knew he had no right to them. And that stung. His brain wanted him to admit that Jade was doing the right thing by keeping him away, but his heart told him otherwise.

"Okay." Harlan wrapped an arm around Wes's shoulder and steered him away from the other christening guests mingling around the Silver Bells Ranch. "It's time you tell me what's really going on."

"What are you talking about?" Wes attempted to shrug him off, but his brother refused to lessen his grip.

"For starters, you showed up without a date. You rarely come to dinner without one, let alone a big event. And something seemed off with that whole car seat situation yesterday."

And here Wes had thought his brother would commend him for putting the children's safety first. "I told you the truth. Liv's sister is here watching the kids."

"I get that. But why isn't Jade using Liv's car and where is Liv anyway?"

Wes faced his brother. "Look, if I tell you, I don't want it to go any further. Not that it won't be public knowledge at some point anyway. For now, I'd appreciate you keeping this quiet."

For the next half hour, Wes explained the circumstances surrounding Liv's disappearance, conveniently leaving out his role in the triplets' parentage. "And because of my friendship with Liv, Jade asked me for some help. Now that she knows her sister is safe, she's trying to make the best of a very difficult situation. I'm here, so I agreed to pitch in whenever she needs me."

"After Molly walked out on me and Ivy, I had questioned if she had postpartum depression and if I had missed it."

"Wasn't Ivy a year old?"

"If untreated, it can manifest into other disorders. When Molly finally returned, she told me how unhappy she had been in our marriage and that she hadn't been prepared to have a child. To this day I still wonder if PPD played a part in her disappearance. And she had disappeared just like Liv. Only Molly was gone for years. Liv had the sense of mind to get help."

"But Molly's fine now, right?" Ivy's mother had popped back into their lives last year shortly after Harlan and Belle's wedding. Liv's baby drama had just begun to grab hold of Wes at the time and he had selfishly ignored what was going on in everybody else's lives.

"Molly's great. Her relationship with Ivy is still strained, but she missed seven years of her daughter's life. It's a work in progress. And I can't say for sure that she had PPD. I don't think she could, either. But I can tell you Liv is not alone. I've gone on more than a few calls relating to the baby blues as some people ignorantly refer to them. The baby blues and postpartum depression are two different things."

"I saw that mentioned on a few websites too. I watched the girls alone for a few hours when Jade met with the attorney yesterday, and it was overwhelming to say the least."

"I think it's hard for people who've never carried a child—both men and women—to understand all the changes a woman's body goes through postpregnancy. Physical and emotional. Personally, I find the entire process fascinating and beautiful. Granted, I haven't always felt that way. I made a point to be home for a month after Travis was born so I have a better appreciation for it this time around. I can thank Molly for that."

"I didn't realize you and your ex had become such good friends." Wes hated the growing distance between him and his brothers. He and Harlan especially. Wes was a little less than a year older and they'd always been close. But ever since Ryder accidentally killed their father, he'd found it next to impossible to escape their family's dysfunctional past. His brothers' memories differed widely from his because they'd either chosen to ignore it or they'd been that oblivious. Ryder had understood. Until the night he'd made the Slade family the talk of the town. Now that distance seemed impossible to close.

"I don't think Molly and I will ever be good friends." Harlan laughed. "Let's just say we have a newfound respect for one another. She pointed out how absent I had been when she had Ivy. Liv carried triplets, almost to term if memory serves me correctly. Her body alone had a lot to recover from. It's too bad she didn't have a partner supporting her through all of this. Kevin would have made a great dad if he hadn't turned out to be such a jackass."

"She definitely loved him." Wes grabbed two beers from an ice-filled horse trough and handed Harlan one.

"He loved her, just not enough." Harlan twisted the cap off his beer. "He's getting married sometime next month."

"You're kidding." Wes had only been gone for six months and the Kevin he knew had been loving the single life when he ran into him on New Year's Eve. "To who?"

"Some woman from Kalispell. I haven't met her personally, but I hear she's nice. She has a couple kids from a previous marriage."

Wes froze, the bottle halfway to his mouth. "Wait a minute. That SOB divorced Liv because he didn't want to raise another man's kid and he's marrying someone with kids?" Wes had to tell Jade.

"Yep." Harlan took a long tug of his beer. "In all fairness to Kevin, I think there's a difference between watching your wife carry and give birth to a stranger's child versus coming into the picture years after the fact."

"Still, that had to have hit Liv hard. You wouldn't happen to know when they got engaged, do you?"

Harlan removed his hat and wiped his brow with the back of his arm. "Not sure, but I received the wedding invite probably a month ago. I'm surprised you didn't get one. They just about invited the entire town. I think it's still in the envelope it came in. I can check the postmark when I get home. You think this was a trigger, don't you?"

"Amongst other things." Wes had read the risk for postpartum depression increased when the woman had a weak support system, had difficulty in breast-feeding, relationship problems and stressful events in their life. Those are just the things Wes knew Liv had battled. He loved his friend dearly, but she wasn't ready to be a single parent. And certainly not a single parent of three children. He should have said no. "Excuse me for a second while I call Jade and fill her in."

"Fine, but don't run off somewhere tonight." Harlan clapped him on the back. "We have a lot of celebrating to do and you're a part of it. You've been gone for too long. It hasn't been the same around here without you."

Wes's head started to pound with guilt. He doubted Dylan or Garrett would take the time to visit him in Texas. He could already hear the excuses about how they were too busy running Silver Bells. Even though Harlan had stuck his head in the sand right beside their brothers, he desperately tried to keep what was left of their family together. Surely Harlan, Belle and the kids would spend the holidays with him in Texas. Of course, it wouldn't be every year, but maybe every other one. Despite the past, his chest ached, already longing for the family events he'd miss.

"I didn't want to say anything earlier in front of Dylan and Garrett because I was afraid it would start an argument, but where's Mom?" She hadn't visited after either of Holly's or Travis's birth and now she'd missed the christenings. "This is the first time in years that all of us are together and she can't drag herself away from her new family and precious California to see us. Ryder killed Dad. Why is she punishing us?"

Wes competed in the Golden State a few times a year, and during the rare times his mother made an appearance at one of his events, she brought along her new husband and his adult children. What should have been a nice visit always turned into Wes feeling like an outsider with his own mother.

"We asked her to come and Dylan sent her a wedding invite. She responded tentatively. Considering she missed this weekend, I'd wager a guess that she'll miss the wedding next Saturday." Harlan turned away and watched Belle sitting under one of the ranch's shade trees breast-feeding Travis. She caught his gaze and smiled. Their love for one another radiated across the pasture. Wes had been so hell-bent on never getting himself tied down, that he hadn't given much thought to the sweeter side of marriage. He'd never even come close to that level of commitment with anyone.

"You're a lucky man." Jade's face clouded his vision. No! Jade would not become the first, either. He took a swig of beer. "Let me make this call and I'll catch up with you in a minute."

"Sure thing." Harlan's eyes remained transfixed on Belle as he hopped the top fence rail and walked toward his wife and baby. A love like that was rare. Just because three of his brothers had stumbled upon it over the past year didn't mean anything. They were meant to be family men. He wasn't.

He pulled Jade's number up on his phone and tapped the Call button, praying she'd shoot him straight to voice mail.

"Hello?" Her voice, sultry and deep, reverberated

in his ear. Good Lord! One word, two syllables and he was already a goner.

"It's Wes. I'm sure you're busy, but I had to tell you what I just heard about Kevin."

"Kevin? As in my sister's Kevin?"

"As in someone else's Kevin. He's getting remarried. The invites went out about a month ago."

Jade sighed through the phone. "That had to have stung. I wonder why Maddie didn't mention it."

"Maddie moved to town after the divorce. She doesn't know Kevin and I doubt Liv would have mentioned the wedding to her."

"I wish she had confided in me."

"If I hadn't left, I'm positive she'd have told me." Wes chose his next words carefully, not wanting Jade to feel bad about her strained relationship with Liv. "The circumstances surrounding my friendship with your sister leant itself to many all-night discussions about her ex and my family. I moved away, but I should have stayed in contact with her. I own that. That being said, I think this goes beyond Kevin getting married again. His fiancée has kids, so—"

"That jerk!" Jade shouted into the phone. "So he'll be their stepfather."

"You see where I'm going with this, right?"

"My poor sister. She battled everything silently. I shouldn't be surprised. She always has."

"What do you mean?" Once again, the Liv who'd been his friend for almost five years and Jade's version of the same woman were two very different people. She'd been raw and honest, and their talks had been extremely therapeutic and cathartic. If something had bothered her, she'd told him.

"We bounced around a lot when we were kids. Whenever our mom got out of jail and claimed us—" Jade snorted "—as if we were a piece of luggage, Liv became the parent. Constantly babysitting Mom and trying to keep us safe. Between cleaning up drug paraphernalia and hiding our mother's own money so she couldn't blow it all, she took the brunt of the abuse. But I never heard her complain. Not once."

"No child should ever be subjected to that."

"Just like no teenager should have endured the teasing you did because of me. I didn't want to do this over the phone, but I can't wait any longer to apologize to you. I'm sorry."

"That's it? That's all you have to say?" Wes turned away from prying eyes and walked toward the stables as he fought to keep his voice low despite the resentment bubbling beneath the surface. "I understand your grudge against me and I admit, I was wrong to do what I did. But, sweetheart, what you did was a lot more than teasing. You telling everyone I was gay not only got me beat up at school, it followed me on the rodeo circuit and home. Dammit!" Wes tripped and caught himself before he hit the ground. He couldn't walk as fast as he wanted to run. Hell, he wanted to fly far and fast. He unlatched the tack room door and swung it wide. Cradling his phone between his chin and shoulder, he grabbed a saddle and blanket off the wall racks.

"Wes, I—"

"My father looked at me with disgust." Wes interrupted whatever excuse she had in her arsenal. He had to finally tell her how she'd ruined his life. "I won't repeat some of the names he called me, but your little game incited fights at home. Not only between me and my dad. But between my parents because my mom defended me. My dad could be a loving man, but he could also be a bigot. You have no idea what that did to us. What *you* did to us."

"I didn't—" Jade swore under her breath. "I never told anyone you were gay."

"The hell you didn't."

"Wes, please hear me out," Jade pleaded.

Wes held the phone from his ear, tempted to hang up.

"Wes?"

"Fine." He had no idea what compelled him to give her a chance to explain, because there couldn't possibly be any justification for her cruelty. "Go for it."

Jade sighed heavily. "I was labeled a slut after you told everyone we had slept together. After everything I'd been through, that really hurt. Here I was the new kid and I already had a reputation for something I didn't do. One afternoon when I was changing for gym class a few girls started calling me names. I wasn't going to take that, so I stood up for myself and I told them we never slept together, and that you had broken up with me because I wasn't your type."

Wes scoffed. He didn't even know what his type was back then. "That's not what I heard."

"I know. One of the girls had twisted my words and inferred that I was saying you were gay. All I wanted to do was get out of that damn locker room, so I didn't respond. By the end of class, the rumor had spread and instead of correcting it and telling everyone that wasn't what I'd meant, I said nothing." Her voice broke. "My silence perpetuated the rumor and for that I'm truly sorry. If I had known what was going on with you at home, I swear I would have been there telling your father it wasn't true."

Tension eased from his jaw as the anger began to slip away. "Even after what I had done to you?"

"Yes. No one deserves what you endured." Her voice soft, barely above a whisper. "My assistant and truly my best friend, Tomás, is gay. He's told me some horrific stories about how he'd been treated when people learned of his sexuality. I would never wish that on my worst enemy. I'm sorry. I realize that doesn't mean much today, but, Wes, I am so sorry for not setting the record straight from the beginning."

For years, he had wanted to rip into Jade and tell her exactly how he felt. To force her to see how bullying affects not only the person being bullied, but everyone around them. While she was wrong to let the rumor get out of hand, he was just as much to blame. He'd lied and told one person they'd slept together, and she'd paid a steep price. If he'd kept his mouth shut and his pride at bay, she'd never have been in the position to defend herself and the escalation wouldn't have happened. They'd both suffered greatly at the hands of the other.

"Wes, are you still there?"

He entered Bonsai's stall, and rested his head against the quarter horse's neck. The animal bobbed his head and nickered, welcoming the human contact.

"Honestly, Jade, I get it. I know all too well how easy it is to lose control of a situation. I also need to accept my part in this. What was it we learned in physics class? For every action there is an equal and opposite reaction. I don't know if you'll ever be able to forgive me. I certainly don't expect it, but I—" Wes swallowed hard at the words he never thought he'd say.

"I forgive you. I think we need to put our resentment aside and end this here."

Silence echoed through the phone for a long moment before she spoke. "End this? You make it sound like we won't see you again."

"You made it very clear last night and earlier when I called that I'm not needed. The girls are in very capable hands. But I wish you had come to this realization before you involved me in their lives. I can't unsee what I've already seen. I can't unfeel what's already in my heart."

"You need to spend time with your family. I believe that even more now than I did before. And I'm sorry for getting you involved, but come on, Wes, we were already involved. Who else could I have turned to? You were the only person who knew everything."

"Almost everything. I didn't know about you."

"And your reaction to the news was justified. You told me your initial connection to my sister was misery loves company. I can relate. I didn't want to be alone. I wanted someone who understood. Someone in the same position I'm in. Maddie—" Jade lowered her voice to a whisper. "She's a great help, but she doesn't get it the way you do. I saw that you were struggling with this so I set you free. I don't know what the right thing to do is."

"The right thing is to say goodbye." Wes blinked away the moisture forming in his eyes as he smoothed the saddle blanket over Bonsai's back. "It's better this way."

"Wes—" Her voice was barely audible.

"Goodbye, Jade." Wes disconnected the call and turned off his phone before shoving it in his pocket. He lifted the saddle on the horse and tightened the cinch straps. Nothing cleared a man's mind like being alone with his horse. And since his Tango was in Texas, his uncle's beloved horse was the perfect stand in.

He slid his boot in the stirrup and swung his other leg up over the saddle. He took the reins and exhaled, already feeling like he'd made the right decision to walk away.

A few days ago he'd been itching to jump on the next plane out of town. Now the thought left him empty. He wanted to see his brothers' children grow up. To be there for their birthdays, Thanksgiving, Christmas or whatever special event they had going on. But in doing so, he'd see Audra, Hadley and Mackenzie. He'd have to. He wouldn't be able to stay away and he didn't want to confuse them. He needed to stay anonymous, for their sake and his.

The house was quiet except for the sound of Jade's fingers tapping on her laptop keyboard. The girls had a 2:00 a.m. feeding a little over an hour ago and had fallen asleep shortly afterward. Even with Maddie's help, Jade struggled to get work done. Two days had passed since she'd last spoke with Wes, three days since she'd seen him. It felt more like a month. She'd promoted Tomás, giving him authority to run the office and hire two more employees. They'd lost a couple lucrative clients over the weekend because Jade wasn't personally there to oversee their event planning. No amount of video chats made up for one-on-one client relations. Tomás was good, probably even better than she was at the job. She had faith in him.

She'd confided in him about how she had severely

affected Wes's life. And Tomás pulled no punches when he told Jade that her silence had been just as damaging as if she had actually said the words. He also told her to forgive herself. She laughed at the mere thought. Forgiveness had to be earned and she'd done nothing to deserve it.

Jade slammed her laptop closed and spun around in Liv's übercomfortable office chair. Her purse and keys hung on the door handle, mocking her. She hadn't left the house since her trip to the attorney's office on Friday. Three days. Well, technically four since the night had already crossed into Tuesday. She'd never been that reclusive. Not even when she had the flu last year. She wanted to go for a ride. Not a long one. Just long enough to feel like she'd really gotten out of the house. What if Maddie woke up? What if the girls woke up? And what if they didn't?

Jade grabbed her bag and tiptoed to the back door before she realized Maddie's car blocked hers in the driveway. Crap! Normally she parked at her own house next door, but Maddie had gone grocery shopping after work and it had been easier to park closer and carry the bags into the house. She turned to head back into the office when she noticed Maddie's car keys on the counter. She could move the car, or…she could borrow it. It was borrowing, right? After all, it would be more responsible of her to leave behind the vehicle with the infant seats in case of an emergency.

Okay, logic aside, she was about to steal Maddie's car. The need for an escape—however brief—won out. Was this how Liv had felt? Walking out the door was simple when you were alone. She couldn't imagine doing it with three little ones in tow. She still hadn't taken the girls out of the house. That probably wasn't healthy. This was why she needed a nanny. Unfortunately, finding one qualified enough to care for multiples had been challenging. They were in high demand.

Jade removed a pad from the kitchen drawer, wrote Maddie a note and left it on the counter along with the keys to the SUV…just in case she woke up. Easing the door closed behind her, Jade practically skipped down the drive. She glanced up at the nursery window, guilt weighing heavy on her chest. Jade never felt guilty for anything. She was cutthroat in business and her personal life. Yet she'd been back in Saddle Ridge for less than a week and she'd worn guilt like a push-up bra. And it was every bit as restrictive and uncomfortable.

Five minutes into her escape, Jade realized she was on her way to the Silver Bells Ranch. It was the middle of the night—correction, it was the wee hours of the morning and she had no idea where Wes even stayed on the ranch. For all she knew, he could have left early for South Dakota.

Doubt aside, Jade pulled onto the main ranch road. Except for the other day when she'd first confronted Wes, she hadn't been there before. The full moon glinted off the roof of the picturesque three-story log lodge reminiscent of a Thomas Kinkade painting. Beautiful as it was, it didn't take her breath away like the cowboy walking out the front door did. Jade froze, framing Wes in her headlights. Broad shoulders, lean waist, long legs. No man should look that good. He approached the car and tapped on the passenger window.

"Are you looking for the Silver Bells Ranch lodge?" he asked as she reluctantly lowered the window. "Jade, what are you doing here?"

She groaned, uncertain of the answer herself.

"Is this Maddie's car?"

He leaned in the window, close enough for her to smell the sharp, clean scent of soap. Had he just showered? Maybe he was returning from a tryst with a ranch guest. She felt heat rise to her cheeks and thanked God the car's dark interior shrouded her embarrassment. Why couldn't she have taken a quick drive into town and back?

"Jade?"

She gripped the steering wheel tighter and braved a glance at him. Between his hat and the darkness, she could barely make out his features. "It was the last vehicle in the driveway, so I borrowed it. I have a lot of work ahead of me tonight and I needed to clear my head for a bit. I pulled in here to turn around. I hadn't expected to see you." *Good Lord, why was she rambling?* "What about you? I'm surprised to see you wandering around this late."

"The ranch still isn't operating with a full staff and I'm trying to fill in wherever I can. It makes for long nights." He tried the door handle. "Can you let me in? I wouldn't mind a lift back to my cabin."

"Um, sure." Jade pressed the lock release and he slid in beside her. His bicep brushed against her arm as he set his hat on the dashboard. She now understood the meaning of *compact car*. Mistake number two… she should have flip-flopped vehicles and taken the SUV instead. At least he would've been an arm's length away. "You'll have to tell me where to go."

When he didn't respond, she lifted her gaze to his. The dashboard lights turned his warm hazel eyes a deep, dark chocolate brown, drawing her into their depths. The man was too much, on too many levels. They didn't even like each other, so why the sudden attraction?

Because it wasn't sudden. He had been her first crush fifteen years ago, before he screwed it up. Crush or not, she hadn't been ready for anything sexual back then. She'd spent years hating him, only now she wasn't sure how she felt. Knowing the truth had lessened that hate, if she could even call it hate anymore. That anger had been redirected toward Burke, where it should have been all along. She had no right to feel anything toward Wes except remorse. While she'd endured bullying and slut-shaming for four years, the physical attack had been swift. Wes had endured far more because of her silence.

"I wanted to call you."

Jade rested her head against the seat and laughed. "You're the one who said goodbye."

"That doesn't mean I don't still care."

Jade ignored the sincerity in his voice and shifted the car into Drive. "The girls are fine. I haven't found a nanny yet and there's been no word from Liv or the treatment center."

Wes covered her hand with his. "What about you? How are you doing?"

Jade gripped the gearshift tighter under the heat of his palm. "I, um, I've been busy trying to keep my company going. It's a bit tough to do this far from home."

"I can imagine." He gave her hand a light squeeze before releasing it. "That's quite an operation you have there. I hope you don't mind. I looked you up online."

Nervousness crept into her chest as she shifted the

car back into Park. "Hey, it's fair. You already know I looked you up. I noticed you haven't posted any photos for the past few days."

"I haven't been in the mood. I haven't wanted to do much of anything since…since I last saw you." He hooked her chin with his finger, gently forcing her to turn toward him. "You've been on my mind. Constantly."

"We're enemies," she whispered.

"We were enemies." His breath, warm against her cheek, sent a shiver through her body. "We are so much more than that and as hard as I try, I can't forget the lives we've created together, however unknowingly. We will always have that connection and no one can take that from us."

"Wes." Jade choked back a sob. "There's nothing we can do about it. They aren't ours to keep. As much as I fear my sister won't get better, I have to believe she will. We can't acknowledge that they came from us. And nothing can ever come from that connection. Liv didn't want us to know about the other. It was her secret, and a friendship or whatever is impossible."

"Now we can't even be friends?"

Hurt reflected in his eyes and it took every ounce of restraint she had not to touch him and attempt to ease his pain.

"No. The risk is too high. And it would hurt Liv. I still need to find a way to tell her you've seen the girls and have spent time with them. I'll discuss it with her doctor when I visit her. I think it's a big enough problem to warrant a third party. I can't imagine her not being threatened by it."

"No chance of keeping it secret, huh?"

Jade shook her head. "If I never planned to see her again, then maybe. I can't look at my sister and lie though. The truth would come out eventually."

"Let me ask you something." Wes shifted in his seat and leaned against the door. "Twice now you've mentioned the truth coming out. Were you and Jade planning to tell the girls that you're their biological mother?"

"Possibly. It depends on the situation." It broke her heart knowing the girls might one day learn their mother and aunt had lied to them for years. Regardless of how well-intentioned the lie had been. "There are a number of factors I wish I had considered before agreeing to this. It's been a lot harder than I imagined. For all of us."

"I have an idea, but I want you to hear me out before you say no."

"Okay, should I be worried?" She laughed nervously.

"If you moved to the ranch—"

"Are you insane?" He must be to propose the one thing that would send her sister into orbit. "Absolutely not."

His brow furrowed. "It's a good idea if you'll let me finish."

"Okay." Jade bit back a retort and raised her hands in surrender. "Go ahead."

"You obviously feel isolated at Liv's house because you're driving around in the middle of the night. You don't have a nanny or any other help during the day. Now I may not know of any professional child caregivers, but I can personally vouch for many of the teenagers living on this ranch. I've known them their entire lives from when their parents worked on my father's ranch and then came here. They are home from school for the summer, looking to earn some extra cash. I'm sure one or two of them would be more than happy to give up cleaning guest quarters to help you with the girls. The few I have in mind helped raise their little brothers and sisters so they're not inexperienced."

Hiring them wasn't a bad idea. But move to the ranch? No. "Why can't they come out to the house?"

"Because they don't have cars. They would need someone to transport them back and forth. Their parents work, and it would be too much of a strain on you."

Okay, he had a point there. "Your idea has merit, but I think it's better if I wait and find a professional nanny. I'm flattered, but after the things you said the other day, I'm confused why you're asking me to move in with you?"

"You wouldn't be living with me because I won't be here. I head out to South Dakota tomorrow...well I guess it's already tomorrow, but I'll be back in time for the wedding on Saturday. Then I head home to my job and life in Texas."

Jade's stomach knotted at the thought of him leaving. "Do you have a girlfriend waiting for you there too?"

Wes's features softened as a slow smile eased across his face. "Aw, sweetheart." He ran the back of his fingers lightly down her cheek. "I'm flattered by your jealousy, but I am one hundred percent single."

"I am not jealous." She smacked him away.

"Ouch!" He rubbed his hand. "You're cute when you're riled up."

"You are so asking for it." The man infuriated her more than a bridezilla with a bathroom emergency. He also turned her insides to mush. Only he could make her feel like a lovesick teenager again. Not that she was lovesick. *Love* was *evil* spelled backward...okay...misspelled *evil*. Regardless, it was close enough and she wanted no part of it. Love came with attachments and commitments. She had enough of that at work. She was married to her job and that was all she needed. "You can't just install me in the lodge and leave me with a bunch of strangers."

"I was thinking more along the lines of one of the guesthouses that are not in use. My brothers are still rebuilding Silver Bells. Business is much better than it was a year ago, but we're still not fully booked." Wes ran his hands down his thighs and Jade wondered if he was as nervous as she was. "Of course, I would have to discuss it with them first, but I don't see it being a problem. If you're worried about people gossiping about Liv being in a PPD treatment center, I promise you, my family is not like that. Harlan understood and even enlightened me about a few things."

"You told him?" Jade closed her eyes, silently adding one more item to the list of things she had to tell her sister. "Why did you do that? Liv should have an opportunity to say what she does and doesn't want people to know."

"Harlan didn't give me a choice. He knew something was wrong when I showed up at the sheriff's department with your rental SUV instead of your sister's. I have a hard time lying to my brothers the same way you have a hard time lying to your sister."

"Fine, but I can't move cribs and whatever else I need to your family's ranch."

"We have cribs. Emma—the woman my brother

Dylan is marrying on Saturday—wanted families to think of Silver Bells as a second home when they visited. She personally redecorated a few of the larger guest cabins with mothers in mind. We have five brand-new cribs at the ready. Those particular cabins have full kitchens with dishwashers, washing machines and dryers, guest bedrooms, rocking chairs and all the creature comforts of home."

"Wow." She planned events at guest ranches with similar amenities and they didn't come cheap. "Your brothers must have some budget to do all that."

Wes shook his head. "That was all Emma. She bought into the ranch as did many of our employees over the last six months. Silver Bells was on the verge of bankruptcy after my uncle died. Now it's a thriving family and employee-owned business. It still has a way to go, but it's getting great reviews and by next summer there will be a reservation waiting list."

"The way you speak so proudly of the ranch, I'm surprised you aren't a partner."

Wes rested his arm on the open window frame and stared out the windshield. "They asked me, but I think they felt obligated to. I had to say no anyway."

"Because of Mackenzie, Audra and Hadley?" Jade hated how three innocent children were the cause of so much misery. It wasn't fair.

"They were a part of it, but I had already planned to leave. I see my father wherever I go in this town. Some of those memories are really good and others not so much. I hate Ryder for what he did. And I hate my father for the way he treated me. For the way he treated my mom. I hate my mom for leaving and never coming back. She wasn't even at the christenings. Those are her grandchildren, but she couldn't do it."

Jade reached across the armrest and entwined her fingers with his. "Maybe the pain is too much for her to return. The same way you said it would be too painful for you to come back."

"I've told myself that a thousand times. She's remarried and I'm happy for her. I truly am. And please don't get me wrong, as much as I hate some of the things my family has done, they are still my family and I love them with all my heart. Just like I love Audra, Hadley and Mackenzie."

"I think it's impossible not to." Jade wanted to comfort him...to find comfort in him, but the barriers were too great for her to cross.

"I didn't want to. I tried not to. But the truth is, I loved them the minute Liv showed me the ultrasound. Something changed in me that day and I can't explain it." His fingers tightened around hers. "I realize I hurt your sister by severing all ties with her after that, but I was afraid to stay friends. If that was my reaction to a grainy black-and-white photo, I could only imagine what it would be like seeing them once they were born. Let alone in person. And I was right. They took my breath away. I may be heading back to Texas on Sunday, but I will never be the same after these two weeks."

"Neither will I." Jade released him and covered her face with her hands. The tears she had carefully held in check over the past few months finally broke the dam. "I feel so guilty for regretting my decision to do this. But I would never take it back. I would never trade their lives in for anything."

"I know, honey. I know." Wes wrapped his arm around her shoulders and pulled her to him. "Neither would I."

"How do I do this?" She sobbed against his chest. "And how am I supposed to do it alone?"

"Move in here."

"How can that possibly work? If you see a resemblance between the girls and your nephew, don't you think your family will? Never mind that my sister would freak over the arrangement."

"You're forgetting that one of your sister's best friends is engaged to my brother Garrett. She may notice a resemblance whether you're here or not. Granted your sister had started the process before Delta and Garrett got together so she couldn't have predicted that connection. But she knew about Harlan and Belle's baby because I told her. Harlan told me when Belle was only four weeks along."

"What did she say?" Jade asked against the softness of his shirt.

"She was thrilled for them. A few days later she had our embryos implanted. But she didn't think this through. I have a lot of respect for Liv, but I think she was so in love with the idea of having a baby, she didn't see the whole picture. Like what happens when Travis and her daughters are in the same class together? Someone's bound to comment on the resemblance. What happens if one of those girls wants to date him when they get older? They're cousins. What is she going to do? How will she explain that?"

"Oh my God! I hadn't thought of that." Jade pulled away from him.

"You shouldn't have to."

Wes brushed her hair away from her face, allowing it to fall behind her shoulder. His touch tender and kind, as if they'd actually been friends. She hadn't thought he was capable of so much compassion.

"You were a donor. I was a donor," he continued. "I can't tell you how many times I've replayed that scenario in my head these past couple days. Your sister either has to move out of town, or she needs to face the cold reality that people will discover the truth. As much as I don't want to reveal my role in this, I realize I can only control a part of it."

"That had to have weighed on Liv." People had babies every day without complication, yet Audra, Hadley and Mackenzie were surrounded by it. Any decision she, Wes and Liv made affected them.

"I'm sure it did. It's too big of a secret to bear. Up until five days ago, she was the only one who knew the entire truth."

"It's killing me not to be able to talk to her." Ironic since she had subconsciously avoided speaking with Liv for weeks. "I have so many questions."

"She may not have any answers."

"I got so mad at her this afternoon." Jade hugged her arms to herself. "I lost another major client because I'm not in LA. Tomás is wonderful and I trust him with my life, but I had contracts with people who expected me to handle their events personally. And to a large degree I had. There's a lot I can do remotely, but I can't hold someone's hand through a catering or cake testing or walk them through a venue. My face on Tomás's iPad just wasn't enough to convince them to stay. We had already invested quite a bit of money in this one. I took a big hit."

"That doesn't seem right. Can't you fight that?"

"Sure." Jade bitterly laughed. "And then that celebrity will tell their friends not to use us. LA may be a large city, but it's a small town at heart. Everyone knows everyone else and reputations can be destroyed with one phone call. I have to suck it up." She inhaled deeply. "I'm mad at my sister for putting me in this situation. I'm not mad she has postpartum depression. But let's be honest, she made some big mistakes. And let me tell you, I pass some of that blame on the fertility specialist she went to. Counseling should be mandatory, especially when implanting three embryos in a single mother. I find that irresponsible. So, yeah, I'm mad. And the guilt eats at me for feeling that way because Liv had to be a complete wreck over this."

Wes gathered her into his arms again and held her tightly. "You're human first. That's why I'm asking you to move in here." His voice smooth and insistent as he rested his head on hers. "By staying at Liv's you're doing exactly what she did. Let me and my family help you. And if they figure out the truth, we'll handle it then. Hopefully it won't come to that. Don't wait until you're so strung out, both emotionally and financially, to do something."

"What about Maddie? She's personally invested in this. She loves the children."

"She should come with you so you're not alone at night."

Because you'll be in Texas. Jade wanted to be selfish and ask him to stay. A small part of her loved the connection they shared. Wes Slade, of all people, was the one person who completely understood. The pretense had slipped away and she wanted nothing more than to lean on him for support.

She lifted her head from his chest and looked into his eyes. Could she really put the past aside and trust him?

"Maybe moving here isn't such a bad idea. But it's only temporary."

Wes cupped her chin, his mouth inches from hers. "It's going to be okay. I'll talk to my brothers and we'll figure this out. Together."

"Together?" Jade had never yearned to kiss a man so badly. "But you're leaving."

"I'll call you every day." He stroked her cheek, brushing away what remained of her tears. "You'll still have me."

If only she had him... Her sister would never forgive her. Jade sat up straight and gripped the steering wheel. "Okay, um, yeah, talk to your brothers and we'll take it from there. How about you show me where to drop you off."

Wes cleared his throat and adjusted his jeans. "Make a left at the stables and follow that road to the end."

Jade shifted the car into gear and stepped on the gas. The engine revved, but didn't move. "Please tell me I didn't break Maddie's car."

"Try putting it in Drive instead of Neutral." Wes laughed under his breath.

Jade stared down at the glowing *N* on the shifter. What was it about Wes? She took pride in always remaining in control, yet whenever she was around him, she made a fool of herself. He was charming, thoughtful, handsome—okay, downright sexy—but he was off-limits. A relationship, even a fleeting, one-night sexual one, was out of the question with the father of her children.

Damn.

She braked the car abruptly in front of his cabin. "Get out."

Wes laughed, making no move to open the door.

Jade flipped up the armrest and reached across his lap for the door handle, pushing it open. "Get out before I do something we'll both regret."

Before she could retreat to her side of the car, he gripped her waist and tugged her onto his lap, the full extent of his arousal evident against her hip. "What if we don't regret it?"

"We can't." She splayed her hands on his chest and pushed away from him, her back against the dashboard.

"Because you don't want to, or because of your sister?"

"Oh, I definitely want to." Her eyes wandered down his abs to his belt buckle as his thumb grazed the side of her breast. In seconds, she could have his jeans unzipped and end the tension between them. She closed her eyes, relishing the thought. She'd never understood that deep sexual yearning she'd heard her brides talk about…until now. A shrink once told her it had been because of her past. She'd always believed she just hadn't met the right man yet. But despite the unfamiliar desire raging deep within her, she couldn't betray her sister any more than she was already.

"We can't do this to Liv. It's not fair to her."

"Okay." He nodded silently and released her. "Just for the record, I don't think it's fair that your sister gets to dictate how we feel about each other." Wes reached for the door. "Before I say any more, I'm going to go take a cold shower."

Jade slid back to her side of the car. "You and me both."

"We could always take one together." Wes snatched his hat from the dashboard. "But then we'd get all steamy again. Good night, Jade. I'll call you after I speak to my brothers." He stepped out of the car and closed the door, giving her a pleasant view of his backside in the process. He leaned in the window before walking away. "Sweet dreams, sweetheart."

"You too."

"I do believe you're blushing."

"Good night, Wes."

Jade pulled away from the cabin before he tempted her further. If he could melt her resolve without even kissing her, she could only imagine what would happen to her if he did. Wes was right, he needed to go back to Texas. She was safer that way.

Chapter 6

Jade stepped outside the large log guest cabin and admired the rising sun over the Swan Range. Okay, maybe Wes was right, the view was photoworthy. She sipped her mug of coffee as Belgian horses grazed lush green grass in the corral twenty yards from the expansive wraparound porch. Dylan and Garrett had been gracious enough to offer her the place for free, but she refused. She could afford to pay their more than reasonable rate, although a part of her wondered if they had discounted the cost. Wes had been insistent on paying the entire bill, but Jade relented and allowed him to share half the expense.

Wes had only been gone a day, and she surprisingly missed him. The ranch, vast as it was, seemed empty without him there. Not that they had spent any time there together, except for the day she arrived and their heated exchange in Maddie's car.

She glanced over at the maroon Ford parked alongside the cabin. Her body began to tingle at the memory. She'd almost had sex with Wes Slade in the front seat of a car. What the hell was happening to her? They weren't in high school. Regardless, the man had already affected Jade and the girls. He hadn't been a part of their lives for very long, but the triplets seemed more content and settled when he was around. Nothing would replace their mother though.

For infants, they'd had so many changes in their little lives and Jade was grateful Maddie agreed to stay at the ranch with her. She had been their one constant. It also didn't hurt that the woman had a major crush on a ranch hand she met at the christenings who just happened to live on the other side of the property.

"Here you are," Maddie said from the open doorway. "Wow. That view's worth a million bucks and then some."

"Are the girls awake yet?"

"Not yet." She padded barefoot to the railing and inhaled the fresh scent of morning dew. "This has to be the first night they've slept more than four hours in a row."

"Maybe it's the country air." Jade had the best sleep of her life after feeding and putting the triplets to bed around two thirty. "I should brace myself for the dirty diaper onslaught while you get ready for work."

"I don't know." Maddie, still in her sleep shorts and T, flopped into one of the porch rocking chairs and closed her eyes. "I may play hooky today and just admire the landscape."

"You mean admire Jarrod."

Maddie glared at her and narrowed her eyes. "Do you see Jarrod anywhere, because I don't."

"No, but I'm sure you'll know his schedule by tonight. And if you get dressed fast enough, you can catch him at the breakfast buffet up at the main lodge."

"Really?" Maddie shot upward. "I mean, breakfast sounds like a good idea."

Jade stifled her laughter as Maddie ran back inside the cabin. She wished she had a friend like Maddie in LA. Tomás and his husband were always around for business or pleasure, but Jade felt like a third wheel whenever they went out together. Her social calendar was packed almost every night so she couldn't complain, but most of those events were business related in some way. She had to out-network the competition to remain relevant, which didn't leave much time for dating.

"Good morning!" A woman called out from an ATV as she drove up to the porch. "It's refreshing here, isn't it?"

The voice and the face were familiar, but Jade couldn't place the woman. Then the realization hit her. "Delta?"

"I know, I look different with a pixie cut, but I didn't have much say in that." She eased off the ATV and unfastened a large tote from the back before climbing the steps. "How are you? I'm sorry I wasn't around when the babies were born."

Jade gave the woman a hug, then held her at arm's length. "Wow! You look amazing." Delta had been stunning before, but her deep mahogany close-cropped hair accented her slender neck, perfect breasts and mile-long legs. "You look more like a supermodel than someone recovering from cancer."

"Well, thank you." Delta mock-strutted a mini catwalk and spun around. "Cancer forces you to take better care of yourself. Besides eating healthier, I'm working out more and kicking some major butt. Life's too short not to. I'm really sorry to hear about Liv. I wish I could have been around more during her pregnancy."

"No, no, please. You had your own struggles. I get it."

Delta nodded, her eyes brimming with tears.

"I have something for you." She held up the bag. "Belle—Harlan's wife—has been teaching me how to bake whole grain bread and muffins, so our kitchen is overflowing with all sorts of yumminess. I thought you and Maddie would like some."

"Absolutely. She's inside getting ready for work."

"Ready for work or ready for *Jarrod*?" She fanned herself as she said his name.

"Oh, you know, huh?"

"Honey, I had a ringside seat to the drool fest. And yes, dear Maddie was drooling."

"Why don't you come in and you can tell me about it over coffee." Jade opened the screen door and held it for Delta. "We may actually get a chance to talk before the girls wake up."

Delta followed her to the large family-sized eat-in kitchen. Jade loved the cabin's thoughtful little details, like easy-to-sterilize solid core countertops and child safety latches on all the cabinets, top and bottom in case someone's child was a climber.

"Besides wanting to pawn my food off on you, I sort of have a favor to ask."

"Okay." Jade poured two mugs of hot coffee and set them on the table. "Do you take cream or sugar?"

"Just black, thank you."

Jade peered into the tote and pulled out a bag of blueberry muffins. "Oh, these look amazing," she said before taking a bite. "These are incredible. I love the addition of the orange zest. It really brightens the flavor."

"I thought so too. Normally you see lemon and blueberry paired together, but the orange is a nice citrus twist."

"I'm sorry. I guess I'm hungrier than I thought." Jade wiped her fingers on a napkin. "Please ask me the favor."

"Um, okay." Worry lines creased Delta's forehead as she death-gripped her mug. "I'm sure you can imagine the first half of the year was really rough for Garrett, me and the kids."

Jade reached across the table and covered her hands. "What is it? Did something else happen?"

"It's nothing bad at all." Delta's caramel-brown eyes met hers. "It's just a big favor to ask. June has been our turning point of sorts. I'm done with chemo, my scans look great and we can finally move on with our lives."

"I have an idea where this is going." Jade hoped she was correct.

Delta returned her enthusiasm. "Garrett and I have been talking and we really want to get married this summer. The problem is, the kids leave to visit their grandparents in Wyoming on Monday, and they won't be back for a month which would give us more than enough time to squeeze in a honeymoon. It's important his kids are in the ceremony, so eloping is out of the question."

"And you want to have the wedding this week."

Delta's smile widened. "After the christenings on

last Saturday, we asked Dylan and Emma if they would mind us getting married this weekend too. We thought it would be the perfect time since many of the same people we'd invite are already in town. They loved the idea."

"I'm so happy for you!" Jade gave Delta another hug. "Dylan and Emma have their wedding planned and set for Saturday afternoon and the reception goes into the evening. We don't want to disrupt that, but we also realize that many people are flying or driving home on Sunday. We just want a simple ceremony, at sunrise Sunday morning and then a quick breakfast reception before everyone leaves."

"It sounds wonderful. I'm jealous I haven't thought of that idea before. I've planned a lot of double ceremonies, but yours is a much better idea. One wedding doesn't encroach on the other."

"Exactly. And we'd each have our own anniversary date."

"So." Jade folded her arms over her chest. "Are you going to ask me or what?"

"Okay." Delta beamed. "I know you're super busy with the triplets and your company in LA, but would you be willing to help plan our wedding? I realize it's only four days away, but—"

"But nothing. I would love to." This was the pick-me-up Jade needed. To physically get her hands on a project instead of doing it remotely. "I have a ton of ideas already."

"We're on a tight budget though." Delta winced. "I know you do big, lavish Hollywood ceremonies. That's just way out of our reach."

"You'd be surprised how many celebrities want

small weddings. My assistant had an intimate ceremony last year, and it meant so much more than the bigger ones." Jade lowered her voice to a whisper. "But don't tell anyone I said that. It would kill my business."

"I promise I won't." Delta giggled. "I feel bad that Liv won't be here for it though."

"Liv's happy if you're happy. I won't even tell her when I see her. I'll leave that for you."

Delta nodded. "Thank you for doing this for us. One more thing, my dog Jake has to be in the ceremony. I can't get married without him."

"You're welcome and I've added many dogs to wed—" The sound of one baby, followed by another, rang out from down the hall. "They're playing my song. I think Emma had the right idea putting us so far away from the main lodge."

"It's loud when there's three of them, isn't it?" Delta stood with Jade. "Do you mind if I help? I haven't seen them in a month."

"Sure." Jade swallowed hard, hoping Delta didn't pick up on the similarities between the girls and Travis, especially Mackenzie. "Just be forewarned, they can pack an odoriferous punch."

"Oh!" Delta waved her hand in front of her face as they entered the bedroom. "That they do. Chemo annihilated my sense of smell and taste buds, but I'll tell ya, I can definitely smell that. Is that normal?"

"For Stinker One, Two and Three, yes. Wes said Travis's was slightly better, but not by much. I don't know if it's their formula or what. They have a two-month checkup at the pediatrician's next week, and it's at the top of my list."

"Oh hey, Delta." Maddie wrinkled her nose as she

entered the room. "Welcome to the danger zone. Enter at your own risk."

"You think after working around horses and their manure for most of my life, a baby would smell like roses. Okay." Delta squared her shoulders. "Where do we begin?"

Jade bet if Delta had goggles and a hazmat suit, she'd have put it on. "Neither one of you need to help me. Go get some breakfast and ogle your men."

"Nonsense." Delta hip checked Jade out of the way. "Three babies, three of us. Let's do this before they claim a victim."

As if on cue, Audra, Hadley and Mackenzie stopped and stared up at the women laughing at them for a brief second before continuing to cry.

"Oh, did we insult you?" Maddie lifted Audra out of the crib. "We're sorry. Just like Aunt Jade is sorry she labeled you with a Sharpie when she first got here."

"You did what?" Delta's eyes widened at she lifted Mackenzie.

"Ah, I'll take her." Jade eased the infant out of Delta's arms. She didn't want her getting that up close and personal with the triplet that resembled Travis the most. "Mackenzie's the fussiest."

"She is?" Maddie asked. "Since when?"

Jade scrambled for an excuse. "Monday. You were at work when I noticed it. I've been double-checking to make sure she doesn't have a rash or anything. I should have mentioned it before." Jade hated having to lie to the one person who'd been the greatest and most unexpected help to her over the past week.

"I think all three of them have been a little more gassy than usual." Maddie grabbed a diaper blanket from the dresser and knelt on the floor to change Audra, giving Delta the changing table. "Definitely let Alyssa and Megan know when they come today."

Jade had met with two of the sweetest teenage girls after Wes had helped move her onto the ranch. His future sister-in-law, Emma, had personally used them many times and highly recommended them. At first Jade wondered if hiring two people was overkill, but she liked the idea of them having each other for companionship so they wouldn't get bored. Jade needed to devote her full attention to work, and she didn't want to feel compelled to entertain a babysitter.

"Someone please tell me the baby labeling story," Delta asked.

"Maddie will never let me live this down. I was afraid of mixing up the babies so I wrote their first initial on the bottom of their feet."

"With a permanent black marker," Maddie added.

"It washed off...eventually." Jade rolled her eyes. "It's not like I had them tattooed."

"Why didn't you use nail polish?" Delta asked as she changed Hadley.

"Because I thought they'd chew it off."

"Not if you put it on their toes." Delta held her nose and shoved the offending package in the Diaper Genie. "They're not coordinated enough to reach them."

"In case my sister hasn't told you already...babies were never my thing. Liv wanted a big family. I wanted the big house in the Hollywood Hills."

"And now you have the kids and you're living in a log cabin on a ranch." Delta refastened Hadley's onesie and rubbed her belly. "There you go, little one. All clean and sweet smelling."

"I'm here temporarily," Jade quickly added. "I have a lot invested in my business. I can't be away from it forever. I'm already taking major financial hits after one week."

At least when she had visited Liv when the babies were born that had been planned. Her clients had known in advance she wouldn't be around during those dates, with the understanding Liv could have gone into labor early instead of getting induced. She'd had months to plan for her absence and some clients had even chosen to push their events out so Jade would be in town overseeing them. She couldn't blame them for being furious she was gone again.

"Do I hear someone's phone ringing?" Delta asked.

"That's mine." Her assistant's familiar ringtone beckoned from the kitchen. Jade glanced up at the wall clock. It was shortly after seven and she knew he was eager to go over today's schedule. "It's Tomás. We have a big event tonight."

"On a Wednesday?" Maddie lowered Audra into her crib, then gently nudged Jade out of the way. "Go take your call. I can do this."

"Thanks." She stepped aside and walked toward the bathroom to wash her hands. "Hollywood doesn't care what day it is." The phone stopped ringing, and she envisioned Tomás huffing impatiently as he waited for her outgoing message to finish so he could leave a voice mail. Jade hesitated in the doorway, watching Delta's reaction to the triplets. If she detected any family resemblance, she didn't show it. Then again, don't a lot of babies look similar at that age? Maybe Wes had been overreacting. Maybe they both had been and everything would work out the way Liv had planned.

* * *

"What's wrong with you today?" Wes's agent asked as the medics wheeled him through the arena's corridors and outside to the mobile sports medicine trailer. "Your head clearly wasn't in it. I picked up on that before you ever entered the chute. You blew me off when I asked. I hate to say it, kid, but you seem a little soft this week."

Maybe if he could get the image of Jade sitting on his lap out of his head, he might be able to concentrate. He'd never been more attracted or infuriated by any other woman. And yeah, in a perfect world, he'd like to see where things might lead with her, but their lives were far from perfect. Once he'd explained to his brothers yesterday about Liv's disappearance and asked if Jade and the girls could move to the ranch, it had raised all sorts of questions. Adding Maddie to the mix had been the only reason they stopped. His brothers didn't even think he'd keep two girlfriends in the same house.

"I've been in Montana and I haven't had a chance to ride or work out for over a week." The multimillion-dollar rodeo training facility he taught at in Texas had a top-of-the-line fitness center and both real and mechanical bulls for training. The pay was great, but the perks were even better. He'd taken every advantage of it when he wasn't on the road.

"That's no excuse," Pete argued. "You lived in Montana up until you moved six months ago, and you were fine then."

He was right, and Wes couldn't fight the truth. "Look, man." Wes reached with his good arm and tapped the medic's leg. "I'm fine to walk. I dislocated my shoulder, not my feet."

"You know the rules," the man said without slowing down. "We can't do that in case you have other injuries. Just be glad we didn't take you out strapped to a stretcher."

"Very funny." The dig was a not-so-subtle reference to an injury he had last year during finals. He'd been furious at himself for miscalculating the bull's rotation and wound up unconscious on the arena floor after the animal headbutted him. He knew the second he'd awoken he'd been eliminated from the competition. He'd gone out kicking and screaming louder than Audra, Hadley and Mackenzie.

"What's got you all in knots. Is something going on with your family that I don't know about?"

"You could say that."

"As long as it doesn't involve a woman," Pete scoffed.

"Try four."

"Four what? Four women?" Pete almost tripped over his own feet.

"Right on!" The older medic walking alongside them tried to high-five Wes before realizing he was on his dislocated side. "Whoops, sorry. My bad."

"You've gotten in more trouble with women than anyone I know." Pete clucked his tongue. "Don't let them get in the way of your career."

Once they reached the trailer, Wes insisted on walking up the steps himself. He refused to be wheeled up a ramp despite the medical team surrounding him. After he stripped off his safety vest and shirt, Dr. Shelton began assessing his injuries.

"What's this…your third dislocation in two years?"

he asked, reviewing his charts on a tablet. Deceiving from the outside, the forty-foot-long trailers housed state-of-the-art mobile medical centers that traveled nationwide treating sports injuries. Competitors no longer had to go to the emergency room since they could perform everything including X-rays, minor surgery and casting on-site. They were also his largest sponsor and trying to hide any injury was futile.

"Just pop it back in, Doc." Wes ground his back teeth from the pain.

Dr. Shelton handed his tablet to one of the nurses. "You know the drill. Sit up straight and shrug your shoulders." The man gripped Wes's wrist and eased his elbow into a 90-degree angle, keeping it close to his body and in line with his shoulder. He slowly began to rotate the arm outward until the pressure increased on the dislocation. "Now try to relax as much as you can."

"I'm feeling that, Doc." Wes exhaled slowly and looked up at his agent hovering nearby. Pete had helped him build his career from junior rodeo greenhorn to champion, and he hated disappointing the man even more than he hated disappointing himself.

"We're almost there." The doctor gripped his upper arm and slowly moved it out and upward. "Good. Now put your shoulders back, your chest out."

Wes closed his eyes trying to focus on anything other than the pain. He didn't remember any of his other dislocations hurting this bad. Then he heard a pop, and the pain began to subside.

"Keep your back straight. It's not quite all the way in yet," Dr. Shelton said as he rotated Wes's arm toward his chest.

"There we go, there we go." Wes tilted his head back at the release.

"And you're done." The man let go of his arm. "Let's get you into X-rays so we can see what's going on in there."

Wes stood, the tension draining from his shoulder. "I'm fine."

"Look," Pete said, stepping in front of him, "you didn't qualify, so it's not like you're riding again. Let the man do his job."

"I made eight."

"No, Wes. You didn't. Your time was 7.8, and it was a sloppy 7.8."

He missed it by two-tenths of a second. "Dammit." Wes kicked the chair behind him. "I thought I had it." He rarely missed qualifying. His sponsorships were coming up for renewal and a few younger competitors had been slowly pushing him down in the ranks. This was not the time to screw up.

"We'll talk about it later." Pete pulled out his phone and tapped at the screen.

"Come on, Wes. Chaps off, gown on," the doctor ordered.

"Fine."

"I'll be outside waiting." Pete's phone rang, and he was out the door before Wes had a chance to respond.

He unfastened his chaps and kicked off his boots. He suspected Pete was already looking to poach one of the younger riders from the lesser known agents. He may not like it, but he couldn't blame the man. Wes intended to retire at the end of next season, even though he hadn't told anyone of his plans yet. He wanted to have two solid final years and another championship under his belt before then. The higher he went out, the more money he could earn training the next generation of competitors. He had nothing else to fall back on.

After two hours of tests and endless waiting, Dr. Shelton's grim expression told Wes all he needed to know. Controlling the argument building in his head, he sat patiently and listened.

"Three dislocations, extensive ligament damage and now a rotator cuff tear, the only thing I see in your immediate future is surgery."

"No." Wes shook his head. "Absolutely not. I'll just rehab it again. The Ride 'em High! Rodeo School where I work in Texas is connected to the Dance of Hope Hippotherapy Center. They have the best physical therapists in the state. You know the place, Doc, and you know their reputation."

"Tell me something." Dr. Shelton clasped his hands. "On a scale of one to ten, what was your pain level when you rode today?"

"I don't know." Wes had thought the week off from teaching and competition would have given his arm and shoulder a rest. He didn't want to admit defeat. And he wouldn't. Not yet. Besides, it hadn't been bothering him this bad. "Maybe a five, possibly a six."

"Compare that to a year ago. What was your pain level then?"

"None." Wes snorted. "I don't get the question, Doc. I wasn't injured then, so of course it would be zero."

"Exactly. You weren't injured then, now you are."

Wes stood. He didn't appreciate games, let alone one at his expense. "I'm not having surgery."

"What's this about surgery?" Pete asked from the doorway.

Dr. Shelton's brows rose as he stared at Wes. His medical records were private and the man couldn't legally say a word to Pete. But his sponsorship contract stipulated they were to be informed of any and all injuries affecting his ability to compete. In the end, the sponsor would tell Pete and there was no sense in delaying it.

"The good doc is recommending surgery."

"What kind of surgery?"

"We haven't discussed that yet." Dr. Shelton removed his glasses and rubbed his eyes. "Your client refuses to hear what I have to say."

"Because I know you're talking rotator cuff surgery and that will take me out of competition for six months."

"Probably longer," Pete muttered.

"Not happening. At least not now. I choose rehab and at the end of the season, I will have it reevaluated and we'll take it from there."

"That's months away," Dr. Shelton said. "If you have surgery now, you'll have a strong chance of recovering and competing in a full season next year. I can pretty much guarantee that won't happen if you wait much longer. You can't ride without pain."

"I'm tough enough to ride through it."

"Thank you, Dr. Shelton." Pete clapped Wes on the back and gave him a gentle shove toward the door. "We will definitely consider all options."

Wes opened his mouth to argue and received another shove.

"Cool it," Pete growled under his breath. "Thank the man and let's be on our way."

Wes hated being corralled like a head of cattle, but

Wes paid the man a hefty percentage to keep him from sticking his foot in his mouth so he might as well shut up.

"Thanks again, Doc. Seriously, I'll consider what you said." *Just not so much.*

Once outside, Wes thought Pete would strangle him. "What's the matter with you? You don't argue with the sponsor."

"I don't take orders from them, either. Besides, he only works for the sponsor."

"And now they know you're injured and you're re-fusing surgery." Pete pulled a pack of cigarettes out of his pocket and lit one. "If they don't pull your sponsor-ship now, they sure as hell won't renew it next year." He took a long drag and exhaled slowly. "We're talking a lot of money, Wes. And that's just from one sponsor. I know you don't like the idea of surgery, but Dr. Shel-ton's right. You get it done now, you're only out for part of the season and next year you'll be as good as new."

Wes snatched the cigarette from his mouth and snapped it in half. "Don't you dare badger me about my well-being while you're blowing smoke in my face."

"You're right, I'm sorry," Pete said sheepishly. "I just feel for you."

"Yeah, well, this is my career we're talking about, not yours. There's no guarantee I'll recover from sur-gery before next season just like there's no guarantee I'll be able to compete at all. If I wait, I have a shot. I'll get through the pain." Pete opened his mouth to speak, but Wes cut him off before he had a chance. "You can walk back in that arena, snatch up one of the young kids you're so hot to get your hands on and they'll get my sponsorship because I'll be home while they're competing."

"You think I'd be that disloyal to you?"

"No, I think you'd be that smart. You have your own bottom line to watch out for and I can't blame you. I need some time. I need to finish the season and see what happens. I can't even teach after rotator cuff surgery. What am I supposed to do? Ride 'em High! didn't hire me for my good looks."

"Not with your ugly mug." He laughed.

"Do you want me to fire you now or wait till later?"

"Sorry." Pete cleared his throat.

"I need time." If this was his last season, then he needed to make plans. He had to discuss it with his boss in Texas and see what their doctors and physical therapists had to say. More than anything else, he had to keep his head clear and away from all things Jade and the girls.

He'd fly to Montana in the morning, get through Dylan's wedding on Saturday and then fly out that night. Three more days. He'd keep his word and check in on Jade. He'd make sure they had whatever they needed until Liv came home, and then that was it. The girls weren't his to raise and he couldn't get involved with Jade knowing what they'd created and couldn't have. He had to move on. He had too much riding on the next few months and the sooner he got into physical therapy, the better. Nothing had ever interfered with his career and he wasn't about to let anything or anyone start now.

Chapter 7

Emma and Dylan had been gracious enough to invite Jade to the rehearsal dinner Friday night at the lodge, but she declined. After handing Tomás every key to her queendom along with check-writing capabilities, she was on the verge of a mini-meltdown. She thrived on control, as did Liv. Even though she had promoted Tomás last week, it wasn't the same as giving him access to the business bank accounts to pay vendors and their employees along with the power to make both business and financial decisions in her absence. After a caterer almost bailed because she couldn't transfer funds into their account on time, she realized something had to give.

She trusted Tomás, she just didn't like relying on someone else to run her company or any other aspect of her life. Which must be driving Liv crazy, because that's exactly what Jade was doing for her. She wished her sister would call. They'd never gone this long without some form of communication. Whether it had been a brief text message or a voice mail, they'd kept in contact with each other. Every morning she reached for her phone and fought the disappointment of the deafening silence.

"How about we go for a walk?" Jade asked the girls, who were happily rocking in the new infant seats Wes had bought them. He was right, they really were a godsend. Emma showed her how she used hers with her six-month-old daughter, Holly, who Jade was relieved to see looked nothing like the triplets. Feeding and naps were much easier and she was sure Liv would appreciate that when she returned home.

Jade bundled the girls in their triplet stroller and set off on the paved path that wound around the ranch. "Your mommy would love it here." It was unfortunate Wes and Liv hadn't been a real couple. The girls would have enjoyed growing up on the ranch with family. It was ironic in a way. Liv wanted family so desperately, and even chose a man to father her children from Saddle Ridge's largest, yet they both wanted to keep the girls a secret from their cousins, aunts and uncles. Jade and Liv never had any of those people in their lives. Maybe if they had they would have grown up loved.

Her sister's poor decision making still bothered her. It had been one thing to ask Jade to be the egg donor. But Wes? Lookswise, there was no arguing he was a fine specimen of a man. But his attitude…maybe not so much considering she hadn't seen him since before he left for South Dakota on Tuesday. He'd come back last night, according to Maddie, who had seen him while she was locking lips with Jarrod behind the stables. He texted her and had even called twice, but she had been on the phone with Tomás and a client and couldn't answer. When she called back, it went straight to voice mail, as if he'd turned off his phone.

It didn't matter, anyway. Wes was leaving for good in a few days and so would she once Liv came home. Although she should probably stick around for a month—if not more—afterward to make sure Liv was truly okay alone with the girls. Jade still couldn't quite pocket the anger she had about that. It would be much easier if the four of them came back with her to California. With the exception of her ex-husband, her sister had no other ties to town. She worked remotely and could do the same job from Los Angeles. Jade didn't think it was selfish to point that fact out to both the doctor and Liv. Jade had been more than reasonable so far.

Up ahead in the distance, Jade saw Wes atop a beautiful black-and-white quarter horse giving a group of guests a riding lesson in a large, dirt-covered outdoor arena. *Damn, he looked good.* She checked her watch, surprised he wasn't at the rehearsal dinner. She set the brake on the stroller and crouched down beside the girls. "Look, that's your da— Oh dear!"

I can't believe I almost said daddy. Jade stood up and quickly released the brake. If she could slip up that easily now, what would happen if she made that kind of mistake when the girls were older. As she turned the stroller around, she noticed Wes watching them. Within seconds, he was at the fence and Jade noticed a sling around his neck and arm.

She tried to tell herself she didn't care, but the cold, hard fact was she did. "What happened to you?"

Wes smiled down at the girls who were intently

looking up at his horse. "I had a run-in with a bull and dislocated my shoulder. This is just a precaution while it heals."

Jade's palms began to throb from gripping the stroller handle too tight. "I still don't understand all the fuss over eight seconds. It's so dangerous."

His expression hardened. "Those eight seconds require a lot of skill and athleticism."

"Don't get your boxers in a wad." Jade hated when men got touchy about sports. "I'm not saying anything to the contrary. I just don't get the attraction."

"I wear boxer briefs, thank you. I'm not going to lie…there's an adrenaline rush every time I compete. But it's also my job, and those mighty highs are sometimes accompanied by devastating lows." Wes nudged his mount closer to the fence. "Is this the first time they've seen a horse?"

Jade peered over the top of the stroller, trying desperately not to picture Wes wearing nothing but boxer briefs. "They've um—they've seen the Belgians from a distance. I think they may be more fascinated with you though. We—uh—they haven't seen you in a few days."

His mouth curved into a cocky grin. "You're cute when you're flustered."

He shifted in his saddle and Jade wondered if she affected him the same delicious way he affected her. His eyes perused her body before stopping at her breasts. She'd always been self-conscious of their generous size, but Wes's appreciative gaze made every nerve ending in her body prickle with desire. Definitely not thoughts she should be having about the man who defined *complicated*.

A muscle twitched along his jawline as he returned

his gaze to hers. "I've been busy helping my family with the upcoming weddings this weekend. I heard you're planning Garrett and Delta's ceremony."

"It's going to be so sweet." Relieved by the subject change, Jade began to relax. "There really wasn't much to it since they stressed simplicity. But it will be uniquely different from Dylan and Emma's wedding."

"I've never seen your face light up so much before." Wes's devastating smile made her bite her bottom lip to prevent her jaw from hitting the ground.

"I love event planning. It brings people together and makes them happy. Speaking of which, why aren't you at the rehearsal dinner?"

"Because the ranch has guests and my brothers have their hands full. I went to the ceremony rehearsal and told Garrett I would take his evening lesson. I thought you'd be there."

"I guess Emma told you she invited me. Is that the real reason you didn't go?"

Wes averted his eyes, giving Jade her answer.

"Well, we'll be seeing you, then." She spun the stroller around and started back to the cabin.

"I told you the truth but that wasn't good enough. You had to dig deeper."

"Go away." Jade waved to him over her shoulder.

"Jade, stop. It's not like that." Wes paced her on his horse. "It's complicated."

"Seriously?" Jade continued down the path. "You're going to talk to me about complicated when I've uprooted my life more than you have. You get to go home in a few days." Jade stopped herself from adding, *while I'm stuck here*. She didn't want to think of Audra, Hadley and Mackenzie that way despite feeling like a prisoner of sorts.

"At least you still have your career."

"What?" Jade stopped and looked up at him. "What happened?"

"There are a lot of factors involved, but the short of it is, my competing days may be over before my planned retirement and I'm not sure what to do. Chirp on all you want about giving up more than me, but I may have just lost everything." He ran his hand down the horse's neck and gave him a scratch. "This is one of those days I wish Liv was here. She was the best sounding board."

Jade knew she should maintain a friendly distance from Wes, but couldn't fathom having to give up her career. Especially at such a young age. "I realize the girls and I are part of your problem, but if you're willing to join us for dinner, I'm willing to listen. I can't replace her advice, but I'm here."

"You're not a problem, Jade. I'm sorry I ever made you think that." He glanced over his shoulder at the guests. "Where's Maddie tonight?"

"On a date with Jarrod. And Alyssa and Megan are babysitting your brothers' kids." Jade still had work to finish, but she craved adult conversation more. "I wouldn't mind the company."

He nodded. "Give me an hour to finish here and clean up."

"Great." A giddy rush swept over her at the thought of cooking for him. "Do you like Italian?"

"Love it. I'll see you soon." He winked before riding away and she couldn't be sure if it had been at her or the girls. Probably the girls, although she secretly wished otherwise. There were a thousand reasons why she should stay away from Wes Slade, but they had suddenly escaped her brain. And she was okay with that. At least for one night.

"I didn't realize you could cook like that." Stuffed, Wes willed himself to stand and help Jade clear the kitchen table. "It definitely beats the pizza we ordered last week."

Jade had fed the girls before he arrived, giving them time to enjoy their meal. It hadn't been candlelight and champagne, but between her vintage yellow floral dress and the wine, it bordered on romantic to him. He tried to ignore the ever-increasing emotions churning in his gut, drawing him to her like a bear to honey. He was failing. Miserably.

"Chicken scaloppine is one of my specialties. A perk of working with some of LA's finest chefs and caterers is I get to learn how they prepare many of their signature dishes."

"I think I would gain ten pounds a week if I ate your cooking every day." His hand brushed hers as he handed her another plate, causing the hair on his arm to stand on end at the jolt of excitement she sent through him. If this was her effect on him without trying, he'd be a goner if they were an actual couple.

"No, you wouldn't," she said as she rinsed the silverware and dropped it in the dishwasher basket. "Half the time I skip dinner because I've been nibbling throughout the day and the other half of the time I order out because Tomás and I are working an event."

"How is he managing without you?"

"I guess I should say he's doing great. The problem

is we're losing clients because I'm not there. He's over-worked because he hasn't found a suitable replacement for his old position. It's going to take an extraordinary candidate to do what he does, which is why I told him to hire two people. While he's interviewing, he's also doing a large portion of my job. He has the mentality of 'I'd rather do it myself than delegate it' and he's quickly learning he has to let go of the smaller things. On the flip side, Tomás and the rest of my team have managed to bring in some lucrative last-minute clients like a movie wrap party the other night. Filming finished way ahead of schedule and they needed something large, lavish and fast. With my contacts and Tomás's vision, he pulled off a quarter-of–a-million-dollar party in under twelve hours."

"That's incredible." Wes couldn't imagine wasting that much money on a party. "Then why do you still seem nervous?"

"The company is my baby, my spouse, my everything. The day I graduated, I bought a one-way bus ticket to Los Angeles and the following week I got a job at an event planning company. The job itself sucked. The pay was horrible. But I loved seeing how we took nothing and turned it into something beautiful." Wes may not person-ally care for frivolous spending, but he enjoyed the way Jade's features grew more animated as she spoke. "At the end of the day, no matter how tired we were, we had something spectacular to show for it. I worked my way up until I was ready to start my own business."

"I didn't realize you left right after high school." Wes had an inclination she'd left because of the mis-ery he'd unknowingly created for her.

"I couldn't get out of this town fast enough. It's not like I had good memories here. That's why I don't understand Liv's attraction to it. If it was all about Kevin, then maybe I can convince her to come back to California with me."

Jade poured two mugs of coffee and handed them to Wes. "Can you bring these into the living room while I move the girls' chairs?"

"Why don't you let me do that?" Wes watched their content faces as Jade lifted the first chair off the dining room floor.

"It's okay, I got it."

Audra and Hadley looked around the room and continued to discover the taste of their own hands, while Mackenzie peacefully snoozed.

"They really love those things, don't they?" Not seeing any coasters, Wes set the hot cups on a parenting magazine on the end table.

"I think I may love them more than they do. I switch the chairs on and once they fall asleep, I put them in their cribs. Usually they're all asleep by now, but you're their favorite shiny new toy. I can't thank you enough. Liv will love them too."

"Shiny new toy, huh?" Wes laughed. "I can't say I've ever been described that way before. All kidding aside, maybe you shouldn't tell Liv they're from me."

"Why? Maddie said she was hurt when you ended your friendship. I would think she'd be happy you gave her this gift."

"Maybe, maybe not. I still wonder if she saw us with the kids that night."

"If she did, she's in the right place to deal with it." Jade shrugged her shoulders. "I don't mean that to sound as harsh as it does. The reality of the situation is, whether she did or didn't is out of our control. I can't keep dwelling on it and neither should you. I'm having a difficult enough time mentally preparing for the pediatrician on Tuesday."

"What's so scary about a pediatrician?"

"I'm afraid if she thinks I'm doing something wrong, they'll take the girls from me. I know it sounds irrational, but I can't shake the thought." Wes noticed a slight tremble in Jade's body as she spoke. "I've read my sister's books at the house, and I think I'm following every parenting blog on the internet, but I have nothing to compare it to. Even Maddie said the same thing. We've never done this before. At least she has a little more experience from helping Liv. Then again, Liv never did it before, either. What if the doctor feels I'm not qualified to care for them? And why are you laughing at me?" She swatted him.

Wes gently cupped her face in his hand. "Because it doesn't work that way and you're doing an amazing job. Look at them." His hand slid down her shoulder, turning her body away from him. His chest pressed lightly against her back as he eased behind her. The fingers on his good arm lightly trailed down her waist and settled on her hip. "Those are three very blissful babies." He leaned into her, wishing he could pull her even closer and shield her from the pain of the past and erase her fears of tomorrow. "They are healthy, well-nourished children. They're clean. They have clean clothes and a small village of people willing to pitch in. Nobody is going to take them away."

"I want to believe you." Her voice broke as she whispered, "It's so hard."

Wes shifted behind her and lifted his sling over his head.

"Don't you need to wear that?"

"I'm supposed to keep my arm as close to my body as possible. Unless I'm—how did you put it?—bouncing on the back of a bull, I'm not really in any pain without it. The sling just makes me aware of what I shouldn't do with my arm until it heals. I think I can make a small exception."

Wes moved to the corner of the couch, softly tugging her to join him. Wordlessly she settled between his legs, her back still to him. He was pushing the boundaries of their relationship more than he should, but the overwhelming need to protect and care for the four females who'd interrupted and taken over his life won out.

"I know you went through hell growing up. But what your mom did and what you're doing are worlds apart from one another. You're not the same person she was. No one is going to compare you to her."

"Why not? I can't help comparing Liv to my mom." Jade's voice pitched. "I'm disgusted with myself for even thinking it. What if that's what happened to my mom?"

"Your mom was a drug addict." Wes wrapped his arms around her, inadvertently resting on top of her breasts. One lone part of his body twitched at the skin-on-skin contact and he prayed the reaction didn't become too evident.

"Maybe that's why. She got pregnant with me a year after Liv was born. What if she had PPD after me and didn't know how to handle it? I've read numerous reports citing a genetic link to postpartum depression. She said our dad wasn't around. That he was some loser drifter, but he had to have been around for at least two years because Liv and I have the same father. At least that's what she told us."

"Have you ever attempted to contact him?" Wes tried to imagine what life would have been like never knowing his father.

"I can't. Our mom never told us who he was, and we have no idea where she is or if she's still alive. There's no father listed on our birth certificates. I cringed when I had to show it to get my driver's license and passport. The woman at the post office had the nerve to argue with me over the blank field on my passport form. Everyone in line behind me heard me explain I didn't know who my father was. I was so embarrassed. Stuff like that happens, even in this day and age. That's another reason I'm surprised Liv chose the route she did. She hated that growing up."

"By the time the girls are old enough to know what a birth certificate is, I'd like to think people will be more educated to the changing family dynamic."

"I like that you get it." Jade tilted her head and looked up at him. His eyes trailed over her face, stopping on her full red lips. How did her lipstick manage to stay on through dinner? He wanted to kiss her to see if it would survive the heat between them. More than that, he wanted to kiss away her worries and promise her everything would be all right.

"I agreed to be a donor so the fact I accept a modern family shouldn't surprise you."

"Nothing should surprise me at this point, but every time I turn around something else does." Her sultry voice, whether intentional or not, only heightened his desire.

"Like what?" The selfish part of him secretly wished she'd say her attraction to him, while the logical side of him hoped she didn't.

"Like your comment earlier about your career possibly being over."

Wes's heart thudded to a jarring stop. He had managed to forget the realities of his job for the past hour. "A bull rider has a short shelf life as do many other sport professionals. By the time you hit thirty, your body starts feeling every fall three and four times more than you did in your early twenties. Especially when the same injuries keep reoccurring."

"Is that what happened with your shoulder?" Concern etched deep in her features as she frowned up at him.

"Pretty much." Wes rested his head against the back of the couch and stared at the ceiling, not wanting to see the pity he was certain would follow. "Now I need to make the decision to either have surgery and sit out for the next six months, possibly longer, or try to finish this season, then rest for a few months and try it one more time."

"Six months?" Jade twisted sideways, draping her bare legs across his jeans as the hem of her dress rose, exposing her more to him. Her toned thighs begged to be caressed and his inner voice begged to comply. "I can't imagine not being able to work for that long."

Unable to tear his gaze from her body, he allowed himself the pleasure of studying it without physically touching her. He wanted to memorize every inch, every curve. And the woman had curves. Luscious Marilyn Monroe curves that tested the seams of the cotton dress's bodice. The tops of her full breasts rose with each breath. He silently thanked God the zipper was in the back because the urge to set them free quickly became a test of his willpower.

"I'm glad you see it that way." Wes wished he had kept on his sling. It would have given him a place to rest his arm. He lifted it to drape across the back of the couch and winced. Silently he cursed, at the pain and the effect Jade had on him. He patted the cushion next to him, hoping the steady beat would force his heartbeat back on track. "My doctor and my agent don't. It's not just a financial thing. I've made quite a bit competing and I've socked a lot of it away. Not being able to compete means not being able to teach. It also means someone younger can come in and take my place both in the arena and at the rodeo school. Big names attract spectators, sponsors and students."

"Humor me for a second and allow me to play devil's advocate. If you are planning to retire at the end of next season, what is so bad about retiring this year?"

"For starters, I wanted to retire on my own terms. To go out on top, with another championship win. I haven't had one since I was twenty-six. I've been chasing my own success for three years. If I retire with the championship, I'll have more options afterward."

"What kind of options?"

"Endorsement deals and collaborations with equipment manufacturers, my own bull riding clinics, TV analyst gigs." Everything his father said he could be if he worked hard enough. The man may have questioned teenage rumors and have been cruel with his words at times, but he believed in Wes's ability to win. "There are a lot of options when you're one of the best. And I was one of the best. And then I made mistakes."

"Mistakes as in your agreement with Liv?"

"If you had asked me that question a few weeks ago I would've answered yes." Wes still couldn't believe how attached he'd grown to the girls in a little over a week. "Liv, my uncle's death, moving to Texas and their birth…they were all distractions. But no, helping to bring Audra, Hadley and Mackenzie into this world definitely wasn't a mistake. Even with all the past issues between us and your sister's postpartum depression, I'm glad I did it. I just want them to grow up happy."

Jade laid her head on his shoulder as they watched the three beautiful lives they'd unknowingly created together. "So this is what normal feels like."

Wes started to laugh. "I'm not sure if I'd call our arrangement normal."

"No, I mean two adults at home on the couch while the little ones drift off to sleep. The closest I've ever gotten to the experience is on a TV show. It's nice."

"Yeah, it is." Wes buried his nose in her hair, never wanting to forget the scent of her shampoo. Contentment washed over him as he held her while watching their daughters. It was wrong for him to think of them that way, but he wanted that pleasure. Just for one night. He'd never be this close to having a family ever again. And that was okay, because this was the only family he wanted to remember. That realization welled in his chest. He didn't want to be a dad. He didn't want a wife or a family. His career and livelihood were collapsing around him and all he wanted to do was stay in this moment and not let go.

instead of her. She just wished the ceremony wasn't happening on the most remote part of the ranch where she couldn't even catch a glimpse of it.

Jade stepped onto the porch. It was still surreal to her to walk out a front door and see wide-open spaces. Even when she lived in Saddle Ridge as a kid, there had always been other houses surrounding them.

The ranch was quiet this afternoon. At least where the cabin was. She envisioned the bustle of the bride and her attendants as she got ready, and the guests filing into the newly constructed wedding venue overlooking town and the Swan Range. Jarrod had picked up Maddie an hour ago, giving her a chance to give her friend her seal of approval. She'd spent fifteen minutes with them and she could already envision their wedding.

Jade had developed a sixth sense about relationship longevity years ago and she had a pretty good track record at picking the odds. She could also tell when her own relationships were doomed and had learned to eliminate the heartbreak by getting out early on. The problem with Wes was, if she removed Liv and the girls from the equation, she didn't see that heartbreak potential. She genuinely liked him and wanted to spend whatever time they had left together. But her sister and the triplets did exist and no amount of justification would make any relationship with Wes right.

It wasn't fair. She'd made a career of planning happily-ever-afters and her life was more of a lonely-ever-after. Los Angeles was the land of opportunity. Where big dreams were made and realized. For the most part, Jade lived that life and she'd been satisfied. Now that she'd had a taste of family, she wanted it. Only the family she wanted wasn't hers to keep.

Jade stormed back inside, annoyed for worrying about her love life instead of Liv's recovery. She wasn't in Montana for herself. She was there for her sister and no sacrifice should be too big. Then why did it already feel like it was?

"It's all temporary, Jade," she said to no one as she pulled out a kitchen chair and sat at the large round table covered in wedding paraphernalia. Any feelings she had for Wes were only in the here and now. In a few months, they would be a distant memory. She shook her head to clear him from her brain. "Okay…time to focus on Delta and Garrett's wedding tomorrow."

Jade checked and rechecked her lists. Even though the sunrise ceremony was much more casual than tonight's wedding, there was still a lot involved to pull it together before the guests arrived. Normally she'd schedule vendors to come in and do all the setup, but Delta and Garrett's budget left Jade doing much of the work herself. It had been a long time since she'd planned an old-school wedding, and she secretly loved every minute of it. Even with teams of people helping her back home, the intense stress to coordinate every event was exhausting. This wasn't. From assembling table centerpieces in mason jars, hand folding silverware napkin pouches and arranging a bridal bouquet from flowers grown on the ranch, Jade welcomed this new level of stress. She enjoyed her celebrity events in Los Angeles, but she loved the close family atmosphere of this more.

It's only temporary.

"Go away." Jade didn't need her inner voice reminding her none of it was hers to keep.

"How did you even know I was here?" a man said from the doorway. "I haven't knocked yet."

"Wes!" Jade shot out of her chair so fast she almost knocked it over. "You scared me half to death." She quickly grabbed the baby monitor to see if she woke the girls. "What are you doing here?"

Good heavens! Jade gripped the table for support. Wes's tall silhouette in the open door frame was a memory she never wanted to forget. His broad shoulders, lean waist and muscular long legs made her breath catch in her throat. But it was when he took a step forward and she saw him standing before her in his black cowboy hat, dress Wranglers and boots, white button-down shirt and silver-gray vest that her tummy flip-flopped a thousand times over.

"You look great." Had she just said that out loud? *Get control, girl.*

"Thank you." He touched the brim of his hat and nodded.

Now, that was something she didn't see in LA. "What are you doing here and where's your sling?"

"I refuse to wear that thing today. I'll be fine if I don't overuse my shoulder or arm. And I'm here to escort you to the wedding."

"Did Emma or Maddie put you up to this?"

"Nobody puts me up to anything. Emma would like you to be there, though. Megan's mom is on her way over to babysit the girls and before you argue with me, she said she's happy to do it."

"I appreciate the offer, but I need to work on tomorrow's wedding. I have to start setting up as soon as the reception ends tonight. Delta and Garrett put together a group of volunteers for me."

"I know. I'm one of the volunteers."

"You?" Jade mentally kicked herself for not realizing Garrett would ask him for help. It was a given. Yet in the back of her mind, she couldn't wait to see Wes's appreciation for her contribution to his brother's wedding. Especially since she refused to accept any payment beyond the necessary supply and rental fees. This was her gift to Delta for being such a good friend to her sister. She would have preferred to cover all the expenses, but the bride and groom refused.

Wes crossed the room to her. "I won't take no for an answer." He placed both hands on her shoulders and turned her toward the hallway. "By the time you're ready, the sitter will be here. Just don't take too long, I have to be there in twenty minutes."

"Twenty minutes?" Jade tried to look at him over her shoulder as he continued to push her toward the bedroom. "Nothing like giving a girl short notice." Truth was, Jade had mastered the art of getting ready for a formal event in under ten minutes. It was a requirement in her industry, especially on the occasion she juggled multiple events in one day.

"I will spend the rest of the night helping you with whatever you need." He stopped and released her shoulders as they reached the girls' bedroom.

"Wes?" Jade whispered. The smile he'd worn only moments ago had faded to sadness. "What is it?"

"In twenty-four hours, I'll be on a plane to Texas. I'll never see them again."

Jade rested her hand lightly on his arm, uncertain

how to console him. She couldn't even begin to comprehend the thought of walking away forever.

"Liv's original plan may have been to keep you out of their lives, but she may not feel that way now. There's still hope."

"That's a big if, and until I know for sure, I can't allow myself that hope. I made an agreement with your sister and I have to stand by that unless she says otherwise. I can't just watch from a distance, though. You should go get ready," Wes said before walking back to the dining area.

Jade didn't know which was harder…remaining in their lives and always wondering what could've been, or never having the opportunity to see them grow up. Either choice was a tremendous sacrifice and there was no alternative.

She sealed herself in her room and leaned against the door. The realization she may never see Wes again struck her heart like a lightning bolt splits an oak. Attending the wedding with him would be the only *date* they'd ever have. Not that dating Wes was ever a possibility. Then why did it hurt?

She quickly tugged her shirt over her head with one hand while opening the closet door with the other. She'd found the sweetest vintage clothing store in town the day she met with Liv's attorney. The shop owner had been setting out a display of '50s dresses and other outfits, all in her size. They'd fit as if they had been made for her and Jade couldn't resist buying the whole collection.

She removed a red-and-white rose dress from the hanger and slipped it on. The tailored bodice, nipped waist and full, flared skirt accentuated her curves and made her waist appear smaller. And she was all for anything that thinned her out a bit. The accompanying petticoat added a touch of extra volume and made her feel ultrafeminine and a little giddy about attending the wedding with Wes. Of course, he would be up front with his brothers during the ceremony, but a small part of her looked forward to a dance afterward. Jade hadn't allowed herself that pleasure in years because it was a rarity she was a guest at anything. Tonight, she'd make an exception. It was the last chance she'd have to enjoy Wes's company on a personal level and she wanted to savor it, because come tomorrow night, she'd miss him and what could never be. Tonight was theirs.

Wes strutted prouder than a peacock down the white pine walkway of the wedding venue with Jade on his arm. He heard a few gasps, a hint of a whisper here and there and quite a few "they look lovely together" from the older crowd as they made their way to the front of the outdoor ceremony site.

Dylan had designed and built the gazebo and surrounding venue seating as a wedding gift for Emma on the very spot they had fallen in love. It had been six months of hard labor to complete it on time, but the location overlooking Saddle Ridge with the majestic Swan Range before them was their declaration of love to one another in front of everyone and heaven above.

For a man who'd never cared about sentiment or long-term relationships, these past two weeks at home had forever altered Wes's sense of family. He wanted someone to look at him the way Emma looked at his brother. He wanted someone to plan the rest of his life with and children to watch grow up and raise families of their own. He wanted the woman who was ever so slightly pressed against him. The woman whose perfume tickled his nose in an "I can't get enough" kind of way. He wanted the chance to see where things could lead with Jade. Even an early retirement didn't look so bad with her in the picture. Only she wasn't in the picture. At least not past tomorrow.

Wes clenched his fist against the painful vise slowly squeezing the life out of his heart. Twenty-three hours and counting before he stepped on that plane. It would be all right once he was away from Jade and the girls. It had to be because he couldn't live with the agony of always wondering *what if.* He just needed some time to shake it off. And since he refused to retire early, he needed to focus all his attention on winning the championship.

"I'm so glad you decided to join us." Dylan hugged Jade. "Emma will be too."

"You did a beautiful job." Jade glanced around at the long, curved pine benches Dylan had permanently built into the ground. "It's absolutely breathtaking here. I never knew Saddle Ridge could be so beautiful."

Neither could Wes.

"Emma and I hope to one day see our children get married here. And maybe the rest of both our families will choose this place too." Dylan nudged Wes. "You're next, little bro."

"Yeah, that's not going to happen," Wes said, feeling as if his tie was suddenly about to choke him to death. As he adjusted it, he noticed Jade's shoulders sag as she turned away from him. *Crap!* Even though they both knew they had zero chance of a future together, he could've chosen his words a little more carefully. He looked up at Dylan, who stood there shaking his head. *Double crap!* "Why don't I show you to your seat?"

"I can manage, thank you." Jade hurried to her seat before he had a chance to stop her. He would've appreciated a private second alone to explain himself, although what explanation was needed? Neither one of them could possibly be that disillusioned to believe they had anything past tomorrow.

"Go after her." Dylan gave him a friendly shove.

"No." Wes took his place beside his brother. "It's not like that between us. We're just friends."

"I don't know who you're trying to convince, but there's a lot more between you and Jade than friendship."

"Are you ready?" Reverend Grady asked Dylan. "I just got word your bride is on her way."

"I've never been more ready." Dylan excitedly rubbed his hands together.

Garrett squeezed in between them. "Let's get you married."

Once again, neither of his brothers had chosen him to be best man at their weddings. It was such a petty thing, but considering they had been each other's best man at their first weddings, it would have been nice if they could have chosen him and Harlan to stand up for them this time around.

Harlan clapped him on the back. "Hey," he whispered. "The other day Belle and I decided to renew our vows and I want you to be my best man. I didn't have one last year and I'd really like you to do the honors."

Leave it to Harlan to pick up on his insecurities. "Are you sure you don't want to ask one of them?"

"Nope. I choose you and you better be there. August 1, no excuses. We're going to have a real wedding this time. Maybe Jade will still be here since it's only five weeks away."

"Not you, too." Wes smoothed the front of his vest as a white, antique horse-drawn carriage crested the horizon. "Jade and I can never be more than friends."

"Who knows, maybe she'll move here." Garrett chimed in on his right.

Wes tugged at the collar of his shirt. "She has a lucrative business in LA and I have no intentions of ever going Hollywood."

"She isn't going to want him after what he said earlier," Dylan added. "Poor guy doesn't know what he's missing." His smile widened as Delta's father helped her down from the coach. "Love, marriage, kids…it's everything."

"It sure is," his other two brothers said in unison before Harlan leaned over and whispered, "What did you say to Jade earlier?"

"Shh." Wes brushed him off. Getting ganged up on by his siblings was the last thing he needed. Especially with Jade watching him from three rows away.

She looked beautiful today and he hadn't even had the decency to tell her. Her retro glam made his heart race every time. A part of him longed to go back in time to the decade she wore so well. Where life was simpler and modern science didn't complicate matters. If they had been a couple, they wouldn't have had Hadley, Mackenzie and Audra at the same time, but Wes was a firm believer in destiny and the girls would've been born regardless. Of course, all the stars would have had to align in order for them to be together today.

Emma's best friend led Garrett's children down the

aisle, followed by Belle and Delta pushing Travis and Holly in white strollers ahead of the bride. Every member of his family—both blood and extended—were a part of Dylan and Emma's wedding. Everyone except Audra, Hadley and Mackenzie. They could have been right beside their cousins in their own strollers and included in all the wedding photos the family would pose for later. Photos that would hang on walls for decades to come and grace the pages of albums for future generations to look through.

Liv had wanted a family, but in creating that family, the three of them had collectively and knowingly excluded the girls from their *true* family. That had always been the plan. Wes had never wanted anyone to know he'd fathered his best friend's children. Now that plan seemed so shortsighted.

At the time, he'd only factored in his own feelings and hadn't considered the bigger picture. That's not to say he would have changed his mind and done things any differently. But maybe, just maybe, he would've come up with a solution that included his family in the girls' lives. He was powerless to change the situation now. He'd made his decision a year ago and was legally bound to it. The law may prevent him from calling them his girls, but in his heart, they would forever be *his girls*. And Jade would always be the mother of his children.

"Friends, family and neighbors," Reverend Grady began. "We are gathered here today to celebrate the union of Dylan Slade and Emma Sheridan. Over the past year, I've come to know the Slade family rather well. I've officiated over two of their weddings, two christenings and sadly one funeral. During that time,

I've noticed one common thread interwoven throughout this family. The thread of love."

Love. All four of his brothers had fallen in love and had been married at least once. Three of those marriages had ended in devastating heartbreak. Love and heartbreak were two concepts that had eluded him for twenty-nine years. It was impossible to get your heart broken if you didn't fall in love. Yet somehow, in a few short weeks he'd learned the meaning of both words. The love he had for his daughters was like nothing he'd ever experienced before. And tomorrow he'd experience heartbreak for the first time when he walked away.

Jade sensed Wes's unease during the ceremony and she wondered if the same thing she'd been thinking ran through his head, as well. That a massive family celebration was missing three new members. She couldn't help questioning her sister's logic once again. She understood Liv's desire to personally know her children's father, but why Wes? Why did she choose the man with the largest family in town? And why did she choose the one man Jade couldn't get out of her head.

She'd only been around him for a week and a half and she found herself tempted by the forbidden fruit. Her sister had spent almost five years with him. Their friendship had lasted longer than Liv's marriage. Despite Wes believing Liv was still in love with Kevin, she couldn't picture her sister pining for anyone that long. They hadn't even missed their mom for more than a few months and she was the only family they had outside of each other.

As the reception began, Jade attempted to slip away

unnoticed. The ceremony itself was the most important part of a wedding, although she hoped no one ever told her bridal clients that. The money was in the after party.

"Excuse me." A woman lightly tapped her shoulder. "Are you Jade Scott?"

Jade turned to see Molly Weaver, Harlan's ex-wife. "Wow, I wasn't expecting to see you here." The last she had heard, Molly had left town shortly after her divorce.

"I moved back to town last year. I'm sorry to hear about your sister."

Jade's hackles rose. "Um, okay what did you hear about Liv?"

Molly paled. "Oh, maybe Harlan shouldn't have told me."

Nice. Real nice. Wes had assured her that his family wouldn't broadcast Liv's illness around town and his brother had done just that. "Liv is a fighter and this time away will only make her stronger. She'll be back before we know it."

"I'm sure she will. And just so you know, the only reason Harlan told me is because I walked out on my daughter when she was only a year old. He asked me the other day if I'd felt the same despair postpartum depression women experience."

"Did you?"

"Possibly. It was seven years ago and I was very overwhelmed by the prospect of being a parent. My pregnancy wasn't planned like your sister's was. It happened, and nine months later I found myself married to a man I didn't love with a daughter I wasn't sure what to do with. And I tried. I did. But walking away was easier than trying harder. It took me six years to figure that out. Even if PPD had been a factor in the beginning, the rest was all on me and my selfishness."

"Why are you telling me this?"

"Because regardless of why you leave your children for someone else to raise, that guilt stays with you. Even after you do the right thing whether that be returning or staying away—and I firmly believe some parents should stay away—the guilt never leaves. I just wanted you to be aware of that when your sister eventually comes home. She'll have to live with that for the rest of her life. You'll understand that bond one day when you have children of your own."

Jade's stomach knotted. "I appreciate your candor. What is your relationship like now with your daughter?"

"We're still navigating the waters. I don't know if she'll ever forgive me completely. I've always heard kids are resilient, and they are to a certain extent. But you never forget your mother walking out on you."

"Oh, believe me, my sister and I understand that all too well."

Molly's hands flew to her mouth. "Jade, I'm so sorry. I totally forgot you and Liv had been orphaned."

Orphaned. The word irked her. Orphaned meant the child hadn't had a choice in their fate. Both Liv and Jade had decidedly concluded they were better off without their mother and had said as much in court. "No worries. Our mother didn't exactly walk out on us, she walked out on herself."

"I didn't mean to bring up any bad memories. I guess I just wanted to say I'm here if you want to talk. Maybe I can give you some perspective from the other side. Again, my situation differed from your sister's, but I'm sure a lot of the sentiment is the same." Molly looked past Jade. "I think someone wants your attention."

Jade turned around to see Wes walking toward them. So much for her slipping away unnoticed.

"Molly," Wes said through gritted teeth.

"Hi, Wes. I'll leave you two alone. Think about what I said."

"I will. Thank you."

"What did she want?" Wes asked as Molly walked away.

"She heard about Liv and said she could sympathize. She really has changed since high school. She's trying, Wes. If Harlan can give her a second chance, you can too."

His brow furrowed. "She really did a number on my niece and brother."

"And forgiveness is hard-won, but sometimes when you look deep within your heart, you realize you've already done it."

Wes's jaw hung slack. "Are you saying what I think you're saying?"

Jade exhaled slowly, relieved to finally release the last of her resentment. "I have forgiven you for the past."

"That means the world to me to hear you say that."

"Now, if you'll excuse me, I need to get back to work." Jade turned away, not wanting to spend any more time around Wes than necessary. While there was no denying his physical attraction to her, his earlier comment to his brother before the ceremony served as a not-so-subtle reminder they could never be anything more than what they were.

"Please don't leave." He touched her arm, sending an instant shiver through her body. "The reception is just starting."

"I have a lot to do for tomorrow."

"No, you don't. While you were getting dressed, I saw your numerous lists on the table and everything was checked off."

"Your brazenness aside, I have other lists for tomorrow morning I still haven't touched on top of the events I'm working on in LA."

"I told you I would help." Wes jammed his hands into his pockets. "This is not going how I planned. Let me start over and begin by apologizing for the way I acted earlier. I was also hoping you would sit with me and my family for the reception. You already know everyone."

"Thank you for the apology, but it isn't necessary. I know where we stand. And I appreciate your offer to help, but the only thing I'll need from you and the others is some assistance setting things up in the morning. Megan and Alyssa are coming over after the reception and spending the night. They'll help with whatever little things I have left."

"What about Maddie?"

"Since she's Delta's maid of honor, she decided to stay with the rest of the wedding party at the main lodge." Jade doubted anyone would sleep tonight with all the excitement of two weddings. "Could you meet me here at three sharp? That will give us three hours before the ceremony begins."

"Of course." Disappointment registered across his

face and Jade wasn't sure if it was because she asked him to meet her at the ungodly hour or if he'd hoped to go back to her place after the wedding. "If you plan on going all night long, you'll need to eat. You're already here and the lodge chefs have prepared an amazing menu. I snuck a taste of a few things this afternoon. Besides, you look amazing in that dress and it would be a shame if people didn't see you wearing it a little longer."

Jade couldn't help herself from smiling at the compliment. "By 'people,' do you mean you?"

"Yes." The stubborn set of his chin told her there was no getting out of dinner. "Shall we?"

Wes offered his arm and for the second time that night, she allowed him to lead her through the maze of familiar faces she hadn't seen since high school. Friends, not-so-friends, store owners and even a teacher or two. She'd known the entire town would be there, but she hadn't taken the time to process who all that would entail. After the thirtieth "it's been so long" over dinner, Jade began to enjoy catching up with people and hearing what they'd done with their lives. She'd even met the woman who'd originally owned the dress she wore and other outfits she'd bought at the vintage store. For the first time, she felt comfortable in Saddle Ridge. The bright lights of LA seemed so far in her past she almost couldn't imagine going back.

Midconversation with her old English teacher, Wes's palm settled on the small of her back. She leaned into the intimate gesture, luxuriating in the heat emanating from his body. Inhaling deeply, she allowed herself the pleasure of his touch. They'd never see each other again after tomorrow and she didn't want to deprive herself of their last moments together.

"Dance with me," he whispered.

His velvet-edged voice against her cheek sent a shiver of excitement straight to her core. Powerless to refuse him, she smiled at her former teacher. "Please excuse me."

Wes gathered her in his arms and elegantly guided her to the dance floor like a seasoned professional. She knew the man had mad skills in the rodeo arena, but she'd never expected him to know how to waltz.

"Are you enjoying yourself?" he asked. His hold firmed as his muscular chest flattened against her breasts and the length of his growing arousal pressed against her belly.

"Immensely," she purred, not meaning the word to sound as sultry as it had. "Are you?"

Wes twisted his face indecisively. "There's just one thing that can make this night better than it already is."

Without waiting for her to respond, he lowered his mouth to hers, branding her with his lips. His embrace tightened as her trembling limbs clung to him. His kiss, surprisingly gentle yet dangerously erotic, intensified with each stroke of his tongue. Her heart drummed against his chest in unison with his as the rest of the wedding guests slipped away. She had never wanted a man as much as she desired Wes. The ache so great it bordered on unbearable. The man she'd once despised shared a bond with her no one could ever break. In the safety of his arms, nothing could hurt her. If only it could last.

Jade broke their kiss and looked up at him. "We can't do this."

"Yes, we can." Wes dipped his head again and kissed the side of her neck.

She flattened her palms against his chest. "Wes, we are not alone. And I won't be alone all night."

Wes tilted his head back in frustration and groaned. He widened his stance to lower his height closer to hers and held her face between his hands. "Then allow me one more kiss before we say good-night."

His lips claimed hers once more. His kiss, surprisingly soft yet commanding, melted away what remained of her defenses. For once in her life, Jade wished she could hold time in the palm of her hand so this moment would never end.

Chapter 9

Sleep had alluded Wes in the handful of hours between their kiss and sunrise. A sense of renewed hope grew inside him as he once again stood alongside his brothers in front of their friends and family. He was leaving for the airport in less than twelve hours, and even though he'd sworn never to return to Saddle Ridge, he now looked forward to Harlan's recommitment ceremony in August. A part of him had even considered flying out to visit Jade in Los Angeles. He'd never been fond of the city before, but spending more time with her would be worth the sacrifice. And who knew? Maybe nothing would come out of it, but he wasn't ready to walk away without trying.

Just as the ceremony began, Jade removed her phone from her pocket and quickly walked toward the catering tent. Instinct told him it was about Liv or the girls.

He couldn't see her walking away from the wedding she'd meticulously planned for any other reason.

"Do you, Garrett, take Delta to be your lawfully wedded wife, for better or for worse, for richer or for poorer, in sickness and in health, to love and to cherish, forsaking all others from this day forward?"

Wes wanted to follow her, but he couldn't leave mid-ceremony. His insides twisted as a million thoughts ran through his mind. If the call had been about the girls, she would've run. She didn't run. It had to be about Liv. Maybe it was Liv.

"What is wrong with you?" Harlan whispered between clenched teeth beside him.

"Do you, Delta, take Garrett…" Reverend Grady's voice began to sound like the teacher on the *Peanuts* cartoon.

A trickle of sweat ran down his temple as Jade emerged from the tent and quickly made her way back to the ceremony. Her face tight and unreadable. Once seated, he fully expected her to look his way, but she remained focused on Delta and Garrett…as he should be.

"You may now kiss the bride."

The applause and celebratory shouts almost knocked him off balance. The ceremony was over and he'd missed a good part of it. Could he have been any more of an ass? He joined his brothers as they congratulated the couple, fighting the pain that rocketed through him when he gave them a hug. He'd pushed his shoulder to the limit last night on the dance floor with Jade and this morning when they were setting up for the break-fast reception. He was scheduled to compete in Oklahoma later in the week and he seriously doubted he'd be able to.

"Are you okay?" Harlan asked.

"My shoulder's really bothering me." Wes searched the faces in the crowd for Jade, but he didn't see her. "Excuse me."

Wes jumped off the side of the gazebo and beelined for the catering tent, almost running into Jade as he entered. "Was that call about Liv or the girls?"

"It was Liv's treatment center." Jade looked past him to the wedding guests before returning her attention to him. "It's less than an hour from here." Jade laughed sarcastically. "At the very first place I contacted. Actually, I contacted them a few times but my sister didn't feel the need to let me know where she was."

"Why did they call today? Especially so early."

"Sunday is family day, and Liv wants to see the girls." Jade's features clouded in a mix of joy and sadness. "I have to leave in a few minutes. They would like me to be there by eight so Liv can spend the day with them. Something about an assessment, cognitive therapy and reacclimation sessions. I didn't understand it all, but I'm sure I will once I get there."

"Okay, I'll go with you." Wes reached in his pocket for his phone realizing he'd left it in his cabin. "Let me borrow your phone so I can change my flight."

"What? No." Jade shook her head and walked away from him, checking each of the chafing dish burners. "You need to go home."

"I want to be there when you tell her about us."

Jade shushed him and tugged him to the corner of the tent away from the servers. "I'm not going to ambush my sister by telling her I know you're the girls' father, or that we've been playing house while..."

"While what? Falling for each other? After that kiss, you can't deny there's something between us."

"I can't devastate my sister like that. I don't want her to feel like it's two against one, especially when the two are her daughters' biological parents. I refuse to put her through any unnecessary hell. You need to get on that plane today, and return to your normal routine. Once things settle down, I will talk to her about allowing you to have a relationship with the girls. But this thing between you and me—" Jade swiped at a lone tear rolling down her cheek "—was temporary. We both knew that."

Wes wanted to argue. He wanted to tell her they still had each other, but he knew any involvement with Jade would be a constant reminder of their daughters. He didn't fit into their lives. He was never meant to. He didn't know how to walk away, either.

"Saying goodbye is harder than I thought it would be." He lifted her chin to him. "At least let me come back to the house with you to see the girls one last time." A tightness grew in his chest. "Please give me that much."

"What about the reception?" Jade peered around him. "They're headed this way now. This will be over in an hour, maybe two. A lot of people are traveling home today. You need to be here for your family."

"I need to say goodbye to my daughters," Wes demanded.

"Shh." Jade swatted him. "Keep your voice down."

"You involved me in their lives and as much as I fought against it, they grabbed hold of my heart. I refuse to leave here without saying goodbye, with or without you."

"Okay." Jade rested her hand on his chest. "I'm not trying to hurt you. I thought I would spare you the pain, but I understand your need to see them. Meet me at the cabin. I need to tell Delta and Garrett I'm leaving."

"Tell them I'll be back in a few." Wes stormed out the tent's back flap. He wanted time to say goodbye to the girls…alone. He jerked off his tie as he half walked, half ran to his truck. Safely in the confines of the cab, he smacked the steering wheel. Hard. He didn't know how to do this.

Within minutes he parked beside the cabin. Tugging his wallet from the pocket of his jeans, he removed a couple hundred-dollar bills. He had no idea if Jade had promised Megan and Alyssa more or less, but this would have to do for now. He needed them to leave.

He hopped down from the truck and took the porch stairs two at a time, startling the teens when he opened the screen door. "There's been a little change of plans." Wes held out a folded bill to each of them, his eyes settling on the three cherub faces happily rocking in their chairs. "I will settle up with you later if you're owed any more than that."

"Are you sure?" Megan asked. "We're supposed to stay until the wedding is over."

"I'm sure. In fact, why don't you go down to the reception and have breakfast with everyone else. Jade's on her way here, so I have it covered."

Wes tried to stop fidgeting as he waited for the teens to gather their overnight bags and leave. He only had a few minutes left to spend with the girls. He closed the front door behind them and sat cross-legged on the floor in front of his daughters. Unable to hold back his tears any longer, he lifted Hadley into his arms and cradled her against his chest.

"What have you done to me, little one?" He kissed the top of her head, inhaling her familiar baby scent. "I never meant to fall in love with you, but I couldn't help myself." He brushed the back of his fingers against Mackenzie's cheek as her big sparkling blue eyes met his. "I have to go away for a little while, but I'll be back in August. I don't know if you'll still be here or not, so I have to say goodbye now." Wes heaved a sob. "Oh God, how do I do this? You three will always be a part of me. And I will always watch over you. I promise. You won't know it, but I'll be there. You are my three little gifts from heaven and I will love you forever."

Wes heard the sound of a car door outside the living room window. It wasn't enough time. He wanted more. He needed more. He settled Hadley back in her chair. "You're going to see your mommy today. And she loves you more than life itself." He leaned forward and kissed Audra on the head. "You'll grow up and rule the world. You can be whoever you want to be." Wes wiped at his eyes. "I love you, now and forever."

The front door opened behind him. How could his time be over already? It wasn't fair. He kissed Mackenzie on the forehead and rose, his back to Jade. "Will you call me later and tell me what happened with Liv?"

"Of course," she said softly. "And you can call me whenever you want."

"Yeah, not like that won't be too difficult." Wes reached for his phone to take a picture of them, but he realized he must have left it in his cabin and cursed. "I never got to take one photo of them. Not one. I have nothing to take with me."

"I'll send you all the photos you want." Jade's voice broke.

"No." He shook his head, incapable of saying anything more. He closed his eyes and turned away from the girls, his heart shattering into a million pieces. He forced himself to walk to the door, unable to look back. "Goodbye, Jade."

Wes stepped onto the porch, forever a changed man. A broken man. All the things he'd thought meant something in his life were inconsequential compared to the love for a child...and a woman. His life would never be the same.

A counselor named Millie carried Audra's car seat down the hall of the postpartum depression treatment center as Jade followed with Hadley and Mackenzie. "This is where most of Liv's initial reacclimation to her daughters will occur." Millie opened the door to a casual living room–type area and held it for Jade to enter. "The visits will increase, and at some point the children will join Liv here at the center so she can learn how to balance her emotions while caring for them."

"Wait, what? I haven't agreed to overnight visits here." Jade set Hadley's and Mackenzie's car seats on the beige carpeted floor. The place may resemble a warm and cozy guest lodge from the outside, but the fact remained it was a treatment facility and she did not feel comfortable leaving the children in a place where women didn't have complete control of their emotions. "I have guardianship and that's not going to happen unless I say so."

Millie's brows arched as she lowered Audra's car

seat next to her sisters. "It's part of her treatment plan. Don't you want your sister to improve?"

"I find that question rather insulting." Jade folded her arms across her chest, annoyed she was put on the defensive so soon after arriving. "Of course I want my sister to get better, but unless I'm a hundred percent comfortable with the girls' safety here, they will not stay overnight. Honestly, I find this conversation premature. I haven't even spoken with my sister or her physician yet. I didn't even know where she was until this morning."

Millie calmly clasped her hands in front of her. "I apologize. I was not aware of that. Dr. Stewart will be in shortly to speak with you. Until then, do you have any questions?"

Only a million. "How is my sister?"

"Olivia is relaxed and learning new coping skills. Her situation is more unique than most of our patients because her children aren't biologically hers."

"Liv. No one calls her Olivia." Millie's ultracalm demeanor irked her. "Relaxed as in medicated or relaxed as in Zen?"

"Your sister is not medicated. She had the option and she refused, as do many of our patients. Since she is a single parent, it was important to her to not have to rely on medication or worry about its side effects."

A tall middle-aged woman with silvery hair entered the room. "Hello, Jade. I'm Dr. Stewart. It's a pleasure to meet you." She shook her hand before directing her attention to the girls. "And this must be Mackenzie, Hadley and Audra." She crouched in front of them. "I've heard so much about you."

"I wish I knew more about you and this place." Jade

swore every emotion known to man coursed through her body. She hadn't even had time to process Wes's goodbye, before having to run out the door with the girls. She'd known he was leaving today, she just hadn't expected it to be so early or so abrupt. Her phone rang in her bag, wrenching her away from this morning's heartbreak. "I'm sorry. I forgot to mute the ringer on the way in."

"That's fine, just understand this is a phone-free zone," Dr. Stewart warned.

"Of course." Jade silenced her phone, but not before seeing Tomás's name on the screen. He'd have to wait.

After a detailed explanation of the treatment center's protocols and a tour of the ten-acre campus and private grounds, Jade felt more confident her sister had chosen the right place. It was well secured and they even had small cottages with nurseries for the women. By the time they made it back to the visitation room, Jade bore a tinge of remorse for jumping all over Millie earlier.

"Keep in mind, all visits are monitored. We don't want you to hold back your feelings, but we do need you to listen to Liv's feelings. PPD patients have difficulty expressing their emotions, especially when they are overwhelmed. Some exhibit anger while others retreat into themselves. If at any time we believe Liv is struggling, we will step in and guide you both through the process."

"Um, there are a few things I need to tell Liv about the father of her children." Jade had debated having this conversation today during the entire ride there. She relented, rationalizing the more they knew up front, the better they could help her sister. "The thing is, I accidently discovered who the father is and, when Liv had disappeared without a trace, I contacted him in hopes he might know where she went."

Dr. Stewart's eyes widened. "I was under the impression she used an anonymous donor. How did you know where to reach this man?"

"I thought she used an anonymous donor too. When I found out who it was, I was shocked because not only did I go to school with him, his siblings live in town and they have children the girls' age. As they get older, they'll have daily contact with their cousins and not realize it."

Dr. Stewart rubbed the back of her neck and stared at the floor in silence while Millie sat perched on the edge of her chair gaping at her.

Okay. Now what?

"And m-maybe I should also tell you that Wes—that's his name—and his family have been helping me with the girls."

"Helping you?" Dr. Stewart cleared her throat. "So they're aware of their relation to the children."

"Only Wes is. But he left to go home to Texas today. He moved there in January." Jade took a deep breath and recounted the past two weeks in detail to Dr. Stewart and Millie. "We had agreed to tell Liv everything, but I didn't think doing it today was a good idea."

"I can't force you to tell her today, but in my opinion, it's better for her to hear everything now so she can process her feelings. I'd rather have her upset here, early on in her treatment, instead of down the road where she might suffer a setback, accuse you of keeping things from her, or both."

"I wasn't prepared for this today." Jade wrung her hands.

"Like we say here, you can't prepare for everything." Dr. Stewart placed a hand over hers to settle them. "Just be open and honest. State the reasons why you contacted Wes, but don't blame her for the reason. Do you understand what I'm saying?"

"But she is to blame," Jade replied sharply. "I'm not talking about her PPD. I'm talking about the way she went about this before she had the embryos implanted. There was a string of bad decisions and it set off a chain reaction. Choosing Wes for starters. What if her kids got sexually involved with one of their cousins years from now? She lied to both Wes and me and said she used anonymous donors. And then the strain of three children at once. She said that was the doctor's idea... now I seriously wonder. I realize there are other mitigating factors, but I truly believe all of this contributed to her PPD."

"And it probably did."

"Thank you." Jade huffed. "I'll be honest...as much as I love my sister, I'm a little angry. My business in Los Angeles is suffering because I'm not there. If she had come to me, I could have moved her out there temporarily and gotten her the help she needed. I think my sister has been a little selfish."

"Millie," Dr. Stewart said. "Set up a few counseling sessions between Liv and Jade. Let's say three for now, the first one today."

"Do you want it before or after she sees the children?"

"Ah." Dr. Stewart pursed her lips and tilted her head from side to side. "After. I want her to be distraction free when she's with her daughters." Dr. Stewart returned her attention to Jade. "We're going to ask Liv to come in, you two can catch up a little, then we'll ask you to leave for an hour or two. We have a Families Dealing with PPD seminar at eleven o'clock if you're interested. I think you'll find it very informative. Families eat together on Sunday, then we'll regroup in the afternoon and you and Liv will have a session together."

"Okay." Jade mentally ran through her list of things to do. She'd left in the middle of Delta and Garrett's wedding. She still needed to do teardown, on top of readying the linens and other rented items so they could be returned to their vendors. Never mind all she had to do for her own business.

Dr. Stewart nodded to Millie. "We're ready for Liv."

Jade ran her hands over her jeans, not knowing what to expect from her sister. Liv appeared in the doorway, dressed casually in a pair of khaki shorts, a white cotton T-shirt and tennis shoes. Her eyes darted from Jade to the girls and back again. While she looked healthy, her cheeks appeared hollower than they had been when Jade had last seen her. The high ponytail only accentuated her weight loss. She didn't look like someone who'd carried triplets two months ago.

"It's good to see you." Jade rose from the couch and crossed the room to her. "I've missed you. And I love you."

"I love you more." The corners of Liv's mouth lifted slightly at their familiar words. "You must think I'm a terrible person."

"Absolutely not." Jade held her sister's hands between her own, uncertain if a hug would be too much, too soon. "I think triplets are a bit overwhelming for a single, first-time mom. It's impossible to do it all alone."

"How are you managing?" Liv asked, careful to avoid looking in the girls' direction.

"I have a small team helping me."

"A team?"

Jade sucked in her breath. She'd said too much. "Maddie at night and a couple of sitters during the day. Like you had talked about hiring a nanny once you returned from maternity leave. That's what I've done. I need to work, so I have someone there with me almost all the time to help. I can't do it alone."

"I guess that makes me feel a little better." Liv's face began to brighten. "Who did you get? I had a tough time finding a qualified nanny to take on triplets."

"They're babysitters. Not nannies. There's two of them."

"Who are they?" Liv's eyes narrowed slightly. "What aren't you telling me?"

Why weren't Dr. Stewart or Millie intervening? "They're two local teens. Emma Slade uses them and sings their praises." Jade didn't see the need to add that Wes had referred them to her.

"Slade?" Liv dropped her hands and took a step backward. "What did you do?"

"I uncovered the girls' paternity while I was trying to figure out where you ran off to." There, Band-Aid off. It's out in the open.

"Oh no." Liv covered her mouth with her hands. "Do they know?"

Jade shook her head. "Only Wes does. And he knows I'm their biological mother." She looked at Dr. Stewart. "Is this okay?"

The woman nodded. "It's not how I would have preferred, but it's okay as long as you both continue to communicate effectively."

"Do you have feelings for Wes?" Jade asked.

"No, of course not." Liv's face twisted. "We were just friends."

"According to him, you were good friends. How would that have worked if he had stayed in town?"

"He wasn't staying in town. He talked about leaving constantly. I knew he was leaving before he did. It just would have been nice if he had said goodbye before taking off. That hurt."

"Help me understand something." Jade mentally rehearsed her words before speaking, not wanting to offend Liv. "Why did you choose a man who comes from Saddle Ridge's largest family to father your children? His brothers have kids close in age. They'd be sitting with, playing with, and possibly even attracted to a relative and they wouldn't know it. I'm having a difficult time understanding your rationale."

"I planned on using a donor. Even after I asked Wes, I still leaned toward one."

"Why did you change your mind?"

"You and I kept having those conversations about medical history and what if something happened to the girls and they needed a donor for whatever reason. You just said it… Wes has a huge family of possible matches. I wouldn't have that with an anonymous donor. I took the risk of losing a great friend in exchange for my children's future health. Especially after watching one of my best friends battle cancer this year. I figured no one would know there was a family connection unless there was a medical crisis. And I would have dealt with it then. It wasn't until after the babies were born and Belle had Travis that I realized one of the girls might want to date him. Garrett moved to town with his children after I was already pregnant. The idea that of one of the girls might want to date his son one day terrified me. It was too late at that point. I just wanted my children to have options. I don't regret that part. When Wes and I first discussed this, there weren't any Slade children in town with the exception of Ivy, and she was seven at the time. The chance of them interacting was slim. Regardless, I regret not being more prepared for the what-ifs."

"Liv, you couldn't have been more prepared. You knew everything there was to know about having children except the emotional aspect of it and I don't think anyone can ever prepare for that. What about Kevin? Did you think he'd come back once you had the children?"

"Kevin." Liv sighed. "He was my one true love. A part of me will always love him, but I knew he wasn't coming back. Even if he wanted to, I doubt I could ever trust him not to walk out on me again. Besides, he's engaged to be married soon."

"I heard all about it. You're okay with that?" Jade didn't want to bring up the fact she knew Kevin was marrying a woman with children. She assumed her sister already knew.

"It doesn't involve me." Liv's lips thinned and Jade sensed a renewed tension in her words.

"If you weren't in love with Wes, why did you follow him all over the place?"

"Oh, for heaven sake, I wasn't following him." Liv threw her head back and laughed. "Have you seen some of those rodeo cowboys? Those men are hot. I wasn't interested in anyone around town, so I met up with Wes when it was convenient. I enjoyed the atmosphere. I enjoyed getting out of town for a day or two. And I certainly enjoyed the eye candy. So let me reiterate one more time, I'm not in love or attracted to Wes. Are you asking about Wes because you're interested in him?"

Jade opened her mouth and quickly shut it. She didn't want to lie to her sister. She didn't want to hurt her, either.

"Oh wow." Liv paled. "You and Wes. I never saw that coming."

"There is no me and Wes. He's gone and he doesn't plan on returning."

"Ever?"

"That was the original plan, wasn't it?" Jade's defenses began to rise. "You knew he was leaving town, that's why you used him as a donor. How could he possibly come back? It was extremely difficult for him to see the girls." Liv had been in the room with the girls for ten minutes and she still hadn't touched, hugged or even looked their way for longer than a second.

"It sounds like he spent a lot of time with them." Liv's voice remained even and Jade couldn't get a read on her emotion.

"He was a great help to me."

"Liv," Dr. Stewart said. "How do you feel about Wes spending time with your daughters?"

"I don't like it." Liv held Jade's gaze. "She can have any man in the world, just not the father of my children."

Jade inhaled deeply, trying to collect her thoughts.

"You should have told me you weren't using a donor. Wes and I have a history."

"You what?"

"We dated in high school. It was brief, but it didn't end well. You would have known that if you had told me you were fertilizing my eggs…with someone from town. Especially someone my age. Didn't you think the likelihood we went to school together was pretty high?"

"All the times I talked about you, Wes never once mentioned knowing you." Liv's voice broke as her hurt turned to anger.

"Because he hated me. We did some terrible things to each other back then. But that doesn't matter now. I had a right to know. You violated our agreement and you violated my trust."

"Okay." Dr. Stewart crossed the room to stand between them. "Jade, you're blaming Liz."

"I don't know how to do this and not blame her." She glared at her sister. "This part happened before her postpartum depression. Honestly, Liv, your actions have terrified me. I'm still trying to figure out why you packed away all the girls' things in the downstairs closet?"

"I needed normalcy. I felt myself spinning out of control and I thought I could regain it if I confined everything baby to the two nurseries." Liv's face reddened in anger. "Clearly it didn't work. And despite whatever you feel you're entitled to, I was under no obligation to tell you who I chose to father my children."

"Our legal agreement says you were going to fertilize my eggs with an anonymous donor. Are you really going to split hairs and say it was anonymous to me and not to you? I think any court would frown on that."

"Oh, so now you want to take me to court?"

"I'm not saying that at all." Jade forced herself to stay calm despite her flaring temper beneath the surface. "Wes and I are the same age and we grew up in the same town. The chances were pretty high we knew each other. The point I'm trying to make is, I may have given you my eggs, but I still had certain rights. You should've told me what you were doing."

"You're right. I had blinders on all through this. I was so excited about finally having a family of my own, I didn't take anyone else's feelings into consideration."

"There is something else I need to tell you."

Liv's body went rigid, bracing herself for another onslaught. "I'm listening."

"I've been living at Silver Bells with the girls in one of the larger family guest cabins."

"You took my children out of their home? Why?"

"Because Maddie and I couldn't do it alone. I am so grateful she offered to stay with me but she has a job and a life of her own. I think you may have forgotten I have a business to run, and it's been difficult to do long-distance. The two girls that babysit for me live on the ranch. It's very convenient for me to stay there."

"I bet," Liv said sarcastically. "Don't you find it a bit hypocritical? You just finished preaching to me about the girls growing up in the same town with their cousins and all these what-if scenarios…yet you have them all living on the same ranch."

"They're infants. They don't know what a cousin or even a relative is. I think there's a difference. If it makes you uncomfortable, I will move back to your house. I only went to the ranch because I needed all the help I could get. I didn't do it to hurt you. I did it for their safety and well-being. If there was a fire, I wouldn't even be able to get the three of them out of the house at the same time. This way there is usually two people watching the girls."

"I'm not asking you to leave. I gave you temporary guardianship because I trust you. So I have to trust you're making the right decisions." Liv crossed the room to her daughters. "With so many people around, they probably don't even miss me."

"They have definitely missed you."

"How do you know?" Liv said in a broken whisper.

"Because they're never settled. Not completely. They always seem to be looking for someone."

"Really?" Liv glanced back at Jade. "You're not just saying that?"

"No, I mean it. You're their mom and they love you."

"But I left."

"You left to get help." Jade wondered if the guilt Molly had told her about was what Liv was experiencing now. "They don't feel the same way toward you that we felt toward Mom. It's different, Liv."

"Thank you. I needed to hear that."

"It's the truth." Jade moved to stand beside her. "I have something funny to tell you." She nudged Liv's arm. "When I first got to your house, I was so afraid I'd mix them up, I wrote their first initials on the bottom of their feet."

Liv tried to suppress a laugh. "You did what? They're not identical."

"All babies look alike to me." Jade shrugged. "I used permanent marker so it wouldn't wash off when I gave them a bath."

"No, you didn't!" Liv said, half laughing, half crying. "Do their little feet still have writing on them?"

"No. It eventually wore off." Jade smiled, relieved to see her sister in good humor. "See, they're very intrigued by you. And I think Audra has your eyes."

"I can't believe how much they've grown in such a short time." Hadley brought her tiny hand to her mouth and smiled up at her mother. "Oh my God, they're smiling now."

"I'm still trying to figure out if it's a genuine smile or gas. They've been a little stinky. They have their two-month checkup on Tuesday so I'll ask the pediatrician about it."

"It's probably the formula again." Liv's shoulders slumped. "I thought the last one was the right one. It would have been so much easier if I had been able to breast-feed them."

"Liv," Dr. Stewart interrupted. "Remember what we talked about. Your inability to breast-feed was not your fault."

Liv nodded and knelt on the floor in front of them. Jade was glad to see her sister interact with the girls, but it also meant her time with them would soon end. That's what she wanted, wasn't it? Then why did it hurt?

"I'm going to head out for a little while and give you some time with them."

Liv smiled at her over her shoulder. "Thank you for coming today."

"Anything for you."

By the time Jade locked the car seats into their bases in the back of the SUV, she felt physically and emotionally drained. She slid behind the wheel, turned the key in the ignition and switched on the AC to cool the vehicle down since it had been parked in the sun all day long. The clock on the dashboard glowed quarter to four. No wonder she was tired. She'd been going since two in the morning.

"Oh shoot!" Jade dug through her bag for her phone. "I forgot Tomás."

She flicked off the side mute button and tapped at the screen. Thirty-two missed calls, nine of which were from Tomás, twenty-seven text messages and over a hundred emails.

Nothing from Wes.

It wasn't like she had expected him to call. She said she'd call him later and she would once she got home. She glanced at the clock again. He was probably mid-flight, and if she called him now, she could get away with leaving a voice mail. It would be easier on them both after this morning's emotional goodbye.

She pulled up his contact and pressed Call. Straight to voice mail as she figured.

"Hi, Wes, it's Jade. It's almost four and I'm just leaving the PPD center. Liv saw the girls, but it was extremely slow going. After about half an hour, she got very overwhelmed. The doctor feels she'll prob-ably need to be there for longer than thirty days. I told her that I knew about you and that you had spent time with the girls. I also let her know we were living on the ranch. She was upset at first, but she understood. Okay, um, well, I just wanted you to know, so I'll talk to you when I talk to you, I guess. I—I miss you, Wes. I'm sorry it had to be this way."

Jade disconnected the call. Maybe she shouldn't

have told him the last part. Maybe she should have said more. No. It was better this way. She shifted the SUV into drive when her phone rang. Tomás.

She answered the call. "Hey, I'm sorry. I'm just getting ready to head home from the postpartum depression center, can I call you back when I get there?"

"I hope that means you're sitting down, because we have a problem."

Jade shifted back into Park. "Tell me."

"We lost the Wittingfords."

Jade gripped the phone tighter. "Lost as in they canceled or lost as in they went with someone else?"

"They went with someone else."

"No, no, no." Jade rested her head on the steering wheel. "What happened?"

"Word has gotten around that you're not in town and our competition is poaching our clients."

"But the Wittingfords have been with us for years. Their parties are the cornerstone of our business. Who did they go with?"

"Margot Schultz."

Oh no, not Margot. She was smart, savvy and had a world-class reputation. She was one of the best, if not the best, in the industry. "If she managed to take them, there's no telling who else she'll get. She has the potential to destroy us."

"When are you coming back? I can do a lot of things, but I'm not you."

"I don't know. Liv's first visit with the girls did not go well. And they're telling me she'll be there past thirty days. Possibly sixty or ninety days."

"Wow, love, I'm so sorry to hear that. I still don't understand why you can't check her into a facility here."

"If I had known about this in advance, I would have. She's comfortable where she is and it seems like a great place. I just have to do the best I can from here." She turned in the seat to make sure the girls weren't too cold. "I know you're trying to find the perfect candidate, but I want you to hire two people by tomorrow afternoon. No exceptions, Tomás. I refuse to lose my business because you're picky. You can train whoever you need to train and mold them into mini yous. If you think you need to hire three people, then do it. But I need you to be me. Your reputation in this town is just as good as mine. There is nothing I can do that you can't."

"I appreciate the confidence you have in me, but—"

"But what? Is it money? Is that what you want? More money? I've already given you a raise, but if that's what it takes—"

"Jade, breathe," Tomás ordered. "I was going to say, it's not the same without you here. I miss you, love."

"I miss you too. And thank you. It's nice feeling wanted."

"Uh-oh, problems with your cowboy?"

"He flew home to Texas today."

"And are you okay with that?" Tomás asked.

"I haven't had time to think about it. Dwelling on what could never be is an exercise in futility. We spent some time together, we shared a few kisses and that was all it could ever be. After the way Liv reacted today when I told her Wes was in the girls' lives, I feel even more guilty."

"Whoa, I'll let you tell me about the kisses later, but you two shared a lot more than that. You have children together. Donor or not, you're always going to be connected. I can only imagine that loss. And we don't have to talk about it. You can choose to ignore it all you want, just know, I'm here for you if you need a shoulder to lean on."

More like cry on. Jade missed Wes. Watching him walk out the door hurt more than losing her biggest client. She hung up and steered the SUV onto the highway. She had Tomás, Maddie, everyone on the ranch and she had the girls, yet she'd never been more alone. She did feel a loss. Whether she wanted to or not, she had fallen hard for the cowboy. Her sister was right. She could have any man in the world…just not Wes.

Chapter 10

The warm Texas sun felt good on his shoulders as Wes strode across the Bridle Dance Ranch's parking lot toward the Ride 'em High! Rodeo School's outdoor arena.

"Oh, I know that look," Shane Langtry said from the top fence rail as a teenage version of him demonstrated technique in the center of the ring. "Either you just got bad news or you just got your heart broken."

"What are you, clairvoyant?" Wes watched Shane's son execute a smooth dismount after a successful eight second ride. Something he may never do again. "Hunter looks good out there."

"Thanks. I have no doubt he'll take the championship one day." Shane swung his legs over the fence and jumped down. "Well, am I right?"

"About Hunter? Most definitely. He's the finest young rider I've ever seen."

"I'm asking if I was right about you."

"Yeah, a little."

"From the expression on your face I'd say whatever's on your mind is more than a little. Did you see Dr. Lindstrom?"

"I'm just returning from there. Thank you for the referral. She's really nice, although I didn't want to hear what she said."

"You know who she's married to, don't you?" Shane pushed his hat back and propped an arm on the fence.

"No, who?"

"Brady Sawyer."

"*The* Brady Sawyer? The Brady Sawyer who works here?" The man had been a legend on the circuit until an accident paralyzed him from the waist down. They never thought he'd walk again, but he not only walked, he went on to compete until he retired. Now he works helping others to recover at Dance of Hope, the nonprofit hippotherapy center Shane's mother owned next door. "I had no idea."

"She was one of his doctors who put him back together. They fell pretty hard for each other while he was recuperating. If she could fix him, she can fix you. What did she say?"

"She confirmed what my first doctor had suspected." Wes watched another teen climb into the chute, remembering back to when he was that age. He thought he was invincible. If he got bucked off he just shook it off and got right back on. "There's no way I can compete again unless I have the surgery. And then I'm looking at six months to a year recovery."

"So it's not a matter of if you're going to have the surgery, it's when you'll have it."

"It's scheduled a week from today. Next Wednesday." Wes hadn't even told his agent yet. As much as he had wanted to wait, the pain had become too intense. If it meant his biggest sponsors not renewing his contracts this year, then so be it. He would just have to work twice as hard next year. He'd been debating his options since his last competition. While the surgery alone terrified him, not doing what he loved most terrified him more. "That will leave me without a job though. I won't be able to teach for a while. I guess I'm giving you notice since I can't expect you to keep my position open for that long. But don't worry, I have enough money to cover my rent here on the ranch."

"You're just Mr. Doom-and-Gloom today, aren't you?" Shane gripped Wes's good shoulder. "You need to relax, man. I can temporarily fill your position until you are able to come back to work, however long that takes."

"Thank you."

Wes had feared his only other option would be to move back home and partner with his brothers at Silver Bells, if they still wanted him. After the other day, he never wanted to step foot in Saddle Ridge again. He couldn't risk running into Jade or the girls. She updated him daily through voice mail and text messages and that was enough for him. But Harlan had asked him to be his best man at his and Belle's renewal ceremony, so he had to go back. Why did they have to get married again, anyway?

"There's something I want to run by you. I've been tossing the idea around for a while, but I haven't found the right person to help me with it. Your extensive recovery time may work to both of our advantages."

"Sounds intriguing. What do you have in mind?"

"Between rodeo clinics and my son's competitions I'm on the road a lot. I really need a rodeo school director and if you're interested, I think we can work something out. It would be full-time, more money and full benefits."

"Seriously?" The deal seemed almost too good to be true. "I've only been here six months. Are you sure you don't want to choose someone else?"

"I think you're the best fit. You've shown an interest in the business side of things and that's what I need. Somebody who can see the business beyond today. Walk with me." Shane motioned for Wes to follow him down the wide path leading toward the Bridle Dance Ranch's stables. The quarter-million-acre estate housed three of Hill Country's most successful businesses, including one of the state's largest paint and cutting horse ranches. "Between running the ranch and the rodeo school with my brothers, I can't do everything I need or even want to do. You'd be helping me immensely. And I don't know how much thought you've given to retirement, but you always need to have something lined up past today in case an injury sidelines you. This will give you that opportunity to compete for another year or two after you've recovered and have something solid to fall back on."

"I'd say that sounds like an offer I can't refuse." Wes held out his hand. "Thank you."

Shane shook on it and laughed. "I'll take this as a tentative yes. I want you to really mull it over and get through your surgery before you give me your final answer. From what I understand those initial few weeks after a rotator cuff repair can be pretty painful. You're privileged to have access to some of the best physical therapists and nursing staff here on the ranch. Don't hesitate to ask for help."

"Thank you. I knew moving here was the best decision I ever made."

"Just do me one favor. Don't accept the job because you're running away from that broken heart you're trying to hide. You asked me earlier if I was clairvoyant so don't try to deny it. I've been there, done that and then some. If you have something unresolved with your woman, you owe it to both of you to see it through."

"There's nothing left to resolve." Wes's mind still burned with the final images of Jade and the girls. Despite the love he had for them, he wouldn't—couldn't—go through that pain again. "It's over."

Jade froze at the sight of Emma and Belle pushing their baby carriages down the road toward the cabin. She had just returned from her second family day at the postpartum depression treatment center and hadn't even had the chance to get the girls inside. She fumbled with the latch release on Mackenzie's car seat, trying desperately to separate it from the base.

"Need some help?" Harlan's wife asked. Without waiting for an answer, she opened the door on the other side of the SUV and released Audra's car seat. "They are so adorable. I never get a chance to see them."

Mackenzie's seat finally popped free. "I know. Between your schedule and my schedule—" *and the fact I'm trying to hide the girls' paternity from your family* "—we keep missing each other. We just came from visiting Liv."

"Here, I'll take her." Emma startled Jade as she reached for the car seat's handle.

Jade snatched it back. "Would you be able to get Hadley instead? This one has a dirty diaper I need to change."

"Sure."

Jade quickly climbed the porch stairs and shoved her key in the lock. She needed to get Mackenzie out of sight as quickly as possible. The whole "hide the baby" routine had worn thin and a part of her wished the truth would come out now. Because regardless of what Wes and Liv wanted, it had to come out eventually. Whether on purpose or by accident it would happen one day and it was better for the girls if it happened before they were old enough to understand what was going on.

Jade sat the car seat next to the changing table and unfastened Mackenzie. How could such a sweet, innocent child have so much drama surrounding her? She eased the infant into her arms, kissing the top of her sleepy head before laying her down. She unsnapped her pink-and-white unicorn pajamas and checked her diaper. Surprisingly, she didn't need a change. Ever since the pediatrician had switched their formula, the girls had been significantly less gassy and odiferous. Liv had been right. They were having a reaction to the formula and Jade had missed it.

"Do you need me to heat their bottles or anything?" Belle asked from the nursery doorway. "I'm exhausted just running around with one baby, never mind three."

"Um, actually, that would be great." Jade choked back the tears threatening to break free.

"Hey, what is it?" Belle wrapped an arm around her. "What happened?"

Jade shook her head, fearing she'd cry if she opened her mouth.

"It's okay." Belle pulled her into a hug. "This has to be so hard on you."

If she only knew all the reasons why.

"I'm sorry." Jade pulled away from her. "I'm just a little overwhelmed today. Of course it's nothing compared to my sister, so I just need to quit my complaining."

"How is Liv doing?"

"Better, but not great. Today was her third session with the girls. We went in the middle of the week for a brief visit, but on Sundays the residents spend the entire day with their children, including feeding and changing them. She's capable of doing that, but she worries she's doing it wrong. If she's with one child and the other starts crying, she feels guilty because she's not there for both of them or not doing something fast enough. She gets very overwhelmed with it and blames herself for everything."

"Wow, I can't imagine. I mean as a new mom I always wonder if I'm doing the right thing. Even with my animal rescue work, I'm constantly questioning myself."

"And that's normal." Jade finished changing Mackenzie's diaper and refastened her pajamas. "A lot of it is a hormonal imbalance and Liv refuses to take any medication. I respect her reasons for not wanting to, but it's delaying her progress."

"And the longer she's there, the more stress on you."

Jade didn't want to think that way. She was the only

family her sister had and she needed to be there for her, regardless of the sacrifice. "I can't worry about me. I have to worry about her and the girls."

"You are allowed to worry about you. Let me tell you something. I don't feel the least bit guilty leaving Travis with Harlan so I can go out with my friends. Do I do it every night? Absolutely not. But every couple of weeks, I need a girls' night out. And Harlan and I need our date nights. That's the beauty of having family so close. We all watch each other's kids. In fact, you need to come out with us. Between Harlan, Garrett and Dylan, they are more than capable of watching the kids and you, me, Emma and Delta will go out."

"I wouldn't want to intrude on your family time." Nor did she think the Slade men could handle Audra, Hadley and Mackenzie at the same time.

"Honey, above all else, we're friends and friends support one another. Friends have dinner and drinks together. Besides, I don't think this one will mind you going out for a few hours." Belle smiled down at Mackenzie. "Hmm. I hadn't realized how much she looks like Travis."

"Really?" Jade held her breath. *I'm sorry, Liv.*

"Babies are funny that way." She trailed the back of her finger down Mackenzie's cheek. "I ran into a woman just last week at the pediatrician's office whose daughter looked identical to Holly. You would've sworn they were the same child."

"Wow." Jade tried not to show the relief leaving her body. "That had to have been unnerving."

"It was a little." Belle spun around and headed to the door. "I'll start on their bottles."

"I'm right behind you."

Just as soon as I pick myself up off the floor.

After she'd finally managed to get her pulse under control, Liv joined Emma and Belle in the living room. They already had the girls out of their carriers and on the play mats next to Emma and Travis.

This was why her sister and Wes needed to tell everyone the truth. Not only did Audra, Hadley and Mackenzie deserve to grow up knowing their extended family, Liv needed the companionship of other moms.

"I hear you're going to join us for girls' night this week."

"I'm considering it." Jade lowered Mackenzie to the play mat, burying any fear she had of the women discovering the baby's paternity. If the truth came out, it came out. She would deal with the fallout later. "I'm still trying to juggle everything in Los Angeles, although my assistant managed to bring in one of Hollywood's biggest producers. I'm not going to name names, but let's just say he has billions to spend."

"Oh! I know, I know." Emma raised Holly's little hand in the air. "Do you want to tell us or should we *phone home* for the answer?"

"I can't tell you that." Jade was barely able to keep the laughter from her voice. "At least not yet. Nothing is finalized—but fingers crossed—by tonight it will be."

"What kind of event is it?" Belle lifted Hadley in her arms and held the bottle to her lips.

"An award show after party." Jade grabbed a few towels from the kitchen and joined them on the floor. She placed Mackenzie in one of the chairs Wes gave them, tilted it back slightly so she could prop a towel under the bottle, allowing Mackenzie to drink on her own.

"Okay, now I'm jealous." Emma frowned. "That means you'll get to meet all the stars that night?"

"Would you guys hate me if I told you I've already met a lot of them?"

"No wonder you're anxious to get back to California," Belle said. "That makes what I was going to ask you kind of underwhelming."

Jade cradled Audra and offered her the third bottle. "Don't be silly. Go ahead and ask."

"Harlan and I are planning to renew our vows on August 1. Last year's wedding was a little rushed and unexpected. We didn't even have a chance to invite anyone. People heard about it through word-of-mouth and showed up, but it wasn't exactly our dream wedding. Our anniversary is on a Wednesday so we don't want a full-fledged wedding, but we want to have a really big party here at the ranch."

"Basically the wedding reception you never had."

"Exactly." Belle gently rocked back and forth on her knees as Hadley sucked happily on the bottle. Jade had always sat rigidly still while feeding them. "I was going to ask you for some ideas, because I know you're busy and I'd really like to plan this party with Harlan. We just want to make it special. Our track record with weddings isn't exactly the greatest."

"I'd be happy to help you."

"Really? Thank you. I have some ideas, but I'd like some professional input. And we'll pay you. I don't want you to think we're taking advantage of your knowledge."

"You'll do no such thing. Your family stepped in to help me in place of the family I don't have. I've never experienced that before. All of you have shown me a different side to family life. A happy side I wasn't sure existed."

"Does that mean you're ready to settle down and have children of your own? Because you and Wes would have beautiful kids."

Jade began to cough. "Wes and I—" She cleared her throat. "Wes and I are not a couple."

"You two sure looked like a couple at my wedding. That was some kiss." Emma winked.

"And sometimes a kiss is just a kiss."

"I call baby doody on that one," Belle laughed. "There is definitely something between you two and you'll have another chance to find out when he comes home for our ceremony. Harlan asked him to be his best man."

"Will he be able to fly so soon after surgery?" Emma asked.

"Surgery?" Jade looked from Emma to Belle. "What surgery?"

"I'm sorry, I thought you knew." Belle grimaced. "Wes is having rotator cuff surgery on Wednesday. He'll be out of commission for six months to a year."

"I didn't realize he had made a decision already." Wes's shoulder must've gotten worse for him to abandon his plan to wait until the end of the season. "What is he going to do for work?"

"His boss in Texas offered him a director position," Belle answered. "But he's taking a few weeks to decide."

"I know Dylan wishes he would move home, but he's already offered him a partnership twice and he turned it down. It's a shame you and Wes both don't live here permanently." Emma stretched out on the floor next to her daughter. "Silver Bells and Saddle Ridge could really use an event planner. I don't mean just little small-time weddings like ours. We're surrounded by ski resorts and other large guest ranches that would benefit from your services. Plus, I think Wes would move here if you did."

"Can't you open a second location?" Belle asked. "Saddle Ridge can be your satellite office."

Leave Los Angeles? Even if she wanted to—and a small part of her was excited by the prospect of opening a second office—she couldn't. It would be great for her sister, but horrible for her. Saddle Ridge already held too many memories. And while she had made some sweet ones during this visit, it was just that…a visit. Saddle Ridge would never be home without Wes and there was no way he would ever move back.

Chapter 11

Wes knew it would be difficult seeing Jade after five weeks away, he just hadn't expected her to take his breath away when he did. He'd managed to avoid her during Harlan and Belle's vow renewal, but once the reception was in full swing, he found her repeatedly in his line of vision. And what a vision she was. Her vintage cream-and-pale-pink dress caused his heart to flutter. And nothing on a man should ever flutter.

Despite his family's best attempts to get them together, Wes and Jade had managed to stay on opposite sides of the wood plank dance floor. The sun had just begun to set and he finally understood the meaning of the phrase *golden hour*. It was as if an ethereal light shone upon her, making him long for the kisses they had once shared.

Wes shook his head and reached into the front

pocket of his jeans and pulled out his prescription bottle. "What the hell did they put in these things?" Dr. Lindstrom had renewed his painkillers before his flight despite his protests. He was glad she had. The cabin pressure and change in altitude had bothered his shoulder to the point he'd had to take one earlier that day. It should've worn off by now.

"Have you given any more thought to our offer?" Garrett handed him a bottle of Coke. He would've much rather preferred a beer or two, but he didn't want to chance mixing alcohol with his meds. "It's a serious offer, Wes. We don't want you to think it's out of pity."

"I know it's not. And I appreciate it, but I just can't move back here. It's too hard."

"Believe me, I totally understand. I felt the same way before I moved back. I saw Dad on every street corner. Everywhere I turned…he was there. Now that I've been home for a while, other memories, new memories, have taken their place. When I walked past the feed and grain, I don't see Dad with the sack of feed over his shoulder. I see Bryce racing through the door to see the baby chicks they have in the back. Just like when I used to go to the Iron Horse for dinner, I saw Rebecca and me on the dance floor." Garrett swallowed hard at the memory of his deceased wife.

"I know you did." Wes slung an arm around his brother's shoulder feeling the distance close between them for the first time in years.

"The point I'm trying to make is you can create new memories. Now when I walk in there, I still see Rebecca, but I also see my first date with Delta."

Wes wanted desperately to confide in his brother. To tell him exactly why he couldn't move home. He loved his brothers. And as their families grew, he had more people to love. But it wasn't enough to make him stay. The love he desperately wanted would never be his.

"I still want you to consider it. Please give us the same courtesy you're giving your job offer in Texas. Look at all the pros and cons. And talk to us. Every time I see you, you seem more distant. Let me tell you something, life is short. No one knows that better than me. You remember that. We are your family and we love you." Garrett took a step to the side. "I believe this lovely woman is waiting to speak with you."

Wes turned around to see Jade standing there. It reminded him of the first time he saw her when she came back to town. Only a month and a half had passed since then, but it seemed like a lifetime ago. He wanted to ask his brother to stay and tell Jade he had nothing more to say, but he needed something from her and it couldn't wait.

"Hi," Jade said.

"Hi," Wes replied.

"Oh, come on. Please tell me you two have progressed further than this over the past couple months." Garrett placed a hand on both their shoulders. "I have an idea...try to com-mun-i-cate with one another. Take it from an old pro like me. It'll get you places." He winked and walked away.

"How have you been?" Jade absentmindedly twisted the ring on her middle finger. "Emma and Belle told me about your surgery. I tried to call you, but I always get your voice mail."

"I got your messages and thank you." Wes had wanted to return her calls, but self-preservation had come first.

"Why didn't you call me back?"

"Because talking to you…texting you…looking at you now just reminds me of what I'll never have. I didn't want a family or to settle down, yet that's all I can think about. You complicated my life."

Jade's eyes blazed. "I complicated your life? Oh no, no. You did that on your own when you went along with my sister's plan."

"Your sister's plan didn't involve me falling in love with you."

Dammit. He hadn't meant to say the words. He tried not to even think them. But they were there, every day at the forefront of his mind.

"Wes, I—"

"I need to see Liv." Wes purposely cut her off not wanting to hear that she didn't love him in return. "I tried calling the treatment center, at least the one that I think she's at, but she's never called me back."

"They're not allowed to talk on the phone. They have computer and email privileges along with old-fashioned snail mail, but most of their communication takes place in person and is supervised."

"Sounds more like prison."

"I wasn't a fan of it myself at first, but I've gotten used to it over the past five weeks."

"I take it things are improving." Wes kept hoping Liv would see that moving to California was best for all of them and leave Saddle Ridge for good. No Jade, no triplets, no heartbreak.

"Definitely. She'd even had a few overnight visits with them and while they were difficult, they went well. She'll be ready to come home soon, and then I'll head back to California. Out of all the crap I've been through in my life, that will be the hardest. I never wanted children and now that I've been caring for them, I don't want to give them up." Jade held up her hands. "I know, I know. I'm perfectly aware that they're not mine to keep, even though they are mine."

"They're ours." Wes wanted to hold her, to console her, but any touch would be too much to bear. "I want to talk to Liv. I need answers."

"I can tell you exactly what she said." Jade's tone flattened.

Wes sensed an argument about to erupt if he wasn't careful. "I need to hear them from her. We were each other's confidants. She was my best friend and there were a lot of times I was closer to her than to them. We owe it to each other."

"I will call the center in the morning and see if I can get it approved. If they say yes, you can come with us on Friday."

"'Us' as in you and the girls?" How could she still not get it?

"Yes."

"No. I can't see them again." His heart squeezed at the thought alone. "Please respect that. I appreciate you keeping me updated, I hope you never stop doing that, but I can't continue to talk to you."

"So that's how it's going to be? You tell me you love me and then nothing. What is there, then?"

"Nothing. There's nothing. There can never be anything more than that unless…" Wes couldn't say the words out loud. He couldn't risk his heart turning to dust in case Liv refused to allow him to be a part of the girls' lives. The chance was small, but he had to try. "I fly home on Saturday. Please let me know when I can see her."

"Fine." Jade stiffened her spine, her face a bright shade of pink. "I'll text you. Don't worry, I don't expect a reply."

She spun away from him and stormed across the dance floor, almost taking out a couple in the process. He'd rather she be mad at him than hurt. He'd take anger over heartbreak any day.

Wes hadn't expected Liv to meet with him so soon, if at all. After meeting with her counselor and physician, a woman named Millie escorted him to a sitting area that reminded him of his old living room at Silver Bells.

When she walked in, he was surprised by how great she looked. He hadn't known what to expect, but based on what Jade had told him, he assumed she'd either be in a hospital gown or some sort of a uniform.

"You look fantastic." Wes took a step closer to give her a hug, then froze when she crossed her arms. "No? Okay. I gotcha." He cleared his throat. "So, um how does this work?"

"You talk to me like I'm a human being."

Liv's words smacked him like a hot tuna on a grill. "Haven't I always?"

"I thought you moved to Texas. What are you doing here and what happened to your arm?"

"Harlan and Belle renewed their wedding vows so I'm here for that and I had to have rotator cuff surgery."

Concern flashed in her eyes. "What does that mean for your career? When will you be able to compete again?"

"Hopefully by next season. I'm being cautiously optimistic and realistic at the same time. I may be forced to retire early."

"What are you going to do?" Liv sank onto the couch across from him.

"I have a few options." Wes sat in the chair in front of her. "The rodeo school I work at in Texas offered me a director position that would still give me the time to compete if I'm able to."

Liv's shoulders dropped slightly. "That sounds like a nice opportunity."

"It's not the only offer on the table. My brothers asked me to partner with them again." Wes watched Liv's left eye twitch ever so slightly as she white-knuckle-gripped her thighs. Now it made sense. She wasn't concerned about his well-being. She wanted to make sure he wasn't moving home.

"So you haven't decided yet?"

"I'm leaning in one direction, but I promised my brothers and my job in Texas that I would take the next couple of weeks to think it over. It's a big decision." Wes inhaled deeply. "I didn't come here to talk about that. I came here because when I agreed to father your children, you told me you were using an anonymous egg donor. I would like to know why you didn't tell me the truth."

"I told Jade all of this."

"I haven't spoken to Jade other than asking to meet with you. You and I were best friends. I think I'm owed some sort of an explanation."

"And I was owed a goodbye."

Hurt registered in her eyes. He had known their

friendship would end, but he never meant to hurt her in the process.

"I couldn't say goodbye to you, Liv. If I saw you... pregnant with my children, I was afraid I'd want to be a part of their lives. It was better for both of us if I just left and told you afterward."

"Now that you've seen them, you do want to be in their lives?"

"Most definitely."

Liv inhaled sharply at his admission.

"But I know I can't be, despite my love for them. Unless for some reason you've changed your mind." He had hoped to ask her more delicately, but no matter how he chose to do it, he feared she'd see him as a threat.

"Why, because you're dating my sister? That was inappropriate. You knew she was the biological mother and you put the moves on her."

"For starters, I did not put the moves on Jade. Second, your sister and I are not dating, and third, my attraction to her grew out of the bond we have over those children and the concern for your well-being."

"You're telling me the kids and I are the reason you're attracted to my sister." Liv rolled her eyes, her voice heavy with sarcasm.

"I'm telling you it was an impossible situation. I'm not blaming you. I just want to know why you didn't tell me the truth."

"Because I was afraid you'd say no. I had an anonymous donor picked out. He was perfect on paper. Except he was as cut and dry as Jade and I are, meaning there was no family to fall back on in case my children got sick one day."

"I don't understand, you mean if something happened to you and Jade?"

"No, like if they needed a kidney or bone marrow transplant. I know it sounds illogical, but I've read so many things about donors being hard to find and children who die because they were on a waiting list for years. I wanted to make sure my daughters were covered for everything so they can have the best possible life. And if that time ever came, God forbid, I would have told the girls and your family the truth."

Wes leaned forward. "I just wish you had been open and honest with me. I wasn't just an anonymous donor from the fertility clinic. I was your friend and I had a right to know who I was creating a child with, even though I signed my other rights away, I did still have that right."

"It wasn't the perfect plan I thought it was. It's taken me a while to realize how selfish my actions were." Liv pushed her shoulders back and stared directly at him. "I realize I was wrong. I apologize, and I hope one day you can forgive me."

"Apology accepted. That doesn't change how I feel about Audra, Hadley and Mackenzie."

"They're my children and I decide who is and isn't in their lives. You were so determined to move away from Saddle Ridge, I knew you were leaving when I chose you. I always knew Jade would be a part of their lives. She's their aunt. But I can't have both of you involved or involved with each other."

"Why not?"

Liv ignored his question. "I thought you were dead set against having children."

"I've changed my mind." Wes stumbled for a way

to explain it to her. "It's like the couple who has the wild hookup and the woman gets pregnant. Just because the guy never planned on having kids doesn't mean now that he has one on the way that he doesn't love his child."

"You're conveniently leaving a few factors out. You knew what you were doing at the time, so the fact that I was carrying your children wasn't a surprise. And then there's Jade. What do you think it does to me knowing the biological mother and the biological father of my children…the children I carried and gave birth to, are in love with each other?"

"Who said anything about love?" Wes couldn't believe for one second that Jade had emailed her sister and told her what he said last night.

"Sometimes you really are clueless. My sister's in love with you. I can see it in her eyes. I can see it every time she mentions your name, which thankfully isn't all that often. Your involvement with my sister makes me feel like an outsider with my own children. I can't have that. I've worked hard to recover from my postpartum depression. I haven't told my sister this yet, but they're releasing me tomorrow. I'm going to go home to my children and resume my life at my house. Not Silver Bells. I'm sorry, Wes, but I need you to honor our agreement. I don't want you in my daughters' lives."

Chapter 12

Sunny Southern California had never seemed so gloomy. Jade had been home for a month and despite trying her hardest, she still couldn't shake her Montana routine. She constantly checked her watch to see if it was time for the girls' feedings. She carefully listened to every sound in the middle of the night thinking one of them had woken up. And she hugged her pillow tight as she lay alone in her bed, wishing Wes was by her side.

She wanted to fly to Texas and tell him how much she loved him. She should have said it the night he told her, but she had been so scared. She'd never said the words to anyone except her sister. Loving Wes meant hurting Liv. And her sister had been hurt enough.

The day Liv came home had been one of her proudest moments. Saying goodbye to Wes and leaving the ranch had been one of Jade's saddest. After two weeks with her sister and the girls, Liv sent her packing… in the nicest way possible. She had hired a full-time nanny and was receiving outpatient therapy. Jade had no doubt her sister would be a wonderful mother to the girls. It didn't make missing them any easier.

The doorbell rang and Jade forced a smile on her face as she crossed the cold marble foyer of her Hollywood Hills home. She had everything she'd ever wanted. Turned out it wasn't what she wanted, after all.

"Hello, love," Tomás said as she answered the door. "You look simply smashing tonight."

The epitome of tall, dark and handsome, her new business partner kissed both her cheeks and offered her his arm. "Shall we? I still can't believe Margot Schultz invited us to one of her parties."

"I still say she's up to something."

Jade had promoted her longtime assistant to partner when he began snagging Hollywood's wealthiest clientele. Despite losing some clients in the beginning, in the two months she had been gone, he took her business to immeasurable heights. Nobody deserved a promotion more than him. With the addition of their three new employees, Jade had a chance to step back and breathe a little.

"I think tonight's the night we'll find you Mr. Right," Tomás giggled as they slid into the limousine waiting at the curb. "Listen to me. I'm a poet."

"There is no such thing as Mr. Right." The only man who came close was gone forever. Jade's clutch vibrated in her lap. She pulled out her phone and tapped at the screen. "Liv sent me a text message."

"I hope it's another picture of those adorable girls." Tomás leaned closer as she opened the message.

Need you here...please come now.

"Oh my God." Jade covered her mouth and quickly dialed her sister.

"Driver," Tomás called up front as he typed wildly on his phone. "Turn the car around."

Please answer the phone, Liv. Please answer the phone. Voice mail. "She's not picking up."

"I'm booking you on the next flight out of here." Tomás gave her hand a quick squeeze before returning to his phone.

Jade frantically dialed Maddie. Again, voice mail. "What the hell is going on?"

"Driver...take us to LAX. It looks like there is only one flight and it's leaving in an hour. You're going to be on it."

Jade looked down at her black evening gown. "I'm not exactly dressed for the occasion." There was nothing like trying to get through airport security with strappy four-inch Christian Louboutin stilettos.

"At least they won't accuse you of concealing any weapons in that dress."

"Give me your jacket," Jade said as she tried her sister again. "Where can she be? She just sent me a text message."

She called Delta next. No answer. By the time she got on the plane and had to turn off her phone, she'd exhausted her Saddle Ridge contacts. "Something's not right."

* * *

Eight hours later, she swiped her credit card on the cab's handheld reader in front of her sister's house. "Thank you for getting me here so fast." She palmed him a fifty-dollar bill. It was the only cash she had left in her small clutch.

Gathering the hem of her dress in her hand, she climbed the porch stairs, careful not to break her neck. Just as she reached for the doorknob, Liv swung the door wide.

"It's about time you got here." Liv's eyes widened. "Wow! Where were you coming from in that dress?"

Jade pushed past her and down the hall to the first-floor nursery. "Where are the girls?"

"They're upstairs sleeping." Liv sucked in her lips. "Um… I need you to come into the living room."

"No." Jade stomped past her. "I need to see them." As she flew past the living room archway, a familiar cowboy hat caught her eye. She spun on her heels, twisting her ankle in the process. Before she had a chance to hit the hardwood floor, Wes wrapped his arm around her and pulled her hard to him. "Wh-what are you doing here?"

Wes stared down at her, his mouth inches above hers. "That's what I'd like to know."

"The girls…" Jade whispered, her mind reeling from the man holding her upright and the pain in her ankle.

"I've already checked on them. They're sleeping peacefully."

"You saw them? You physically saw that they're okay?"

"Yes."

Jade turned her head to demand answers from Liv, only her sister was gone. "What is going on?"

"I don't know." Wes helped Jade into the living room and eased her onto the couch. "I got a text message last night telling me to come right away," he said as he unlaced her shoes. He held her calf as his eyes trailed up her thigh, exposed by the high slit in her gown. "That's some dress." He stopped just shy of her cleavage, closing his eyes and cursing under his breath. "I tried calling Liv and then Maddie, but no one answered."

"I even tried calling your sisters-in-law, but there was no answer there, either. I was about to call Harlan when I had to board the plane."

"I'm glad you didn't call the police," Liv said from the doorway, holding an ice pack and a towel. "That would have been awkward to explain, even though your family is well aware of why you're here."

"They're what?" Wes sat back on his haunches as Liv handed him the ice pack.

"Sorry about your ankle." Liv wrinkled her nose. "That wasn't part of the plan."

"What plan?" Jade and Wes said in unison.

"After you both left and I started getting out more with the girls, a lot of people came up to me and told me how you two made a lovely couple. Maddie had already been singing both of your praises, but she filled me in on all Wes had done for the girls. And then Delta came over, and Emma called." She nervously laughed. "And then it hit me…the family that I wanted was much bigger than me and the girls. It was you." She pointed at Jade. "And all of the Slades, including you, Wes."

The sun had just begun to rise and filter into the room as Liv rose from her chair and looked out the window. Was her sister having a relapse? Was that possible with PPD?

"Liv, sit next to me." Jade patted the couch. "Oh, that's cold." She jumped when Wes rested the ice pack against her ankle.

"It's already starting to swell." Wes held her foot firmly. "Liv, I can't tell if you're trying or not trying to tell us something, but my patience is wearing a little thin. When we last spoke, you told me you didn't want me in your daughters' lives. Now you're saying their family is my family. You didn't tell them, did you?"

"Well…" Liv gnawed her bottom lip. "Yes, I did. I felt I owed them the truth. My actions not only threw your lives into total chaos, it had the potential of hurting the girls and Wes's family in the future. I hadn't thought about the school issue, or that the girls and their cousins would be friends. I was laser focused on having a baby. In hindsight, that destroyed my marriage more than our inability to have children."

Jade felt Wes's grip tighten slightly on her foot. "Liv, I love that you did the right thing, but that was Wes's place to tell his family. Not yours."

Wes exhaled slowly and stood. "I'm not concerned that you told them. I'm more concerned with what comes next."

The front door opened, and Harlan poked his head in. "Is it okay for us to come in now?"

"What's going on?" Jade tugged on Wes's arm. "Help me up. What are they doing here?"

"I called them."

Wes slid his good arm under her and lifted Jade beside him. "I'm almost afraid to believe what this might mean," Wes whispered.

One by one, the entire Slade family filed into Liv's small living room.

"Thank you for coming. And, Jade and Wes, please forgive my little trickery. I didn't think you would come otherwise. Especially Wes." Liv walked over to him and held his face in her hands. "Dear Wes. I am so sorry for the way I treated you. You gave me the greatest gift in the world, and I was so cruel. You asked to be a part of their lives. And today I'm giving that to you." Liv cupped her sister under the chin. "To both of you."

"Liv," Jade sobbed. "What are you saying?" She knew her sister would never relinquish her rights to the girls. If that's what she was doing, then there was something seriously wrong. "Liv, please."

"I've already contacted my attorney and he will meet with us later today to explain in further detail, but…"

"Liv, no." Jade pulled her sister into her arms. "You can't. I won't let you. You love those girls." She didn't care what she had to give up in California, she'd stay by her sister's side every day and make sure she was okay.

"Jade, sweetheart." Liv soothed her hair. "Because I love them, I'm asking you to become de facto parents."

"De what?" Jade released her sister. "I don't understand."

"De facto parents. In Montana, a child or children can have more than two parents. You and Wes would assume day-to-day parental roles with me."

"This isn't a sister-wife thing, is it?" Wes asked.

"I think I might be able to explain this." Harlan stepped forward. "If you two choose to reside here in Montana, and like Liv said, assume the day-to-day parenting of the girls alongside her, her attorney can petition the court to have you named de facto parents. Because you're their biological parents, you have an excellent chance a judge will sign off on it."

"And considering my father is the judge—" Belle winked "—your odds are pretty good. We took Liv to meet with him and he detailed everything that needed to happen in order for the court to grant the arrangement."

"You both have to live in Montana though," Dylan said. "That partnership is still open if you want it."

"And I still say Saddle Ridge needs an event planner," Emma added.

Jade blindly reached behind her for Wes's hand. She needed to feel his touch, to know she wasn't dreaming.

"And you need a place to all live that's not too sister-wifey." Garrett laughed. "We talked it over with Liv, and we have two side-by-side guest cottages on Silver Bells that we'd like to offer you. They need to be renovated, but—"

"But the sale of this place will more than pay for them," Liv said. "You two would have your space, and I would have mine. The girls would have both houses to call home."

Jade's heart hammered in her chest. "Liv, are you sure about this? You love this place."

"I love you more." Liv clasped her hands over theirs. "Do you two love each other?"

"Yes," Wes said as he wiped away a tear. "I love those girls more than life itself." He started to laugh. "And I really wish I had use of both arms right now."

"Oh, Wes." Jade wrapped both of her arms around his waist and looked up at him "I've got you. And I love you."

"I love you too, with all that I am." He looked across the room to his family. "I love all of you. And, Liv, thank you. This means everything to me, but there's just one problem." He sighed heavily.

"What?" Jade pulled away from him. They were so close. How could he possibly back out now?

Wes lowered himself on one knee and took her hand in his. "I don't have a ring or some grand speech prepared, but I have a lifetime that I'd like to share with you and our crazy, unconventional family. That is if you'll marry me."

A wave of euphoria bubbled inside her. "Yes! Yes, I'll marry you!"

The shadows in her heart had finally disappeared and she was happy. Blissfully happy with the father of her children and a family to call her own.

* * * * *

"You're welcome to join me if you'd like. Unless you have plans. It's Saturday, after all."

Plans as in a date? Yeah, not so much these days. In fact, she hadn't been in a serious relationship since she and James had broken up over two years ago.

"I don't date," she blurted before she could stop herself. "I mean, I can, but I don't. Or I haven't been. Um, lately."

She consciously pressed her lips together to stop herself from babbling like an idiot, despite the fact that the damage was done.

"So, dinner?" Desmond asked, rescuing her without commenting on her babbling.

"I'd like that. After I shower. Meet back down here in half an hour?"

"Perfect."

There was an awkward moment when they both tried to go through the kitchen door at the same time. Desmond stepped back and waved her in front of him. She hurried out, then raced up the stairs and practically ran for her bedroom. Once there, she closed the door and leaned against it.

"Talking isn't hard," she whispered to herself. "You've been doing it since you were two. You know how to do this."

But when it came to being around Desmond, knowing and doing were two different things.

Don't miss
Before Summer Ends *by Susan Mallery,*
available May 2021 wherever
Harlequin Special Edition books and ebooks are sold.

Harlequin.com

Love Harlequin romance?

DISCOVER.

Be the first to find out about promotions,
news and exclusive content!

f Facebook.com/HarlequinBooks

y Twitter.com/HarlequinBooks

◉ Instagram.com/HarlequinBooks

ⓟ Pinterest.com/HarlequinBooks

You Tube YouTube.com/HarlequinBooks

ReaderService.com

EXPLORE.

Sign up for the Harlequin e-newsletter and
download a free book from any series at
TryHarlequin.com

CONNECT.

Join our Harlequin community to
share your thoughts and connect
with other romance readers!
Facebook.com/groups/HarlequinConnection

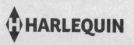

HARLEQUIN

Heartfelt or thrilling, passionate or uplifting—Harlequin is more than just happily-ever-after.

With twelve different series to choose from and new books available every month, you are sure to find stories that will move you, uplift you, inspire and delight you.

HNEWS2021